ALL MY
MOTHER'S LOVERS

ALL MY
MOTHER'S LOVERS

a novel

ILANA MASAD

DUTTON

DUTTON
An imprint of Penguin Random House LLC
penguinrandomhouse.com

Copyright © 2020 by Ilana Masad
Penguin supports copyright. Copyright fuels creativity, encourages diverse
voices, promotes free speech, and creates a vibrant culture. Thank you for buying
an authorized edition of this book and for complying with copyright laws
by not reproducing, scanning, or distributing any part of it in any form
without permission. You are supporting writers and allowing
Penguin to continue to publish books for every reader.

DUTTON and the D colophon are registered trademarks
of Penguin Random House LLC.

LIBRARY OF CONGRESS CATALOGING-IN-PUBLICATION DATA

Names: Masad, Ilana, author.
Title: All my mother's lovers : a novel / Ilana Masad.
Description: [New York] : Dutton, [2020]
Identifiers: LCCN 2019031340 | ISBN 9781524745974 (hardback) |
ISBN 9781524745998 (ebook)
Subjects: GSAFD: Love stories.
Classification: LCC PS3613.A7926 A78 2020 | DDC 813/.6—dc23
LC record available at https://lccn.loc.gov/2019031340

Printed in the United States of America
1   3   5   7   9   10   8   6   4   2

BOOK DESIGN BY ELKE SIGAL

To Ima/Andi, my mother,
who is not the mother in this book
ולאבא/אורי, שתמיד איתי

What you do to children matters.
And they might never forget.

  —Toni Morrison, *God Help the Child*

The truth is, the world will probably
whittle your daughter down.
But a mother never should.

  —Meg Wolitzer, *The Interestings*

I'll tell you a secret. A lot of times,
parents are not the best at seeing their
children clearly.

  —Celeste Ng, *Little Fires Everywhere*

ALL MY
MOTHER'S LOVERS

Maggie is in the midst of a second lazy orgasm when her brother, Ariel, calls to tell her their mother has died. "Don't pick up," Lucia says, the lower half of her face glistening. But Maggie doesn't listen; she lives for moments like this.

"Hello, Brother. I am currently being eaten out. What are you up to?" And when Lucia pulls her face away, peeved, Maggie leans up on her elbows and says, "No, don't stop."

But then she listens, and she sits up and pulls away from Lucia, tugs her knees close to her body, protective. She can feel her face turn stony, is sure the color is draining from it as her brother talks. She sees how she must look through her lover's shifting features, Lucia's eyes widening with concern, her mouth hanging open a little, chin still wet.

"Okay," Maggie says. She repeats it. Then: "I'll text you my flight details." She doesn't say "I'm sorry," though she is, nor "I love you," though she does. She can't think clearly enough to say the things people are supposed to say in such moments. Not because she's stuck—she isn't. She isn't even thinking about her newly dead mother, nor of the violence of her death, a car crash along a route she can picture well. Instead, Maggie is several steps ahead, thinking of the funeral, of who she needs to call, of what will happen to her father. She's thinking about whether they need to print programs, whether the synagogue will do that, and whether that's even really a thing, or just something people do on TV. She's thinking about her planner, sitting in the kitchen, so far from where she needs it.

"Mags, you're scaring me," Lucia says. She's sitting very close to Maggie now rather than between her legs, kneeling, her brown breasts hanging heavy, nipples grazing Maggie's knees. "Where are you going?"

Maggie stays hunched into her phone, looking at flight options, prices and times. "Home," she says, and she leans forward to kiss Lucia, whose lips look especially swollen, though it's just that her lipstick is smeared despite its no-smear promise. "You've got a smudge," she says, and thumbs it away. "My mom died."

"What?" Maggie tends to shriek when she's surprised, but Lucia goes soft and still. It makes people lean forward to hear, and somehow amplifies her presence. It's one of the things Maggie likes about her so much. Her solidness, the space she takes up without trying. "Babe, your mom?"

"Yeah," Maggie says, lowering her eyes to her phone again. "A tree crashed into her car. Can you hand me my wallet?" But Lucia pulls the phone out of her hands instead. "Hey—!"

Lucia holds Maggie's face in cupped palms, looks into her eyes like she's trying to find something there, something that isn't. "I think you're in shock."

"No, I'm not." Maggie jerks her head away and gets up. "Fuck it, it'll be easier on the laptop." She grabs her underwear from the ground, pulls on the baggy Babadook T-shirt she wears to sleep, and walks out to the living room where her laptop is still hooked up to the TV, paused on the credits of the documentary she and Lucia had been watching. It's Monday already, the night having turned early morning without her realizing. She needs to compose an email to her boss to explain why she won't be at work for a few days. She needs to call her dad. She needs—

"What can I do?" Lucia has followed her, still naked, and hands Maggie the wallet she left in the bedroom, on the chain she keeps attached to her jeans.

Maggie doesn't know what to say, because she doesn't know what Lucia can do. Her mother has never died before. She's never before had a girlfriend for this long, this many months in a row. She doesn't know what having a person help her in this intimate way should look like. She can't ask Lucia to call her dad for her. She can't ask Lucia to look up flights for her. She can't ask Lucia to figure out how to get hold of the will and whether her parents still have the same lawyer now as they did a decade ago, a plucky blond woman named Janice, whom Maggie had the displeasure of meeting when she got arrested for smoking pot at age seventeen. She isn't even sure what she's told Lucia about her mother, whether they've really talked about their parents. It seems like they've been too busy fucking the life out of each other for most of the past five months.

When Maggie's foot begins to fall asleep, she realizes how long she's been sitting with it underneath her on the couch. The same position her mother always sits, an inherited trait, or maybe a picked-up habit. *Sat*, she thinks. The same way her mother sat. The tense change feels like a fist around Maggie's esophagus, its permanence making the edges of her vision cloud. But no—she can't fall apart yet. There are practicalities to attend to. She's been staring at flight options for far too long, switching to another tab and googling "how to plan a funeral fast" and "Jewish funeral" and "what to do when your mom dies." She pulls her credit card out of her wallet, inputs the numbers. The tips of her fingers are numb.

A mug of tea appears next to the laptop, not steaming, which is good, because Maggie can't drink anything hot. She usually puts an ice cube in her tea to avoid needing to wait fifteen minutes before drinking it; Lucia must have seen her do this, or maybe it's been that long already. "Here you go, babe," Lucia says, and sits on the couch next to Maggie, her hip—now underpantsed, her torso T-shirted—pressed close. "Did you find a flight?"

"Yeah, in the morning."

"We should get a few hours of sleep before I drive you to the airport. Come on, let's go to bed."

"You're driving me?" Maggie looks up from an unhelpful listicle of ten things no one expects when losing a parent. Lucia's irises are usually two different shades of brown, one deep and rich and the other golden in the light, almost like an eagle's eye. In the shadow of the dark living room and the glow of the laptop screen, they just look black, as if all pupil, like on the night she and Maggie met, both of them on molly and dancing to EDM at an overpriced warehouse party.

"Of course. I mean, if you don't want me to, I won't, but I'm here, babe."

Maggie wants her to. She also doesn't. This is not where they're at yet. This is what she usually considers too real. This is when she bails.

"Look," she starts, but she can't go on, and so she doesn't say that Lucia doesn't have to, or that she should leave, or that Maggie wants to be alone, because it isn't true. She doesn't want to sleep alone, if she can even sleep. She wants Lucia's teddy bear warmth. She exhales. "Okay."

In the barely there light of early morning, Maggie pulls her medium suitcase out from under the bed. She doesn't know if there's going to be a shiva or not, doesn't know what her mother would want, if she wanted anything, if she had any plans. Was she too young for that? Maggie has to stop what she's doing and calculate from the birth year in order to zero in on her mother's age. Sixty-three, she thinks, sweat pooling in her armpits at the shame of not remembering.

"Can you turn that off?" she snaps at Lucia, who's making coffee in the kitchen, her phone playing a soothing acoustic guitar playlist. "I need to concentrate." The music stops mid-strum, and Maggie feels even worse.

She'll pack enough clothes for ten days, just in case they do a shiva. Her dad is a lapsed Catholic, and she and Ariel weren't raised particularly anything, though when she was small, when her maternal grandparents were both still alive, they would visit from New York to celebrate the High Holidays, going to synagogue and eating lavish meals at the rarely used dining room table. She has only glimpses of those years, the softness of Bubby's hands, how everyone said Maggie looked just like Nonno, which confused her because he was bald. She does remember her mother crying when the calls came about their deaths, barely a year apart. And she remembers her mother packing, though that seemed to be a constant activity.

Now it's my turn, Maggie thinks. She packs work clothes because those are appropriate, some of her all-purpose jeans and tank tops for lounging around or doing errands in, and the obligatory black dress and heels. Why women need to wear heels to funerals, she doesn't know, especially when everyone ends up poking holes in the grass when they reach the cemetery. What she does know is that it's expected.

"Are you ready? Got your ID? Money? Phone?" Lucia hovers at the door, clutching a thermos of coffee for them to share. Her hair is pulled back into the severe ponytail she wears on a day-to-day basis, so tight that it flattens her curls to her scalp, leaving the hennaed highlights looking like squiggles in a word processor, and then flares into a kinky puff right outside the hair tie. Maggie often thinks about how lucky she is that she first saw Lucia with her hair free and wild and flying as she danced. She's attracted to Lucia any which way, but she looks less approachable with this ponytail, more adult and businesslike. Of course, Maggie tends to look similarly grown-up when she goes to work, where she still feels like a kid playing dress-up.

"I'm good," she says, patting her pockets for the items Lucia listed. Her wallet is there. Her ID is in her wallet. So is her debit card, her credit card, and the emergency card connected to her dad's account, which is all the money she tends to carry outside of bar- or club-hopping, which is the only time she'll make the effort to carry cash. Her phone is in her back pocket. She nudges Lucia into the hallway and begins to lock the door. But she remembers—"Wait, shit, I gotta get my weed."

Lucia grabs her arm to stop her. "No, are you crazy? You can't fly with that."

"No, I know," Maggie says, her voice trembling. Of course she can't. Though people do. And she wants to. She can't handle this sober, can she? "But maybe? I can stick it up my vag, I've heard of people doing that."

Lucia shakes her head and yanks the door shut all the way. Maggie doesn't know what just came over her. She's always in the mood to get high, but she's not an idiot. This would be the worst time to find out what the TSA would actually do if they caught her. She doesn't fight Lucia on it again, and they walk downstairs and get into Lucia's car. She'll get some when she arrives, she consoles herself.

On the ride over, Lucia tries to ask Maggie about her mom, like how old was she, and does Maggie know what happened exactly, and how close were they, but Maggie doesn't really answer beyond sixty-three and car accident, *splat*, a sound effect she hopes isn't accurate the moment she utters it along with a loud clap.

"We weren't," she tries, "I mean, she— I loved her, obviously, but she was weird about, you know." She waves a hand between her body and Lucia's, and Lucia catches it, holds it fast. "She always thought it was a phase. Rebellion or something. And she was gone a lot. We weren't super close."

Maggie doesn't know what else to say. Her mind is already in California, picturing her dad sitting in his office, but he wouldn't be there now, would he? She hasn't talked to him yet; it's an impossible task, to pick up her phone and call him. She texted Ariel the details of her flight before she went to bed, so she knows someone will come get her, and she'll figure things out from there.

"We're here," Lucia says, interrupting the silence that fell between them. She puts her hand on Maggie's bouncing knee, stilling it. Maggie stares at the hand, a few shades darker than her own skin, which seems to wear a permanent tan. There were jokes throughout her childhood about her father not being the father. But he is, of course. Maggie's Italian *nonno* was a Sephardic Jew—his ancestors banished from Spain or Portugal to North Africa or Greece, maybe, intermarrying or having affairs along the way, as people did, before eventually ending up in Italy. At least, that's what the family always speculated. Maggie's eyes feel dry, as if she's been staring at Lucia's hand without blinking for hours when she's pulled back to reality. "Babe?"

7

"Yeah. Okay. Hey, thanks," Maggie says. "You didn't have to do this." She moves to open the door but Lucia pulls her back and kisses her, softly, and Maggie yields to it, kissing back harder. But her desire is shut off, something that she doesn't think has ever happened to her before, certainly not with Lucia. She pulls away, uncomfortable. Kissing seems like an odd thing to do right now. The slapping of lips together, the lapping of tongues—such a strange way to show affection, to express want. Maggie touches one of Lucia's breasts and squeezes it a little bit. "Everything is so weird."

"I know. I'm sorry. I'm so sorry, Mags." Tears are gathered in Lucia's eyes, and Maggie knows she has to keep moving. She hasn't cried yet, and can't let herself now; there's much too much to do.

A loud tap on the window saves her. It's a man in a neon orange vest, one of the traffic attendants meant to move folks along and prevent loitering. "This is a drop-off zone," he says sharply when Lucia rolls down the window. "So drop her off and move or you'll get a ticket."

"Yes, Officer," Lucia says.

"What a prick," Maggie fumes when the window is shut again. "And he's not an officer, you know, he's just some security dickwad," she adds.

Lucia shrugs. "Be safe, babe," she says. "I'll check in with you, okay? Tell me when you land?"

"Sure." Maggie forgets this as soon as she's out of the car with her suitcase and her Trans by JanSport backpack, the same style she's had since high school, the only purse she ever wants or needs.

ON THE PLANE, the pilot talks about how they're all going to miss the complete solar eclipse. "You won't see it right in California," he admonishes. Maggie and Lucia were planning to video-chat during her lunch break to watch it together. Oh well, she thinks, as the plane begins to accelerate. She has a row to herself, since apparently a Monday morning in August isn't prime flying time. She's grateful for it, and once the plane is in the air, toe-ankles her way out of her Converse, the same pair she's flown in since moving to the Midwest for college. A good-luck charm.

It was her first, that flight nine years ago. She was eighteen and fluffy-haired after shaving her head the year before, intending to donate her lengthy curls to a cancer charity, though her braid in its plastic bag was returned in the mail due to some postal mistake and ended up staying on her bedroom floor, forgotten. She was scared when the plane took off from the small Oxnard Airport—still in service back then—and her mother, Iris, had taken her hand and squeezed it. "You're doing great," she said. She'd surprised everyone by insisting that she should be the one to help Maggie move in. It wasn't just that Iris almost never took time off work, it had also been a bad year for the two of them: Maggie's increasingly flaunted weed smoking causing endless fights, her coming-out evoking uncomfortable silences. But Iris took her hand on that flight, told her she was doing great.

Maggie's left hand reflexively tightens on her jeans. The denim is coarse or soft, depending which direction her fingers move along the lines of its weave. It feels nothing like a human hand. Self-consciously, she holds her own hands together and closes her eyes, tries to imagine that her right hand isn't hers but her mother's. Just for a moment, she manages to divorce herself from the touch of one hand, focusing so completely on the other that it's as if Iris really is there, really is holding her hand again on that onetime bonding experience.

But then the illusion disappears and a heavy warmth settles on Maggie's chest, the kind that comes before crying. Her mother is dead. She will never again comfort Maggie on a flight, or any other time. She'll never again tell her that she's doing great. Not that Iris was quick to express love, or that Maggie has needed her all that much in recent years; it's that the option was there. The nest existed. Her parents, cocooned in their separate and busy lives but coming together for their children, at least most of the time.

No more.

She shuts her eyes and breathes deeply, swallowing past the lump in her throat as best she can. She decides to deploy the relaxation method she uses when she's smoked something unfamiliar that makes her paranoid or when she has a bad hangover that makes her feel half dead: recalling her work scripts, the things she tells people when she's trying to sell them more insurance or when they have questions about the things they want to purchase. The scripts are relatively new, because the agency she works for changed a bunch of their product titles a couple of years ago, and everyone had to practice replacing the earlier language. Auto-Death Indemnity, for instance, became Medical Payments Coverage.

"No one," the company rep in charge of retraining explained, "wants to hear the word 'death' when buying insurance." Insurance is a tricky business that way; it prepares people for the worst, which they hope won't happen, but it also makes them aware that it could. "Don't remind people of their mortality," the rep said. "Or remind them how vulnerable they are. Explain how vulnerable they *could be* if they don't purchase our product. Ultimately, you're selling them a promise that nothing bad will happen to them. That's really what we're about."

It's a soothing lie, Maggie knows, but it was a novel one when she started working there—her parents rarely made promises, even down to little things like reasonable birthday gift requests, so she never learned how empty so many of them could be.

Medical Payments Coverage, she explains to an imaginary faceless customer while trying to maintain her steady breathing, *is a no-fault auto-insurance coverage for the worst-case scenario.* She hopes Iris had the right kind of insurance. *What if you and your loved ones are driving down I-55 . . .* They have some savings, but a lot was lost in 2008, and they had to take out a second mortgage on the house at one point . . . *and some asshole—excuse my French, ma'am—is texting behind the big wheel of his truck and he plows right into you?* That's not what happened, though, was it? It was a tree, Ariel said, not anyone's fault. *Well, if you choose this coverage* . . . What a strange word: "coverage." Like a blanket . . . *we'd be able to help pay medical and funeral expenses for you or your passengers* . . .

Maggie feels the plane lurch and sits up straight, yanking her earbuds out, heart pounding. She must have fallen asleep.

"We're descending now to LAX, folks," the captain's voice comes on the overhead speakers, crackly and soft. "The weather is sunny and mild, with southwesterly breezes and a lovely seventy-eight degrees."

IRIS

AUGUST 20, 2017

Stillness. Darkness. Waves of passing sound. Death, she discovers, is like being taken out to sea by the tide. Peaceful once she stops fighting the pain of it. Or is this just the story she tells herself in order to handle the sharpness running through her?

But no, before that. Before the end.

It was Iris's day off. A Sunday. She'd just returned from the first half of a corporate weekend in Las Vegas, leaving the last couple of days in the hands of her capable assistant, Anya. She disliked Vegas, but more and more companies seemed to be making semipermanent homes there, for tax reasons she assumed, and still others just liked flying their people out for lavish yet well-contained vacations. The thing about Vegas, Iris felt, was that it was predictably glitzy, which made it lose its teeth. No, that wasn't quite right—after all, the Strip was just one part of the city. It was the tourists who were predictable in Vegas. You could often tell, she thought, what people would want to do there, and what services bosses would want to provide. Her clients tended to underestimate the prices, though, as if Vegas being a place of clichés built upon other clichés made it cheap. There

13

was the toilet-paper manufacturer who brought his corporate office to a retreat and wanted everyone to get free massages, then balked at the price and complained to Iris about his budget. There was the head of a bridesmaid-model company who insisted on finding not just one but three separate male revues for her girls to go wild at and then got peeved at how much she was billed for lap dances. Iris always tried to warn them, but it seemed people forgot money's worth in Vegas. Part of Iris's job as a corporate events planner, of course, was to keep things inside the client's budget and she almost never strayed out of it, keeping a section cordoned off for extra expenses that her clients never thought to consider.

This latest excursion—a boutique-winemaker conference—had been relatively simple, but she was relieved to be home. She had a whole week ahead of her without traveling, a rare treat, and she meant to take advantage of it. Peter was already up and at it when she got out of bed—she could tell because the house smelled deliciously of coffee, the hazelnut kind he indulged in on weekends. Ariel was still asleep, she was pretty certain. She hoped so—she didn't feel like getting fully dressed yet, and she knew that her bralessness inside one of the many ratty T-shirts she slept in made him uncomfortable. She'd noticed him averting his gaze before. It was heartbreaking, how she'd become old and repulsive to him at some point, her body's existence embarrassing him. She wasn't sure when it had happened, and she knew it was normal, but she still felt a twinge of pain when he looked away from her like that. A reminder that the last link of intimacy between their bodies, once babushka-dolled one inside the other, was severed for good. She put her hand on Ariel's shut and locked door and silently bid him to sleep a little longer, just until she had the energy to get dressed.

"Hello, sleepyhead," Peter said when she passed his office. Iris waved but kept going to the kitchen and coffee. He followed her there and hugged her from behind as she poured herself a mug.

"Mmph," she said, elbowing him to let her go, and got the milk from the fridge. He put his hands up, surrendering with a grin. "It's *Sunday*, and it's *morning*, stop being so perky," she groaned at him. But she didn't mean it. This was Peter, and she loved how unfairly upbeat he was.

"What are you up to today?" he asked, leaning against the kitchen island. Without waiting, he went on. "I have some errands to do, and I'm catching up on that project for the museum, they've asked for some more adjustments, but—"

"Honey, why oh why don't you put it in your contract that you'll only do two or three rounds of changes before adding an additional fee?" Iris shook her head. Peter was a good artist, a good graphic designer, but not the best businessman. She should know; she was the one who did their taxes and dealt with their finances. Some years he barely made a profit, what with the subscriptions to various software and the way he took his time with projects. She was the one who'd really kept them afloat. Peter's income was chump change in comparison to the fees she charged her clients.

He shrugged. "They're a nonprofit. I'm okay with doing a bit more work."

Iris didn't understand him in this way, how much he seemed to enjoy the work in itself and how little monetary value he placed on his time. She took a sip of coffee and decided she didn't care. This was an old argument, a boring one, and they were doing all right right now, still paying the mortgage, alas, but also building their savings back up, preparing a small nest egg they could hopefully leave their children. Which reminded her. "You know, Anya asked me yesterday when I'm planning to retire."

"No!"

"Yes, she really did. I don't think she meant it to sound so rude. But she's more ambitious and grasping than she realizes."

"Are you dangling that in front of her now?" Peter asked. Iris raised her eyebrows. He knew her well. It was a good way to keep the excellent assistant around, hinting at a possible promotion, a passing of the baton she wasn't planning on anytime soon. "Anyway, sorry, what did you say you were doing today?" he asked.

"I didn't yet, but yeah, I have to take my stuff to that dry cleaner that's open on Sundays, you know the one, the Ocean Breeze place or whatever it's called. Other than that, I'm going to relax a bit. Oh, and volunteering tonight," she added, offhand, though of course she hadn't for a moment forgotten about it.

"Ah, yes, my wife the do-gooder," Peter said. "Well, I hope you relax in my office at some point. I'd love a nap on the chaise with you."

Iris palmed his cheek before hugging him. She reveled in the way his arms squeezed her torso just a little too hard, anchoring her. She'd been gone only three days, but still, it was always so good to be home.

BY THE TIME Ariel emerged from his bedroom, Iris was dressed in her weekend clothes—a pair of loose-fitting slacks and a light cotton long-sleeved shirt—and was lounging on the living room couch with the latest Faye Kellerman novel. He traipsed in with both his hands scratching around inside his gray sweatpants and yanked them out when he saw her, like a child caught with his fingers in the cookie jar.

"Hi," he said. "I thought you were coming back tomorrow?"

"Nope. How're you doing, kiddo?"

"Ugh."

"Still no word from . . ." She struggled to recall the name. Lena? Leonora? Leanna? ". . . that girl you like?" she ended up saying.

"I don't *like* her, Mom. It's not like that. We're friends." Ariel stomped to the kitchen and put his head in the fridge.

"Right," Iris murmured, only half to him. The girl in question had been friends with Ariel all through college so far, and had visited with him for Thanksgiving once and for spring break another time, and Iris was fairly certain Ariel was in love with her. She could picture the girl's sweet face, her clean-cut girl-next-door looks, the drab brown hair that always looked like it just needed a good shampoo-commercial makeover to make it shine.

But her name—Iris was bad with names, some days. She always had been, especially outside of work, but she wondered idly if it was getting worse. Or if she was being paranoid because she was in her sixties and was expected to be decrepit. Her own mother at this age had looked and acted so much older than Iris looked or felt, which made sense, of course. After all, being humiliated and marked and moved around, suffering a terrible loss, living through a war, and then immigrating to the United States ages a person. "Hey, Ariel, want to come with me to the dry cleaner's?"

He lowered a bottle of orange juice from his mouth, where he'd been sucking on it ravenously. "Um. Not really?"

Iris laughed, loving him for his honesty. "Fair enough."

IN THE EVENING, Iris gathered her purse and keys and set out for the second time that day. Peter didn't know what she was really doing at the Caring Place, the assisted-living facility she'd been visiting almost weekly for the past couple of months. There were plenty of things that Peter didn't know about the way she spent her time, and she was sure there were just as many things she didn't know about how he spent his. Still, she felt uncomfortable— she wouldn't say guilty, but only because she'd tried to scrub that useless emotion away a long time ago—having a secret so close to home, to Peter. She wasn't worried about Ariel, since he'd never expressed much interest in her life outside of her involvement in his, though as he got older, she supposed that would change. It had for her. But home was hers and Peter's sacred space, and though he was the true homebody of the two of them, Iris had enough respect for him and for what they'd built together to have a modicum of unease.

Not that it stopped her from going.

On the drive there, she caught herself touching the sides of her lips over and over again, making sure her lipstick hadn't strayed or smeared. It was ridiculous, she thought, being nervous now, at this point, with all that history behind them, with him in the state he was in now. But it didn't make any difference; rediscovering him, and them, had kept her giddy for weeks, aching to get home for more than the usual reasons.

She parked in the visitors' section and pulled down the mirror to check her lips one last time. She noticed a bit of sleep in her right eye from the nap she'd had earlier with Peter on his favorite piece of furniture in the house, the jade-green chaise longue, its velvet long since hardened and scratchy. Still, he loved the angle, the way he could hold her on his side just right without his shoulder pain getting in the way, the way he could scoop her close to him and wrap one leg over hers. She was truly one of the luckiest women alive, she thought, though she knew only a fraction of it was luck, really—she'd created circumstances for herself over and over again. Like this, here, now.

Her low heels clicked across the smooth parking lot, the lines of the spaces recently repainted and sharply white, almost gleaming in the twilight. Inside, Darlene, the Sunday evening nurse, greeted her with a smile. "Harold is having a good day," she said. "He's in the rec room."

"Oh good, thank you," Iris said. At the doorway to the rec room, she saw Harold sitting, a bit slumped, watching a rowdy card game that several gentlemen were engaged in, along with a lady Iris hadn't seen there before. She smiled at the curses the players were hurling at one another as they demanded the woman make her move to call or fold, but she was holding her cards in her lap and waving a disapproving finger at them, insisting they give her the proper time to consider her odds.

"She's counting cards, you idiots," Harold boomed suddenly, and Iris laughed. He heard her—he was blessed with better hearing than Iris's own, which was beginning to fail, a fact he relentlessly teased her about, since he was two decades her senior. When he turned to look at her, his face, normally a distinguished craggy mask, spread wide with his smile, causing his cheeks to further wrinkle up toward his eyes even while his jaw seemed to smooth out. Iris was herself fairly lined, but she'd been watching the people here since she began visiting, fascinated by the many ways skin could weather the years. "Well, look who it is!" Harold called out.

Deliberately, slowly, Iris walked forward, her thick hips swaying, and released her hair, which had been up in a high bun, from its clip. Her wavy almost-black hair with its unevenly dispersed streaks of gray tumbled down to her shoulders, and Harold wolf-whistled as she shook it out behind her. She knew other women her age who felt at peace with their looks, but she could never quite tell if that meant they also still felt sexy at times. She did, at least in moments like these. The cardplayers clapped and whooped for her, the lady winking and grinning widely, showing off a single missing tooth.

"Hello, Iris," Harold said as she pulled up a chair and sat down. The cardplayers included a couple of Harold's new friends, though she couldn't recall their names. The woman just waved and then asked the others if they were ready to play or if they wanted to keep gawping at young women. Iris laughed at this. She was certainly not young, and her skin showed far more wear than some other women her age. Still, the lady had a point—every time Iris came here, she registered a shock at seeing so many old people in one place, before reminding herself she too could be considered old, that people on the street probably thought of her as such.

"It's busy here tonight," Iris said. The room was relatively full, visitors sitting with residents, children running around with the kind of pack men-tality that kids thrust together seem to acquire quickly.

"No busier than usual," Harold said. "But let's go to my room and open a bottle of wine, shall we?"

"Hubba-hubba!" one of the men sing-songed, raising extremely bushy gray eyebrows.

"Now, now, be nice," Iris said as she helped Harold up. He leaned on her, the exertion of rising showing in his pained face. "Where's your walker?"

"I got here without it today," he told her proudly, but she could tell that he was tired, his knees wobbling a bit. Darlene had said he was having a good day, but Iris wondered how much of that was Harold feeling well and how much of it was shame over his need for assistance. His face began to redden as they walked slowly toward the elevator in the hallway by the rec room, and Iris wanted to suggest a rest, or that she borrow a walker from the room they'd just left, but he looked determined, mouth set in a hard line. She didn't want to ruin his good mood.

The elevator was equipped with a small bench, and Iris maneuvered Harold to it and sat with him for the short ride up to the third story, where his room was. He wasn't panting, but he wasn't comfortable, and even as he gripped her hand, he looked away.

"Penny for your thoughts?" she said.

"Darling, pennies are worthless and you know it. Make a man a better offer than that."

The elevator door opened and there was Harold's walker on the landing where he must have left it earlier. Iris knew it was his because his grandson, a fifteen-year-old whom Harold said was in his monosyllabic phase, had decorated the dull silver with skateboarding stickers, wrapping every surface but for where Harold gripped it with the black-outlined, neon-colorful graffiti fonts. It looked ridiculous, but Harold loved it. His grandson must be special, Iris had thought when she first saw it. How many teenagers would try to make their grandparents' walkers look hip?

They got to his room fairly easily after that, Iris taking small paces beside Harold, but it was hard seeing him like this. She'd first met him over twenty years ago, and while he hadn't been young then—he'd been only a bit younger than she was now, in fact—he had been vibrant and athletic, that late-fifties type of man who wore his middle-age like a bespoke suit. Now he was old, truly old, and she could tell he hated it. She thought he'd hate being dead more, though.

"All right, here we go," he said, trying to turn his energy back on as he settled himself on one side of the couch that sat by the window. The curtain was pulled back and the sky was a magnificent indigo, not yet entirely dark. "A room with a view, some good wine, and an old flame—what could be better?" He'd already positioned the bottle, an opener, and two glasses on the coffee table and was now working on opening the wine while Iris settled beside him.

"Excuse me, who're you calling an *old* flame?" she said, trying to be playful as he struggled with the cork. When it was out, he poured a generous glass for each of them so that the bottle was almost half-empty when he set it down.

"Iris, what are you still doing here?" Harold asked after taking a sip. His charm was dimmed, his eyes suddenly very tired, the pouches underneath making him look like a hound.

She considered his question, surprised he'd asked it. He was the one who'd reached out to her, after all. He'd tepidly googled her, found her email on LinkedIn, told her he was moving to this place near where he knew she used to live. Where she still lived. He'd never been to her house, didn't know her address. She'd looked him up too some time back, had figured out where he was located, had written his address out on a white envelope. She kept forgetting she needed to change it. "I thought you wanted me here," she finally said, turning her glass between her palms, watching the light bounce off it.

"Well, sure I do. But I'm old. And this place is depressing."

"It wasn't so depressing last time I was here," she said softly. They'd made love then, the first time since they'd become reacquainted. Harold had needed to take a pill, which had somehow surprised her, though she knew it shouldn't. His body was different, of course, his pubic hair sparse and white, his skin loose around his joints, his stomach and thighs heavier than she remembered them being. She'd been on top for most of it, but he'd flipped her over with more strength than she'd expected toward the end, and the weight of him had felt almost suffocating, heavy with nostalgia. She'd been weepy after, but he kissed her tears away and made her gasp with his fingers until she was moaning. He'd whispered in her ear, calling her beautiful, sexy, delighting in the feeling of her wet and warmth. When she'd orgasmed hard around his fingers, he'd shuddered alongside her, urging her on, breathing raggedly with her.

A shiver passed through her now, and she reached for him. "Harold," she said softly. "Don't we have the right to enjoy each other? Haven't we earned that?"

He barked a laugh and looked away from her, though he leaned his cheek against her hand. "I don't know about earn," he said. "But yes, we have the right." He nodded at the bedside table where the Viagra sat in the drawer. "Maybe we should get started before it gets too late."

It was only eight, but visiting hours ended at nine thirty here, and she didn't want to overstay her welcome. She got him the pill, a glass of water, and sat beside him, stroking his long fingers.

It wasn't the same this time. Neither of them came. There was a feeling of futility and frustration in their actions, an attempt to recapture the magic they'd only just rekindled last week. Once he got tired, he pulled out and tried to make sure she, at least, was satisfied.

"It's okay," she said finally, as she reached a precipice she couldn't get beyond for the third time. "I can't. It happens."

"Are you sure?" he asked, and Iris almost laughed. It was such a juvenile question, one she'd answered so many times. It was always her responsibility, somehow, to make every encounter with a man end up all right. She'd made her peace with it a long time ago, though a vestigial twinge of resentment lingered.

"I'm sure. Tell me something nice," she said, wanting to revel in the intimacy between their damp unsatisfied bodies before she had to get dressed and go. She laid her head on the plumped pillow, with his outstretched arm under her neck, so that he could hold on to her without her weight hurting him.

"Like a story?"

"Sure."

So he told her about his eldest son's dramatic divorce from a health guru in Sacramento, how they'd split their community of yoga-class attendees and juice-bar regulars and how he'd gotten the rotten end of the friend deal, because, and Harold smiled as he relayed this reasoning, his son couldn't put his foot behind his ear like the ex could. Harold made the story funny, though Iris imagined the whole thing had been quite painful, but that was Harold—he was a spectator of human behavior, his years working as a psychologist always with him. Iris felt herself drifting off into semi-sleep, and only when the soft chime announcing visiting hours coming to an end sounded from the hallway did she rouse herself.

"I can't come next week, I'll be packing for a trip, but can I come the week after?" she asked as she pulled her bra and panties on. Harold was on his side, watching her with his always damp-seeming blue eyes.

"Only if you promise me something," he said. Iris looked up, trepidatious. "You need to tell me more about you. Your family. Your kids. I think your daughter was, what, two? When we first met? And you said you have a son. I want to know about them."

"That wasn't ever part of the deal before," she said, turning her back on him as she finished getting dressed.

"We're in a very different place than we were before, Iris," he said, tone serious. "I don't know how long I have to live, and I know, I know, I'm in great health for a man my age, but that doesn't matter. Living here is a reminder that people can go at any time, sick or not. It just happens. Old age is a real thing, Iris, and you're lucky that you're not afflicted with it yet."

"What?" she said, holding a hand to her ear, mocking herself. "I'm a little deaf, what did you say?"

"Har har. You heard me very well." He lay back. "I don't want to know just this one part of you. If you want to spend this time with me, you have to be willing to share more. Let me get to know more of you, not just this ephemeral sexy pixie-dust-throwing apparition." He was laughing by the end of this descriptor, and so was Iris.

"I missed you, you know," she whispered into his mouth when she kissed him. Something inside her felt loose, as if the hinges of the cage containing her other life when she was with Harold were rusting, but it didn't frighten her. She thought it would be nice, actually, telling him about Ariel, about Maggie, about what they taught her. He would understand, she knew now, about the terror that was parenting, and the elation, and he would smile indulgently. She was, she realized, looking forward to it.

"I missed you too," he said.

"Two weeks, okay?"

"See you then, darling."

AND THEN. THEN the drive home, one hand on the wheel and the other fiddling with her necklace, a little elated, a little melancholy, that space of in-between that she felt was becoming more and more a part of her life as she aged. She both wished for things to be as they once were, and accepted quicker than ever before how they were now. And then the dog, or maybe it was a coyote, she wasn't sure, running across the street. Her senses just a tiny bit duller from the large glass of wine. Her hands gripping the steering wheel hard, her eyes wide open, swerving, swerving, until she crashed, the car crumpling in front of her, her head whipping back, seat belt tightening around her torso and the crack of breaking a rib as her body rocketed forward, and the airbag popping into her face and breaking her nose, and as she tasted blood, as the broken rib punctured a lung and she began to drown, she heard the cars still driving by in the opposite direction, and in the soothing tide of life going on as normal, she died.

Maggie collects her suitcase and walks out to the curb. Ariel said he'd pick her up, but she doesn't know yet how a mother's death changes responsibility, whether he'll forget or oversleep or show up. She doesn't know what home will be like, whether it will feel like it used to or like a nightmare reflection. The world is atilt. LA's air smells faintly of tar. The sky is so blandly blue it could be a tarp, the kind set up to provide shade for the outdoor picnic tables at the park where Maggie's classmates had birthday parties when they were all little kids and the most exciting rush was sneaking third and fourth slices of birthday cake when the adults weren't watching. The distance Maggie still feels from the existence of her grief makes her intensely self-conscious, as if she's acting in a movie about a woman who goes home when her mother dies rather than actually experiencing it. She runs her hands through her hair, styled in a curly top fade to accommodate both her thick waves and her workplace—she slicks everything straight back and flat for the office—and considers texting Lucia to tell her she's arrived, but a car honks at her and she sees it's Ariel in his 1994 Jeep

Wrangler, a car older than Ariel himself, but which someone sold him in high school when he worked at an OfficeMax that has since closed.

"I can't believe you're still driving this thing," she says when she opens the door and heaves her suitcase into the narrow space of the back seat. Ariel rolls his eyes, and again, the entire scene feels unreal, too normal. "Hey, are you okay?" she asks as he tears away from the curb. LAX is as bad as the St. Louis airport about letting people sit and wait. Everywhere is. This constant coming and going of humanity, Maggie thinks, makes it impossible to pause anywhere. *We're all just going-going-going until we're gone.*

"What do you think? Are *you* okay?" Ariel spits at her. He turns the radio up. It's something she doesn't know, a rapper tossing out lyrics and rhymes in Spanish. She recognizes the curl and curve of some words, but can't grasp the overall meaning. Maggie wants to tell Ariel that yes, she's okay, more or less.

Instead, she says, "Jeez, okay, just don't take it out on me," and wonders what she means by that. Who else is Ariel supposed to take things out on? It's not like he has a girlfriend, as far as she knows, and then is disgusted with herself for assuming she's supposed to take things out on Lucia. Although hasn't she already? Just in the last sixteen hours or so? But it's a good thing, really, she thinks, pulling absently at the yellow-brown foam poking out of the seat. It's good because now that Lucia has seen how cold Maggie can get when something bad happens, she'll know she should leave. And that's good too, Maggie tries to convince herself as Ariel plucks the chunk of foam from between her worrying fingers and asks her sternly to stop. It's good because this way Maggie will at least know that she didn't cheat this time, that she didn't fuck it all up half on purpose.

The drive is longer than it should be because of the traffic getting away from the airport, but eventually the 101 clears up enough for it to feel like they're actually moving again, and Maggie watches the hills that always look dry, burned-out—some of them really are, the fires have been bad lately—with what greenery there is lying low, fighting for its life and the few drops of water it can get from the arid land.

"Remember when Mom took us sometimes when she had work in LA?" she asks, the words tumbling out of her mouth. Ariel's hands tighten on the wheel and he nods. He pushes his fist under his thick black-rimmed glasses and rubs each eye with a tight twist, as if shutting off a faucet, as if this'll keep him from crying. "That was so fun," Maggie continues. "Well, for me it was. You were so little, you usually just watched whatever I was doing and then fell asleep."

"Yeah, but you'd tickle me to try to wake me up. You know that's why I'm not ticklish? I trained myself to ignore you because if I looked like I was asleep Mom would pick me up and bring me to the car. I mean, everyone fakes that, right? Like, do kids really stay asleep when grown-ups pick them up like that?"

"No idea. I also pretended," Maggie says. They fall silent again, and she thinks about that feeling of being wrapped in the warmth of an adult, a person she could trust. She knows she's an adult herself now, technically. Usually, she's proud of this, that she's made it, as if growing up is an achievement rather than a force of nature, but now, she wishes she could go back.

WHEN ARIEL PULLS up to their childhood home, Maggie sighs, relieved. It looks the same as it always does, the same as it always has, and though she grew up thinking it was ugly and old and was always jealous of the kids who lived in the newly built houses, she realizes now that she was lucky to live in a somewhat vintage place, even though it's still ugly on the outside. Ariel parks in front, without opening the garage door, essentially blocking it, and on any other day Maggie would have told him off for this annoying habit, but at the moment, she feels a rush of fear. Ariel hasn't mentioned their father once, and she's been too scared to ask. She has to wait for Ariel to open their front door, which is littered with several wreaths of flowers delivered apparently in the past couple of hours.

"Who are these from?" she asks, and Ariel grunts something and bends down to pick one up and check, but she doesn't wait. She walks straight through the foyer, doesn't glance at the kitchen or living room or the backyard where her mother left out a birdfeeder that was usually used by the squirrels. She goes right to the door of her father's office, which is ajar, and pushes it open.

"Dad?"

She drops her backpack. It thunks loudly, the metal water bottle at the bottom landing hard. Her father doesn't look up. Ariel mutters from behind her, "He's been this way since last night."

Peter is sitting at his work desk, the place where Maggie and Ariel have seen him a thousand times before, but it's all wrong. Rather than the busy, harried focus on paper or screen he usually had when they were kids—or the pacing that accompanied his bouts of creative frustration—he's still. Peter isn't a still man, or never used to be. The death of his wife appears, Maggie thinks, to have made the clockwork inside him run down.

Throughout their childhood, Peter was the one who cooked, who cleaned, who picked them up from after-school tutoring sessions or sleepovers on the weekends with friends. Peter was the one who made their house a home, always welcoming them when they arrived. He was a stay-at-home dad, a work-from-home dad, a dad like no other dad they knew. He was good with his hands but wasn't handy, and he hired people to fix things when they broke—plumbers and electricians and car mechanics. They weren't wealthy, but they were in that middle-class place where they could weigh time against money—Peter knew, for instance, that instead of trying to learn how to pull things out of toilet piping or attempting to figure out his car engine on his own, he could cook for his children or find a new client to work for. He was good that way, knowing when to extend himself and when to keep to the things he knew.

When Maggie first came out, there were those kids at school who asked her why she hated men. She didn't answer them, because they didn't deserve an answer, but she thought about the question. Did she hate men? No, she didn't. She hated male dominance and the patriarchy, of course, but that was different. Men, on an individual level, she didn't hate. How could she, when she joined in the boys' games all the way until puberty, disliking the girly things she was supposed to like back then? She simply wasn't attracted to masculinity, though she adopted some of it for herself. She wanted to tell those kids in high school that it was impossible to hate men as a category when she had a father who was distinctly male—in the essentialist way she would later reject as being true, because the binary was bullshit—a father who had been nothing but a gem to her. They had their share of fights about curfews and dating—both before and after she came out—and the way her mom could be a total bitch, but still. He was the best dad she'd heard of. He was there. He was paternal and maternal, making up for Iris's long work hours and frequent business trips.

And he was talented too, though she didn't really register this until much later. She was just used to seeing new lettering, logos, and designs hanging around his office, not quite thinking about the fact that Peter was creating them entirely from scratch for his clients. It wasn't until she took a graphic design class in her first year of college and hated it—the software was so finicky, and doodling on notebooks was very different from creating consistent shapes—that she realized the extent of her father's abilities. That he was, though he didn't call himself that, an artist.

But now—now Maggie looks at her father sitting at his desk, still, his head lowered, reading something, not moving, not reacting to her voice.

"Daddy," she tries again, and begins stepping toward him. He lifts his head, an expression of mild surprise on his face.

"Oh, hello." He sighs and looks back down. "This isn't very good. But I can see why Iris loved it so much." Peter and Iris almost never used each other's names when speaking to their kids, usually saying "your dad" or "your mom," and it's strange for Maggie to hear the way her father says her mother's name, like she's some woman Maggie's never heard of.

She walks closer and says gently, as if speaking to an invalid, "What are you reading?"

He lifts up the book and shows her. It's a detective novel, one of the many her mother read and loved. She had shelves and shelves of them, collecting all the books by the same author, becoming obsessed with one for a while, reading everything they wrote, and moving on to the next. LA noir, Florida noir, medical thrillers, psychological thrillers, literary crime, spy novels—she collected and read all of it. Maggie's never been the reader her mother was—Ariel inherited that trait far more clearly—but she sees the appeal, though she prefers true crime to fiction and viewing or listening to reading.

"Dad, you need to get up and do stuff," Ariel says from the doorway. His face is screwed up and angry, and as he speaks, his voices rises. "There's shit to do, stuff to plan, you can't just sit there!" Ariel's arms wave around as he yells this, and Maggie knows she needs to stop this and control the situation.

"Okay, now, Ariel, come on—"

"No, no, don't you do that, Maggie, don't you dare, it's not your responsibility, it's Dad's, he's the parent—hello? Are you still a parent?" Ariel is full-on screeching now, and Maggie wonders what the last eighteen hours have been like in this household without her. Ariel is supposed to start his junior year of college at UC Irvine in a month and is still home for summer vacation, and he was here when it happened, when their mother's car was found rammed into a tree, probably after swerving to avoid something, a child or animal. This is what Ariel explained happened last night, but Maggie realizes she doesn't actually know many of the details and needs to regroup, to get things figured out. The body, for instance—where's the body?

First order of business, she thinks, is to get Ariel out of here, get him doing something useful. She's pretty sure her hands are shaking, so she balls them up into tight fists, clenches hard. "Ariel," she says, turning to him. They're virtually the same height, and she stands close so he can't see Peter and has to focus on her face. "Go get those flowers from the front door. Make a list of all the people you think we need to call. Find out how we get an obituary in the paper. Can you do that for me?"

Ariel stares, his jaw working hard as he tries to stop himself from crying again. Maggie flashes back to when he was a young teen and she'd just become officially legal; back then, whenever she told him to do anything, he'd respond with a loud, sarcastic "Okay, *Mom*." She wonders if he's thinking of this as well, of how he can't say that anymore. Without a word, he turns and slams the door of the office shut behind him. Maggie's shoulders jump at the sound, and she feels a surge of anger, or maybe just adrenaline, but tamps it down. She can't fall apart now. She's the oldest child, the independent one, and apparently the most capable grown-up in the house at the moment. And she has to deal with her father.

"Daddy, have you eaten anything?" she asks him. He shakes his head and murmurs a no. "Okay, let me get you something. Also, is your lawyer still Janice, the woman who helped with my arrest that time?"

"Arrest?" Peter asks mildly. "Oh, that. That was so long ago."

"Janice, Dad. Is she still your lawyer?" Maggie asks. It's hard to keep from shouting, but she manages.

"Mm."

Well, okay then, she thinks, and swallows again, pushing away the panic, anger, adrenaline, whatever it is, because she has to believe that Peter will be all right again eventually, that he'll be normal, recognizably her father. She doesn't have time or energy to consider the alternative. "I'm going to call her, okay?" she says.

He doesn't respond. She leaves his office, wanting very much to slam the door like Ariel did but restrains herself. She knows, without really thinking about it, that she will restrain herself a lot in the coming days.

MAGGIE SITS IN her childhood bedroom for a moment, on the single bed her parents never agreed to graduate her out of. She isn't out of breath, but she feels she has to catch it. She isn't dizzy, but she needs everything to stop spinning. She isn't jet-lagged, has never been jet-lagged, but she feels like daylight savings has just happened and that she's flown across the Atlantic to boot.

Her room looks nothing like her anymore. It's a reflection of a past self. On the wall above the bed are taped-up pictures of an androgynous Johnny Depp torn out of the teen magazines she would buy—until recently, he was the one exception to her disinterest in men, but when she found out he was an abusive asshole, she had let him go, not without regret. Beside Johnny are pictures of women—Uma Thurman in *Kill Bill,* Gwen Stefani in her most punk No Doubt phase, Janet Jackson pre–Justin Timberlake Super Bowl. There's a hole in the center of Gwen's picture from where the poster was ripped out of the magazine, cutting off her cocked hip.

"Don't you want to take these down already?" her mother had asked the last time Maggie visited. "It's been long enough. Almost a decade."

At the time, Maggie had tightened up, had answered something sarcastic or glib or possibly mean. She can't remember, but she knows her mother thought it was silly that this room remain a shrine to her teenage self. Maggie didn't know how to explain that she found comfort in her unchanging room. She liked the teenager she'd been, the raw newness of discovering her desires, the things that made her angry, the causes she became passionate about. She doesn't think high school was her happiest time, and she's pretty suspicious of anyone who thinks it should be, but she knows she was more open then, more willing to extend herself. Everything else shifts, changes, moves, grows up—and dies, she thinks now—so why not keep one thing the same, especially if it isn't hurting anyone?

She takes a deep breath and lets herself sink back, her Conversed feet still on the floor. *Just for a moment,* she thinks, and shuts her eyes.

SHE WAKES UP groggy a full two hours later. She's shocked Ariel has let her sleep this long. Her mind tries to wrap around the discomfort, the disconnect of being in her old bedroom on a Monday afternoon when she should be at work, sharing a muffin with Simon. She checks in on Peter again, remembering she'd meant to get him to eat, but he says he isn't hungry. Her phone has pointless news alerts about the now-finished eclipse, two texts from Lucia—Did u land safely? and Babe?—and some Facebook messages that she swipes away without looking at who they're from. She checks her work email to make sure that her leave is being handled smoothly. Her boss has answered her, expressing her sorrow for Maggie's loss and telling Maggie that she'll get three days of bereavement leave and can use paid or unpaid vacation days thereafter, and gently suggests that she hopes to see Maggie back after Labor Day. Maggie has been working at the agency for four years, and her boss likes her; she's good with younger clients who don't really get how insurance works or what the point of it is. They can connect with Maggie, her nose stud, her slicked-back hair, her clear hipsterness even inside her button-down and slacks. She's newly grateful for having this often sneered-at job, a stable one with a salary and benefits, rather than the freelance or barista and server life some of her friends lead—unlike them, she thinks, she's isn't worried about being fired when something like this happens and she has to leave.

In the kitchen, she sets up her battle station, plugging her laptop in so she won't have to think about its battery life, laying her planner and several pens beside it. This will be her base of operations. She waits for the tabs to load, the feeble beginnings of her research from early that morning. An air bubble rising up her esophagus makes her pay attention to her body—she must be hungry, even if Peter isn't.

"Ariel!" she shouts into the house, which is silent but for the hum of the refrigerator behind her. She calls his name again and gets no response. Reluctantly, she lowers herself out of the tall chair and checks the cupboards and fridge. There's plenty of food, but most of it requires actual cooking. Peter taught her how to cook a long time ago, and it's something she occasionally enjoys, especially recently because she and Lucia do it together a lot. Maggie had cooked with friends before, in the sad dorm kitchens in college and with roommates in St. Louis before she got her own place, but never with a lover, and the experience kept surprising her with its tenderness. Lucia cooked with care, and Maggie found herself increasingly doing the same, wanting to nourish Lucia in some way, to make her feel full, comforted. Just after they'd agreed they were officially together, Maggie prepared a marinated pork shoulder dish they'd shared at a restaurant; Lucia had taken one forkful of meat, held it in her mouth for a moment, and gently spit it out into a napkin before bursting out laughing. Maggie had mixed up the olive oil and vinegar ratios in the sauce recipe. At least the plantains she'd fried came out perfectly.

She can't muster up the energy to cook anything now, so she grabs a cereal bar and scarfs it down. For Peter, she gets a yogurt and some bread and cheese and a banana and puts it on a plate, which she brings to his office. He's leaning back in his chair with the book open on his stomach, which has grown rounder over the years into a distinct potbelly. His eyes are closed, and Maggie thinks he may be feigning sleep.

She heads to Ariel's room. The door is shut, and she can't hear anything inside. She knocks, and when she gets no response, tries the handle, but it just turns uselessly. Ariel convinced their parents to get him a real lock for his birthday when he was fourteen, with a key and everything so he could lock it from the outside as well as inside. Maggie had helped, mentioning to their father—she'd never say as much to Iris—that Ariel probably just wanted to jerk off in peace. Ariel has always been fiercely private. It's why she likes shocking him so much. She wanders through the house, which seems bigger than it ever has before, so different from her one-bedroom apartment in St. Louis, which feels spacious enough for her and more. She begins to hear Ariel's voice as she approaches the backyard and sees the door to it is open. But he's not there; she walks toward his voice and realizes he's on the phone, walking up and down the gravel-filled side yard. Shoeless.

"Why?" she mouths, pointing to his bare feet. He tries to wave her away but she stays there, listening.

"Yes, Mrs. Gershon. That's right. She really was. Okay, thank you so much for your help." Then, to Maggie, "You know who's the man? This man. This man right here. And you know why? Can you tell me why?" He cocks his ear toward her, cupping a hand around it. "No? I didn't think so. Well, I just got this whole funeral thing taken care of and we don't have to do a thing. Boom! How'd you like that!" He lifts his hand for a high five but Maggie leaves him hanging.

"What do you mean?" she asks.

"I mean," Ariel says, "that I just called the synagogue, and Mrs. Gershon is still there, and you know she and Mom—" He pauses for a moment, looks down at his bare feet, which must be both burning and uncomfortable on the hot and prickly gravel. "She knew Mom for a long time, like since way back when," he pushes on, determined to ignore the quaver in his voice. "And she said the synagogue will take care of everything, and she just needs us to get the death certificate from the hospital and scan a copy of it for her by tomorrow afternoon, and then the funeral will be day after tomorrow, which is as soon as she said they can make it. Wait, where are you going?"

Maggie began backing away around the words "death certificate" and now is sliding the door to the backyard shut behind her—*he always leaves it open, that fucker,* she thinks, *wasting the air-conditioning, wasting electricity, he never listens to Mom when* . . . though of course it didn't matter, because

Iris never seemed to get mad at Ariel, the goody two-shoes nerd who liked school and D&D and books. She half-heartedly hopes the door will lock behind her, that Ariel will get stuck outside, that he'll need to wake Peter from his stupor to come and let him in, but no such luck. Ariel is behind her now, asking again where she's off to.

"I'm taking your car," she says.

"No, you're not. What if I need it?"

"Fine, I'll take Mom's car then." She stops. Realizes. "Ariel," she says quietly, "what actually happened last night? I mean, how? How'd you find out?" She meant to ask Peter, thought asking the adult was the right thing to do, not the twenty-two-year-old junior in college. But now that she's seen what their father's like, how monosyllabic he is, she feels lost.

Ariel's bottom lip is shaking again, his eyes shining. His hands go back in his pockets. He begins to tell her, right there in the hallway. Maggie thinks this is a sitting-down conversation, a hands-wrapped-around-a-mug-of-tea conversation, but she stills and listens.

"I was watching the new season of *Episodes*, you know, that show with that guy from *Friends*? Anyway, I was watching, and Dad was getting ready to go to bed because he's getting to be old and whatever, and someone knocked at the door, and I thought it was Mom, because she was driving back from doing her volunteer work at the retirement home, you know how she started playing bingo or whatever it is with them on Sunday nights—"

Maggie doesn't know this, actually. She has no idea her mother volunteered or had the time to; Iris wasn't a person generous with her time, as far as Maggie knows, but she listens, trying to absorb what Ariel is saying, though she can't keep away the thought that her mother never told her about this, and she can't remember, suddenly, when the last time they spoke was, when she last heard her mother's voice.

"—and yeah, well, it wasn't her, it was this cop, and he had his hat in his hand and shit, which was really weird, and yeah, I dunno, I guess Mom was just driving home down North Rose Ave, and the police dude said they think she must have been speeding and that something, like an animal or something, ran into the road, and she must have tried to swerve and she hit that big tree, you know, where the sign to Camino de la Luna is? You know, before the turn?"

Maggie doesn't remember the sign, not having driven around the area regularly in years, but she knows the stretch of road he means. On one side are fields, the big square historic park commemorating the early farmers to settle Oxnard—or colonize it, probably; she isn't actually sure who lived here before. On the other side, separated by a broad boulevard, are the backs of the houses in the West Village neighborhood. Such an innocuous stretch of road.

"And?" Maggie asks. "I mean . . ." She doesn't know what she means. Ariel just shakes his head and shrugs, like that's that, like he's told her everything there is to know.

"Anyway, the car is totaled, obviously," he says.

"Where is it? Where is *she*?"

"St. John's. I, uh, I don't know about the car."

"Okay," she says. But it isn't. "I'll take Dad's car, then." She grabs the keys from the hook and shuts the door to the garage closed in Ariel's face. This time he gets the message and doesn't follow her.

In Peter's Prius, she rests her head on the steering wheel for a moment. She'd already emailed a funeral home last night through their online form, during her spate of busyness. When she got off the plane, she saw they'd written back, ungrammatically but swiftly:

Yes, we can accommodate a jewing funeral. Has your loved one past? we can
have the burial permit issued within 24 hrs along with an all wood casket.

She thought she had things under control already, or at least had the steps to get them under control. And now Ariel's taken the whole thing away from her, from all of them. She should be grateful he's taken this off her list, but isn't. It's too easy, she thinks, fobbing the job off to someone else, like it isn't their responsibility. She wonders whether she can even trust Mrs. Gershon. She vaguely remembers the woman occasionally calling to chat with her mother about this or that function, but the family so rarely went to the synagogue that Maggie doesn't really know what her mother's advice was being used for.

Pulling out of the driveway, Maggie decides that she'll call this Mrs. Gershon whom Ariel so blithely trusted with their mother's remains and ask her some things. Not that Maggie knows what Iris would have wanted, but funerals aren't for the people who've died; they're for the people who are still alive. Her mother said that once, she realizes. About her father's, Maggie's grandfather's, funeral. Maggie was only about seven, and Ariel would have been around two. Iris had told them the story from New York, her voice crackly over the landline speakerphone. Someone had whispered behind Iris that Benami would have wanted to be remembered in a more elaborate fashion and Iris had told him that funerals weren't for the dead but for the living, and that Benami's family wanted a simple funeral and if he, the stranger, didn't like it, he was welcome to leave. Maggie remembers feeling mortified by her mother's anger. She'd witnessed Iris's saltiness in public before, and it was always embarrassing, even then.

Maggie isn't entirely sure where she's driving at first. She just knows she had to get out of the oppressive atmosphere of the too-quiet house and that she didn't want to encounter any of the neighbors by walking around. She realizes soon that she's heading to the beach. Something she misses terribly in St. Louis is the ocean, after years of taking its proximity for granted. It isn't a place where she particularly remembers her mother—they didn't do much together, really, her mother always so busy with work—but it's the first image that usually comes to her mind when she thinks of the word "home." She spent long afternoons and weekends with her friends at the beaches, with Anthony, Kyle, Morgan—she hasn't thought about them in so long—and Gina, the only one from high school she still keeps in touch with. They'd all sit around, both complaining about and celebrating how far they were from the tourists who flocked to LA and San Diego and La Jolla's beaches. Tourists, she and her friends thought, meant good-looking people who didn't go to their school or the other school or the other other school. There were a few more, but somehow, it seemed like they always knew everyone, like there was no one new to get excited about. Maggie wonders if everyone feels that way in high school, like they know everyone worth knowing.

The beach is also where Maggie first fell in love—well, what she thought was love when she was fourteen—with a surfing instructor. Pulling into the mostly empty parking lot, she wonders idly if Cleo still works here, but surely not.

The sun is just starting to go down. It's hot and orange and impossible to look directly into. Maggie takes her shoes and socks off for the first time since putting them on this morning back in St. Louis, which seems forever ago, and leaves them in the car. The sand on the beach is warm, but no longer hot, and there are cool spots where uneven dips and mounds have created pockets of shadow. She plops herself down close to where the tide is coming in. Some swimmers' heads bob around in the sea, and there are a fair few people lying on blankets around her, but it's quiet. No one is playing loud music from their cell phones or Bluetooth speakers, no one is playing volleyball at the nets—it's as if everyone is choosing to respect this moment, Maggie thinks. Like they know.

Her lips curl with a half smile, and she shakes away the dramatic sentiment. Pulling her phone out of her back pocket to get more comfortable, she sees a missed call from Lucia. She texts her: Hey I'm here safely just a lot going on and dad isn't being helpful like at all.

She doesn't wait for a response. She figures Lucia can cut her some slack right now. And if she can't, then screw her, right? It's been too good to be true, anyway, Maggie knows. No one, until Lucia, ever made her feel like her parents felt about each other. She never talks about it, because it seems like an utterly ridiculous thing to complain about, what with people's broken families and divorces and parents who drank too much or died too young or left or hit or hurled violent words, but she's wondered whether seeing such a good example in her parent's marriage has been detrimental, made her standards too high, her expectations over the top. Lucia is the first person Maggie's been with who hasn't made her feel inadequate, but surely that won't last.

A cloud partially covers the sun, breaking the light into the kind of rays that look like they belong in a Disney movie. It's too pretty, Maggie thinks, and her eyes are burning, so she shuts them and listens to the waves instead.

BUT SHE DOESN'T manage to stay at peace for long. Maggie ends up scrolling through her social media feeds instead of watching the ocean and the sunset. Lucia spent the day hard at work in her studio, it seems; there's a picture of her hunched over her pottery wheel, a beautifully captured and sharply focused bead of sweat at the back of her neck. Maggie wonders who took the photo. She knows Lucia shares the studio with several other artists, but the couple of times she's been there have been at odd hours—late at night after their third date, when Lucia showed her some of her work; an early weekday morning when Lucia realized she'd left her wallet there— and when there was no one else around. Maggie hearts the picture, then unhearts it, thinking it'll look weird, like she's thinking about her still-newish girlfriend instead of about the fact that her mother has just died.

She swipes the screen down to reload the app and get fresh stories at the top, and a jolt runs through her when she comes across Ariel's post from last night.

An hour ago the cops came to my parents house to tell us my mom died in a
car crash. I don't really know what to do right now. My sister is coming home
and my dad isn't talking, he's just sitting there not doing anything, if anyone
has any advice on how to handle this kind of thing, let me know. Sorry to be a
downer tonight.

The post has been heavily loved, liked, teared over. Someone wrote
"fuck the police" in a comment, to which Ariel replied, "sure, but irrelevant
right now they didnt kill my mom kthxbi." Most of the comments are sympathetic, with some overly long ones in which people share their own experiences with sudden death, or with long illnesses, or with anything that
makes them feel like they're doing something by commenting. At least
that's what Maggie assumes is the point. It's not like any of this is really
going to help Ariel feel better, is it?

She wonders if she's supposed to post something similar. If she's supposed to reach out and tell the whole world that she has suffered a loss. But
no, she thinks. It's nobody's business but her own. Ariel's post at least explains how people already knew to send flowers.

Hollow and numb, Maggie gets up. She pounds the sand off the back
of her jeans as she heads to the car, ignoring the marvelous colors stretched
across the sky behind her. So fucking what, she thinks, it's all pollution
anyway.

BACK HOME, SHE opens the door to Peter's office and finds the food she left
for him untouched. He's moved from his chair to the chaise longue, where
he lies on his side, knees curled up toward his chest. He looks very old and
very young at the same time, and Maggie feels a rush of something that she
can't untangle, something that feels like love, pity, and also anger. This isn't
fair, she thinks. Life isn't, her mother would counter whenever Maggie said

that, whether it was about not getting roller skates for her birthday or having her rent raised every year. And Maggie would say that just accepting that doesn't change anything, doesn't make anything get better, ever. But maybe, she thinks now, Iris had a point; maybe accepting some things as unfair is as good as it can get.

Maggie takes the old fleece blanket that lies at the foot of the chaise and spreads it over her father, who is shivering slightly, his arms wrapped tightly around himself like he's trying to hold on to something. She kneels next to him and stares at his face, its expression so unfamiliar, so unlike the parental, caretaking mask she needs it to be.

"Daddy," she whispers. "We'll make it okay. It's going to be okay." She doesn't know how or why she's making this promise—she has no idea how to keep it, what will make him okay. Once, when Maggie had another flameout with a girl she was dating, she'd asked Peter how he and her mother did it, and he'd vaguely talked about communication, about absolute trust, about giving space, about loyalty. Maybe they weren't just platitudes, Maggie thinks now. The tense sadness radiating off him seems to highlight, perversely, just how much he loved Iris.

She finds Ariel outside again, sitting at the eroding round metal table with its attached curved metal benches. It's always been there, as far as she knows. They never fixed it or replaced it, even though it smells strongly of metal and rust and is impossible to sit on during the day because it gets too hot in the sun. Ariel is smoking a bowl, to Maggie's immense relief. He hasn't turned the outside lights on, and though he has an open book beside him, it's flipped pages-down.

"Hey," she says. "Can I join?"

He shrugs but holds out the bowl to her.

"I didn't know you smoked," she says, then positions the lighter he hands her above the bowl, and draws deeply. It's weak stuff and tastes kind of old and stale and makes her cough. But she hasn't eaten in hours, and she's already in a strange emotional space, so she feels her head beginning to float almost at once.

"Rarely," he says. "Shit's been in my room since last summer."

Maggie gets it; getting a little fucked up is as good a way as any to figure out what they're supposed to be feeling right now. "You're saving my ass here," she tells him. "I almost tried to bring some on the plane."

Ariel says nothing, not really paying attention to her. He's staring at the sky, properly dark by now, with some of the brightest stars visible despite the light pollution. They sit together in the cricket-filled quiet, Maggie taking another couple hits, trying to keep her mind occupied with the tactile habit of what she's doing.

"This can't be real," she says eventually. "I mean. It's Mom."

Ariel picks up his book and turns toward her, and in the darkness she can see only the outline of his face and hair, the glint that signals the whites of his eyes. But his tone is unmistakably acid. "Cool. You think this isn't real? Then you go identify the body tomorrow."

For a moment she is equally shocked by Ariel's anger and the need to identify her mother's body. But of course, she thinks, of course he is angry with her, his older sister who got five more years with their mother than he did; he's probably angry at Peter, at Iris, at the whole damn world. And of course Maggie will go and identify her mother's body tomorrow, and get the death certificate, and do all the unpleasant things that he certainly doesn't want to do. He called the synagogue today and she didn't praise him to high heaven for it, so now he's pissy and resentful. Over something she would have figured out just as well and without boasting about it. And her father, falling to pieces at the worst possible time. How dare they, she wants to shout at them. How dare they grieve themselves into uselessness.

Maybe, she thinks, taking another hit, maybe she does hate men after all.

AUGUST 22, 2017

It doesn't get easier. When Maggie wakes up on Tuesday, it's from a nightmare she can't grasp the details of. She's sweating in her childhood bed, the sheets soaked.

It seems like Peter has been up and about the house during the night. The mac 'n' cheese she'd bought on her way home from the beach last night and left for him in the fridge has been eaten. Ariel must have found the tofu nuggets she'd gotten him, since those are gone too. No thank you, no nothing. Feeling spiteful, she makes just enough coffee for two cups, both for her.

She calls the police, keeps getting transferred, only to find out that she has to go to the hospital but that she won't need to see her mother's dead body, only look at a photograph. She begins to cry, for the first time, and it's humiliating, that this is when it happens, on the phone with someone deskbound who probably has to talk to dozens of bereaved a day, but the androgynous voice on the other end of the line says nothing, waiting her out. This is surprising. Though there is clearly bureaucracy at work, the people she's spoken to have all expressed sorrow for her loss, their tone shifting when she tells them what she's calling about. She's read horror stories online, of funeral directors making fun of the dead person's name, of police officers imitating rigor mortis positions, of hospital staff betraying boredom or impatience—maybe that's where her nightmare stemmed from, she thinks, the articles she was reading before bed. She wonders how much of the niceness from strangers she's experiencing has to do with her being a native English speaker with a flat accent, with her and her mother's names signaling whiteness. She wonders if the reason she's so suspicious is just that she wants to pick a fight with someone.

The doorbell rings, and she expects it to be more flowers but instead finds her brother's friend, Leona, on the stoop. "Oh, hi."

"I'm so sorry for your loss," Leona says, and rushes into Maggie. It's awkward, the force of the hug intrusive, unnecessary. "How is Ariel?" she asks when she lets go and Maggie gestures her in. Her eyes are wet with tears, which Maggie finds distasteful; it's not her loss to cry over.

"He's not great," Maggie says, though she doesn't know if this covers it. Ariel hasn't been out of his room yet.

"Oh my god, yeah," Leona says. "Look, if you need *anything*." She doesn't say what Maggie should do in that case. Just leaves it hanging there, her eyes wide and weepy, then turns her back on Maggie and goes to Ariel's bedroom. He opens the door for her, not quite as hangdog as he usually looks at this prenoon hour. He's smoothed his hair down and is wearing jeans rather than the gross gray sweatpants or boxers he usually sleeps in. He's had a crush on Leona forever, something Maggie finds slightly pathetic, especially as she's pretty sure it's always been one-sided, because Ariel's basically a good kid with so-so grooming habits and he's probably too safe or too nice for Leona, whose vibe Maggie recognizes because she used to be like her in college.

Then again, she concedes, as she watches Leona subject Ariel to the same hug she greeted Maggie with, she doesn't know anything about this girl, this woman really. Maybe she's just projecting, remembering that when she was that age, anyone within reach, who actually liked and respected her, just wasn't good enough, exciting enough. But why should Leona be anything like her? Iris always said Maggie was judgmental. Maybe she was right.

Before Ariel and Leona close themselves away in his room, Maggie asks her brother for Mrs. Gershon's number. "I'll text it to you," he says.

Maggie finds evidence of her mother all over the house. A sweater still hanging from the couch cushions where she must have been reading the day she died—the day before yesterday, how is it still so recent—and, in the bedroom, her mother's Filofax lying on her nightstand, the physical daily calendar and planner she insisted on keeping into the internet age. It's full of her mother's tiny, neat handwriting—Maggie has to swallow hard against the rush of emotion brought on by the familiar shapes—with shorthand notes she doesn't really understand. Things like *Call P.???* and *Caterers— again!* In the back are all the people her mother knows, the phone numbers and addresses and emails, transferred over from one year's Filofax to the next, year after year, some pages so old they're yellowing, the ink fading. She finds the number for Janice, the lawyer, and calls.

"Oh, sweetie, I'm so sorry," Janice says when Maggie explains. "This is truly awful."

"Thanks," Maggie says, because what else is she supposed to say? The line stays silent for another moment, and she finally asks, "So what do I do?"

"I have the will here," Janice tells her, "but I believe the original is at your home. I'll check to make sure and get back to you. How about we meet next week? There's no big rush on this stuff, honey." They make an appointment for the following Tuesday.

She calls Mrs. Gershon next, who says Maggie can absolutely help out if she wants, but that everything is being taken care of. Mrs. Gershon adds that she and Anya, Iris's assistant, already got obituaries with the funeral information printed in the *Tri County Sentry* and a couple of LA papers, since many of Iris's friends and colleagues and clients are based there. At the word "obituary" Maggie feels another surge of panic—she forgot it had to go in fast if anyone was going to make the funeral, Jewishly early as it had to be. "Good," she says, relieved. "I mean, thank you. I totally should've done that yesterday. Or, I mean, Ariel was going to. But thank you, Mrs. Gershon, really."

"Of course, dear. And please, call me Dena. You know," she goes on, "I've known, I mean, I knew your mother a long, long time. Since her first marriage, if you can believe that."

"Oh," Maggie says. And then, as the words sink in, "Wait, what?"

"Yeah, you know, I worked for Shlomo, her first husband, that . . . well, I shouldn't talk ill of him, he was very respected in his community, a very good rabbi, but really, he turned out to be such a putz to your mother. And his second wife too, they got divorced maybe a year after they married. Iris laughed at that one, she was so pleased. We both thought he deserved to end up a miserable old man, all alone with the things he'd done."

All of this is moving far too fast for Maggie. She knows her parents married relatively late, in their early thirties, that she was born when her mother was thirty-six, and Ariel, a miracle baby of sorts, when Iris was forty-one. But . . . a first marriage? How could Maggie not have known about that?

"Mrs. Gershon," she says, "I'm sorry, I have to go. Thank you for taking care of things. What time should we be there tomorrow?"

"Oh, you won't be coming here, dear. The funeral's at the Jewish cemetery in Simi Valley, it's the nearest one, you know. About nine would be good. The service will start at ten, and then we'll direct people to your house for shiva after."

"I'm, uh, I'm not sure we were going to do one of those," Maggie says. She hasn't talked to Ariel or her father about it.

"Nonsense. You must, dear. You'll get to hear stories about Iris, she was so loved, she *is* so loved, and besides, people will feed you, and your brother said your father wants this." Peter expressing anything of the sort is news to Maggie, and again she feels out of control, like she's not needed here, not useful, except she is, she's fed them both, Peter and Ariel, hasn't she, and she's keeping it together and—

"Okay. Okay," she says, trying hard not to lose it as her heart pounds and pounds and her hands begin to shake again. "Okay, thank you, bye."

Maggie begins pacing back and forth in the kitchen, wanting to sit, to lie down, but scared that if she stops moving she won't get up again, and there's still so much to do, even without this revelation about her mother. Why didn't Iris ever mention her first husband? But no, it doesn't matter, Maggie thinks, clearly the man wasn't worth talking about, or he was just so awful that her mother couldn't . . .

The thought of Iris as a survivor of something has never occurred to Maggie, and this is what finally makes her sit down, slowly, in the big armchair in the living room, the one no one ever really uses because it's so deep that it's not really comfortable. A memory pops into her head, a time she and Iris were in total agreement. A family dinner sometime during her prime Myspace years, so she was probably fifteen or sixteen, Ariel ten or eleven, a rare night with everyone at home all at once, no sleepovers or work keeping anyone away, and Ariel was talking about the weird new kid at school, how everyone said his dad hit his mom all the time, and why would she let him do that. Iris banged her cutlery down on the table just as Maggie turned to Ariel and called him something devastating like "you goat scrotum," because she was into weird swears then. Iris hadn't told Maggie off, which was shocking enough, but then she also asked Ariel in her calm-but-stern-voice if he *let* Chad Nelson hit him last year, and when Ariel said no, she said that most people don't *let* anyone hit them and that goes for grown-ups as well as children, and that he should get people at school to knock it off. Maggie remembers saying "Go, Mom," because it wasn't something she ever said, and because she was so rarely impressed with her mother, who never seemed to her very political or opinionated, traits Maggie was beginning to hold in high regard.

Before something close to guilt has a chance to set in, she's up and running and opening the door to Peter's study and demanding to know, "Why didn't you ever tell us Mom was married before? Why didn't *she* tell us?"

Peter is reading another book of Iris's, a woman's silhouette on its cover, her ass shielded by the title *Life Support*. "Oh, that," he says, his tone the same infuriating calm it was yesterday. No, not calm, she realizes. Detached. He's just not entirely here. "Yes, it was a bad time for Iris. She didn't like to talk about it much."

"Bad how?" Maggie sinks to the chaise, stares out the window to the flowering bush right outside and the lawn beyond and the quiet street, the absolute immovability of the neighborhood. It's so solid, like a set piece.

"He was a cruel man. And he made her feel like she didn't matter," Peter says, then leans back again with his book and adds, "Honey, it's rude to interrupt when someone is reading."

"Are you fucking serious?"

He turns the page. She can't fathom what he's thinking. It's scary, like watching her father get pod-personed, taken over by someone else. Whoever is impersonating him is doing a terrible job.

"You know we're having a shiva?" she asks just before she leaves his room.

"Oh, how nice," he says without looking up. "Have fun, honey."

Jesus fucking Christ, she thinks, and repeats it over and over again as she paces the length of the hallway, the words tangling up, *jeezus-fucking-christ jeezfuckrist jeefuckist.* The hall goes from carpet near the bedrooms to square terra-cotta tiles as it opens to the foyer and living room and kitchen. This is a nightmare, she thinks, turns around at the front door, walks back, watches the knuckles of her toes bend and straighten, the littlest one disappearing into the shaggy off-white strands and curls. This is unreal, she thinks, and the words strike her as platitudeness, as meaningless as Leona's offering of *anything*. She wonders if there's a German word, one of those compound nouns that people like to share online, that could describe what she feels, this mix of anger and sadness and the fear looming above it all that nothing will ever feel normal again. She turns again, reaches tile again, feels the cool stone under her feet again. Back and forth, she tries to count how many steps of carpet, how many of stone, but loses track each time.

IT TAKES MAGGIE a good long hour to drag herself out of the house. She showers and gets dressed and knocks on Ariel's door to try to get him to come with her, but he tells her to go away, and Leona emerges for a moment with her T-shirt on the wrong way, with the tag sticking out in front, and apologizes for Ariel, tells Maggie that he is just heartsick and needs to rest. Maggie wants to puke. She starts writing a text to Lucia: While I'm trying to deal w/things, my bro is getting a pity fuck from this chick who's prolly only into him cuz he's all tragic. But then she glances up to Lucia's latest text, from last night— Thinking of u, babe, hope tomorrow isn't too rough—and deletes the message she was drafting, decides that Lucia's implication in saying she hoped to-morrow, meaning today, wouldn't be too rough is that she probably doesn't want ongoing updates. *Stop being so clingy*, Maggie tells herself.

The hospital, at least, turns out to be much easier a process than she expected, though she has to wait for what feels like forever. There are several people ahead of her. A string of mourners, all trying to identify their loved ones. None of them are alone. There are two men speaking Spanish softly to each other, maybe brothers, an older woman sitting, rocking herself, as they hover over her. One of the men is gay, Maggie's pretty sure, his washed-out skinny jeans clinging to his muscled thighs, his T-shirt pink and tight, one of his arms sleeved in dragon tattoos. When she meets his eyes, he jerks a nod at her, a moment of recognition. Farther down the room full of plastic chairs, a hetero couple watches the muted TV, their hands clasped tightly on top of their adjoining armrests. Next to Maggie sits an old white man with wisps of fluffy hair above his ears and a younger man with a hooked nose and an abundance of dirty-blond hair. The only voices are the receptionist's and the brothers' softly curling words.

She checks Instagram while she waits and finds Ariel posted the same thing there as he did on Facebook, the requisite photo of nothing, just a blur with corners that might be his desk or the kitchen island. She goes back to Facebook to see his post has acquired more comments, love, expressions of solidarity. Her own feed is mostly shared articles about queer injustice, climate change, the threats to health care, events she's checked into—most recently, the informational meeting in July for folks interested in serving on committees at the new Pride center that opened in January. There's also an embarrassing amount of pictures and videos of pit bulls, her favorite breed of dog, which is, she believes, deeply misunderstood. It's not an inaccurate reflection of herself, her life, but it's incomplete, almost impersonal. She and Lucia aren't Facebook official, for instance. They haven't even posted a photo of themselves together.

She begins to type something up, an announcement of her own, when her name is called.

It's quick, the medical examiner showing her a picture of her mother's face, which is bruised and looks nothing like her. They also show her a picture of her mother's collarbone with its splotchy birthmark which Iris always said looked like a koala bear clinging to a tree but which to Maggie just looked blobby. Still, it's hers all right.

"There's one more thing," the ME, a wide-faced man with a gold cross hanging around his neck, says. "Her clothes are in pretty bad shape, but if you want—"

"No," Maggie says quickly, the idea of handling her mom's blood-soaked garments making her light-headed. "No, uh, thanks."

"Whoa, there." The ME's hands are gripping her arms, though Maggie isn't sure how they got there, or why she's against the wall when a moment ago she was standing three feet away from it. "You okay?"

She must have almost fainted. She's never fainted, ever, in her life. "Yes," she says, her shoulders tensing, and he releases her.

"There was also this," he says, and reaches into the file-and-folder-filled cart next to them. He hands her a manila envelope, its flap folded back, unsealed. Maggie reaches in and finds her mother's necklace, the silver chain with the raw amber pendant. The one she always wore when she headed on the road. A good-luck charm.

Not a very good one, as it turns out.

"Thank you," she says.

She signs the paperwork and asks about getting a copy of the death certificate to Mrs. Gershon, and whether she needs to do anything else to make sure the body gets to the funeral okay. She tries to forget about the clothes, to banish from her mind the image of her mother's dead face, nose broken and bruised, eyes closed, mouth set low like the disapproving frown Iris wore whenever Maggie spoke about girls.

MAGGIE DESPERATELY WANTS to get high. She wants to stop feeling so much one moment and nothing the next. It is uncomfortable, the welling up of emotion that keeps plaguing her, the intrusive internal mantra that her mother is dead, dead, dead. Dead before her time, dead before she should be, dead so suddenly, so stupidly.

She hasn't eaten yet, so she drives to an In-N-Out, the place she and Iris used to go to celebrate things together, when they were on good terms. Iris took Maggie there when she got her period, when she graduated high school, after her first year of college, when she got a promotion at the insurance agency. They'd usually get something from the secret menu, which

Iris thought was "so cool," as if it were a speakeasy and she was a naughty flapper indulging in the forbidden. Iris would always get the vanilla milkshake, Maggie the chocolate one.

But she gets the vanilla today, and eats and drinks in the parking lot, sitting in the car, sucking the milkshake down until she gets a brain freeze and slams her fist to her head to make it go away. Once it does, she wishes it were back. The physical ache seems easier.

She calls Lucia. "I'm sorry," she says. "For, like, being needy. I'm just all over the place."

"It's not needy, babe," Lucia says. "Your mom died. You're allowed to reach out." There's loud noise in the background but she's moving away from it.

"Is someone like forging a sword over there or something?" Maggie asks.

"Yes, actually. Well, sort of. Soo Min's trying to replicate a spearhead for this project she's working on, it's interesting, actually—but anyway, babe, how are *you*?"

Part of her is convinced that no matter how nice Lucia is being, she's going to leave, because who wants to deal with a new girlfriend whose mother has just died, but for now Lucia is on the phone and talking to her. "How do people do this?" she asks. She hears Lucia heave a sigh.

"I don't know. We just do. We push through it."

"We?"

"My aunt died last year. My grandfathers on both sides the year before."

"Oh. I'm sorry. I didn't know."

She can almost hear Lucia shrugging through the phone. "You didn't ask, babe," she says, and Maggie wonders whether she was supposed to. "You don't usually like talking about pain," Lucia adds, softly.

Maggie thinks back to their conversations, the ones late into the night, the ones before and after they've ravished each other. They talk about politics a lot, about responsibility, personal and societal. They've told each other about prior relationships. Maggie loves listening to Lucia talk about her art, and her friends' art, and Lucia asks Maggie to tell her funny anecdotes from work, and the stories from the podcasts she listens to. They talk about their respective friends' dramas, amateurly psychoanalyze them— those Maggie shares making Lucia laugh, maybe because her close circle is older, mostly, their lives unnervingly adult; her best friend, Isa, had her second child recently. Maggie supposes Lucia is right; they don't talk about their own pain.

"I guess I don't have a choice right now," Maggie says finally. But she doesn't say anything of substance beyond that. Can't get the words moving out of the hole beneath her breastbone and into her mouth. They say goodbye.

Still sitting in the parking lot of the In-N-Out, staring at a large SUV tearing out of the drive-through, Maggie remembers where the will Janice mentioned on the phone must be—in her mother's filing cabinet, exactly where she told her she would put it. A few years ago, her mother had sat her down when Maggie was home for Thanksgiving that time it had overlapped with Chanukah. When Maggie visited, once or twice a year usually, she tried to time it around the Jewish holidays, because she had fond memories of going through the motions with her grandparents, and later, with Iris and Ariel, Peter hovering supportively in the background, whenever any of them remembered to pay attention to the Jewish calendar. Plus, practically speaking, tickets tended to be much cheaper during Chanukah and Passover rather than Christmas and Easter, which they didn't celebrate. Peter was raised Catholic, but he'd long since declared himself agnostic and despised the corporate and capitalist quality of Christian holidays in the U.S.—he claimed that for the three years he'd lived in Germany, Christmas had been entirely different and much more wholesome and lovely.

That year, when Maggie was home, with the big clay chanukia she'd made during a short stint of Hebrew school when she was in first grade taking up prime real estate on the kitchen island, Iris had explained that she and Peter were working on their wills since they were both almost sixty and felt they were overdue in dealing with them. Peter was chopping vegetables for a salad, and Ariel was somewhere else, clearly deemed too young for this conversation. Maggie remembers being incredibly disturbed by the matter-of-factness of it all. "But Mom," she'd said, a knot forming in her stomach immediately, "you're not sick or anything, are you?"

"No no no," Iris had soothed her, cupping Maggie's cheek in that way she did. "No, we're fine, honey, this is just to prepare, to be on the safe side." Maggie had thought then, as she does now, that there's nothing safe about being dead.

WHEN SHE GETS home, Maggie goes right into Iris and Peter's bedroom, into the walk-in closet that her mother transformed into a miniature home office. The file cabinet is neat, with folders for medical bills, legal things, taxes, and even a folder that's titled, in the same block lettering Iris used in crossword puzzles, MARGARET AND ARIEL—CHILDHOOD. Maggie finds report cards, drawings, little notes she and Ariel wrote to their parents and to each other. There's a drawing of Jasmine from Disney's *Aladdin*, only recognizable because of the turquoise of her clothes and the orange and black striped thing by her side that's meant to be her tiger. There are hearts all over the page around the misshapen drawing. Maggie's very first crush. Did Iris know that's what it was?

There are two slim baby books tucked into this folder as well, one for her and one for Ariel. All their early statistics are there: weight and length at birth, first smile, first laugh, first crawl, first step, first word. Maggie's was, apparently, "boots." She smiles. She still loves boots. The first thing she'd bought herself with the money she made babysitting when she was fifteen was a pair of Dr. Martens. She was such a baby gay cliché, she thinks. And, apparently, a pretty gay baby too.

The will. That's what she needs to find now. She puts the folder full of nostalgia back and keeps looking, but it's not in the top drawer. She opens the bottom one, which is almost empty, save for two folders. One is labeled OLD MENUS, which looks like it's full of exactly that—takeout menus graying with age, edges crumbling. Maggie has no idea why her mother would save those. Behind it is a folder that reads, simply, WILLS. There are two files inside, and Maggie leaves Peter's alone, opening her mother's. The blur on some letters suggests it's a photocopy, or maybe just a bad printing job.

She skims past the legalese, some of which is familiar to her from work—the shalts and theretos and mentions of estates, rests, and residues not as daunting as they'd been before she learned how to read and explain the contracts she was having clients sign—but most of it seems standard, the surviving husband, Peter, being the beneficiary. Her eyes lock on a section titled INSTRUCTIONS that mentions Iris's request that the letters enclosed be sent out in the case of her untimely death. Maggie checks the folder again, but Peter's will is the only other thing there. She leans up and looks into the drawer again, and yes, there they are, a small stack of letters at the back, under the hanging organizer. She takes them out and turns back to the will. On the next page, under the section that reads SPECIFIC BEQUESTS, she sees that her mother has left Ariel her engagement and wedding rings. She's left Maggie the amber necklace, the one that's still in her pocket.

She's not sure how long she sits there on the floor, cross-legged, staring at the brief paragraph. Blood drums in her ears; she can feel her pulse at the base of her throat; she's furious. Of course Iris left the rings to Ariel, valued his prospects of marriage over Maggie's. *It's 2017,* she wants to shout at Iris, *I can marry whoever I want! I can propose to a woman and marry a woman and we can have children together!* But no, of course, even beyond the shadow of the valley of death or whatever, her mother is disapproving of Maggie's quote–lifestyle choices–unquote. But it's worse, really—until now, Maggie has never had a committed relationship. And Iris didn't know about Lucia.

Could she have smelled something on Maggie? An inability to commit? A failure at love? She tries to push this away. Iris knew nothing about her.

And the necklace. What is that, she thinks, some kind of pity gift? She knows it was her grandmother's, but it's nothing special, just a stone and chain without a story. She never even saw Bubby wearing it, Maggie thinks, bitterness rising in her esophagus. Just an arbitrary good-luck charm her mother wore on trips, a charm that failed spectacularly during Iris's last and extremely brief one. It's so *gendered* too, Maggie fumes, like what, boys can't wear necklaces? But no, apparently, the big, obviously expensive rings are for Ariel to bestow upon his future boring bride so he can have future boring kids in boring suburbia.

Iris never made a secret of her discomfort with her daughter being gay, but she'd stopped being so overt about it in recent years, which Maggie took as a sign that she'd given up trying to change her. There was still an edge to her mother's tone when she asked Maggie if she was dating "anyone," always the implication being that perhaps, just once, the anyone would be a man. But still, Iris had listened without obvious judgment when Maggie told her about the occasional work she did with queer youth in St. Louis, the college-prep tutoring at an affirming church and the local LGBTQIA2S+ suicide-prevention hotline she volunteered with for a couple of years before they merged with a larger, national organization. She even sounded mildly interested when Maggie told her about the Pride center opening. But now Maggie realizes that Iris was preparing for this spiteful act the whole time. It had all been a sham, Iris just biting her tongue rather than actually accepting any of it.

"Fuck you too, Mom," Maggie tells the filing cabinet. She imagines Iris sitting at the small desk chair beside her, tapping on her phone in that slow, older-lady way, not listening because she's dealing with work. "Fuck you very much."

She stuffs the will back in the drawer and slams it so hard it bounces back.

Tomorrow morning is the funeral, she thinks, and Ariel's pot sucks. She finds Gina's number in her phone and calls. Calling isn't a thing she and Gina do, much. It's not a thing Maggie really does with anyone anymore. She's pretty sure today was the first time she talked to Lucia on the phone, though they did have video-chat sex a couple months ago when Lucia was out of town for two weeks at an artist's residency.

"Gee," Maggie says. "Yeah, hi, I'm in town. Yeah. I know, it wasn't planned. My mom died. No, not shitting you. Yeah, thanks. Look, I want to see you, for sure, but also I really need something to get through tomorrow. Are you still selling?"

"Up, Daddy. You've got to get up." Maggie pulls on Peter's arms. It's almost six thirty in the morning, and she's already high. When the alarm rang, she rolled over and began toking, right there in her bedroom, which she'd never done before. Even in St. Louis, in her own apartment, she can't smoke inside because someone got evicted for stinking up the place before. She usually goes out onto the porch of the four-apartment house, or if the weather is nice, climbs out her kitchen window onto the sloped roof. But Peter as Dad is MIA, leaving behind only Peter as new widower, so Maggie figures he's not going to care. And if he does notice the smell and smoke, well, maybe it'll snap him back from wherever he's gone.

Peter responds to her tugs, agrees to get up from the chaise he slept on all night again. His face looks like it got left in the washing machine too long, the wrinkles unfamiliar, like they'll need ironing out. Maggie steers him toward his bedroom and its en suite bathroom, but when they reach the doorway and he glimpses the large bed, the shared bureau, Iris's vanity, the open walk-in-closet office, the filing cabinet with its half-open drawer and Iris's will and those letters lying on the floor, he stops. He puts his hands up and holds on to the doorframe, pushing against it, refusing to go in. He shakes his head over and over like a child and Maggie almost laughs. An inappropriate response, weed-driven, surely, but she knows she wouldn't be able to handle this role-reversal thing sober.

She brings him to the other bathroom. Tells him to wait. She gets the clothes he most hates from his closet—his monkey suits, he always called them, the business attire he had to wear to rare meetings. In recent years, as more and more of his calls and meetings take place through video chat, he's only needed to wear the top half, the white shirt and black blazer. She hopes the pants still fit him. Back in the bathroom, she finds him leaning over the sink, staring at himself in the mirror. "Shower, dress, got it?" she says. He nods, and his eyes well up, and he mouths something that might be "I'm sorry," but she isn't sure and doesn't stay to find out.

Ariel's closed and locked door is hiding, mercifully, only Ariel himself. Last night, when Maggie came back from her brief meeting with Gina in a McDonald's parking lot—where Gina hugged her tightly and refused payment for the weed and the two MDMA capsules she'd added in there in case Maggie needed to let loose sometime before she left California—she saw that Leona's car was still parked on the street and had shuddered at the notion of needing to deal with Ariel's crush first on this of all mornings. But it isn't there now, thank goodness.

"Is she coming to the funeral?" Maggie asks when Ariel finally opens the door to her pounding. He looks exhausted, as if he hasn't slept a wink, but also over the moon at having gotten lucky. "Also, get dressed, we have to leave in like an hour, and you're driving."

"No, she's not. She said it was too triggering for her." Maggie snorts and Ariel glares at her. "Fuck off, you're not the only one who matters," he tells her and slams the door. It's like they're back in his teenage years, his prime banging-things-around days. She gives his closed door the finger and goes to shower in her parents' bathroom.

. . .

MAGGIE SITS IN the back. She wants Peter and Ariel to handle getting to the cemetery. It's the least they can do, she figures. She closes her eyes for most of the silent ride, willing them to speak to each other, to her, to curse at other drivers, anything. Finally, when they arrive, she realizes the socializing is going to fall to her.

"Please, please, please just be nice," she tells them when she opens the car door. She doesn't wait for them to follow because she knows they will, but also she has no idea what she means with her directive. They don't owe it to anyone to be nice, she knows this, and yet—and yet, don't they? Isn't there an obligation of sorts? A need to be present and aware? Socially acceptable grief, she thinks, is fucked up, but she feels like she needs to perform it anyway. Mostly, she wants this to go smoothly, so that they can get it over with and go home. She hasn't bought her return-flight ticket yet, but she's going to have to stay for the shiva, and after that, well, she isn't entirely sure. She can't think that far ahead, though, or she'll panic.

They walk into the chapel, and a woman dressed in a dark blue skirt suit introduces herself as Dena Gershon. "I met both of you when you were very young," she says, then turns to Peter, "and you I haven't seen in years." She hugs him and says something softly, touching her forehead to his in a way that looks far too intimate, but he nods at her and wipes tears away from his eyes. She takes them through how the ceremony will go, the brief service in the chapel and then the drive to the grave site, where a rabbi will say some words. Mrs. Gershon tells them that they can stand near the doors and greet people or sit in front and choose to disengage. "Both options are quite all right," she stresses, but she gives Maggie a look, and when Ariel and Peter head to the front row of the chapel, heads bowed, she grabs Maggie's hand and pleads, "You'll come stand with me? It's good to have someone from the family there."

"Yeah, of course," Maggie says, though she doesn't want to at all. "But we've got a bit of time before people show up, right? Is there anywhere here I can get some coffee?"

Mrs. Gershon shows her a small back room with coffee and tea fixings, and Maggie gets herself a Styrofoam cupful and reluctantly brings two out for Peter and Ariel as well, though she thinks they could have figured this out themselves if they wanted. They both have brought books with them and are sitting in companionable silence in the front pew, reading, like this isn't a funeral, like they've just gone out to a café or are sitting in their living room. Ariel is dressed in a black metal-band T-shirt and cargo pants, and seeing the outfit again makes her angrier. She's pretty sure that he didn't get the kind of talks she got from their parents about the difference between what they were okay with—"Wear whatever you want!"—and what the world was okay with—"Oh, you can't wear that to a job interview/nice restaurant/the theater, though." If he did, the lesson has clearly passed him by.

She smokes more outside before needing to greet people coming in. Her buzz is on, her heart palpitating a bit too fast with the addition of the caffeine, when she sees the first two cars come in one right after another and prepares herself next to Mrs. Gershon.

IT'S A WHIRLWIND. Most of the people who arrive knew Iris professionally or are old friends, and they almost all remember Maggie or claim to have heard a lot about her. Anya, whom Maggie is certain she has never met, says it's good to see her again. The assistant's narrow face is pinched, and she makes a valiant effort at smiling, but her eyes are red and she excuses herself with what sounds like a choked sob. Peter's stepbrothers arrive, the first truly friendly faces because Maggie actually recognizes them, though they're not close. But still, they have children around hers and Ariel's ages, none of whom could come but who Maggie is Facebook friends with, and so they have something to banter over, which allows her to relax for a moment.

But then they're seated and she continues greeting the attendees, occasionally casting her eye toward Peter and Ariel. People keep walking up to them, touching them, trying to make a connection. Ariel kneels backward in his pew and talks to one of the stepuncles while the other sits next to Peter and wraps an arm around him, though Peter doesn't appear to notice. The awkwardness of tangential grief is palpable in the room.

"Iris? No, of course, I'm so sorry."

Maggie whips her head around. An old man with a walker is in front of her, his forehead broad and deeply grooved, his cheeks softly pock-marked. His suit jacket is as baggy as the pouches below his eyes, but those seem clear and his red tie is crisp. "Hello," she says, shaking the man's hand and giving the little half bow she's been perfecting over the past twenty minutes, a kind of shorthand for thank-you-for-coming and yes-this-is-very-sad-and-shocking.

"You must be the daughter," he says. His grip is warm, firm, but not trying to prove anything. "Iris's hair looked like yours when she was young."

This stops Maggie short. "It did?" Her mother hated it when Maggie buzzed her hair. She claimed to love Maggie's tangle of curls.

"Yes, in the late nineties, she was very hip," he says. Mrs. Gershon is greeting other people and casts a glance at Maggie, as if she should hurry this man along.

"Who are you?" she says instead, rather rudely.

He smiles, and she can see he was handsome once. Maybe he still is. "Oh, you wouldn't have heard of me. I'm an old friend of your mother's." He looks into the chapel, then back at Maggie's face. The room is fuller than she expected it would be. Some young people have shown up, looking uncomfortable and out of place. No one she knows; she hasn't kept in touch with anyone who lives in the area except for Gina, who couldn't make it—Anthony lives in Oregon now, predictably working on a pot farm; Kyle got weird in college and moved to Yogaville in Virginia, where he married a waifish blonde; and Morgan . . . well, Morgan and Maggie don't talk anymore, not since Maggie made the mistake of sleeping with her one spring break when she was twenty and found out Morgan had been pining after her quietly for years and was hoping the sex meant they'd U-Haul. No, Maggie has no one here. The young folk must be Ariel's friends from college and high school. "Are your father and brother here as well?" the man asks, startling her out of her resentful musings.

"Yes, they're in front," she says. And then adds, because this man seems nice and understanding, "But I don't think they're up for talking right now. It's, you know, a hard day." She feels flustered. No one else, she realizes, not even her step-uncles, not even the two sets of neighbors from their street, has really looked her in the eyes since she started this farce. They've looked down, away, past her into the chapel. But this man feels present. Maybe it's his age, she thinks. Maybe the older you get, the more you can be present in the moment with people.

"Of course, I completely understand. It's good of you to tell me, though. Kind. Maybe I'll come by during the shiva, if the stuffy nurses let me out again." He's still standing there, and his genial expression changes. "She was a very special woman," he says. "I'll miss her." Then he bends a little, as if returning her bow, and turns to walk slowly into one of the back pews.

THE SERVICE ISN'T long. There are some prayers, the shapes of Hebrew words surprising Maggie's tongue. The body remembers, she thinks, the melodies rising through her, familiar from her childhood, from funerals of distant relatives, from her mother's yearly insistence on saying the kaddish on Maggie's grandparents' yahrzeits. Ariel is holding Peter's hand, though it doesn't seem that Peter is reciprocating the pressure. Sitting on Peter's other side, Maggie holds her fists tightly in her lap, pushing them down between her knees, denting the dress. She hates dresses. She hates dress-up.

Ariel and Peter are called on to be pallbearers, but Maggie isn't. Four men rise from the crowd, volunteering to help carry the casket, but Maggie refuses this sexism. Not now. Not here. Come on, she thinks. She stands behind Ariel and stares down one of the men. He walks back, hands held in front of him like she's a rabid dog. She, Ariel, Peter, his stepbrothers and a stranger to her lift her mother's casket together. It's heavy, even with six of them, and she feels her shoulder muscle strain as they shuffle out together to the hearse that will drive to the burial site. The pain is good, though. It makes her feel like she's doing something, even if inconsequential. She wishes her brain would shut up, void itself of all current thought, but that's not going to happen, so she tries to accept the strange floating thoughts like she does when she's smoked too much and is paranoid. Then she remembers she probably has, probably is.

After the casket is deposited in the hearse, they climb into Peter's car again with Ariel at the wheel and drive at a snail's pace through the winding paths of the cemetery. Maggie finds it terribly ugly here. Almost all the headstones are nestled flat into the earth, making it seem like some Swiss countryside, like Julie Andrews will run up from beyond the horizon and burst into song at any moment. Cemeteries have never bothered Maggie, really, but she prefers the ornate Catholic style, the run-down churchyard look. This place, clean-shaven, seems polite and apologetic about the decomposing bodies under the earth.

When they arrive at the grave site with its mound of freshly turned dirt smelling like rain and gardening, things begin to go awry. Peter refuses to get out of the car. He's mumbling into his hands, "No, no, no, I can't, no, Iris, no," and Maggie looks at Ariel with alarm, sees the blood has drained from his cheeks, his eyes fixed on Peter's helplessness. Neither of them have ever seen their father this way, and while he's been bad the last couple of days, this despair, the ache in his voice, is worse than anything Maggie has ever heard.

No, she realizes moments later, it's not. Peter follows Maggie and Ariel out of the car eventually, accepts the shovel from the rabbi, picks up the first bit of dirt, and lets it go over the hole the casket has been lowered into. As the earth hits the wood and makes a terrible, muffled thump, Peter lets out a cry that is more animal than human, and that—that is the worst thing Maggie has ever heard. It's then that she begins to cry and doesn't stop until halfway through the ride home when Ariel curses loudly at another driver in exactly the same way that Iris once did, which is when Maggie's sobs turn into a blissfully brief bout of hysterical laughter.

"WHAT'S THE PLAN for this shiva thing?" Ariel asks as he pulls into their driveway. "I mean, do we have to do anything?"

Maggie shrugs and gets out of the car. She's empty, depleted from crying, from the laughter, from the silence that reigned again after it was over. "I think we just leave the door unlocked and hang out and people come if they come."

"But one of us has got to always be around then, right?"

"Pretty much."

"Fuck."

"Yeah." Maggie isn't thrilled about this either but it appears that they don't have much of a choice. The idea of a shiva makes sense to her, in theory, because mourning rituals are important, a conviction that has only grown from keeping up with the news in the past few years; every time there's some kind of mass shooting or hate crime, people gather to mourn, after all. When she was a junior in college, a kid named Rudy from one of her classes died by suicide, jumping off Eads Bridge; Maggie hadn't known him well, but she and her friend Allison and Allison's boyfriend at the time all went to the candlelight vigil that Rudy's friends organized on campus. Even the professor who taught the class Maggie shared with Rudy was there, wearing a white salwar kameez. Maggie had felt something like virtue then, or self-satisfaction, for attending and sharing a space of grief with others. Now she wants nothing of the sort, no matter how much sense it makes. She sighs. "I mean, I guess we can like put a sign on the door or something if we're out?"

"Gone grieving," Ariel says, and they both smile at the lame joke. Peter shuffles after them into the house, saying nothing.

People start showing up soon. They bring Swiss rolls and croissants and casseroles and hummus and bottles of juice. Maggie helps lay these out on the kitchen island, finds paper plates and plastic cups in the bowels of a cupboard, lugs the big trash can from its corner into a more prominent position so that people throw things away properly. She doesn't absorb much of what is said to her. Ariel and Peter sit in the living room on separate couches, and people make conversation with them, though Peter seems mostly silent and those sitting around him turn uncomfortably to talk to one another instead. They ask Maggie if he's okay, if she's okay, if Ariel's okay, as if there's any possible answer to this question. There isn't. She says yes, she says no, she says they will be, anything but the real answer, which is that she has no fucking clue.

In the late afternoon, after all the other first day's visitors have left, Mrs. Gershon helps clean up, washes the mugs that were used for the several pots of coffee Maggie brewed, covers dishes in cling wrap and puts them in the fridge, dumps out the flattening bottles of soda and puts the empties in the bin for recycling. Before she leaves, she cups Maggie's face firmly in her palms and tells her, "Breathe, mamaleh. Breathe and eat and sleep and you will get through this."

The house is quiet again and Maggie feels like she's run a marathon. Peter is asleep on the couch in the living room and Ariel emerges from the bathroom freshly showered—his second in one day, an anomaly—looking lost. "What now?" he asks her.

"I found Mom's will yesterday. She left you her wedding and engagement rings. Guess she wants you to get hitched."

Ariel looks stunned, but he follows her to Iris and Peter's bedroom. The rings are on the vanity, where Iris left them since menopause made her fingers swell and they became uncomfortable. Ariel picks them up and puts them down at once, like they're hot. "What am I supposed to do with these?" he murmurs.

"Keep them somewhere safe. You might want them someday." *Maybe I do know something,* Maggie thinks. Her detachment surprises her, this feeling of adulthood, as if losing a parent was something she's been readying for since turning eighteen and leaving home. It isn't, though. Nothing has really prepared her for this—Iris wasn't sick, she wasn't that old, she was just . . . Mom. Mom doing her thing far away while Maggie lived her life in St. Louis, not all that different, if she's honest, than Mom doing her thing while Maggie was in grade school, middle school, high school. It doesn't feel real yet, even though she's carried her mother's body on her shoulders, maybe because Iris not being in the house isn't all that strange. A story Peter finds funny—or did, when he was coherent—was how Maggie asked him, when she was four or five, where Mommy lived. It's funny only because the day she asked that, Iris, who was pregnant with Ariel, was ordered on bed rest for the next few months. Maggie remembers running to her parents' room after kindergarten during that time, hoping her mother would be awake so they could cuddle and watch whatever old police procedurals were rerunning on the couple of channels that didn't play daytime soaps, which Iris didn't like.

Ariel moves the rings around the blond wooden surface of the vanity, making them shush and clink. "What about you?" he asks, and picks them up again, the engagement one with its small pink diamond in one hand, the plain gold band in the other. He thrusts the hands forward as if offering them to Maggie.

"She left me her amber necklace," she says.

"Oh?"

"Yeah, remember that one she wore whenever she went out of town? I don't know, man. Fucking whatever," she says, trying to shake off the slight, and recalls something. "And there's also letters we're supposed to mail, apparently?" She points at the facedown stack on the floor.

"Okay, well, I think I'm going to go call Leona," Ariel says. "I mean," he pauses, half-turned away from her already, "do you need me? It's just like, sticking them in the mail, right?" Maggie nods that she can handle it and lets him go. She doesn't need him, not if he doesn't want to be there.

Having something to do feels better than not, so she decides she'll take a walk to wherever there's a mailbox. Her legs are stiff from standing in place, shifting from foot to foot most of the day, and it feels like she hasn't really moved in days. She kneels on the floor and flips the letters over, looks at the names on them.

KARL JELEN

ABRAHAM K. OKAFOR

LIAM AINSWORTH

HAROLD LAKE BROOKS

ERIC BAISHAN

Who *are* these people? Maggie hasn't heard of any of them, never heard her mother mention them. Were any of them at the funeral? Were they clients? Friends? She finds her mother's Filofax again and flips to the address book at the back. Next to the names of her work-related contacts, Iris wrote their roles: caterer, photographer, client, manager, concierge, and so on. But these men, when Maggie finds them, aren't designated as anything, so they're social contacts, not professional.

"Huh," she says aloud into the empty room. She wants to ask Ariel if he's heard of them but can hear him talking to Leona through his closed door. Peter is still asleep, or pretending, in the living room.

She takes the letters outside with her and sits down to roll herself a joint, even though she's reached peak high. The float in her head just feels normal now, not really a relief anymore. It's as if there's a threshold, a point beyond which she simply can't get more fucked up. This is partly why she prefers it to alcohol—booze has no real limit, and the couple of times she's blacked out were awful. The first time was when she was in high school, after prom, which she'd gone to dressed in an ill-fitting secondhand suit she'd found at a vintage shop. The knees of the pants were ripped, purposefully she suspected, and held together with ancient safety pins that seemed rusted shut, and Iris had hated it, asking Maggie why she was bothering at all if she thought the whole thing was a mockery. It was one of their big fights. When Maggie woke up the next morning in her room with no memory of how she got there, she was wearing only her underwear and the dress shirt, which was stained with something that smelled awful. When she made a muffled noise at the ache in her head, Peter popped in to tell her Iris had put her to bed when she'd stumbled in at two in the morning, and then he went to get ice water and a bucket, which Maggie used liberally over the next two hours. She'd expected Iris to crow about it, but her mother seemed to think that puking six times was punishment enough.

Maggie licks the end of the rolling paper and seals the joint, which is thin and crooked but there's no one around to prove herself to. She lights it, inhales, and looks at the letters again.

Four of the addresses are in California, and one is in Las Vegas. She pulls out her phone and begins googling them.

It corrects Jelen to Jelenic at first. When she fixes that, she still finds nothing, really. No Facebook profile, one Google+ account with four followers and zero posts. Abraham K. Okafor finds pictures of basketball players, though she assumes that's just Google racially profiling, since there aren't any players with that exact name. She does find a doctor with the last name Okafor but in Florida, and his first name doesn't match. Liam Ainsworth brings up an actor who looks about twenty who's appeared in several movies she's never heard of. His Twitter puts him in Manchester, the one in the UK, and besides, she can't imagine her mother having anything to do with a One Direction lookalike. There are several dead Harold Lakes and one dead Harold Brooks, but she has no idea if any of them are the right one. Eric Baishan finds her absolutely nothing relevant, but his address is different from the others. Before the name is ATTN and it appears the letter is addressed to a company, DRAKE & CARDINAL, in Los Angeles, which is also where Karl Jelen's address is. Okafor is in Sacramento, Ainsworth in Las Vegas. Brooks just has a PO box number in somewhere called Palo Verde, California.

Later, Maggie won't remember how it happened, how she found herself in her bedroom, piling the things she'd scattered back into her suitcase. She won't remember the leap of excitement in her stomach at the plan forming in her mind, a plan that will get her out and away from the eerie house her mother will never return to—because, no matter how often Iris was gone, Maggie always knew that she would be coming home soon, and this will never again be true. Maggie won't remember ignoring a call from Lucia, too scared that if she picked up and told Lucia about it, she'd chicken out or be convinced that she should stay and do her duty. She won't remember thinking that it'll serve them right, Peter especially, that he should be forced to deal with the half-strangers showing up to the shiva. But in the moment, as she keeps moving the stack of letters around the room while she packs, as if they might disappear, as if she might lose her excuse to get the fuck out of there—in the moment, she's a jumble of nerves, her hands shaking as she tells herself that this is the right thing to do. That she needs to know what these letters are about. That Iris owes her this much after giving the rings to Ariel. That, strangely, she owes this to Iris, no matter how mad she is, because a will is a kind of last request. She finds the amber necklace in her jeans pocket from yesterday and tucks it into a small zipped compartment inside her backpack.

Once she gets her toothbrush from the bathroom and locates her deodorant, which rolled under the bed, she dashes to the living room.

"Dad, I'm—"

She stops short as she turns the corner. Her father is lying on the floor in the middle of the room, curled up like a child, holding something to his face and wracking with quiet sobs that make his back jump and shake. Maggie kneels down beside him. "Dad," she whispers. The cloth clutched between Peter's hands is Iris's sweater, the one that was still on the couch yesterday. He must have noticed it when he got up from his sleep. "Daddy, oh, Daddy." She lies behind him and spoons him. She's never been his big spoon before.

When she was nine, almost ten, after Columbine, there was a while when she was so scared of what might happen in her school that she stayed up most of every night worrying about it, and got on the yellow bus every morning exhausted. When she nodded off in class one day, she was sent to the principal. She had never gotten in trouble in school before, ever, and as nervous as she was about what would be said in the office, she was more concerned with what the principal would tell her parents. Ms. Fermina ended up treating her kindly, but she called Peter to come and take Maggie home, and told him what had happened.

He wasn't mad, but he wanted to know why she was so tired. Maggie didn't want to tell him at first, but eventually he broke her down with a stop at the frozen yogurt place she loved because they had green sprinkles that reminded her of the slime from Nickelodeon. That night, Peter climbed into bed with her, and spooned her, and sang her the lullaby he'd been singing her since she could remember herself:

Hush, little baby, don't say a word,
Papa's gonna buy you a mockingbird,
And if that mockingbird don't sing,
Papa's gonna buy you a diamond ring . . .

It helped, though it took another couple of weeks of Peter staying with her, cuddling and singing, before she was able to fall asleep on her own again.

And now here she is, spooning her tall father with his softened body and thin, receding hair, as he cries into her dead mother's sweater.

She manages to get him up, makes him drink a glass of milk warmed in the microwave—another trick he used to calm her when she was little—and tries to get him to bed. He won't sleep in his bedroom, though, so she settles him in his office, on the chaise, and brings him his dorky pajamas, the 1950s kind with buttons and piping and everything. He holds them in his hands like he doesn't know what to do with them, but she's not going to help him get dressed. It feels like one step too far, and besides, he's not actually physically feeble. So she leaves him there and goes back to her room, to her packed bag.

She can't do this, can she? But the thought of another day talking to people she doesn't know, who barely knew her mother, chaperoning Ariel into being social and moving her zombie of a father around . . . It's unbearable.

She definitely shouldn't drive yet, though, she realizes. She'll nap, write a note, then go.

IRIS

JUNE 2, 2013

Iris rarely considered her death a real possibility, perhaps because she spent much of her life making sure to avoid it. It was one reason she read detective novels, crime novels, all the literature she could get her hands on that explored the bloodiness and depravity and confusion of the worst of human nature. By being aware of it, of all its infinite—if predictable, as she discovered over the years as she devoured more and more such books—possibilities, Iris was able to feel in control. In restaurants, she sat with her back against the wall or at a corner table far from the windows. During air travel, she sat behind the wing, even when she could afford the occasional business-class seat, because she'd read that you have more chance of surviving a crash in the back half of the plane. If she'd ever needed to take a long bus ride, she was sure she would have looked for the seat belts. She drove carefully, never more than five miles above the speed limit. She double-locked motel and hotel room doors, added the chain if it was there. And, because she wasn't one to dismiss harmless superstition, she wore her amber necklace, handed down from her mother, whenever she had to travel farther than a five-mile radius from her home.

But soon after Iris turned fifty-nine, she had a fall. That's all it was. A fall. She was walking along Abbot Kinney in Venice, where she'd just met a prospective client for lunch, and was pretty certain she was going to get the job. It had been a nice meal, perfectly pleasant. She and the prospect, the owner of a chain of coworking spaces, discovered they'd both gone to the same temple back when she lived in LA and might have crossed paths. He knew her friend Dena—not well, but he liked her; she'd recommended a decorator that he and his wife ended up using—and they had fun playing Jewish geography, trying to see who else they might both know, whether they'd lived near each other or had relatives who did. She wanted the assignment, even though it meant going up to Sacramento a few times, which would be sad.

When they finished, the prospective client insisted on paying, implied she'd probably be charging him expenses soon anyway, and shook her hand before handing his ticket to the valet. Iris had found parking on the street, and she walked toward her car, hoping there wouldn't be unexpected traffic on her way home.

And then she fell.

It was a tiny jut in the sidewalk that tripped her, and she only got a small run in the pantyhose she was wearing. Her hands were a little scraped, stinging without bleeding. But the moment in which the concrete rushed toward her had felt endless, and her body's reaction hadn't been instantaneous like she was certain it should be, like she was sure it once was. Instead, her body froze, her reactions slowed, and she thought she was about to die.

"Lady, are you okay?" A white guy with dreadlocks had a hold of her elbow and helped her up. He was her height, but he seemed to be gazing down at her, and she imagined how he must see her, as a middle-aged—no, probably old, if she was being honest—woman, silver-streaked hair, frail, even though she never pictured herself this way, never felt this way. "Ma'am?" he pressed, looking concerned, if stoned, and when she said she was fine and thanked him, he nodded and said, "Well, be careful, yo," and walked away, his dreads swinging behind him as he approximated a sloped and sideways walk. She thought of Abe, of the stories he told her about his son and their bickering over things like cultural appropriation in fashion, Abe rolling his eyes and saying that there were more important things in the world than white guys wearing dreads, his son trying to tell him that wasn't the point, that many things could be important at once. She'd never mentioned it to Abe, but whenever he talked about his son, she thought the teenager would get along with Maggie. They seemed to share an indignation with the world that she couldn't muster in the same way anymore. She missed Abe. She wondered if she'd ever conveyed how grateful she was to him and how much she appreciated their time together.

She missed all of them, really, all the important ones, except Shlomo, of course. She fiercely missed Peter in that moment after the fall, and made herself start moving again so she could get to the car and back home to him. Her body was stiff, as if still seizing up on the way down. Nothing had happened to her, but she felt like something had changed, irrevocably. She was faced with the fact that her body wasn't going to be getting stronger. She should be getting more calcium. She should get a bone-density test. A physical. She'd been neglecting herself for years, thinking she was going to last forever on sheer willpower. This small fall, a stumble, an uncharacteristic slip in her never-before-clumsy life, reminded her she was mortal and aging.

In the car on the way home she tried to calm herself. After all, she'd had some existential moments when she started going through menopause years ago. But mostly she'd been worried about her sense of desire back then, concerned that with her hormonal changes she would also feel less of the lifelike substance that was her sexuality. She'd been relieved to find that while certain bodily functions worked less vividly than they used to—for the first time in her life she'd begun using lubricating substances besides condoms—her desire remained. Now, she didn't even care about her desire, the fear coursing through her instead entirely devoted to the time she had left on earth.

On a whim, while stuck in traffic on the 101, she tried calling her daughter, but the call went to voice mail and she realized it was almost four in St. Louis and Maggie would be working. Ariel was on a weeklong trip with some buddies of his, attending an amateur Magic: The Gathering tournament, and she'd see Peter soon enough. She called Maggie again and left her a message.

"Hello darling, it's Mom," she began in her singsong phone voice. "I just wanted to see how you are." She considered telling Maggie that she'd fallen, but decided against it. What else could she say, though? "Oh, and I watched the first part of that documentary you recommended, about the West Memphis Three, and you know, those boys really were railroaded, weren't they? Imagine if someone had seen how you dressed in high school and decided that meant you'd done something terrible! Anyway, I'm rambling. Stuck in traffic. I'm sure you never miss that in Mizzerah." She slurred the word the way Maggie did when she was making fun of the local accent. "Anyway, love you, bye! It's Mom, if I didn't say before. Okay," and she hung up.

She wondered, sometimes, why talking to Ariel always seemed easier. They had more in common, she supposed, in that they were avid readers and could talk about books for hours; they read wildly different genres, usually, but would occasionally read one of the other's favorites so they could talk about it. But it wasn't just that; it was something to do with privacy, maybe. Ariel was the one with the lock on his door, but Maggie's heart and mind were closed books, and she was independent enough not to open them unless she wanted to. Iris envied her daughter, sometimes, for being able to seize at her own strength so soon, so young—she'd started insisting on wearing what she wanted to nursery school when she was four; she'd told Iris firmly that she had no interest in ballet when she was seven; she'd come out to friends at school before telling her parents. Mostly, Iris was proud, of Maggie and a little bit of herself for managing to raise her to be this person. She wasn't sure her daughter recognized their similarities, or how lucky she was to have had her independence encouraged, but it didn't really matter. If Maggie were to ever have a child of her own, surely she'd set a good example in other ways and also not receive credit for it. Iris wasn't sure she would—as far as she knew, Maggie wasn't interested. And if she was, well . . . Iris couldn't help but worry about a child raised without a father. She could almost hear Maggie yelling at her just at the thought.

She wondered if it was too late for them. She hoped not.

When she got home, she entered Peter's office, but he was on a video call and could only glance up at her and half smile in the midst of his chatter about banner widths and necessary resolution. She went to the bedroom and rolled off her pantyhose and took off her skirt and blouse and got into her comfy home clothes, the yoga pants and overlarge T-shirt. Last of all, she removed her necklace. She fingered the raw amber in its setting, bought by her grandfather long ago and given to his youngest daughter, Iris's mother, who wore the jagged edges smooth with years of worrying it. She gave it to Iris when she married Peter, because, she said, Iris had finally given her *naches*, and she didn't have to worry about her anymore. It was only after her mother died, though, that Iris turned it into the regular companion it became—it had felt somehow like tempting the evil eye to wear it before, like stealing her mother's luck before it had run out.

Iris stared at the mirror, at her face that looked no different than it had that morning but which seemed to symbolize a whole lot more. The crow's-feet, the way her lips were grooved all over, the loose skin below her cheeks that weren't quite jowls but implied them. She had to write a will, she realized. It was time. She was sure she and Peter had some boilerplate thing, probably made when the kids were little, but she needed to write something proper. She needed her children to know she loved them. Come to think of it, she needed everyone she'd loved to know it.

AUGUST 24, 2017

Dad, Ariel,

I've gone to carry out a few of Mom's wishes. Not sure how long it'll take, but I'll update you. Hold down the fort. Be nice to people (please) and eat their food because there's going to be a lot of it. Kick them out early if you need to. Love you.
—Maggie

She leaves the note in the middle of the kitchen island, anchored by the black and red salt and pepper shakers, which, when put together, look like two vaguely humanoid blobs hugging. She deposits her suitcase in the trunk of Peter's Prius and puts the Sacramento address into her phone. If she takes the I-5, it'll take her less than six hours. But she remembers that the scenic route, up the 101, is supposed to be much prettier, and besides, she isn't sure she wants to be back so quickly. She chooses the longer option, despite the map's dire warning of tolls—she doesn't remember there being any a decade ago when she drove up the coast with Morgan and Kyle to see a queer punk band in Oakland. If she comes across any tollbooths, she can afford to pay, she thinks, a luxury she never really expected when younger, assuming always that she'd live a hand-to-mouth artist's life. Not because she had any artistic passion, let alone talent, but because that's what she thought being a queer millennial meant. Her friends from college all seem to be actors or artists or musicians—Allison sings and plays piano in an all-girl band called Twatter; Micah is doing a Fulbright in Nicaragua, collecting the oral histories of the Sutiava *Primitivista* painting workshop participants from the 1980s; Blair works at a coffee shop and does community theater on the weekend; Harper freelances as a technical writer and self-publishes young adult novels—and for a long time, Maggie wanted to be like them. She tried, sort of, but nothing stuck. Instead, she works in insurance and has benefits and vacation days and actual weekends, which gives her time for brunches with friends and concerts and movies and getting involved in local queer stuff.

"Let's go," she says to the empty car.

As the garage door opens in front of her, revealing shadowy six o'clock light, she has the uncanny feeling of being inside a movie again. Lone girl in search of the truth, she thinks, or child looking for her mother's secret life. Grieving woman out for revenge, maybe. Of course, she realizes, this may all be moot. These guys may turn out to be some professional contacts. Maybe they're Mafia dudes her mother owes money to. That'd be the day, she thinks; her mother was always careful with money, which is why they didn't come out of 2008 in worse shape than they did, she supposes, unlike many middle-class families they knew. Iris had a good money-manager person, some woman named Glinda, like the good witch from *The Wizard of Oz*, which Maggie always found very ironic. During high school, when she had a rudimentary obsession with Communism that mostly had to do with sticking it to the capital-M Man, Maggie had made fun of this Glinda person, saying that no good witch would ever use her powers to make money out of nothing—which was what she understood of the stock market and investments—and that Glinda must be an impostor, that she was actually the Wicked Witch of the West and killed the Good Witch and taken over her life. It was a whole narrative she'd spun herself, and it was one of the best ways to get Iris into a fight with her. "How's Glinda the Wicked Witch?" she'd ask when her mother was doing something innocuous like heating up meat loaf in the microwave. Or "Have you stolen from the poor yet today?" when her mother was washing her bras in the sink.

Maggie fiddles with the air-conditioning setting, smiles. She can laugh at herself about it now, if sheepishly. She's not proud of it. After all, she's learned since that everything her mother hurled at her at the time was true: she and Ariel were a big part of the reason her parents invested and saved money; it was them the money was meant to protect, educate, and eventually go to, if there was anything left; her life had been incredibly easy, all things considered, her needs always met. She'd never wanted for anything necessary. She had absolutely no right to complain to her mother about her own privilege. It was naive, and it was stupid. She supposes most teenagers are, in one way or another.

How incredibly lucky she was in life had become clear to her only when she was in college already, in St. Louis. During her first year she had two roommates, all of them in a cramped triple with another triple across a dilapidated common room that held only a three-seater couch whose cushions were sky blue and stained and made of some scratchy woven fabric. The six of them shared one bathroom. The school required all freshmen to live in the dorms, and one of her roommates had needed to work two jobs to be able to afford it because her scholarship didn't cover room and board. This seemed patently unfair to Maggie, that the school would require a student who couldn't afford it to live in campus housing when, as Tiffany pointed out, there were cheaper accommodations in town. Maggie ranted about it drunkenly to some people during orientation week, and Tiffany had been there too, holding a forty and raising her eyebrows. She tossed her long, overly straightened and dyed blond hair back and said, "You must be pretty rich to be this surprised." Then she'd walked away, and a boy wearing a flannel shirt followed her, and Maggie realized how stupid and lucky she was, had always been.

She's less stupid now, she knows that, but lucky? The last few days seem to indicate that whatever luck she's had in the past is gone now. It's bad enough that Iris . . . but then with Peter the way he is . . . "Nope, not now, drive, focus, drive," she says loudly, gripping the steering wheel hard enough to see her knuckles whiten.

Merging onto the highway is strangely liberating. It's not empty, and plenty of people are on their way to work, but traffic is moving swiftly, and she opens the front-seat windows a crack on either side so she can feel the air, which is still cool and smells just a little bit like the ocean amid the exhaust and dust. She wonders if this is why her mother liked to travel. Alone, that is. Iris liked to travel alone. She took Maggie and Ariel occasionally when they were little, but they never took a family vacation all of them together, not once, even though Maggie saw her parents' friends and her friends' parents doing exactly that. She remembers Ariel being jealous, but by the time he was old enough to be, she was a teenager and pretty relieved not to need to trek around with embarrassing parents and a geeky brother. She isn't sure whether she'd complained like he did when she was younger; if she did, she can't remember it now.

When Maggie turned thirteen, her father took her on a sorta-kinda bat mitzvah trip—they didn't celebrate it in any other fashion—to wherever Maggie chose. Ariel got to do the same thing when he turned thirteen. Maggie had asked to go to Joshua Tree and also to Disneyland's new park, Disney California. Ariel had thought much bigger—he'd chosen Vietnam, but he'd gotten a terrible stomach bug on the plane, before ever setting foot in Hanoi, and had spent three of the five days there lying in a hotel bed, running to the bathroom every so often to puke or shit whatever he'd attempted to eat each time he thought he was feeling better. It was still a sore subject for him.

But Iris didn't do this with them. Instead, she stayed behind, first with Ariel, and then with Maggie, making sure to be home so that the house wasn't empty. But Maggie was eighteen when Ariel took his trip, about to go to college, and she had no interest in hanging out with her mom. At other times during her childhood, Iris would suggest the four of them take a short trip somewhere in the United States, somewhere kitschy like the Grand Canyon, which neither she nor Peter had ever been to, or New York, where they could see where Iris grew up. But those trips never actually happened. Everyone was busy, Maggie and Ariel had their own activities and social circles, Iris rarely refused any work that came her way, and Peter seemed perfectly content at home.

Maggie tries rolling down the window down further but the wind buffets her and makes the gelled curls on the top of her head whip stiffly sideways, so she rolls it back up. There's a knot of traffic ahead, and the GPS tells her to get off at Exit 101B to avoid some of it. She drives down what appears like a smallish back highway named San Marcos Pass Road just as the morning fog begins to lift enough to open the view of the mountains in front of her. She can see their broad bases and their not-so-high tops with a band of cloud cutting them right across. Maybe they're hills, she thinks, and not mountains. Lucia grew up in Colorado, and she's scoffed at Maggie's puny idea of what mountains are. She misses Lucia. She texted her this morning, finally, telling her about the letters and her plan, but Lucia hasn't texted back. It's Thursday, though, and Maggie reminds herself that Lucia is probably just busy, because it's the day she teaches simple claywork and pottery to kids at a summer arts camp. It's probably the last week of that, though—the school year must be starting soon.

A growl of hunger announces itself in Maggie's gut, so she pulls over to the shoulder and searches for somewhere to turn off and eat, but the closest places are all behind her, a detour barely forty-five minutes into her journey. She considers—and decides, fuck it. She can treat this as a vacation of sorts, can't she? Just like her mother treated her trips. She makes a U-turn and heads toward a Mexican place that says it's open and where the reviews recommend the breakfast burritos, which sounds perfect just about now.

Iris used to regale them with stories of inconsequential things that happened at work. Peter never needed to tell stories like that, the type with a beginning, middle, and punchline-end, because he was always right there, right in Maggie's line of sight. She didn't know details, but she knew vaguely what he was working on at any given time because his office was basically decorated with his own ongoing work. Other than the bookcase holding his heavy, overlarge art books at the bottom and a combination of old and new well-thumbed design books above that, there was a large bulletin board on one wall and a magnetic white board on another. Here he would pin and magnetize a variety of printed and hand-drawn sketches of logos and banners and office stationery borders and doodle new ideas and notes beside them. Even though he did all the real work on his computer, his office was still a big signpost for whoever his current clients were.

But Maggie remembers how the stories Iris told always sounded so scripted, a narrative that she built carefully to pass along. One tale that Maggie remembers, because Iris liked to tell it again and again, was about her love affair with a particular out-of-the-way Mexican restaurant that she'd accidentally ended up at twice in one trip—once because she'd been driving around aimlessly, starving, after a client had missed an appointment that morning in Soledad. "There I was," Iris told them over dinner more than once, though she usually only repeated stories for company, "all alone in a place called Soledad—so fitting, right?—and I ended up finding the least solitary place imaginable."

She'd walked into the restaurant on a day that a beloved community member was retiring from the local police force, and there was a huge celebration underway. She'd tried to leave, feeling like she was encroaching on a private party, but instead she'd been welcomed by two young servers and invited to sit right along with everyone. Iris claimed it was the only time she'd ever gotten drunk during the day, and she didn't regret a minute of it, though she'd needed to nap in her car for an hour before setting out on the road later in the afternoon.

"And the second time? You said you went there twice," someone would always prompt.

"The second time," Iris would say, smiling, "was the very next morning. The client I was supposed to meet the first day took me there. He was so sorry for missing our first meeting he said he'd take me to the best-kept secret in the whole county, which was this place. But I'd already discovered it all on my own."

Maggie wishes she knew what it was called, that place. Iris said they served the best enmoladas she'd ever tasted, the mole sauce so delectable, smooth and bitter yet fiery, that she wanted to let it sit in her mouth forever. But, of course, Maggie has no idea where exactly the restaurant was, if it's even still there. It's been ages, probably a decade, really, since she heard this story.

I'm at the age where I can remember conversations over a decade old, she thinks as she pulls into the parking lot of Papa Cantina. It's basically empty, with a bright turquoise-painted bar along one side and tables with red-and-white-checkered tablecloths on them spread neatly around a small central stage. The fliers by the door advertise a range of musical performances, including, she's tickled to see, a drag show special tomorrow. Maybe she'll make it back to see it, she thinks. Alone, though? She's not sure she's ever gone to a drag show, or any queer event really, without thirsty undertones. But Lucia and she have lasted twice as long as any former quote-relationship-unquote, and she doesn't want to screw it up. Not that she hasn't cheated before—she has. But usually as an excuse to end whatever unsatisfactory dating experience she'd found herself in.

"Hi, anywhere is fine," a young man tells her. He's sitting at a corner table along with two men wearing big white aprons, one of whom slowly raises himself up and heads into the kitchen. The other one keeps staring at his phone, and the young man gets up and picks out a menu to bring to her. They hover around each other, awkward, as she dithers between tables stupidly, wondering where would be easiest for him in terms of cleanup and delivery—she waited tables during her summers off from college and hated it, but is grateful for one thing that came out of the experience: she'll never again take for granted the servers and busboys and cooks anywhere she eats. She chooses the table closest to the kitchen, which is just to the right of where one of the cooks is still sitting, and hopes that he doesn't think she's encroaching on his space.

"Thanks," she says, taking the menu. "But I know what I want, actually. I hear you make good breakfast burritos?"

"We do. Seven kinds." He grins and leaves the menu with her. A moment later he's back with a glass of water and asks if she wants coffee.

"Omigod, please. And, um, the mushroom-and-mozzarella burrito?"

"You got it."

The coffee, when he brings it, has a hint of cinnamon in it, she's pretty sure. And it isn't too hot, so she can actually drink it without surreptitiously pouring in some cold water or waiting until after her meal. She leaves it black to better enjoy the flavor. It beats the five-dollar lattes and cold brews she's grown accustomed to drinking; it makes her mouth feel warm even after she's swallowed, the sweet bite of the spice making her think of her mother's beloved mole sauce.

Unexpectedly, tears prickle in her eyes. She takes out her phone as a distraction, to check text messages; Facebook, where she keeps up with a mix of faraway friends and acquaintances and older work buddies; and Instagram, where she mostly follows her close local friends like Allison and Micah and Harper and Blair, as well as various queer news, joy, and fashion accounts. She takes a photo of the mural across from her, which shows a stone wall in the forefront and behind it a small square building in the middle of a broad sandy lot, which she realizes is meant to be this very restaurant before the whole area was developed—she can see the tablecloths through the painted building's windows, and the flags hanging across the window frames, and even, in a kind of mind-bending move, a corner of this very mural on the inside of the painted building. She captions it "improv road-trip mindfuck" and posts it.

A few friends from St. Louis have texted her—Simon from work, asking her if she'll be coming to Friday night happy hour tomorrow; memes and pictures in the years-long shit-posting group text she has going with Allison, Micah, Harper, and Blair; and a clearly very drunk booty call message from Jolie. Oops, Maggie thinks, she hasn't told Jolie she has a girlfriend. It all seems so far, so foreign to where she is now. Only her work crew knows she's gone, and they probably just think she's sick, because she asked her boss to keep the whole my-mom-died thing quiet. There's nothing from Peter or Ariel yet. Must still be asleep or clueless that she's left, she supposes. It's not like they're used to having her in the house anymore.

She texts Allison, the closest of her friends and also an ex, about what's going on. Just as the server puts her burrito in front of her on a plate with a blue and yellow rim that she instantly wants to find and buy for her apartment, her phone rings. It's Allison. Before she thinks too hard about it, she answers. "Hey."

"Em, I'm so *so* sorry about your mom. I can't believe it. Are you okay? Of course you're not okay. But, like, are you surviving? Is it—"

"It's okay, Ally, stop. It's okay. I mean, yeah. It blows. Super blows. But I'm surviving. Actually, I'm taking a road trip."

"Yeah, I just saw your post. What's that about?" Maggie tells Allison about the will, about the necklace, about the letters. "So, wait, your mom just had these random letters to dudes? What, were they like waiting for her organs or something?"

The possibility of Iris's organs being placed with these men—or with anyone—never occurred to Maggie, but she doesn't think that's how it works. No one knows who they're donating to before they die, do they? Wouldn't that imply Iris knew she was going to die? The image of her mother's body cut open, her organs carefully being harvested, is horrible, even if Maggie has the box checked on her own license. She isn't actually sure if her mother did, or if there was anything salvageable. She gulps, pushes her plate away for a moment, the smell of food overwhelming her.

"Uh, I don't think so," she says.

"Shit, Em, I'm sorry, I didn't mean to—I'm horrible at this, I'm really sorry. I love you. I'm sorry."

Maggie tries to shake it off, even as irritation prickles down her back. "Anyway, look, I've been stewing in my own shit for days. Tell me something about your world. What's going on with the Devon and Alexa situation?"

As Allison regales her with the latest drama going on with the couple she's dating—her being poly is one of the reasons she and Maggie didn't last long—Maggie only half listens, but the familiar voice and safe topic have their desired effect and she manages to eat the rest of her burrito. She waves her hand at the server, who's sitting across from the off-duty cook again, and mouths "Check" at him with a lift of her eyebrows that she hopes indicates a request rather than a demand.

"Wow," she says when Allison explains how they worked everything out in a two-hour conversation last night. "So that's good then?"

"Yeah. It is. I'm so emotionally exhausted, though. I think I may cancel my hookup tonight."

Maggie rolls her eyes, but doesn't say anything. She's frankly impatient sometimes with Allison's determination to live a polyamorous lifestyle, feels like it's unfair of her to keep taking all the good people. Besides, it seems like Allison spends eighty percent of her time with her lovers just talking about their relationships rather than actually experiencing them.

"Are you really okay, though?" Allison asks after a moment of silence. "This whole road-trip thing—you're being safe?"

A surge of rage rises in Maggie's stomach and she says, much louder than she intended, "I'm not cheating on Lucia, if that's what you mean, and even if I did, you're one to talk." The server and the cook both begin turning their heads toward her but manage to keep their eyes on their newspaper and phone, respectively. She's embarrassed, and waves to the server again with her card and the curling check he put in front of her.

"Whoa. Dude. Chill. I didn't mean anything like that. I meant like, are you hitchhiking."

"Oh," Maggie says, sheepish. "No. I've got my dad's car."

"Okay. And also," Allison adds, "I know you're not in a great place, and I'm not mad, but like, I've literally never cheated, so while I know what you're implying, please don't."

"I'm sorry, Ally. I just . . . I don't know."

"It's okay," Allison says, a little too magnanimously for Maggie's taste. "Em, I love you and I'm here for you, okay?"

When they hang up, Maggie stares at her phone a bit. She decides it's time to follow Ariel's example. She takes a selfie—it's not great, but she chooses a filter that makes her look less wan, which she hadn't even realized she was looking. She posts it to Instagram and shares it to Facebook, along with her announcement:

Hallo frands. On the night of August 20, my mother, Iris Judith Krause, died in a car accident. The funeral took place yesterday. If I'm out of it or don't answer for a while to messages that's why.

As reactions, messages, texts, and comments start flowing in, she turns off her notifications.

. . .

BACK ON THE road, Maggie listens to KCRW in the car, the second airing of *Morning Edition*. Charlottesville is still in the news, and her blood boils remembering the incident—no, the atrocity.

The night it happened, she and Lucia had been out together, which rarely happened, after their first few dates, they tended to snuggle up and watch movies or fuck and talk and smoke and pass out. But that night, they'd gone to see *Newsies*, which Lucia had enjoyed and Maggie had hated for its twee love of boy orphans. On the way back, they were debating the merits of the musical, when both their phones buzzed, which meant, Maggie knew, they were probably getting the same alert. "Uh-oh," Maggie said, mostly joking. "What's the *New York Times* saying now?"

Lucia had her phone in her lap, and she didn't say anything for a long minute. "What is it?" Maggie asked, a knot in her stomach. Everyone she knew—well, everyone she knew and liked—had been dealing with anxiety and fear since the election. They discussed it often, trying to figure out how to keep going when they felt the fabric of the cushioned world around them fraying, exposing the rotting underside that had been there all along, except that people like Maggie—white, middle-class people—had been willfully unaware of the extent of this intense, ugly reality. But that night, something further shifted for Maggie when Lucia leaned back in her seat and said quietly, "The Nazis are marching. I want to sleep at my place if that's okay."

They stayed up half the night on their phones, propped up next to each other in Lucia's bed. Her cat, who usually hid when Maggie was over because she didn't like the noises the women made, came out that night and curled up next to Lucia, intuitively knowing that her person needed comfort.

"Honey, I—" Maggie had tried at one point. She wasn't sure what she wanted to say. *I know I'm white, but I'm not one of* them? *I'm Jewish, plus I'm queer, and they hate me too?* No, none of that would have been right or relevant. The Jewish part was true enough, and whenever Maggie let herself think about it for too long, about the history, about what could happen again, she found herself dismissing it, because surely—not here. It was impossible. And anyway, she still had the day-to-day privilege of whiteness. Lucia— Afro-Latina, daughter to born-and-raised Puerto Rican parents, a lesbian to boot—was so much more visible to these hateful people. Her and Maggie's relationship was still new enough, raw enough, that they had so far skirted the issue of how different their lived experiences as queer women had been.

"You're what?" Lucia asked, her eyes red-rimmed; they'd been smoking out her window every half hour or so.

"I'm here," Maggie said. It felt lame, but it was what she could offer, and Lucia seemed to appreciate it. She bumped her shoulder into Maggie's and went back to her Twitter feed. Eventually, Maggie fell asleep, and in the morning, Lucia told her, with the manic energy of one who hadn't slept all night, about the counterprotest she and some of her friends were organizing. It was the first political thing they'd done together, though Maggie knew and resented that just holding hands together on the streets of St. Louis was political, whether they wanted it to be or not. But this was intentional, and Maggie had watched Lucia that whole day, mesmerized by her energy, her ability to make this happen. As she listens today to a reporter talking to a Democratic strategist, she feels all their words are futile and empty. Lucia and folks like her—activists, people who know how to get shit done, a quality Maggie has been working to gain in recent months—are doing the real work, she believes.

By the time Ariel calls her almost three hours after she finished her breakfast, *Morning Edition* has ended and given way to music, with a feature about an indie rock band from Philadelphia, and the phone's ring breaks Maggie out of her reverie. "Where the fuck are you?" he says, his voice echoey on the speaker, but she can still practically hear his jaw grinding down through the phone.

"Near Greenfield, I think. Just passed it. Never been there, though, have you?" she says. Coming home, talking to Ariel—it always brings out this side of her that she doesn't like. It's as if the voices of her parents and brother, or maybe it's California itself, awakens her bratty inner teenager, the one who fought with her mother, who stayed out past curfew, who resented how amicable her brother was with Iris and how easily he followed rules. It's like a reaction to nails on a blackboard—involuntary.

"Fuck you," Ariel says. "Dad needs us."

"Yeah? Well, so does Mom. I'm taking care of the letters she wanted to send."

"Send, idiot. *Send.* What, there wasn't a mailbox closer than fucking Greenfield?"

"Yeah, okay, well, maybe you're not curious, but I want to know who these guys are she's sending letters to. After her death. So like, people who are important to her, right? Dudes. All of them dudes we've never heard of before. You think that's normal? I don't."

He breathes heavily for a moment. "When are you coming back."

"I don't know. I'll probably stay in Sacramento tonight."

"Jesus fucking Christ."

"Don't take the Lord's name in vain, little brother." There it is again. She's so glad that Lucia has never seen her like this. That Allison, who has seen her like this, has forgiven her.

"Fuck. You. Straight. To. Fucking. Hell," he says. Maggie wonders if he's aware of the way they talk to each other, like animals, like children. Their age gap was always such that she wanted nothing to do with her little brother most of the time, and when he was four and five and six, old enough to be interested in her and her friends, she had no patience for it. She remembers smacking the back of his head, swatting at his little shoulders, shoving him—usually in private, and Ariel, who so wanted her to let him stick around, would rarely squeal. But once, when Peter caught her at it— she was shoving her door closed on the foot Ariel had stuck in to try to prevent her from keeping him out—he'd been livid, the angriest she's ever seen him. Not usually a strict parent, he grounded her for two weeks. No TV, no Game Boy Color, no computer time on the family machine, no seeing friends outside of school. If she was bored after she finished her homework, he would hand her one of the volumes of the children's encyclopedia set she'd gotten for her birthday the year before. She refused to speak to Ariel the whole two weeks, as if it was his fault.

"Mags, Dad isn't doing well, I don't know what to do with him, okay?" Ariel whines. He sounds like he did all those years ago when he begged her to talk to him, and she feels immediately awful. He's her baby brother, after all, and isn't she, on some level, supposed to protect him?

"Just—just make sure he eats," she says, trying to swallow her guilt. "I got a bunch of instant shit from the grocery store the other day so you don't have to cook. Tell people today you're vegan, okay? I bet you someone will pass it along and folks will bring more vegan stuff when they come tomorrow. That's the point of shivas, to get fed, you know? You can do this, Ariel. You can."

"I dunno . . . Like, shouldn't I take him to a doctor or something?"

"Look, so far Dad seems to be good at doing what he's told to do. And it's been like barely any time since Mom—since it happened. So let's give him a minute before we go full-on straitjacket on him, okay?"

Ariel seems calmer by the time they finish talking. She hopes people will show up soon, like her dad's stepbrothers, who said they'd come by at least another couple of times. She hopes Ariel's girlfriend or fuck buddy or whatever she is also shows up to help get him through this.

It occurs to her that what she's doing is extremely irresponsible. She isn't sure Peter has insurance on his car for her specifically or for another driver at all. She doesn't know if it's really a good idea to leave Ariel alone with Peter. And for all she knows, the people she's intent on delivering these letters to could be dangerous. Maybe they're all in a biker gang—but no, she can't see her mother consorting with anyone wearing as much leather as a leather-daddy.

So maybe they're ax murderers, she thinks idly, and wonders, as she pulls into a gas station, whether ax murders are even a thing anymore. A tall, broad-shouldered and stocky white woman with a blond mullet is filling up her truck from the opposite side of the pump that Maggie pulls into, and she smiles, jerks her chin. Her snaggletooth is incredibly sexy, and Maggie is flustered as she turns around to place the suddenly obscene-looking pump into the gas tank. "I like your hair," the woman says.

"Thanks," Maggie says, her cheeks reddening. Normally, she would be flirting back, telling the woman her truck is cool or that her cheek piercing is hot. But she thinks of Lucia, and doesn't really want to. Or she does—does she?—but she isn't doing it. She's not used to this feeling, this keeping herself to herself.

She realizes also that this is the closest she's felt to turned on since she got the call from Ariel on Sunday, and even this isn't really that. She can't believe it's only Thursday. She can't believe it's already Thursday. Her mother has been dead for only four days. She has been orphaned of her mother for four days already. The words feel bland and empty, not sinking in. It's when she lets herself think of *nevers* that the emotion wells up. She'll never hug her mother again; never hear Iris's distracted voice on the phone; never see her lighting Shabbat candles, which she liked doing even though they didn't keep kosher or stop using electricity over the weekend. The things she'll never see or hear or witness keep coming, and she thinks that death isn't about the person who's dead; it's about the people who are still alive. Grief, she realizes, is selfish. It's about what she's losing, not what her mother lost, not what her mother still had time or desire to do in her life—and surely there was a lot. Iris was young, as old people go.

Maggie can handle being existential when she's high, when she can generally accept that the world is complicated and people are both selfish and selfless. It's easier to hold more than one concept as true and valid in her mind when she is less than clearheaded. When she's sober, like now, she just feels the spiral of thoughts tightening, stifling her.

For the next leg of her ride—the dyke with the truck has driven off, and she's glad she didn't need to consider flirtation again—Maggie decides to listen to a true-crime comedy podcast. The voices of three jolly men discussing some terrible crimes that happened in the 1970s soothe her as the highway stretches on ahead, and she drives into the afternoon.

MAGGIE'S BEEN UP to Sacramento only once, years ago, when she was considering going to college there. When she shockingly got a scholarship from the Midwestern school she ended up attending—"I bet," she had said uncharitably at the time, "they're trying to *diversify*"—her parents agreed to let her go out of state. They still had to contribute some, and she took out student loans whose minimum she reluctantly still pays every month, refusing to hurry up and get out of a debt she resents; she hadn't really wanted to go to college in the first place. She may have been a dumb seventeen-year-old—she embraces this fact now, certain that everyone considers their younger selves to be idiotic—but she knew even then that she was a reluctant student, preferring to learn things on her own during long, late-night Wikipedia trawls, a variety of informative podcasts, YouTube videos, and the occasional nonfiction book. But her parents insisted that she had to go, that no kid who could afford college didn't go these days because how else would she get a job, and so she'd applied to a few select schools out of state to try to get away from them.

As she drives into the state capital, she thinks of how Peter and Ariel must be saying goodbye to people by now and her shoulders tense at the thought of what today would have been like if she hadn't left. She pictures herself hurling plates at people who repeat empty platitudes, or yelling at Peter in front of the guests, and she's relieved, again, that she didn't stay to risk that.

"In a quarter mile, turn right," her phone chirps, and Maggie remembers how when she came here last time, with Iris, neither of them had smartphones yet, and Iris's GPS device, a cheap one, pronounced Sacramento with a long *A* at the beginning, making them laugh. Peter had taken Maggie to see other places in-state, and she'd gone with her junior class to a few nearby colleges, but Iris had a job prospect in Sacramento and offered to take her. On the drive up from Oxnard, Maggie remembers Iris admitting that the job interview could have easily been done over the phone but that she'd wanted an excuse to take Maggie on a college visit. Maggie is sure she was dismissive, probably replying with "whatever, Mom," but she wonders now why Iris had needed an excuse in the first place. Couldn't she have just said that she wanted to go with Maggie? Couldn't she have just taken time off work? But no, of course not. Iris was big on work ethic.

Which, whether Maggie likes it or not, is something that her mother clearly instilled in her. Maggie has taken vacation days to travel to California but always for short stints, often arranged around long weekends. She has a bunch of accumulated days off that she's likely using now, since the bereavement leave only covered Monday, Tuesday, and Wednesday. It's a double-edged sword—on the one hand, having a set work schedule allows her to use it as an excuse if there's something she doesn't want to do. "Oh, I have to get up early tomorrow for work," she'll say, or "I've gotta stay a bit late at the office today. Sorry, guys." On the other hand, she tends to take her job a bit too seriously, always going in even when she really shouldn't, like the time she didn't notice she had a fever until Simon pointed out that she was sweating while everyone else was lobbying to turn off the A/C. Maybe her mother just couldn't let loose that world, like Maggie can't. Or maybe, she thinks, Iris used it as an excuse to stay away from them.

"I don't have kids," Maggie mutters to herself. "I'm not hurting anyone." She misses a turn and waits for the phone's GPS to recalibrate.

It's almost six in the evening. A couple of hours ago, her eyes beginning to droop, she stopped at a gas station and napped in the car's back seat for a while. She hadn't slept enough the night before and knew it would be stupid to keep driving. *See, Mom, I* am *responsible,* she thought as she tossed a flannel shirt over her shoulders to keep the sun from burning her. Sometimes, it seems like everything she's done since leaving home—going to college, graduating, buying a good used car, getting a straight job, actually liking it—could be viewed through this lens. As if she's been trying to prove that, despite the weed and the molly and the boots and the androgynous clothes and the haircut and the lesbianism, all the things her mother disapproved of, she's still capable of being an adult, of being responsible. That she's still doing it, not only years after leaving home but now that her mother isn't here to witness it—it's painful, it's pathetic.

Maggie's mouth tastes like the cinnamon gum she bought at the gas station along with a limp chicken sandwich, and she wonders if she should stop somewhere to check out how she looks. But no—this isn't a date. She's just delivering something, isn't she?

She isn't certain what she'll do when she gets there. The streets get smaller and wind tighter around her as she enters the city proper, until she reaches another residential neighborhood that looks, if she's honest, no different from Oxnard. Everywhere is the same, she thinks. Just houses and houses and lawns and commercial districts dotted in between them. She's never lived in a city where buildings are tall and crowd around her, but she's often wondered if that's where she should end up eventually; she doesn't like the lawns, the false aesthetic that feels and looks like all suburbia in movies and television shows.

When her phone bleats out, "Your destination is on the right," she parks and stares at the house. It's bland, a one-story, painted a kind of grayish green above a brick foundation. A little smaller than the houses on either side, and the lawn has been pulled up and replaced by a rock garden with a few dry shrubs and a couple cacti breaking up the pale gray stones. There are lights on inside, peeking through blinds that are mostly shut. The letters, which have been sitting on the passenger seat next to her like a talisman while she drove, seem impossible to look at now. Her hands quiver as she shuts off the car and reaches toward them.

Abraham K. Okafor. This is where he lives. She didn't start out that long ago, but it feels like her journey has been endless already and she's immensely tired.

What am I even doing? she wonders, staring at the house. Someone lives here, someone whose life has nothing to do with hers. She should probably just leave the letter in the mailbox out front, a novelty one shaped like a pig whose curly tail is the handle. She imagines the mailman who comes by here every day, how resentful putting letters in this piglet's ass must make him.

"Just do it," she tells herself. "Fucking coward." She snatches the letter, grabs her phone and grips it tightly in her hand, and makes sure she has her legal-carry knife in her jeans pocket—because what if her mother really does owe some kind of gambling debt or is involved in other shady activity? It's not likely, no, but she can't rule anything out yet—and slams the door to Peter's car behind her. She walks up the path to the house with what she hopes is confidence and determination. Not that there's anyone watching. It's quiet in that way residential streets are in the evening, when everyone has gotten home from their nine-to-fives.

In movies, people always hesitate and turn around and come back and do this several times before they actually knock on the damn door. Maggie won't let herself be this cliché. When she gets to the entrance, heart pounding, palms sweating, she presses the doorbell.

Silence. No ringing sound from inside that she can detect, though she does hear voices. Should she knock? She tries the doorbell again and knocks three times for good measure. The voices inside lower and halt and someone stomps toward the door. She could run, she could leave now—

"Yeah? Hi?" A broad-shouldered black man—no, a boy, she realizes after a moment, a teenager probably—opens the door. He's wearing an oversized T-shirt but his bottom half is clad in what she's pretty sure are those weird tight white pants that baseball players wear.

"Hi," Maggie says, her voice trembling. "I'm looking for Abraham Okafor?"

"That's me," he says.

"Seriously?" she asks, now confused. He draws back a little, like he's nervous. Of course. Of course he would be, she realizes. Some white lady he's never met before at his door asking for him by name? But how could this kid be at all connected to her mother?

"Hey, what's going on—" Another man reaches the door. He's taller than the youth, rail-thin, absent any muscles at all it seems, dressed in what she can only think of as professorial gear: khaki slacks belted to his narrow frame and a black turtleneck sweater that seems too warm for the weather. A delicate salt-and-pepper mustache frames his upper lip. "Can I help you?" he says, shimmying in front of the boy, as if he might need to shield him from something.

"My name is Maggie Krause," she says, and the older man's eyes widen. "I'm looking for Abraham K. Okafor—I have a letter for him?" She holds up the envelope and the man's gaze fixes on it.

"Oh, that's you, Dad," the kid says. He seems relieved.

After another awkward pause which is likely only momentary but feels longer, she adds, "It's from Iris? Iris Krause?"

"Right. I'm Abe," he tells Maggie. "Junior, can you go check on the sauce?" The youth looks between his dad and her, and his mouth purses. He blinks slowly, and she notices he has incredibly long, beautiful eyelashes. Feminine, almost. But he glares at her, a warning, she thinks, which is sweet, really. Protective. "Junior," Abe repeats, his voice quiet but commanding.

"Yeah, yeah," the kid, Junior, grumbles. He lets go of the door and turns inside.

"Um," Maggie says. "So."

"So," Abe says, crosses his arms. "Is this a joke of some kind?"

Fury rises in her, an anger that feels violent. A *joke*? "No," she says. "My mom, Iris, is dead. She died Sunday. She left some letters. She left one for you. I want to give it to you, but I want to know how you knew my mom."

Abe's lips part, his eyebrows knit—he looks stricken. "Dead? I . . . Lord. Was she sick?"

"No," Maggie says, and swallows hard. "It was an accident."

"And you're her daughter? I'm so sorry for your loss. Please, come in," he adds, stepping back.

Maggie steps inside. The ceilings are a bit low in the foyer, making the space look dank at first, but Abe leads her into an airier living room, and she's a little stunned by the art everywhere. Colorful framed paintings and masks in a range of styles hang on the walls, with a long row of hanging bookshelves above them, and stone or clay statues sit on end tables. She wishes Lucia were here to comment on the decor—would she find it intimidatingly classy, like Maggie does, or cluttered? More books lie on the ground in corners, apparently waiting for more shelf space. It smells incredible, and Maggie sees Junior stirring something on the stove—there's a wide window cut into the wall between the living room and a small kitchen nested in the middle of the house. The boy's eyes are glued to what must be a TV or some other screen and she can hear the fast-paced talk of a sports broadcaster.

"Sit, sit," Abe says. His hands are clutched together, making a kind of washing motion. He seems as nervous as she feels. "Can I get you anything? Coffee, tea, water? A beer, maybe?"

"A beer would be great, actually," she says.

"Great," he says, and then hesitates. "You're . . . you're twenty-one, right?"

She smiles. She gets the feeling this man is a bit of a dork. "Twenty-seven," she says.

"Good, good," he mutters. He takes a while in the kitchen, and she can hear him murmuring under the noise of the game. Junior's deeper voice says something that sounds like "But Dad!" and then hushes, along with the broadcaster. She hears footsteps retreating to the back of the house, where another TV switches on and then a door shuts. When Abe comes back out of the kitchen, he snaps the light in there off.

"I interrupted your dinner," Maggie says, realizing that they were cooking and now they're not.

"No, it's all right, it's simmering, don't worry," Abe says. He hands her a Heineken, but hasn't taken one for himself.

"Oh, if you're not having one, I'm okay—" Maggie tries to give back the beer but he shakes his head.

"It's fine, please, drink." He sits in an armchair across from her, his long legs spread apart and his elbows resting on his knees.

"Okay," she says, but she doesn't have a bottle opener and she doesn't want to ask for one, so she just holds the cold glass in her hands, rolling it between them.

"So what does the letter say," Abe says, staring at his feet.

"I didn't read it." The letter lays in her lap. She still hasn't given it to him.

"What?" Abe's head snaps up. "You didn't?"

"I—yeah, no."

He smiles. "Very respectful," he says, though she's not sure if it's with approval, exactly. Maybe she's naive, but Maggie never thought that reading the letters was a possibility. It'd be like finding her mother's journal, or her father's for that matter, and those at least make sense to read after someone's dead—they were writing to themselves, after all.

But Maggie was always taught to respect privacy, and she knows for a fact that, no matter what she and her mother disagreed over, Iris never went through Maggie's things. So when Maggie found these letters, she never thought of opening them, especially since they're addressed to other people, a communication Maggie has no right to infringe on. But she could, she realizes. She could just leave now, and take the letters with her to a motel and smoke up and read them and see what this is all about.

But she doesn't want to. At least, not yet. She wants to hear what Abe has to say.

"Here," she says, and hands him the envelope finally. "I just . . . Can you tell me how you know her? I've never heard of you before," she adds. And then, "Should I have?"

He takes the letter from her and turns it around and around in his hands. "No, I guess not," he says.

Maggie waits. The shaking is back. She isn't sure she really wants to hear whatever he's about to say. But she also can't leave, not now that she's gotten here, not now that she's met him. "So . . ." she says, and this seems like enough prompting.

"I met Iris about, wow, I guess it must be almost ten years ago. My wife—my ex-wife and I had just gotten divorced. My son, you saw him, he used to live with both of us, alternating, but my ex got a job on the East Coast and he didn't want to move, so he stayed with me full-time." Abe pauses, and Maggie wonders what his son has to do with meeting her mother. "The last time I saw Iris was when I told her that we wouldn't be able to see each other anymore, because I didn't want to confuse Junior. That was probably about five years ago now." He stares behind Maggie's shoulder, unfocused, and sighs. "I can't believe she's dead."

"See each other?" Maggie says. The words roll around in her mouth. She is seeing Lucia. Ariel is seeing Leona. Dating. Fucking. Impossible— her parents' marriage is perfect, was perfect, they were the most loving people she's ever met. Look at how Peter is grieving; that doesn't happen when someone is cheating. Right? Her heart is racing, and she wants to throw the bottle clutched between her hands, to see it shatter against a wall. And yet, a part of her is calmly thinking what she's kept herself from ac-knowledging since she found the letters. *I knew it.*

Abe heaves a sigh and she notices his eyes are wet. "I don't know if I should talk about this . . ."

"She left the letters she wanted to send at home," Maggie snaps. "She could have left them with the fucking lawyer. She didn't. Which means—" Maggie feels her voice rising, but she can't help it, she's livid. "Which means that she didn't fucking even *think* about whether my brother or I would have questions, she just didn't care, and my dad is sitting at home barely moving because he's so depressed that his beloved wife is dead and you're telling me you were fucking her?!" She doesn't know when she stood up, but she's on her feet. Abe isn't. He's still sitting, and doesn't look alarmed so much as sad.

"Yes," he says, so calmly that Maggie instantly feels scolded and sits back down. "That's pretty much right."

She waits, refusing to look away from his face, her jaw aching with how hard she's clenching it to keep herself from angry-sobbing. Eventually he starts talking again.

"Look, Iris was a complicated person. She was on Ashley Madison, you know that site? Anyway, I'd made an account when I found out my wife had one, because I was mad. Then, after we divorced, I kept checking it occasionally. One day, I got a message from her. She said she was looking for someone she could talk to and be intimate with. She wasn't looking for a one-night stand, she said, though she wouldn't begrudge me if that's what ended up happening. We started talking. She was fascinated with my work—I'm an astrobiologist." He pauses, and since Maggie is pretty sure her expression betrays that she has no idea what that is, he adds, with the practiced tone of someone who needs to explain his job a lot, "I basically use real and simulated climates and landscapes to consider and test the viability of life elsewhere in the universe—" Maggie has a moment of thinking, *Whoa, cool,* before she focuses again. "—and she flattered me by taking an interest, asking me lots of questions. She came to town a little while after we started talking, and we had lunch and hit it off."

"And, what, you were just okay with her cheating on her husband? A husband she had kids with? You were okay with being the other man? The home-wrecker?" Maggie grips the beer bottle so tightly that her bones begin to ache.

Abe looks at her with something akin to pity. "I was very lonely," he says. "Iris was extremely special." He shrugs. "She had rules, though."

"That's rich," Maggie says. "She was already breaking the rules just by being with you."

"Well, rules for me, I should say. I wasn't allowed to ask anything about, well, about any of you. She told me she'd tell me when and if it was relevant, but that she wanted to keep her family life separate from anything she had with me. She said she had a road life and a home life and that she wasn't going to ever mix the two."

Maggie tries to digest this. Iris had secrets, obviously, but more than that, she wanted to keep them secret. Compartmentalized. Something is nagging at her. "When did you say you met?"

"About ten years ago. I think it was 2007? Fall, probably, or late summer, something like that."

There's something infuriating about his vagueness. She does the math. "Jesus," she says. "Was it in September of 2007 by any chance?"

Abe's eyes squint as he tries to remember. "I think that's right, yes." He looks down at the letter in his hands and runs his fingers over his name. "Mind if I open it?"

"Go ahead," Maggie says, and leans back. She really wants the beer right now. Remembering she has a lighter in her pocket, she gets it out, snaps the beer cap off, and takes a long swig, which isn't as refreshing as she'd like since it's warmed considerably in her grasp.

Iris may have wanted to keep her family life and dating life separate, Maggie thinks, but she met Abe when she was taking Maggie on that trip to see Sacramento State. And maybe that was the real reason she wanted to go in the first place. It wasn't a job, and it certainly wasn't wanting to spend time with her daughter.

Maggie pulls herself out of this mire of thoughts to watch Abe's face as he reads the letter. It's three pages long, handwritten. She takes another swig of her beer, thinks of her own infidelity. It was never this way, never so . . . calculated, is the only word she can come up with. When she cheated, it was, at least in hindsight, deliberate, but it was also spontaneous in the moment, not planned. It was a way to create a confrontation she didn't know how to start otherwise, meaning it was never a well-kept secret. And none of her flings ever looked at her the way Abe is looking at this damn letter, that's for sure.

"Did you love her?" she asks, interrupting him.

When he glances up, his eyes are definitely wet and his voice is thick when he says, "Yes. Yes, I did. It wasn't easy, and I never saw her very often, but yes, I loved her very much. That's why I ended it. She wouldn't leave your father, you see. She told me that from the very beginning, but as time went on, I started to hope. And my son was hitting puberty and I needed to focus on him. If I could have, I would have asked her to marry me and come live with us. But that wasn't going to happen." He looks back at the letter and continues reading.

Maggie thinks she's heard enough. She wants to smoke. She wants to sleep. She wants to call Lucia, maybe Ariel, and she wants to understand what the hell her mother was doing and how no one knew about any of this. She wants to throttle her innocent and loving father and tell him to snap the fuck out of his mourning because there isn't nearly as much to mourn as he thinks there is. Though that would likely make things worse.

She gets up, leaving the half-empty beer on the artfully rough wooden coffee table. "Well, okay. I guess I'm done here."

"You're going?" he says, looking up. "Don't you want to stay for dinner at least? We have a guest room." He hesitates, puts down the letter. His hands begin the nervous washing motion again. "That is, it's yours for the night. If you'd like."

And Maggie, tired, is undone by this kindness. So half an hour later, she finds herself settled in, her bag retrieved from the car and lying on the queen-size bed in the spare bedroom, sitting down to eat ewa agoyin—which she's told are mashed beans with a dark sauce of palm oil, peppers, onions, and ground crayfish—with Abe and Junior.

IRIS

DECEMBER 13, 2012

Every year, Iris tried to do something special for herself on what she considered the Bad Day. It was the anniversary of her first marriage, and if she didn't make an effort at distraction, she inevitably sank into a pit of dark memories. Though, truth be told, those memories invaded anyway, almost no matter what she did, and not always or only on the Bad Day.

That morning, she woke up to a thermos of fresh coffee with a flower-shaped jam cookie propped against it on the bedside table. Under the thermos was a note from Peter. *Good morning, my love,* it read. *Have an easy day. I'm sorry I'm not here to hug you.* For a moment, she was disoriented. Where was he that he had to leave a note? And then she remembered that he and Maggie had driven to LA to meet a friend of Maggie's from college who was visiting the West Coast with her family over winter break. They were going to brunch at a place Iris recommended—she took clients there occasionally—and then to the Huntington Art Gallery to see Ricky Swallow's contemporary abstract sculptures. Iris was originally supposed to go with them, but when she'd realized what the date was, had begged off.

She hadn't explained why, though. Her children didn't know she'd been married before, and she had no interest in telling them. Peter deferred to her in this, knowing that she felt it was a sad and pathetic excuse for a marriage. No matter how many times she was told it wasn't her fault, no matter how much she would tell others it wasn't theirs either, the fact remained that she was ashamed of it, of how long she'd stayed, of how many years she'd spent subsumed in it. She didn't want her children having that kind of example in their lives, and she didn't want them to see her as weak.

She pulled herself up, stretched, and began to get organized for the alternative plans she'd made for the day. The distracting ones. Ariel was probably home—she couldn't imagine where else he'd be—but was probably sleeping late as usual. She'd told the kids that she had an urgent work thing pop up last night, while she and Maggie were watching *Motives & Murders: Cracking the Case,* the newest of the sensational crime docudramas on the ID channel. She'd waited until a commercial break, of course, her and Maggie having forbidden Ariel from talking only moments earlier because he was making fun of the narrator's overly serious tone. Ariel, who'd gone back to his book after that, barely glanced up when Iris explained that she was heading out of town, but Maggie seemed disappointed that Iris wouldn't meet her friend. In her usual way, though, she'd lifted her chin and jerked out a nod of what Iris suspected was feigned indifference. She couldn't confirm it; Maggie would always deny vehemently that she was hurt or bothered by anything Iris did. It used to drive her up the wall, the passive-aggressive way Maggie said "Whatever," or "Never mind," but over the years, Iris had come to accept it, mostly because she had never managed to break through it. She used to try, telling Maggie they could talk, that it was better to discuss these things than keep them inside, but Maggie would just roll her eyes and say that there was nothing to talk about. "She takes after you," Peter used to tell her when she was at her wit's end, crying in their bedroom after another fight with her daughter. "She's stubborn, and she protects herself. She'll come around eventually," he'd say. But so far, Iris was sad to note, she hadn't.

In the kitchen, she grabbed a couple of slices of bread and stuck them in the toaster on low in order to make the emergency snack she always brought with her on drives—a peanut butter sandwich. One of the vestiges of her mother's rearing. An immigrant—or did she count as a refugee, at least at first? Iris didn't know, since her parents refused to talk about so much—her mother had tried to expose her daughter to everything American, and along with TV dinners and Twinkies, she deemed peanut butter especially so. She was forever worried that Iris would get hungry and made sure her daughter had a Wonder Bread peanut butter sandwich—crusts on, only because Iris insisted—whenever she left the house.

Waiting for her toast, Iris began sifting through the pile of mail from the week that had accumulated on the kitchen island. A couple of bills, some requests from museums and theaters for donations—these were all for Peter, since he was the one who got on their mailing lists—and some holiday cards from former clients, one from her accountant. And at the bottom, a parents' newsletter from Maggie's university. She slit the envelope open with her thumb, tearing it unevenly and giving herself a paper cut. "Ow," she said, sticking her thumb in her mouth. She sucked on the metallic flavor of her blood and relished the sting as she skimmed the thick pages of the pamphlet. They described all sorts of student affairs she didn't care about, and then, on the back, in large letters, she saw the word "Graduation" and tugged her thumb out of her mouth. Some guy with a silly name was speaking at commencement, and Iris grinned at herself; he sounded like a fashion model rather than a motivational speaker. She supposed he could be both. Mostly, she couldn't believe Maggie was going to graduate in five months. That is, she thought as she spread Laura Scudder's on the hot toast and pressed the slices together, it made perfect sense that her daughter was graduating college, but was also a totally bonkers concept. And Ariel—he'd be starting soon enough. A warmth filled Iris's chest as she gathered her things to set off. If only her parents could have seen her children—fully American, free to speak their minds and follow their hearts, unconstrained by the kind of oppression Iris's parents had suffered. Even when Maggie went on about the state of politics, even when Iris agreed with her, she knew in a way her daughter didn't that the very ability to voice her anger was a freedom.

She climbed in her car and began the drive to Coalinga, to the resort she had a good discount on since she'd organized a couple of events there for small companies. It boasted three restaurants, a large pool, and was near what she'd learned was the annual Horned Toad Derby, something she knew nothing about but was charmed by anyway. She listened to NPR on the drive as she always did, and the news was dire, of course; there were violent protests in India following a gang-rape. Good, she thought. Rape was nothing but violence, disgusting and disguised as sex rather than what it really was—a destruction of a person's power, an erosion of their will. Her vision blurred for a moment with the force of the image springing before her. Shlomo's face, his scraggly beard oozing off his chin and cheeks, his hot breath filling her nose. A loud honk brought her back to the present—she was going far too slowly for the highway. She pulled over onto the shoulder and endured another extended blare as someone passed her and yelled "Learn how to drive, bitch!" out their window.

Iris sat, hands gripping the wheel so hard that her knuckles were white and the flesh between them beet red. A story came on about the final funerals for Sandy Hook victims. The newscaster's voice was solemn in a way it wasn't a moment before during his discussion of the rape protests. Iris changed the station—Billy Idol's "White Wedding." Oh, the irony, she thought.

When she got to the resort, she realized she hadn't eaten her sandwich. She considered it but decided to toss it in the bin—her mother was probably rolling in her grave—and get some lunch at one of the restaurants instead.

The more casual one; she'd save the really fancy place for later, when Abe arrived.

"Hello, ma'am, can I tell you about our specials today?" a young white brunette woman asked, her apron tied meticulously around her hips and her crisp shirt so clean it was almost blinding. Iris was pretty sure there was a woman like her at every upscale restaurant she'd ever been to—bland, fresh-faced, appealing in the same way as a town car. Recognizable, symbolic, utterly dull.

"No, thanks, I know what I want," Iris said. "The crispy calamari to start, please, and then the Cobb salad?"

"What kind of dressing?"

"Do you have blue cheese?"

"Yes. Excellent choice, ma'am," the server said. She clicked her pen sharply on the pad in her hand and smiled widely, revealing a silver ring hanging from her gums over her front teeth that made Iris shudder internally, and think that maybe she wasn't quite so bland.

"Oh, and a glass of wine, please. Whatever the house white is."

Iris began to relax now, leaning back in the polished wooden booth and feeling her limbs begin to ease from the tension of the drive, which had become overcautious after her vision of Shlomo. She pulled two books out of her bag—one crime novel she was almost finished with, about a corpse found in 1946 in a bombed-out corner of London, and a new one she was about to start that she'd picked up because it was about an old widowed Jewish repairman. Sort of like her father, a jack of all trades who'd been the super of the apartment building she'd grown up in, in Brooklyn. She thought he'd enjoy seeing someone like him starring in a book.

But the books couldn't keep her attention for too long, especially after the second glass of wine. She kept thinking about her imminent meeting. It had been over three months since she'd last seen Abe; they'd texted and exchanged a few emails and talked on the phone once or twice. He'd been busy with his semester—it was a teaching year for him, which he didn't love, but it came with being a researcher with university funding—and his son's full-time move into his house. And Iris had been working, trying to help Ariel study for the SATs, and remodeling the bathroom in her and Peter's room after they'd discovered rot underneath a couple loose floor tiles. As she paid and got up to go check into their room, she pushed thoughts of her family away from her mind, reminding herself that she needed boundaries, even on an emotionally slippery day like this. Without strict separation, she wouldn't have ever been able to keep this up. Instead of home and the guilt she felt at canceling plans with Maggie, she made herself picture Abe's mouth on her neck and wondered idly how quickly they'd fall into bed. One thing they had in spades was chemistry.

"Here you go, two-oh-one, the Canary Room," the desk clerk told her, handing over a key with a large wooden tag on it in the shape of a yellow bird. The rooms at the resort used to only have names, but apparently too many visitors had complained about having difficulty navigating, and so there were numbers now too. Iris wished there weren't—there was something so romantic about the idea of needing to hunt down the Canary Room.

She took the elevator up, because her knees ached in the winter nowadays, and found the room at the end of the hall. It was painted a light, friendly yellow, with the couch and the bedsheets in complementary white and gold stripes. A large TV hung across from the bed, and the curtains were flung open, letting in the winter sunlight, which was already beginning to orange with the passing of the day. She followed her usual routine: kicked off her heels, got her toiletry bag onto the bathroom counter, and turned on the TV to the Weather Channel because it made her feel less alone. There wasn't much exciting about entering hotel rooms anymore, though she remembered her first stay, how stoked she'd been when her parents had taken her to Maine once when she was young, to visit distant relatives. Back then, staying in a hotel felt like the epitome of wealth. Now she stayed in Best Westerns and Holiday Inns almost weekly, and sometimes, if events were taking place in higher-end Marriotts and Hiltons, she'd stay on-site. She wasn't rich, but she was more comfortable than she could have ever imagined being.

In a way, she had Shlomo to thank for that. She hated it, though. She didn't want to owe him anything.

She lay down and let the talk of rain and shine and temperatures and dew points soothe her to sleep.

WHEN SHE WOKE up more than an hour later, her mouth felt foamy, and there were two missed calls from her daughter. She called back, panicked. "Sweetie, what's wrong?" she asked as soon as Maggie picked up.

"What? Nothing, chill, everything's okay," her daughter said, impatient. "Dad wanted to know whether you had renewed the Barnes and Noble membership but he forgot his phone at home like a dingus."

"Don't call Dad a dingus," Iris said, relieved and also beginning to get mad. "When you call twice and don't leave a message it makes me think something awful is happening."

"Yeah, but like, if something awful was happening I'd call nine-one-one, you know?"

"Okay, Maggie." Talking to her daughter was exhausting sometimes. "How was your day with your friend? Are you all still in LA or heading home yet?" There was a long pause. "Honey?"

"What."

"What, what? I asked a question."

"We're heading home. Bye." And Maggie hung up on her. She stared at her phone. What had she done this time? Maggie wasn't one to just hang up like that, not usually—she would normally stay on the line, huffily silent, while Iris tried to figure out how she'd offended her daughter. Last time, it was when Whitney Houston died; Maggie had told her that it was an open secret that she was a closeted lesbian, even if the rumors were being denied over and over again now that she was dead, and Iris had said that sounded like nonsense. It seemed to her that fans were always trying to make famous people into a version that suited their politics. Maggie had gone cold and monosyllabic for the rest of the call. But Iris hadn't said anything about anything this time, had she? The way she and her daughter ran hot and cold on each other kept her up at night sometimes, trying to figure out which of them was being unreasonable.

Her phone, still in her hand, buzzed; it was Abe, telling her he'd just parked. She closed her eyes, made herself sink back into the here and now, into this part of her life that was hers alone. When she sat up, she was smiling, her fingers prickling with anticipation at touching Abe again.

Giddy, she went downstairs in her stocking feet. The carpet felt like a pillow under her soles. It was a luxurious sensation, like being Eloise at the Plaza, and when the elevator opened and she saw Abe standing at his majestic six-foot-three height, she had the urge to run to him, jump on him like someone in a rom-com. But instead she stopped and watched as he looked around, his mouth set. When he caught sight of her, he smiled, but not as enthusiastically as she'd hoped.

"What's wrong?" she asked once his long legs carried him over to where she was standing.

He squeezed her shoulder and shook his head. "Let's go to the room."

In the elevator, she took his hand and squeezed it. He pulled her toward him and kissed the top of her head, taking a long whiff of the smell of her hair. "Abe, I'm worried," she said.

"Don't be." He smiled, more genuinely. "It's just things at home."

"Ah," she said. "Has Lisa gone yet?" Lisa was Abe's ex-wife, who was moving to New Jersey and letting Abe have custody of their son, as long as Junior wanted to stay in Sacramento.

"She's leaving after Christmas. Junior's been with her all this past week even though we already moved all his stuff into my place."

"I'm sorry, darling," Iris said. They were in the room by now, and she knelt before him and began to remove his shoes to give him a foot rub, which was one of his favorite things. But he pulled her up and sat her on him, her skirt riding up to her thighs, and kissed her. "Oh," she said, feeling not so sorry after all.

They fucked hard and fast. There was an urgency to Abe that she wasn't used to. He tended to spend a long time pleasuring her with his lips and tongue first, even if they hadn't seen each other for a while, but this time he got her clothes off, gazed at her, and awkwardly tore off his own while fumbling in his bag for lubricant. He slid his wet hand the length of his shaft and then, with more force than usual, slid two fingers inside her. He picked her up and she wrapped her legs around him. He didn't quite slam her against the wall, but he backed her into it hard enough that he pulled away from kissing her neck and asked her, "Okay?" She nodded, and he pushed inside her.

It was over pretty quickly, as with a shudder he let loose inside her. He held himself there as she rocked against his pelvis, his penis softening but providing enough stimulation to keep her going. Finally, she pushed her fingers between them and rubbed herself until with a stuttering gasp she came. He took her hand and sucked on the wet fingers. Then he laid her down on the bed so gently it made her throat fill with emotion. He settled behind and pressed up against her, a long arm wrapped around her stomach with his hand tucking under her waist.

"Hmm," she murmured, arching back into him. "I missed you," she said.

"I missed you too, Irey," he breathed. "I missed you too." After a long moment, Iris dozily basking in the warmth of his body, he spoke again. "I miss you too much to keep doing this."

"What?" Iris tensed, wide awake in an instant, as if someone had put ice at the base of her spine.

Abe heaved a sigh and rolled onto his back, away from her. She turned over onto her stomach, her head facing him, ashamed all at once of her nakedness in the face of what she suspected was coming.

"I can't do this, Iris. I don't know how else to say it. I can't do this hiding around thing, this seeing you a few times a year and wishing you were nearby for the rest of it. I want this to be real, for you to meet my son, for me to meet your kids."

"Oh, Abe . . ."

"You sound like you're disappointed with me," he said, sitting up and crossing his legs in front of him like an overlarge child in a preschool reading circle.

"To be perfectly honest, I am," she said. She got up and began putting on her clothes quickly.

"Damn it, don't *do* that," Abe protested, darting forward to grab away her shirt. She yanked it out of his hands. "I told you from the beginning that I never wanted this to be something that weighed on you. It was never supposed to be something that would hurt you. And I told you also that I would never marry you, and never move in with you." She was pissed, and she knew she sounded it too, but she'd long ago decided to replace the sadness of rejection and endings with anger. She didn't know if it was the wiser emotion or merely the easier one, but she knew that she had it in spades. Anger, rage, suppressed for years when Shlomo was hurting her, dismissing her, belittling her, and turned into self-loathing and self-condemnation. She refused to feel these things any longer. She knew that Abe wasn't trying to make her feel lesser—he was just being vulnerable with her. He was trying to tell her what he wanted. What he needed. But she had never said she could give him anything beyond what she'd laid out at the very beginning—sex, occasional company, friendship, care, the trappings of love that could at times veer into the real thing. And nothing more.

"So that's it? No compromise? No conversation, even?" He sounded angry too. A petulant child, Iris thought unkindly.

"What exactly do you think I'm going to compromise over? I told you about my situation, my marriage, right at the beginning. To avoid exactly this."

"But it's been five years, Irey! Has nothing changed? Don't you care for me at all?" He stood before her now, naked still, the scattered hair on his chest and pubis coarse and, she noticed, beginning to go gray. He wasn't embarrassed by his bony body, his chest just concave enough to give his stomach the illusion of sticking out in a gentle mound, his legs narrowing so much at the calves and heels that she sometimes got chills when she realized they were only a shade thicker than his bones. She knew his comfort in his own skin was hard-earned. And of course she cared for him. She cared so much that it hurt.

But that didn't change a thing. "Would it be easier for you if I said I didn't?" she asked. He looked like she'd punched him.

"No, of course not." He began wringing his hands the way he did when he was nervous. "I want the truth."

"The truth? The truth is that I can't give you more than this, Abe. I will never leave Peter, and I will never break up the family he and I made together. My children will never know about you, and I will never meet your son. That's the truth. I care about you deeply, I've told you that many times, but this is all you get. Take it or leave it."

His eyes were turning red and his bottom lip shook. She'd made him cry. She wished she could take it back, and the searing pain beneath her breastbone was gathering itself from all over her body, making her feel weak and exhausted with the first symptoms of grief. Abe began to gather his clothes and put them back on, so Iris let herself sink into the couch and look down at her feet to avoid seeing him as he tried to collect himself.

"Okay, Iris. You're right," he said, dressed and shod, as he sat beside her on the couch, leaving a couple of feet between their hips. "You never said you could give me more. Hey," he put his hand on the back of her neck gently, "look at me. Please?"

She did so, wishing, not for the first time, that crying came more easily to her. He wouldn't be able to see on her face that she was sad. He would see only the lines around her mouth hardening and her deeply furrowed eyebrows. Whenever she was like this at home, Peter would put a finger to her brows and slowly massage them until she realized she had her face clenched, as he called it, and made her muscles relax. Abe didn't do this, though. He cupped her cheek and ran a thumb across her thin lips. "I'm sorry, Abe," she said.

"Don't be." Then he amended, "Well, you can be a little bit sorry." She laughed. "Goodbye, Irey," he said. He kissed her forehead like a patriarch would and left the room. The door shut behind him with the softest of clicks, almost as if he hadn't left at all.

HOURS LATER, AFTER she'd ordered pizza to her room and eaten six out of the eight slices, and after she'd gotten an ice cream bar from the vending machine in the basement and devoured it, she lay on the bed in her underwear and a raggedy old T-shirt of Peter's, watching *The Simpsons*. Homer didn't fix a leak at home, which opened up a cavern underneath Springfield, and when the ground collapsed, Marge drove right into the hole. Iris could never complain like Marge could. Peter got everything fixed. She never drove into any pits he created. He would never let her sink into so much as a puddle if he could help it. She'd made the right decision, and she knew it, but it didn't make losing Abe less painful.

Still, it was Peter's voice she wanted to hear more than anything. But when he'd called an hour ago, she'd let the phone ring itself out. Now she checked her voice mail, and sure enough, there he was, sounding warm and sleepy, telling her he hoped she was doing okay and taking care of herself, telling her about the strange sculptures and the delicious brunch and how lovely Maggie's new girlfriend was.

"Girlfriend?" Iris said aloud, her head tensing and then banging back against the headboard. "Ouch." She was glad he couldn't hear her. He would think she was reacting to Maggie, not the pain. Peter rarely got mad at Iris, but her fervid wish for Maggie not to be gay was something they'd fought about more than once. She didn't know how to explain it to him again. She didn't know how he didn't fear his daughter being different, standing out, making herself a target to the hateful people of the world. She didn't understand how anyone could choose that identity—she knew she wouldn't have chosen to be Jewish, for instance, if she hadn't been raised by her parents, no matter how ingrained it was in her now. And yes, Maggie said she was born this way and Iris could concede that this was a possibility, but she wasn't utterly convinced that Maggie wasn't at least partially trying to rebel, that she might still meet a man who would make her happy.

But a girlfriend! No wonder Maggie had been angry at her earlier, disappointed last night. Iris had misunderstood—*Willfully?* she wondered—had really thought that Maggie was meeting a friend, hadn't realized how big a deal this was, or was supposed to be. Iris had never met anyone Maggie was seeing, had never been offered the chance. And now she'd screwed up again, and Maggie probably thought she was purposefully denying her sexuality, that she'd avoided meeting this woman out of disapproval.

Iris didn't know how to fix this. She'd ask Peter tomorrow, she decided, as she listened to his message a couple more times, focusing on his parting words, "I love you, I love you, good night." She let herself slip back into being a happily married mother of two incredible if sometimes infuriating children, and by the time she went to sleep, she was feeling a little better. *Look on the bright side,* she told herself—at least now the Bad Day had a new association that was, if not positive, at least less nauseating than her memories of her ex-husband.

Instead of making dinner awkward, Maggie decides to stuff her face and listen to Abe and his son talk. And they have plenty to talk about. From issues with Junior's team—"Coach is slacking on the relief pitcher, and that just isn't *right,* Dad"—to Abe telling a long and apparently oft-repeated story, if Junior's glazed look is anything to go by, about his grandmother's daily routine back in Nigeria, before she immigrated to the United States with her then-young daughter, Abe's mother, the lesson of which seems to be that Junior should be grateful that he's on a baseball team at all—"She used to walk seven miles just to stand outside the boys' school and listen to their lessons, and here we are complaining about your retired Dodgers coach!"—to the two of them bantering about some reality TV show whose premise, as far as she can tell, is exposing imposters to the real people they're dating on the internet.

"But why pop their bubble?" she asks. Junior grunts, but he's just taken a huge bite. He chews quickly, forcing the food down his throat in a visible lump that makes Maggie look away.

"'Cause people deserve the truth," he growls once he's swallowed, and shoots a look at his father. Her presence must not have been explained to his satisfaction. Abe said only that she was the daughter of an old friend of his, because apparently his son didn't know about Iris, just like Maggie didn't know about Abe. "How would you feel if the person you thought you loved was someone totally different? Like a super fat guy with chin pubes?"

Maggie wants to tell him he's being fatphobic, but she's not sure it's her place to tell him anything. She just nods and brings her spork back to her plate.

"Wait," Junior says and to Maggie's surprise plucks the spork out of her hand. "Dad! Why did you give her my spork?"

"I didn't notice I had. Please give the utensil back to her." His voice changes whenever he gives his son a command, Maggie notices, becoming lower and vibrating a bit, as if he's swallowed a handful of gravel. It's one of the most dad-like things she's ever witnessed and she has to suck on the inside of her cheek to keep from smiling.

Junior tosses over the spork, and it lands on her plate with enough force to spray sauce drops on the table, her face, and Abe's arm. Abe stands up, thunderous, his chair scraping across the floor. "You may be excused!" he barks.

"Whatever," Junior mutters. He takes his plate and fork and leaves the table. His door slams again.

"I should probably—" Maggie starts getting up too. She can't blame the kid, really—she threw plenty of tantrums as a teenager, and only an hour ago she was having to restrain herself from throwing that beer bottle at the wall. But she doesn't want to make this night harder on Abe, or on herself for that matter, and is prepared to get her bags and go if that's what's best.

"No, please, stay, eat, it's fine. I'll talk to him later." He looks depleted when he sits back down himself, and though Maggie takes another few tentative bites, it doesn't look like Abe is going to finish his plate. "I'm sorry about that," he says finally, leaning back in his chair. "He's very emotionally attached to some of his childhood things. My shrink thinks it's because of the divorce." He gestures at the spork. "We've had that since he was about three or four, along with this plate with dinosaurs on it from an old animated movie."

"*The Land Before Time*?" Maggie guesses.

"Yes, yes, that one."

"I used to love it so much. I barely remember the plot, just that I cried a lot." She's doing that thing where she chatters when she's nervous, when people are upset or mad.

"He had a dinosaur phase," Abe says, smiling a little at the memory. "Good?" he asks suddenly, seeing Maggie run a finger around the edge of her plate. She stops, embarrassed at the almost unconscious move, and he laughs. "Your mom used to do that too. She finished everything on her plate, every time. She said it was—"

"Second-generation Holocaust syndrome, I know," Maggie finishes. She smiles at him. He can't be so bad if he still remembers details about her mother. She can't blame him for her mother's actions or choices, anyway; Iris is the one responsible for this betrayal, not Abe. "Thank you for this," she says, and she means the food, yes, and the guest room, but also something more that she can't articulate.

He tells her to leave her plate, that he'll make Junior do the dishes in a minute, and then gets her a towel and shows her how the knob in the shower is marked as if hot comes out if you turn right and cold if you turn left, but that it's really opposite, "like most showers," he says with great seriousness. She thinks he's kind of cute in a delicate, pretty way, though his boniness and masculinity don't appeal to her even a little. But she can recognize why her mother would think he was attractive—not that it's any excuse.

She showers quickly, trying to wash the bitterness away in the hot water, and when that doesn't work, she asks Abe if she can smoke outside. He nods her toward the back of the house where she finds a door to a small yard bordered by tall hedges separating it from the neighbors all around.

It's breezy, so she kneels with her back to the house to use her body as a shield and rolls a joint deftly between her fingers. She isn't usually shy about her pot habit, but she doesn't want to get anyone in trouble, and even though it's recently become legal, Abe looks like a square and she doesn't think he'd want her smoking around his son.

Which is why she jumps nearly out of her skin when she gets up and sees Junior, wearing a stony expression, leaning on the sill of an open window that looks out onto the yard, lowering a vape pen from his mouth. "You too?" he asks, gesturing at her hand cupped around the joint as if it needs her protection.

"Unless that's a Juul, then, uh, yeah, me too," she says, sheepish. His face cracks open and he grins at her. "Damn, girl, you don't have to be all sneaky about it."

"So your dad's okay with it?" she asks. She lights up and pulls deeply.

"If I finish my homework first, yeah. I have insomnia, so."

"Cool dad."

"I guess," he says. "Anyway, how does he know you, really? Are you gonna be my new mom or something?"

So that's why he's pissed, Maggie thinks. She's young enough to be his big sister, and it sounds like Abe isn't really the type to be forthcoming about his dating life. She wants to tell Junior that it sounds like they were actually going to be stepsiblings if his dad had had his way, but knows it's not her place. "No, your dad was telling the truth. I'm just the daughter of someone he knew once. She, my mom I mean, she died."

"Oh shit." Junior's face goes slack. "Sorry for your loss," he says, trying to sound formal.

"Thanks." A wave of exhaustion hits her. She wants to get on the road early tomorrow since her next destination is all the way back down the state, in LA. If she doesn't decide to quit and just go home—but she can't, she realizes, even though the idea seems fetching for a moment. She can't, because now that she knows about Abe, she has to know about the others, about why and how and when. And besides, all that's waiting for her at home is a barely functioning dad and a brother she can't bring herself to be nice to. No, she's not ready to call it quits yet, though she does think it might be a good idea to check up on them. Home is on the way to LA, after all.

She takes a last puff of the joint and puts it out. "Good night," she tells Junior. "Thanks for the company. Oh," she remembers, "and sorry about your spoon, dude. I didn't know."

"It's a spork," he mutters, and withdraws from the window. She thinks he must be pissed still, but when she gets inside, she hears him call through the door, "G'night."

In the kitchen, Abe is doing the dishes himself. "He's a good kid," Maggie tells him. He nods, asks if she has everything she needs, so she says yes, thanks him, and heads to the bedroom. He doesn't need her approval, she thinks. He knows he's raised a good kid. She wonders, as she flops back on the springy double mattress made up in striped blue and silver sheets, if Iris knew she was, too. A good kid. All things considered.

As she's about to fall asleep right there on the covers without taking her clothes or shoes off, her phone buzzes in her back pocket and startles her.

Hey bb how are u? It's Lucia, finally, and Maggie feels relief wash over her—Lucia hasn't gotten sick of her yet.

So Maggie types back a long, tired message, full of typos because the phone feels heavy in her hands as she lifts it above her face. When the rectangle of metal and computer falls and a corner hits the tender spot between her eyebrow and eyelid, she sits up, annoyed and awake.

Omg, Lucia writes back. That's a lot. R u ok? Want me to call?

Its ok, I'm ok enuf, she writes back. Miss u tho.

I miss u too, worried bout u tho bb, its a lot to process, isn't it? Lucia texts. But Maggie doesn't want to talk about it, to process it. She wants Lucia. Her body, moments ago so exhausted, feels electric, aching, and she wants Lucia to know it, to feel the strength of Maggie's desire. She starts telling her girlfriend—and this word is still not entirely comfortable in Maggie's lexicon, but it's more acceptable to her than ever before—how much she misses her smell, the goose bumps that rise up on her areolae when Maggie sucks her nipples, the way she can feel the heat gathering up between her legs through her pants. Lucia plays along, telling Maggie she misses pulling her hair, biting her earlobe, running her tongue slowly around her pelvic bones until she squirms.

Maggie switches off the light and puts her bag in front of the door. There's no lock, but this way if anyone were to come in, she'd at least have a second to gather herself. She strips in the pitch dark—the windows are hidden by blackout curtains—feeling especially naughty to be naked in a house not her own, a house belonging to a man her mother fucked. The tawdriness of it is so appealing that she's clenching around her own wetness already. She climbs under the sheets and brings the phone screen back up, its light beside her on the pillow her only window to Lucia.

Send me a pic, she types. Plz bb. Plz plz plz.

Lucia obliges, and Maggie can tell from the picture that she's at her studio, doing work. She often stays there late, forgetting to eat dinner until ten or eleven some nights. The image is subtle, possibly taken in the company of her fellow artists; just Lucia's lips and teeth biting down on a pencil, but to Maggie it's impossibly erotic. Tell me what to do to myself, she texts. Ill do anything.

The three dots that show Lucia's typing start and stop several times, and Maggie gets a little spooked. Will Lucia ask her to do something complicated? The idea turns her on, even if it's something like masturbating on the living room couch or using something in the room to pleasure herself with. She's much higher than she meant to get, she realizes—what Gina gave her is potent, but it's probably got more to do with being so tired—because she would never really do these things in someone else's home. It's just the idea of it, the wrongness, the disrespect that would morph quickly into shame . . . all of it is appealing.

Finally, the bubbles resolve into text. Do nothing, Lucia writes. Don't touch urself. Wait until ur alone somewhere and we'll do it together. Promise bb?

Maggie's pelvis is still straining, but a heat spreads across her chest and words she's never said in a romantic context strain to come out. But no, not over text. I promise, she writes. After hesitating, she sends a heart. Green, not red. She doesn't want to spook Lucia. With a strange mix of unfulfillment and fullness, she falls asleep.

AUGUST 25, 2017

The birds wake Maggie up. She half falls out of the bed and shoves the curtains open, their tracks making a click-click-clicking noise. It's sunrise, she sees, and there's a tree right outside the window. She pushes herself back under the covers and lays there for a moment, trying to hold on to a dream. She's pretty sure Iris was in it, that they were both running to or from something, but the details are all gone. Was it a nightmare? She isn't sure, but it doesn't matter, because all she can think of is how she can't call Iris and tell her about it.

She and her mom had a tradition, which Iris said came from her own mother; whenever they dreamed about each other, they let the other know as soon as possible. Once, at some point during Maggie's teenage years, Iris woke her up in the middle of the night just to tell her she'd dreamed that Maggie wanted to kill herself. "You don't, do you?" she'd asked, urgently, kneeling beside Maggie's bed. She'd shaken her shoulders, utterly panicked. "Maggie?!" It wasn't as if there was a right answer; Maggie wasn't happy during that time. She was realizing she liked girls, and worse, realizing she always had, and even worse than that, realizing she was in love with her best friend at the time, Sarah, and didn't know how to tell anyone or who to talk to about it. So yes, the thought had crossed her mind. But she told her mother no, no, she didn't want to kill herself, everything was fine.

Things certainly aren't fine now, and she can't tell Iris about it, and she can't go back to sleep because she's crying and very awake and the birds are screaming.

Sometimes they'd try to reconstruct dreams together on the phone. When Maggie was a senior in college, she had a late-morning class every Friday, and it became her Mom-call time. She and Iris almost always ended up talking about their dreams when they ran out of pleasantries.

What does it mean, Maggie thinks, *to dream about you but not remember anything? Do you know what it means, Mom?*

The house is quiet, but not for the reason she thinks. She tiptoes, worried about waking Abe and Junior, but in the bathroom she finds a note taped to the mirror, the handwriting tall and long, kind of like Abe himself. It tells her Abe is driving Junior to baseball training, but that he will be back soon if she'd like to talk more, and that if she doesn't, that's quite all right as well. Maggie puts the note down and brushes her teeth, remembering how perplexed she'd been with Sarah—that best friend she was in love with—about her choice to spend her summers, like Junior apparently, being an athlete. Like nine months out of the year weren't enough.

She wanders through the house, peeking into Junior's room—neater than she'd expected it to be—and into Abe's—messier—before she goes back to the guest room. She sits on the bed and idly swipes through pictures on her phone as she tries to think. Is there anything left to say to this man who loved her mother? Who wanted Iris to leave Peter for that matter? In the bright light of day, after a deep, restful sleep, she isn't sure she can stomach it. No, she thinks. He did her a mitzvah by letting her stay, she thinks, the word coming into her head unbidden, something Iris would say about unearned kindness. But Maggie's done one too, in giving him the letter, and she's fulfilled her duty to Iris to boot.

She decides that it's enough, that Abe will understand that she had to leave. So she clicks the front door shut behind her and gets back in Peter's car. It's going to be a long day's drive.

WHEN SHE GETS near Oxnard, she starts regretting her late-night decision to visit her parents'—no, her dad's house for a bit before driving down to LA. It's late morning and she's taken the faster route, the duller one, alternating between true-crime podcast episodes and music, with stops every hour and a half to pee and buy iced coffee. The heat of the day has risen with the sun, and even with the A/C going in the car, she feels sticky.

Halfway through town, the anger returns—at herself, at Ariel, at her dad. She feels she needs to visit home, she reasons, because she doesn't trust that they can keep shit together. What if they've done something awful to the house? Or offended the people coming to pay their respects? Maybe Ariel is just shut up in his room and Peter is reading or being all comatose and they're ignoring the doorbell or their appetites or their need for sleep and bowel movements. A horrifying image of the house strewn with her father's and brother's piss and shit comes to mind. But why doesn't she trust them? They're grown-ups, aren't they? Grieving, yes, but still. If she can't leave them alone for a few days, will she ever be able to leave again?

This, she realizes, is what she's really concerned about. The idea of needing to move home to take care of Peter. She knows why, too, though she hasn't thought about it in a long, long time. When she was fourteen and Ariel was nine, Peter left home for six months. It was strange but fun to have Iris around all the time—she ordered a lot of pizza and cooked a lot less than Peter. But after a while, Maggie started to miss him. Not just the meals but spending time with him while he made them, learning a little from helping out. And it wasn't just the food, of course. Peter had a way of pulling the details out of her and Ariel when they got back from school— the first answer was always "Fine" when he asked "How was it today?" but unlike Iris, who seemed to accept that her children didn't want to share anything further with her, Peter needled them by asking about details they'd let slip some other time. He'd ask how the math quiz was, and whether Mrs. McKitrick gave the book reports back; he'd ask whether Dan Gonzales was still in the lead for student body president and whether Ariel traded any good Yu-Gi-Oh! cards at recess that day.

Peter always sounded chipper when they talked to him. At first, he and Iris sold it to the kids as Dad needing to travel for work for a while, just like Mom. But Maggie was old enough to understand that if that was all that was happening, her father wouldn't be spending an hour on the phone with her mother every night. She remembers listening to Iris pick up the phone at around ten, Ariel fast asleep by then, and not saying much, mostly "Mhmm" and "Oh, love" and "Peter, I'm *so* sorry." Finally, one night, Maggie snuck into Peter's office and carefully lifted the receiver. It took her a minute to understand that Peter's voice sounded full and snotty because he was crying. "I can't take it, Iris, I want to kill him half the time," she heard him say, and then Iris countering with, "Oh Peter, I know. But you're trying to be a good son, and it can't be much longer now, can it?"

Maggie had always known that Peter didn't talk to most of his family anymore. He had two stepbrothers he talked to occasionally, when one or the other or both of them visited the West Coast. They were the sons of the woman his father married for a brief time after Peter's mother died when he was a teenager, and were in business together, taking over their own father's industrial vacuum cleaner distribution operation. All this was information that had dripped down to Maggie over the years, but Peter's family was largely a mystery to her, one she'd never taken an interest in. But as she listened to her parents talking, she began to understand that Peter was with his father somewhere in Massachusetts, taking care of an old, senile man who had no one else left. She hung up the phone carefully when her parents began saying good night, and tried to sneak back into her room, but Iris's voice—not the one she used on the phone, but clearly addressing Maggie—came loudly from the living room.

"So now you know," she said. Maggie stopped in the hallway, wincing, sure she was about to get in trouble. "It's okay, sweetie, come in here," Iris said. So Maggie did, and she sat on the couch next to her mother as Iris wrapped an arm around her and twisted a lock of Maggie's long hair around her finger. "Dad didn't want you and Ariel to know because he's scared you'll be curious about his father, and he hates the man more than you would believe possible."

"But why?" Maggie asked.

"That's for him to tell you, if he wants to." Iris kissed Maggie's forehead and sent her to bed. When Peter got back a couple of months later, he sat her and Ariel down and explained to them that his father was given a terminal diagnosis some months ago, that his third wife had left him when she found out, and that a neighbor had discovered his father wandering along the road without shoes one day and called Peter. So Peter went to take care of him until he finally passed. He told them his father was a bad, mean-spirited man but that Peter felt it was his duty to do this. He was sorry he hadn't told them beforehand, but he didn't want to burden them with the knowledge. He thought it would be easier this way. He'd hugged them both until Ariel squirmed and asked to go back to his PlayStation.

But Peter, Maggie thinks, chose to do that. He could've paid someone to care for his father, couldn't he? He hated his dad, and he still went there himself; what does that say about her, that she doesn't want to need to do the same thing for a father she loves?

She's too young, she thinks, pounding the steering wheel with her fists at a stoplight, emitting an accidental toot of its horn. She's too young to think about moving back home to take care of an ailing parent—Peter was in his forties already when he did that. But no, maybe it's not about how young she is—after all, Allison's mom died when she was in college, and her dad two years later, by suicide, and Gina still lives at home, has been caring for her father ever since her mother up and moved to North Dakota shortly after he was diagnosed with early-onset Alzheimer's a few years ago. Fact is, Maggie just doesn't want to. She doesn't want to move back home; she doesn't want to leave her life for good, a life that finally feels stable, a part of her steadier since Lucia came along. She doesn't want it all derailed.

But what she wants doesn't matter—it might get derailed no matter what she does, so she might as well do something she wants before that happens. And she wants to deliver these goddamn letters.

On her street, she sees two cars in the driveway, which is a good sign. She parks next to a fire hydrant in front of her house—the cops almost never come by to give tickets—and texts Lucia, Kept my promise last nite ;). Going to check in on dad and bro and then back on the road. how r u? She watches the screen for a moment, but the message stays unread, so she puts her phone away and Lucia out of her mind.

The front door moves at her nudge, apparently unlocked. She's not sure what she'll find, and her heart begins to thrum with the fear of disaster, but when she comes in, she sees the kitchen island is full of food, like it was on the first day of the shiva, and it doesn't appear to be the same food, since it isn't buzzing with flies or anything horrible like that. In the living room, she finds Peter and Ariel side by side on a couch with three women sitting around them, passing photos from hand to hand.

"Maggie!" Ariel jumps up from the couch and runs to hug her. She's surprised by the gesture until he hisses in her ear, "Fucking save me."

She pulls away. He looks haggard, and his beard is growing in. She's always surprised, though it's been years now, that he's old enough to have facial hair. "I'm leaving soon," she warns him. "I'm not done with the letters yet. But go take a breather. And a shower, dude, yuck."

"Thank you, thank you," he says, and runs out of the room.

"Hello," she says to the people who've all turned toward her, except for Peter, who's gazing at the photographs in his hand. "I'm Maggie, Ariel's sister." She isn't sure why she says it this way. Why not Peter's daughter? Or Iris's daughter, for that matter? But somehow, calling herself a sibling feels like it allows her to be a little less responsible, like she'll be able to flee when she needs to, just like Ariel has.

As she approaches the couch, the women introduce themselves and shake her hand. Two of them are her mother's age or thereabouts but they have such perfectly straight and uniformly deep, teddy-bear-brown hair that she realizes they're wearing wigs. Only then does she notice that they're also dressed in long skirts and long sleeves—frummishly, Iris used to say. These two are named Leeza—Maggie isn't sure of the spelling but that's how the woman pronounces it—and Hannah. The third woman, who seems younger, though not as young as Maggie, is wearing jeans but also a long-sleeved white shirt that's closed at the neck and a head scarf covering most of her hair with some wispy bits coming out. Her name sounds like it's in Hebrew and has an unpronounceable letter or two in it.

"I used to be your mom's sister-in-law," the head-scarf woman, who stood up to shake, says. Maggie yanks her hand away without meaning to. She's still wrapping her head around the idea of Iris being married before Peter, let alone having a sister-in-law. The woman seems taken aback, but smiles again, tentatively, and sits back down, glancing at Hannah and Leeza.

"Right," Maggie says. "Uh, I didn't actually know. About her other husband. Until, like, this week." Peter exhales loudly and looks down at his hands, which are twisting an orange rubber band around and around.

Maggie sits where Ariel was, picking up the stack of photos he left behind. She wants to ask about the man who used to be Iris's husband, but she doesn't know where to start, or what would be too rude to ask, or whether Peter wants to hear any of it. So she flips through the pictures, and for a moment, she sees herself in them. Herself as she was at eighteen or nineteen, wearing big flowy skirts and little halter tops that bared her stomach. But no, this isn't her, because she never wore clothes like that. She's always detested skirts, even more than dresses, because at least with a dress it's just one easy item of clothing; if she's going to clad her top and bottom half separately already, then why would she ever choose a skirt? No, this is how Iris used to dress, she understands. A young Iris. A vulnerable-looking Iris, with an open face, mid-laughter, barefoot on the grass with her crooked toes, which she hated, out for the world to see.

"Wow," she says. "Dad, look." She leans over to show him, and he nods, but she notices that he isn't empty anymore. He looks angry, in the only way she's ever seen him be contained and teeth-gritting. He never used to let loose on her or Ariel. If he was mad at them, he would tell them to go to their room and would talk to them when he calmed down. Once, she discovered him in the kitchen banging with a wooden spoon on pots and pans when he thought she wasn't home; he'd told her it was his way of releasing anger without harming himself or anyone else. "The pots deserve it, cheeky bastards," he'd joked. Maggie never heard her parents fighting loudly either, never having arguments. The one time she thought that they were, the way her friends with divorced parents described fights, she'd spied them having a tickle-match on their bed, the shouts and yells all down to wrestling, a four- or five-year-old Ariel giggling and dancing around nearby, cheering them on. So seeing Peter angry like this, knowing him as she does, in this company, means something is very wrong. But she doesn't know what. "When are these pictures from?" she asks the women. "You said you were her sister-in-law?"

"Yes, Shlomo is my brother," the head-scarf woman says. "She was such a precious one, our Iris." She smiles, but there's a shiver in it. "We missed her so much when she decided to leave us. But," she sighs, her bosom rising dramatically under her white shirt, "she had her reasons, didn't she."

"What do you mean?" Maggie asks.

"Well," the woman says, glancing at Peter. "My brother . . . He had a lot of problems."

Before Maggie has a chance to ask what that's a euphemism for, Leeza jumps in, changing the subject. "We also worked with her," she tells Maggie. "We hired her at our synagogue!"

"Yes, when she and Shlomo split," Hannah adds.

"And the pictures," the head-scarf woman says, "they're from when your mother first met Shlomo. I found the album a while ago when I was helping him move; she must have left it behind years ago, I'm honestly shocked it survived. They were both so young when these were taken. It was so long ago. You look just like her," she adds, and leans forward, touching Peter's knee with a finger. "Doesn't she?"

Peter glances at the spot where the woman's hand touched him, then looks away, nodding. Not for the first time, Maggie thinks about how awkward adults are. How when she was a kid, she thought being an adult meant being certain of yourself, sure with your body movements. But what she'd thought then was confidence was just size—adults were simply, for the most part, bigger than she was at ten or eleven. But now that she's a grown-up herself, she knows that there's no innate dignity, only people more or less competent at playacting.

"So, wait, what did you hire her for?" This isn't what Maggie wants to know, really. But it's a way to keep the conversation going.

"Well, now, let's see," Leeza says, pondering. "It's pretty much what she does now—I mean, what she did," she corrects herself, her pale cheeks reddening. "If what Dena Gershon tells me is correct. The first job must've been planning the break-fast we offer after Yom Kippur—you know, getting the tickets printed and sent to everyone who bought one, talking to caterers and getting a good price, hiring extra cleaning staff for after, making sure everything ran smoothly on the day itself, etcetera. We knew she could do it because she did the same thing at Shlomo's synagogue the year before. This must have been, what, the early eighties?"

"No," Hannah says. "No, a bit later. She started working for us after Shlomo . . . well, after she couldn't find other work, remember?" She puts her hand on Leeza's thigh as she leans toward her and leaves it there.

"Oh yes, that's right," Leeza says. "Your mother was a very kind, caring woman, Maggie."

Maggie's eyes are stuck on Leeza's hand, now resting on Hannah's. She notices that Leeza is perspiring underneath too much white facial makeup, though the house is cool with central air. The older woman catches Maggie's gaze and yanks her hand back to her lap.

There is a jittery silence.

"Excuse me," Peter says, stiff. "I am feeling indisposed." *Can you feel indisposed?* Maggie wonders. *Isn't it just a thing you are? Isn't it the kind of thing Victorian women said about having their periods?* She watches Peter march out of the room without a backward glance.

She isn't sure if she's more pissed off at him or these people making him uncomfortable, these people who don't seem to belong here, who Iris couldn't have belonged to, could she? Maggie feels the chutzpah that Iris always says she was blessed with bubbling up.

"So this is awkward," she says, her voice a forced cheerful. "Why did they get divorced?" She stares the woman with the head scarf down, waiting, but it doesn't seem to work. The woman just looks away and fiddles with her hair, pushing the flyaway wisps under the scarf, though they continue to escape.

"Rakefet," Hannah says quietly, her accent Americanizing the name so Maggie now retains it. "She has a right to know."

Rakefet continues to stare at nothing for a moment, but then sighs again and leans back in her seat. "Family is family, you know. I love Shlomo, despite everything."

Maggie wants to scream with frustration when Rakefet doesn't keep going. It takes a good deal of effort to control her tone when she asks, "What's 'everything' mean?"

"Every relationship has its problems," Leeza jumps in before Rakefet can answer. "And it's not for us to judge what—"

"Oh, stop protecting him, " Hannah says, stern, grabbing for Leeza's hand again.

"I'm not, I'm—"

"You don't want to air out dirty laundry, I get it, but this is Iris's daughter and she asked us a question and deserves an answer." Hannah waits, looking at Leeza, who finally nods and looks down at their entwined hands. *Could it be that these two biddies . . .* Maggie wonders, but Rakefet interrupts her line of thought.

"My brother beat Iris," she says bluntly. "At least, that's what we all think. Your father might know for sure, but neither of them ever *admitted* it to anyone. But, you know, she had bruises, and I remember his temper from when I was young. He slapped our own mother once when he was drunk at Pesach and blamed the alcohol. I didn't—I blamed him. So, there, there's the dirty laundry. Even rabbis can be terrible men."

Maggie feels like a stone has plummeted into her belly. She just can't picture her mother ever shrinking before another person. She seemed always like a woman who never had a doubt. Like a woman who knew her place in the world and in her own skin. It dawns on Maggie that whatever else her mother was—and she has some choice words she'd have loved to hurl at her if she were alive—Iris was strong, and that her strength felt like a kind of protection between Maggie and the world, even long after moving out and having her own life. She won't ever have that again. She's a woman without a mother, she thinks, and somehow, the world is a little less safe now.

This makes her feel so melodramatic that she immediately reminds herself that Iris's strength wasn't all good. She never backed down during arguments, and once she had an opinion she could defend, she would defend it to the end—even when she was wrong—or passively aggressively hear the other person out but in a way that always made Maggie feel judged.

But maybe she wasn't always like that, Maggie thinks. Maybe it was leaving that horrid man that made her more secure. Maybe it was surviving him. A rabbi, no less. That her mother was married to a rabbi is . . . bizarre. Or maybe not, she thinks, trying to puzzle it all out. Maybe that's another reason Iris had a lukewarm relationship to religion, that on-again, off-again desire to celebrate holidays, the halfwayness of lighting Shabbat candles occasionally but working through the sabbath.

She doesn't know what to say. So she says something stupid in this room full of Jews. "Jesus Christ."

Hannah nods, her face severe. "You've got that right. Anyway, Iris was much better than Shlomo ever was, and everyone knew it. He doesn't have a congregation anymore, you know. He's just a cheap officiant for hire now. For once, a bad man got his just desserts—a disappointing life."

"Well, that's nice, I guess?" Maggie says. She looks back at the photos in her hands, these images of a woman who is Iris but who isn't her mother yet, a woman for whom Maggie is years and years in the future. It's an odd sensation, looking at them, the first images of her mother's face she's seen since her death—but it isn't her mother's face, at least not yet. She wants to see the just-desserts man, but the pictures are all of Iris alone or with other women. Maggie doesn't know who they are, who Iris was at that time, and she puts the stack down, overwhelmed.

As if she can tell, Leeza gets up. "We've taken up enough of your time, sweetie," she says. "Tell your father that we're available if he needs anything, all right? He should come to our shul sometime." She bobs her head sideways toward Hannah. "She's our rabbi, and we have a very accepting congregation. I'm sure they'd all welcome a goy in mourning."

"Leeza," Hannah admonishes. "He's not just a goy. Besides, he married a good Jewish woman, that counts for something."

"I know, that's what I'm saying!" Leeza says, and they each kiss Maggie firmly on both cheeks before walking out.

Rakefet stays behind for another moment and looks at Maggie with something like regret, or sympathy, or maybe just pity. "Shlomo wanted to come," she says. "I wouldn't let him."

"He did? Why?" This makes no sense to Maggie.

Rakefet fiddles with her scarf again. "I think he was hoping that your mother had a bad life, a bad family, an ugly husband and children, tsuris, you know, like him." She pauses, then adds, "He would have been disappointed to see how well she made out."

Maggie nods. She's crying in that quiet way again. It seems she'll never stop spontaneously leaking tears. She hopes it's true, that Iris considered this life a good one, but then she wants to tell Rakefet about Abe, and the cheating, to tell her maybe this Shlomo would have been happy after all if he knew that Iris wasn't satisfied with any of them. "Thank you for coming," she says instead, reaching for a tissue.

"No, no. Thank you for opening your doors to us," Rakefet says. "The girls meant it, you know. We really are here if you need us, okay? Here, let me leave you my card, just call or email if you need anything, all right? The girls made your brother write down their phone numbers and emails earlier already." Maggie realizes that by "the girls," Rakefet means Hannah and Leeza. She likes that they're still girls to this woman—politically incorrect as it might be, she finds it, in this instance anyway, sweet.

Maggie takes the proffered card, accepts the hug and kiss on the cheek, and walks behind Rakefet to close the door. She looks at the card and smirks, her eyes dry again. Rakefet appears to be a Reiki healer in Los Angeles. It seems like an extremely un-Jewish profession.

MAGGIE NEEDS TO get going, but she's tired. She wants more answers, or at least someone to talk to about this. Why wasn't Ariel around when all this came out? And Peter? Why does she keep needing to deal with these bomb-shells alone? She texts Lucia and tells her that her mother was married to a rabbi who beat her. She tells her that she's exhausted and wants to just come home already. She writes that she is angry at her father and at Ariel and at Iris for dying. The thing about texting Lucia, she thinks, is that it never feels like she's going to be judged.

Until, that is, she's sat there staring at the ceiling, phone in her lap, for ten minutes. And then she starts to feel sheepish. Lucia hasn't written her anything today at all. Maybe she's sick of Maggie's whining; maybe Maggie should chill. So she steels herself, reminds herself that if she really, *really* needs to, she can go to Allison, the only friend she's comfortable approaching with this sort of thing—Blair and Harper are a good time, but Maggie doesn't feel close to them in that way, and she hates burdening Gina, who's usually exhausted from taking care of her dad. But more than that, Maggie reminds herself as she gets up, she knows how to deal with shit on her own.

The rest of this should be easy, she thinks, now that she knows a bit about what she's getting into with these letters. Well. Not easy. But easier.

A series of loud thumps make her drop the car keys she just picked up from the counter. She runs to Peter's office and finds him standing in the middle of the room with the baseball bat that usually lives under his and Iris's bed, surrounded by piles of his big, heavy art books, stacked up to the height of his waist. He's clearly just knocked down one column, which lies scattered across the floor between him and the door.

"Dad!" Maggie yells. "What the fuck? You scared me. I thought you blew your brains out."

He blinks at her slowly. "Margaret Krause, please close the door. I need to be alone."

"No. What are you doing?"

"We had guests. I couldn't access the kitchen. This was the next best thing." His glasses are off, and he looks like a crazed father in a melodramatic scene on TV, his face red and puffy, but he's deflating before her eyes, as if he can tell that he's a ridiculous sight. Maggie feels like she could knock some shit down herself, though, so she steps over the fallen tomes and kisses him on the cheek.

"Take care of yourself, Daddy. I'll be back in a couple of days."

"You're leaving?" he asks. "Again?" He almost sounds like he cares, though his tone is still flat.

"I have to. It's . . . I'm trying to fulfill Mom's wishes," she says.

He nods, takes a deep breath. As soon as she shuts the door to his office, she hears another loud tumble of books. Ariel peeks out of his room and raises his eyebrows at her. "Everything okay?"

"Just Dad being Dad, I guess. I'm heading out. Keep holding down the fort, okay? They're gone, by the way," she adds, gesturing to the now-empty living room.

"Oh. Cool. Wait, no, you're going? You just got back!"

"Yeah, well. I'm not done yet. So did you hear, Mom was married to a rabbi?"

Ariel shrugs. "Yeah. It's weird. Do you have to go?"

"Yeah. You okay?"

"No," he barks. "Are you?"

"Yeah, no. Fair enough." She turns to go, and Ariel trails her all the way to the car outside.

"So did you find anything out? Like, with the letters?" he finally asks, hands balled up in his pockets making visible lumps in the sides of his jeans. He isn't looking at her. She's not sure he really wants to know.

"How about this," she says. "I'll tell you all about it when I deliver all of them, okay?"

He sighs, and his hands come out of his pockets. "Yeah, okay." He waves as she pulls out. Lucky, she thinks. He has a few more days to imagine their mother as the woman they thought they knew, more or less. But, she reminds herself, he's the one staying here with Peter and whoever comes to sit shiva. She hopes Leona is still hanging out with him, for his sake.

She sets Google Maps to the address of the only post office in the zip code belonging to Harold Lake Brooks, and begins to drive.

IRIS

Years later, Iris would remember the first time Shlomo hurt her being April Fool's Day, 1977. But it wasn't. It was the day after and there was absolutely nothing funny about it. That day, Iris walked to the synagogue office to join Shlomo with paperwork—they had written a letter of introduction that they were going to send to the congregation, which wasn't too pleased with the coming transition. They'd known the old rabbi for years, a white-haired, long-bearded man whom Iris secretly compared to the man on the Bridge of Death in *Monty Python and the Holy Grail*. She didn't tell Shlomo this, since he didn't usually find her humor very amusing. She discovered after they'd gotten married that he was really much more serious than she'd thought.

But Iris was ready to be serious. She'd gotten up late to find Shlomo already gone. He'd let her sleep in, a peace offering, perhaps, after they'd argued over something inane the night before. In the bathroom, she was disappointed to see red on the toilet paper after she wiped. They'd been half-heartedly trying to get pregnant. Iris had stopped taking her birth control right after the wedding because early in their courtship, she and

Shlomo had discussed how much they both looked forward to raising children. This was one thing they agreed on wholeheartedly. But as for trying . . . well, Iris had to admit that sex wasn't all it was cracked up to be, or at least she hadn't found it to be so yet. She'd been a virgin when they married, more because there hadn't been anyone else whose intellect she respected enough to be attracted to before. She'd gone out with some boys in Brighton Beach, boys whose families went to the same shul she and her parents attended during the High Holidays, boys who went to the same Jewish camp in the summer as she did. But she'd known most of them since they were all in diapers, and the boys she'd met who weren't Jewish made her uncomfortable, because she couldn't imagine bringing them home to her parents. They weren't religious, really, but they both clung to certain aspects of their upbringing. More than that, they'd made it clear to her that after what they'd seen and gone through in the war, they didn't trust goys and never would. They never talked about what happened in detail, but over the years, Iris had heard stories from friends and their relatives.

But it wasn't the stories that made her parents' reality settle in her mind; the thing that haunted her memory all the way to her marriage was discovering the shoebox under their bed. It was a Saturday, and her mother had gone out to offer some of her goulash to old Mrs. Winceslass, who lived next door and was ill. Iris and her father were playing hide-and-seek in the small apartment, and while he counted loudly to one hundred in their narrow living room, she went to wriggle under her parents' bed, a bold move since she wasn't usually allowed in there; but her mother had left the door open on her way out, and that was enough of an invitation for Iris. While she waited for her father's slow search to begin—"Is she under the table?" he would ask in his hard-won, accented English, and pull the tablecloth up with a flourish, and then sigh dramatically, and say, "No! She is not! Where *is* she?"—she discovered the box. Inside, she found several rubber-banded together rolls of cash, maybe for emergencies, a faded red ribbon, and a photograph that was so battered and old that she couldn't make out the details of the faces. But she could tell it was a family: two tall people and two little ones, parents and children.

When her father walked in and discovered her under the bed with the box open and her hand in front of her clutching the picture, he became very still. He told her to put the photo back and come out. She was scared, since her mother always said her father would whip her if she did something bad, though he had never laid even a finger on her. But the threat was there, the possibility that he was just holding back for something bad enough.

"Come," he said, and sat her on his knee in the living room like he had when she was very little. He patted her back a couple of times and she waited, twisting the silver ring with the little blue stone she got from a cereal box around and around on her finger. The ring had made the skin under it green days ago already, but she refused to take it off. It made her feel powerful, and she pretended it had magic powers and could zap whoever she wanted. If her father tried to whip her, she could *kazzam!* the belt right out of his hand.

But it turned out she didn't need to. Instead of punishing her, her father explained to her quietly that her mother had lost everything in the war. Everything. A husband and two young children. Iris had already known that her mama was much older than many of the other women who bore the same title. Now she understood why. For many years after the war, her father said, her mother hadn't wanted to have other children. She didn't trust in peacetime or safety. But she got pregnant despite their best efforts— and Iris didn't understand until she was older that this meant that she, herself, was an accident. Much, much later, when she would get pregnant with Ariel, part of the reason she decided to have him despite her age and the possible risks to her health was that her own mother had kept her. She felt she owed it to the universe, to the god she wasn't certain of.

After Iris's father told her what his wife had lost and why, Iris became more suspicious of the world around her. It seemed capable of evil, dangerous, in a way she hadn't quite understood before. And when it came to dating, she simply couldn't handle all the goyische brown-haired and blond boys with blue eyes that some of her friends went gaga over. She'd look at them with the understanding that there was only a thin veil between their kindly behavior and the ability to follow orders. And so when she'd met Shlomo, she saw an appealingly haughty Jew who was secure in his faith and his place in the world, a third-generation American, the rebel son of Haredi Jews in Flatbush who saw the Reform movement breach his community's neighborhoods and decided he liked their approach. He wanted to make Judaism more accessible, not less, so he left his parents and siblings and community behind and turned to what he perceived as the intellectually superior, not to mention modern, Reform Judaism, and lived with the conviction that he was doing the right thing, the honorable thing, in the eyes of God. Iris fell for him and his conviction. Both of them were working at the Jewish camp Iris had once attended, she as a girls' counselor and he as a boys'. They were also both in school, though he was older, studying to become a rabbi at Yeshiva University, while she was getting a degree in education at Hunter College, what people called the Jewish girls' Radcliffe, at her parents' insistence. She had no idea what she wanted to do, but they believed teaching was both a noble profession and always in demand. She and Shlomo had gotten along splendidly, mostly because she thought he was one of the smartest men she'd ever met, able to tell her for hours about various texts, philosophies, prophets and scholars of yore, while also expounding on music and movies and theater, much of which he was severely critical of.

It would be years before she understood that memorization and specialized knowledge didn't automatically equal great intelligence, though she continued to be attracted to obsessives of one kind or another.

On April 2, 1977, a few months after Iris had uprooted her life to move cross-country with Shlomo for his new job—he was hired to train under Rabbi Brodsky in LA with the aim of eventually replacing him—she left their apartment in Sherman Oaks and parked near the newsagent's a few blocks away and did what she always did—perused the foreign newspapers as well as picking up the usual *Los Angeles Times* for herself and the *Jewish Press* from New York for Shlomo, who liked keeping up with the goings-on in their old city. She couldn't read any other language, but she liked the look of foreign words. She loved the lettering of the Hebrew and Yiddish newspapers, the Cyrillic alphabet of the Russian ones, the varying curling shapes of headlines from as far apart as India and Egypt, the characters she couldn't distinguish that belonged to Chinese and Japanese and Korean newspapers. Seeing the world in one shop this way was the only kind of tourism she figured she'd ever be able to afford—well, that and books—and she was grateful for it.

Sometimes, Iris would buy a British or Australian or South African paper along with her *LA Times*. She felt reassured learning that local human-interest stories looked pretty much the same everywhere, while on the other hand found it fascinating to see other countries covering American affairs. During the Vietnam War, she noticed there was a clear difference in coverage among various countries, and it didn't always make the front page elsewhere. Of course, those newspapers were often a day or two old, but that was okay.

"Hello, Mrs. Epstein," James, the clerk, greeted her. She suspected he was also the owner, because he was there more often than any of the others who manned the counter, mostly young and bored high school kids with long hair and exhausted expressions chewing gum and reading magazines. She always wondered whether James was the man's given name or the one he used with Americans so they wouldn't butcher the pronunciation of his real name, but she never asked him about it. He spoke deliberately, and she knew English wasn't his first language only because he'd told her. "We have a special rush delivery of the *Guardian*," he said. "They have a wonderful travel section this week." His eyes narrowed with mirth as she picked up the British paper and brought it to the counter. Iris was glad that she could be as chatty in LA as she'd been in New York—she was sure her mother wouldn't be happy about that, since she'd always worried about Iris's penchant for befriending strangers.

"'The Island of San Serriffe,'" she read aloud. For a long moment she glanced at the headlines of the articles about the island and looked at the advertisement from the Kodak Company asking for photos from any tourists who'd been there. How could they run a whole travel section without pictures? It didn't make any sense. Then she understood—it was an April Fool's joke, and so clever, too, to trick an entire country of readers, at least for a little while. "Oh, James, this is wonderful! I bet Shlomo will take longer than me."

"I think so too," James said, and rang up the papers. She paid him and went back out to the car, humming.

At the synagogue, she parked near the small door that led directly into the back corridor and the office. "Shlomy," she called as she walked in, holding the papers. "I got you the paper, and you must look at the *Guardian*, they have a . . ."

She trailed off. The office was a mess, open boxes lying everywhere, drawers open with their contents half falling out, cupboards looking thoroughly rummaged. Shlomo was sitting at the desk pounding on the typewriter keys.

"What happened in here?" she asked.

"I couldn't find the cockdamned tape," he said. He always used the word "cock" instead of "god" in swearwords. Iris could remember a time when she'd found this funny, even endearing. At the moment, she wanted to yell at him. He'd made a sty of this room and just left it for her to clean up. She knew this was her job, just like she knew that when he left towels and socks and underwear and sweat-soaked shirts on the floor of their apartment, it was her job to pick those up and deal with them. It wasn't that Shlomo hadn't heard of women's lib—but he argued, and she usually conceded, that since Iris wasn't making any money yet, she needed to do the housework so he could focus on his very important, not to mention sacred, career opportunity. Iris didn't like to mention that she was also his de facto unpaid secretary at the shul; he was stressed, she knew, and he'd be hiring someone once he moved to the top position, but this was a transitional time.

"You made a mess," she said. She didn't quite dare ask if he was going to help her clean up, but she hoped he'd understand that this was what she meant. Instead, he did something he'd never done, but that from this point he began to do with increasing frequency. He got up from behind the type-writer, walked around the desk, and got very, very close to her. He gripped her with both hands and shook her, and though Iris had heard that it was bad to shake babies, she had never realized just how painful a good, hard bone-rattle could be.

Then he pulled away and grabbed just her face with his right hand, squishing her flesh and making her jaw ache. No longer pinned, she should have—as she'd think later, over and over again—pushed him away, shoved herself out of his clutches, but she couldn't move. Her arms hung stupidly by her sides, limp, and she tasted blood in her mouth from where her teeth were involuntarily biting into her tongue. "Are you just going to nag or are you actually going to help me run this place?" He didn't yell, which was part of what made it so scary. He didn't wait for an answer, just shoved her face and head back and let go, making her lose her balance. She fell, ungainly, right over one of the open boxes, making it break beneath her, scattering the mess of books and papers even further. By the time she caught her breath and noted her splayed legs, how her skirt had ridden up, and the fact that her head had narrowly avoided the corner of a low bookcase, Shlomo was back at the typewriter.

She wanted to ask, *Did you just do that?* She wanted to ask, *Did you just go crazy?* She wanted to say, *What if I hadn't gotten my period and I was pregnant and you made me fall?* She wanted to say many things, but instead, she got up, and without a word she began tidying the mess. When she finished, Shlomo read aloud the letter of introduction he'd written from both of them, and asked her eagerly what she thought. She wasn't sure she could speak yet, so she just nodded, which he took to mean she liked it. He then handed it to her and told her to go and make enough copies to send out to the entire congregation.

She didn't tell him there was a typo, and he never noticed, but it wasn't much of a revenge.

She also started taking her birth control pills again.

Maggie badly miscalculated. She could have sworn Google Maps said it was a three-hour drive, but that remains the time estimate when she exits the LA area and keeps going south. She watches the clock tick closer to five p.m., which she assumes is when most post offices close. She races through the last hour of road, watching her speedometer climb to ninety, keeping a lookout for traffic cams and police cars hidden in plain sight.

But when she arrives at the tiny building with its blue mailbox standing outside like an R2-D2 with tiny legs, she knows that even though it's a few minutes to five, she's likely too late. The place looks deserted. She parks anyway, badly, and exits the car at a run, leaving the driver's side door open, hoping for the kind of movie ending such a scene deserves—that is, she's hoping there will be a kindly elderly person just locking up inside who will see her desperate face and the grief in her eyes and will let her in and tell her where to find Harold Lake Brooks. That's the trouble with there being only a PO box number on this letter: she doesn't know where Harold actually lives. But she assumes—or hopes—that in the kind of community where people pick up their mail at the post office, everyone knows everyone.

Whether she's correct or not won't matter today. The post office, as she sees once she reaches the door, closed at one. She never had a chance of reaching it on time.

"Fucking great." She has a raging desire to kick the door but kicks the mailbox instead and then regrets it immediately as the thing actually moves, shifting momentarily onto two legs before slamming back to all four. She didn't think she had that kind of strength. Then again, the box might just be incredibly empty. Shouldn't it be nailed down?

She gets back in the car. Lucia hasn't texted her back yet. Stop thinking about that, she commands herself, and figure out what to do next. She can't drive home now—funny how quickly her parents' place gets called "home" again in her mind—and she still has to find this Harold. LA, where two other letters are addressed, is a long drive too, and she's tired and hungry. The closest motels, she finds on her phone, are somewhere called East Blythe. There is the usual assortment: Motel 6, Super 8, then another Motel 6 down the road a few miles from the first. She chooses another one, a Knights Inn, because the name is charming and she's never been to one of those. The coloring of the logo, a bluish purple, makes her think of a certain kind of camp—like the way the purple Teletubby was accused of being gay by that conservative nutjob, which only cemented its gay icon status. When she gets to the motel, though, its exterior looks distinctly Californian, with the terra-cotta roof tiles and that particular shade of wall that she associates with the Spanish-style homes from the last century that are found every-where in the state. The inside is bleak, the walls stained with watermarks and the carpet threadbare, and it smells of clean laundry that has been sitting damply in the drier for too long. She feels itchy inside, her nerves tingling still from the rushed drive and the waste it was.

She checks in, pleased with how cheap it is, and asks the long-haired and startlingly beautiful woman working the desk whether there's any-where to eat nearby.

"There's a Del Taco down the road that way, and a grocery," the woman says. She flings her hair back and Maggie sees her badge reads NELLY. "And there's a *really* good Indian place that's like seriously right across the highway, maybe two hundred yards that way."

"Oh, I love Indian," Maggie says, twitching the strap of her bag so it sits more securely on her shoulder.

"Indian Indian," Nelly clarifies, and at first Maggie isn't sure what she means. "Like, from India. Not Quechan like me." She laughs, and Maggie smiles at her, wishing she could call this woman her friend, for no other reason than to be able to hear this laugh again.

"Hey," she says impetuously. "When do you finish your shift here?"

"When no one else comes through," Nelly says, shrugging. "So, like, probably ten? Why?"

"Let's get a drink," Maggie says. She puts both hands on the desk and leans forward, grinning. "I'm in dire need of a good time."

Nelly's face closes up for a moment, as if sizing up the offer. She grabs a pad of paper and a pen from beside her and passes it to Maggie. "Write your number," she says. "I'll text you when I'm done."

"Rad," Maggie says, aware she's flirting like a surfer dude. Then she waves and heads back out of the lobby. The doors to the rooms are all on the outside. Maggie's is on the second floor, so she climbs the staircase to the walkway, and finds her room all the way to the end. It's bigger than she expected it to be—it has two queen-size beds and a couch to boot—and she wonders whether Nelly gave her an upgrade. Could she have been flirting first?

Maybe, maybe not. Maggie rarely trusts her gaydar when she's sober, too nervous to assume things about people unless she witnesses them actually saying or doing something she can confidently read as queer. Then again, when she's high or drunk, she tends to think she has a shot with everyone. And, generally, she's found straight-identifying women are curious enough about her soft masculinity and slight swagger to take a chance on making out with her. Not that this has ever led to the most satisfying of experiences, she has to admit, but there it is.

It isn't until she's on the toilet in the bathroom, which is very small and on which her butt fits uncomfortably, that she realizes that she's actively sought out a date for tonight. She can convince herself all she wants that Nelly is straight and probably won't want to make out with her, but the fact that she needs to at all means that however it turns out, she went into this interaction wanting it to be a date.

The image of her mother meeting Abe surreptitiously while Maggie was having an overnight dorm visit at the college they were looking at makes her shudder. She tries to shake off the dirty feeling crawling over her, the way she's thinking about what Nelly's behind might look like rather than remembering Lucia's. Maggie pulls her phone out of the back pocket of her jeans, pooled around her ankles. Still nothing. It was only last night that she was aching for Lucia's touch. How has today been so long already? How did it go astray in such a short amount of time?

Nelly probably won't even text, she tries to console herself, but the disappointment that rears up at that thought doesn't help.

Food might fix things, she decides.

THE INDIAN RESTAURANT is small but packed from the moment Maggie arrives until she leaves. The early diners are locals, most of them white, old, and dressed in well-worn jeans and T-shirts. They give her—with her nose stud, short hair, and black clothes—surreptitious but disapproving looks. Still, the naan is fresh and warm when it arrives at her table and the tandoori chicken is delicious, just below the level of spice she can't handle. With its heat in her stomach, she agrees to her server's recommendation of a cooling mango sweet lassi as dessert.

From her table in the corner, she witnesses the elderly crowd leave and the slightly younger, later set arrives, ordering more alcohol, talking more exuberantly. The place seems to be family owned and staffed, at least two of the servers sharing a crook in their nose that appears similar to that of the older man who greeted her at the door. She tries to imagine what it would be like, working with her family. There's nothing that all four of them were ever passionate about together, except maybe the first season of the eventually awful crime show about twenty-four hours spent largely in and around Los Angeles, and sitting down to an episode of TV together once a week barely counts as an interest, even. Not that Maggie has ever really had a passion that has lasted for longer than a few weeks, when it got too hard to play the guitar or too boring to keep knitting. Not like Lucia and her art, or Allison and sex education, or Gina and sea-life preservation, or Sarah and cross-country running.

When they first started spending time together, Lucia seemed a little baffled by this. She didn't seem to know anyone—including her family—who didn't have some consistent, long-standing passion project that was always in the works. "I guess I'm just boring," Maggie had said as they stood outside of the Crack Fox, smoking, on one of the first really warm evenings in spring. But Lucia said this was patently ridiculous. A couple of months later, officially girlfriends, Maggie had asked Lucia, "Does it bother you? That I'm not, like, artistic? That I just have a regular job and no garage band?" Lucia had laughed, and Maggie, who was spooning her, could feel the vibration where her sternum pressed against Lucia's back.

"No, Mags," Lucia said. "I've been with plenty of artists." She turned around so she was facing Maggie in bed. "And let me tell you, we're overrated." Maggie smiled, relieved, and Lucia kissed her cheek. "I like how stable you are, you know? Like, not just the job," she clarified, "but in who you are. You're living your damn life, you know? Without trying to always prove something to everyone you meet. It's refreshing, honestly." Lucia turned over again and nestled her body into Maggie's. "Plus, you let me be the little spoon. You make me feel safe."

Remembering this, Maggie can't help but wonder. What's to say that Lucia won't decide that without stability—which is very much lacking right now—Maggie is dull, passionless, not worth putting the effort into?

Trying to distract herself from the tightening anxiety, she takes another sip of the thick lassi and opens Instagram to find a bunch of likes and comments her phone didn't show her for some reason. She still isn't ready to start going through everyone's expressions of sympathy, so she just scrolls through the feed until she sees a picture of Lucia in a demure but lovely deep blue dress standing in front of one of her carved decorative bowls.

Fuck, Maggie remembers—tonight is the gallery opening of the group show Lucia was invited to join a few months ago. Her smile in the photo looks fake, and Maggie bets she's feeling awkward and very nervous, because she knows Lucia hates needing to schmooze with people at these things. So Maggie swallows her pride—her nerves, really, if she's being honest—and sends Lucia yet another text. Break a leg bb, ur doin great! :)

She feels awful for having forgotten all about it. Now she wonders if this is why Lucia hasn't answered her—has Maggie been too self-involved? But her mother has died—surely, surely if there's ever a time to forget . . . Plus, she hasn't been consulting her planner, which she thinks must be in her duffel in the motel.

The thing about Maggie's planner is that she considers it her version of a daily journal. She doesn't record her feelings about events, but she makes sure that everything that's happened in any given day appears on that day's page. So if in the morning she only had plans to go to the gym and see Lucia, but by evening she's also gone grocery shopping and grabbed an early drink with a work colleague, she adds those extra activities in. It serves as a memory trigger, she's found; she doesn't need to write down how miserable her dentist appointment on July 3, 2015, was—just looking at the way she wrote the word "DENTIST" in all caps with a manic smiley face next to it is enough to remind her how bummed out she was that she had to have a surprise root canal.

She has planners like this dating back to her twenty-first birthday, when Iris got her the first one. Maggie had been bitterly disappointed in the gift, feeling as if her mother didn't know her at all. Later, when she began using it during school and fell in love with it, she told her father how useful it had ended up being, and he told her mother, and then Iris had called to confess that it had been Peter's idea all along, that he'd convinced Iris that Maggie would love a planner, and look, he'd been right! Maggie was almost more disappointed in this revelation than she'd been in the gift. For a while, she'd felt a secret bond with her mother, believing temporarily in that power of parents to provide for their kids in ways the children don't even know they need. Peter had always provided for her that way, so it wasn't a welcome surprise to know that he'd figured her out; it was a given.

She hasn't checked her current planner since the day of the funeral, she's almost certain. Which means she hasn't updated it, which means she's also losing everything she's doing.

Maybe, she thinks as she sees a text from a new number pop up, it's not so bad to let certain bits of her life remain only in memory. Maggie can only assume that the Hi now you have my # :) is from Nelly.

U were right the Indian place is AMAZEBALLS, she texts back. She gets a blushing emoji smile back. Oh dear, she thinks. Oh dear, oh dear, oh dear.

MAGGIE AVOIDS THE reception when she goes back to the motel and showers in steaming water that hurts her more than it soothes any of the driving stiffness in her back and legs. But the punishing hard water feels good anyway. She's immensely tired now that she's eaten and showered and, with a pessimism that she half hopes will prove correct, she puts on boxer shorts and a T-shirt and begins flipping between the extremely limited channel selection. Nelly might not get in touch again. Maggie may not need to put her outside clothes back on anyway. Might as well relax for now.

She falls asleep in front of a dubbed-into-Spanish episode of an old

Law & Order, but when her phone buzzes by her head, it wakes her. The TV is showing an infomercial in English now, with an elderly, white and white-haired lady dripping in tasteful jewelry showing how simply wonderful and relaxing the mosaic kit she's working on is. GOOD FOR ARTHRITIS flashes in yellow on the screen.

Come out, the text reads. Maggie jerks her head to the window looking out over the parking lot, relieved that she remembered to pull the curtain closed earlier. She dresses quickly in her usual going out at night uniform—black skinny jeans, a white tank top, a dark blue plaid shirt thrown over it. She finds her pomade in her bag and works the now dry curls into some order. She needs to reshave the sides soon or she'll get that weird triangle shape to her head again.

She steps out and locks the door behind her, because the motel is old enough that it uses actual keys rather than key cards, and at first she doesn't see anyone waiting for her. But as her eyes adjust, she sees that Nelly is also wearing black and sitting on the bed of a black truck that sits in shadow. Her smile gleams when she waves. "Come on!" she yells to Maggie. A man leans out the passenger side window of the truck and watches Maggie jog over.

"Climb up," Nelly says when Maggie reaches her, and puts her hand out. Maggie takes it, the bodily contact heating her underarms even though the hand itself is cool, and jumps up into the truck bed. Nelly crawls toward the back window of the cab and smacks it twice. The woman in the driver seat raises her middle finger but starts the car. A thumping bass begins playing inside.

"So where are we going?" Maggie asks. She likes to think that she's a go-with-the-flow kind of person. Or rather, she likes other people to think that. But she's never entirely certain at the beginning of a mysterious night out what it's going to end up like, and there's always a certain temptation to run back home and into bed and safety. She thinks of Lucia. She should have tried calling her rather than texting again. Shouldn't she? But no, Lucia could have contacted her today—she hasn't. So when Nelly, whose hair is now held up fetchingly in a butterfly clip, leans in to be heard over the sound of the wind and rush of the road, Maggie decides not to think about Lucia right now.

"You said you needed a good time," Nelly says. "So that's where we're going!"

Maggie isn't sure what she means, but minutes later, when they arrive at a smallish-looking whitewashed building with a vast dirt parking lot behind it, she understands. A modest neon sign above the door to the building reads GOOD TIME BAR.

"Very literal," she says, raising an eyebrow. Nelly laughs and looks away. Oh dear, Maggie thinks again.

Inside, it's much like any dive. Two pool tables take up the majority of the floor space with small two-person tables squeezed in along the sides of the room. The bar itself is only big enough for three stools, all occupied by men, two stout and white and middle-aged, wearing trucker hats, and one younger dude whose sharp elbows rest on the bar as he holds court with a few others standing around him.

"Keep going, all the way to the back," Nelly instructs her with a poke to the shoulder. Maggie walks on and sees the second room opens up to a yard scattered with wooden picnic tables and rickety metal tables and chairs, a few beach umbrellas poking up from white bases. "What do you want?" Nelly asks.

"Oh, I can get it—" Maggie starts to get up from the picnic table Nelly steered her to, but Nelly waves her off and says she's a guest, and anyway she can get the next drink. "Okay," Maggie concedes. "Um, gin and tonic?"

When Nelly gets back, the driver and the guy in the front seat are with her. "Cheyanne, Rob." Nelly points in introduction.

"Maggie," Maggie says. They all shake hands, and then the three friends fall right into a conversation she supposes they were having earlier, something she can't follow about a couple who's getting divorced because the dude is a creep who doesn't want his wife going to college. She sips her

G & T. It's very strong, which she appreciates, though she feels self-conscious now because the other three are drinking bottled IPAs; she gets the feeling this is the kind of bar where folks drink beer late into the night and only then get trashed on the harder stuff. She'll switch to beer after this, she decides.

"So what the fuck are you doing in town?" Rob asks when the gossip being discussed has been concluded to everyone's satisfaction. Maggie has noticed that he uses the word "fuck" at least once a sentence, so isn't insulted by the way the question sounds.

"I'm looking for someone," she says.

"Mysterious much?" Cheyanne looks unimpressed. She pulls out papers and a pouch of tobacco and begins rolling herself a cigarette.

"No, just, it's a long, boring story, you know? Also, here, let me contribute," she adds, and pulls out her baggie of weed, tossing it over. "If you want."

"Don't worry, we'll tell you if you're boring," Cheyanne says. She doesn't thank Maggie but begins industriously pulling apart the stems and leaves and crushing them between her fingers, keeping her other hand over the operation to shield it from any stray breeze.

"Oh-kay. Um." Maggie tries to shake off the unsettled feeling. Maybe she shouldn't have tried to distract herself this way. Maybe she should see if there's an Uber or Lyft she can get back to the motel. She begins explaining how her mother died a few days ago—Cheyanne says, "Fuck, omigod, sorry" and Nelly puts her hand on Maggie's arm for a moment, but Maggie doesn't stop because she doesn't know what to do with these reactions that she supposes she's going to start getting from everyone. She barrels on, telling them about the letters, though she doesn't mention that she's already delivered one, and says she's trying to find Harold Lake Brooks. "Actually, none of you would know him, would you?"

Cheyanne shakes her head and takes a long slug of beer. Rob shrugs and says he doesn't know any Harold. Nelly says, "No, but does he live here? In East Blythe?"

"I don't know, actually. The letter is to a PO box a few miles away, in Palo Verde."

"Oh, dude," Rob says, "That's like small-town-city down there." Cheyanne snorts, and Nelly looks like she's trying to hide a giggle. "You know what I mean! It's like, seventy people or something in that zip, they have to go to the fucking post office to get their mail."

"Weird," Maggie says. But it confirms what she was hoping—surely, someone will know the man she's looking for when she goes back tomorrow.

"Not that weird," Nelly says. "It's the same where I grew up, we had to go to the USPS in Winterhaven."

Maggie feels ignorant, like a city slicker who doesn't know to bring bug spray when camping. "I've always lived in pretty big places, I guess," she says. "Though they always felt small to me."

"Doesn't anywhere you grow up feel small?" Cheyanne asks, and the profundity of the question is undermined by Rob shrieking and slapping at something small and winged that landed on his forehead.

"Okay," Maggie says when they've all finished laughing. "Next round's on me. What does everyone want?" She gets up, and Nelly accompanies her back inside. It's louder and thick with cigarette smoke, something Maggie can't remember ever seeing in a bar in her lifetime. Outside, sure, even in gardens that say they're no smoking, she's seen people lighting up when it's late enough and everyone's a bit too soused to care. But smoking inside is something she's seen only in movies and heard about from older dykes reminiscing in the lesbian bar back in St. Louis.

"Harv, come on, don't be a dick, Ha-a-arv!" Nelly is trying to get the bartender, who appears to be studiously ignoring her, to pay attention.

"Everything okay?" Maggie asks.

"Yeah, it's just Harv being a DICK," Nelly yells the word at Harv, whose eyes betray that he's heard her before he flicks them back to the customer he's handing a beer to. "I broke up with his brother a week ago, and though Dylan is totally over it and already fucked Jamie, Harv is somehow still saying I broke Dylan's heart."

"Oh wow. Small town, huh?"

"Small campus, small town, small everything," Nelly says, and rolls her eyes.

"Including Dylan's dick?" Maggie asks.

Nelly lets out a loud cackle. "No, but really," she says, "the community college is small, the CNA program is small—oh, certified nursing assistant," she clarifies when Maggie shakes her head in confusion. "And yeah, there just aren't that many places to go out and chill, so everyone knows everyone and there's all this drama. My mom doesn't like it, but I don't know. I think it's fun, sometimes."

"I get that," Maggie says.

"But if I get into the CNA-to-RN program I'm applying for," Nelly goes on, her fingers tapping out a quick rhythm on the bar, words sounding almost rote, like an anxious refrain, "and pass everything and get my registered nursing license, I might move back to Fort Yuma, try to work at the clinic, help take care of my people. It's not easy there, but at least it's family, you know?"

"Yeah, totally," Maggie says, though she has no idea—she can't imagine moving home in that way, and she doesn't know what kind of hardship Nelly is referring to, beyond the general impressions she has from things she's read over the years. But she's never been on a Native American reservation. She was never invited by anyone, and though Anthony and Kyle always talked about going to Santa Ynez for one of the intertribal powwows hoping to score some ayahuasca, this made Maggie feel itchy with discomfort, even in high school. She didn't want to be a tourist in someone's home, not when that home was taken, reclaimed, and often still threatened.

It wasn't like going to Paris or something. Lucia had mentioned a local arts festival at a reservation in Missouri a couple of weeks ago, and when Maggie voiced her concerns, Lucia had smiled sadly at her and said that yes, she thought about this too, but that an event like this fostered community, for one, and also the revenue from food sales, raffle tickets, and the table space the artists rented would be going to the people who lived and worked there. But it's the kind of moral tightrope Maggie never knows what to do with.

"What can I get you?" the bartender says, finally turning to Maggie, still ignoring Nelly.

Maggie smiles. She can almost feel Nelly's vibrating annoyance next to her. She hasn't picked up on someone else's signals in a while, and it feels good. Lucia reads her, but she can't read Lucia, at least not yet. She thinks she could read Nelly, though. She orders beers for everyone and gets the four sweating bottles pounded on the bar.

Back outside, Cheyanne waits until Maggie sets the beers down and gives her the joint she's finally rolled to her satisfaction. "Your shit, you do the honors," she says, solemn. Maggie smiles, now glad she's come out, and relieved that despite how unstable she's been feeling the last few days, she still knows how to do this, how to socialize with new people and make fair-weather friends. It's what she's always been best at, fitting herself into other people's groups, never becoming the center, retaining the freedom to drift away and back. She lights the joint and inhales once, deeply, before passing it on to Nelly.

There is a strange thing that Maggie discovered with smoking weed when she was in college. By then, she was comfortable enough with the drug that it didn't excite her the way it did when she first started, when it had felt all delinquent and naughty. In fact, she'd gone to the other extreme, pretending a world-weary exhaustion—fuck, she'd been young!—as if she was so over it and just smoked it like a regular cigarette. But she'd noticed in college that smoking with someone you were flirting with turned into an almost erotic experience, especially that moment when you pass it and the other person, if interested in you, makes a point at brushing your hand and looking you in the eyes as they take their toke.

Which is exactly what Nelly is doing, as Cheyanne and Rob look at her, impatient. But Nelly takes her time, drawing the smoke into her lungs and holding it in and keeping her fingers and hand cupped around the joint. As she begins to let the smoke out, she shows off, doing a couple rings before her face changes to surprise or chagrin and she succumbs to a cough. Cheyanne and Rob crack up, and Maggie smiles. The urge to ask Nelly how old she is rises in her, but she tamps it down. She'll ask if it comes to it—right now, it would just be an awkward buzzkill.

When the bartender, Harv, comes out to tell the folks in the back that it's last call, Maggie is good and wasted. She's another joint in and has had three more beers. Her stomach feels full in a familiar, yeasty way. She and Nelly trail behind Rob and Cheyanne to the truck. "Aren't they drunk?" she asks Nelly.

"Chey is," Nelly says. She hiccups, then giggles. "Me too. But Rob stopped after the second beer, like two hours ago. And he didn't smoke at all!" She grabs Maggie's arm and fake whispers, "He's such a good guy. Don't you think he's a good guy and that Cheychey should give him a chance?"

Cheyanne turns and scuffs her heeled boot in the dirt, inexpertly flinging sand at Nelly. "Fuck off!" she says, but she's laughing. When Rob steps on the running board, he turns back to Maggie and Nelly, puts two fingers to his mouth, and flutters his tongue in between. Nelly runs into his chest and hits him all over with her small fists until he pushes her off with a triumphant jeer, and slams the door in her face.

Maggie helps Nelly up into the bed of the truck, and her muscles tense as the younger woman snuggles up into her as they pull out of the lot. The lights are spaced far apart on the road, and they keep passing through patches of dark. "It's so quiet out here," Maggie says.

"Yeah, there's never any traffic this late," Nelly says, sleepy, her breath hot on Maggie's neck. Sizzles run up and down her flesh. The fear and anxiety of attraction, the possibility of maybe touching this person next to her, the proximity—it's all bringing her groin alive, and she can feel the tug low in her stomach that she associates with desire. But she can't make the first move. She always makes the first move, and besides, she isn't in a position to make any moves at all. She won't, she decides. Though she isn't sure what she'll do if Nelly kisses *her*.

At the motel, the truck stops and Nelly gazes up at Maggie's face. Her lips look so soft, so utterly kissable, her eyelids heavy with booze and tiredness from a long and boring workday that was preceded by a full morning of classes, and Maggie wants terribly to lean in and just do it, but she doesn't. She smiles, and scoots away. Nelly grabs her shoulder, and for a moment Maggie thinks, *This is it, she's going to kiss me, it's going to happen*, and she's already ten steps ahead with her face in Nelly's crotch, imagining her pubic hair and her thighs, but Nelly only says, "What, no hug?"

Maggie hugs her, tightly, and feels her own small breasts against Nelly's, and she again flashes to the image of them both naked, pressed into each other. But she lets go. She smiles and waves, and Nelly and the others pull out of the parking lot.

By the time she gets into her room, Maggie isn't turned on anymore. She tries masturbating anyway, imagining what sex with Nelly would have looked like. Would she like her nipples bitten? Would she like being fingered or being gone down on more? Would she eat Maggie out or would she turn out to be one of those bi-curious women who can't handle other people's vaginas? The thought is so depressing that Maggie gives up and pulls her fingers out of her underwear.

Her thoughts turn to Lucia instead. Who still hasn't gotten back to her, not at all, not once. Lucia would tell her to drink water. She would tell her to take two aspirin. She would do everything possible to make sure both of them avoided hangovers in the morning. She would remind Maggie that by the time she's also thirty-five, she'll realize how the body changes and how important it is to care for it when you're young. Lucia will never meet Iris, Maggie thinks. She'll never get to see what Maggie might look like when she's older—Maggie read somewhere once that people unconsciously made choices about longevity with partners based on their partners' parents. If Iris were alive, Maggie could show Lucia how perfect her parents' marriage is, how good Maggie could be for her forever, if she let her. Usually, Maggie pushes thoughts like these away—commitment, future, such serious and dull things—but the cross-fading, the head high and the buzzy-faced drunkenness, let her fantasize about being the steady partner of her creative-genius girlfriend, about cooking for her when she forgets to eat and kissing her nape quietly as people ogle her sculptures at a gallery and murmur flattering things about them. Except now, Maggie thinks, turning over, Lucia will know her mother was a cheater and her father a dupe. That is, if Lucia is even interested in her.

The last conscious thought she has before falling asleep is of Iris. *It isn't so hard to not cheat, even when you really want to, Mom. See?*

When Maggie wakes up to a dry mouth, peeling lips, and a tongue that feels like it's been turned to stone in the night, she knows she deserves it, a conviction that's strengthened when she sees she has new texts from Allison, Gina, and Ariel, but nothing yet from Lucia. Her head is pounding from the inside, like there are people punching the walls of her skull trying to get out. She finds the little cups wrapped in thin plastic in the bathroom and fills one of them four times. Her stomach feels watery and sloshy as she takes a shower, avoiding getting her hair wet because it looks surprisingly punk with its dried gel and the back isn't as flat as she expected it to be.

Nelly isn't there when she checks out. Instead, it's a pasty man with buckteeth and an unevenly balding pate. He's excessively friendly and Maggie wonders if he's a creep or just a social oddball. There is a little area in the lobby with stale bagels and undersized muffins and a few of those single-serving cereal boxes lined up on a shelf. She grabs a sticky corn muffin and the healthiest-looking banana from the sad fruit bowl and scarfs down both before she gets to the car. She texts Lucia one more time, starting to get a little bit worried, despite—or maybe because of—last night.

It's not that Maggie has never stepped out—it's just that the times she did are incidents she deeply regrets. Not because the relationships she imploded were that good—though she supposed she'll never know if they could've been, really—but because she always hurt at least one person, often ended up hurt herself, and the drama was deeply exhausting and, at least in hindsight, not worth it. Occasionally, it happened because of a stupid misunderstanding. Once, her first year living in St. Louis after college, Maggie met an incredible woman who was in town on her book tour, spent three magical days with her, and then assumed that they were each going to go about their lives. But the writer had remembered their drunk postcoital conversations differently, and thought they were going to try to make things work long-distance for a little while since she only lived a few hours' drive away in Chicago. When she drove down for a visit three weeks later, after they'd been texting almost daily, she was furious when Maggie told her about the woman she'd gone on a date with in the intervening time. "You're such a bitch! This is why I don't like dating dykes," the writer had said, putting her shoes back on and grabbing her little rolling suitcase. "You're all like dudes. Bi women at least have the experience of how shitty men are and try to avoid acting like them." In retrospect, Maggie knows this woman wasn't exactly the kind of person she'd want to be with, but she still hates hurting people when it isn't her intention.

But then, of course, there was the time she'd cheated very intentionally on her only longish-term relationship other than Lucia, Sasha. But that was different, and Maggie barely counts it as a relationship anymore, because she'd discovered a few weeks after introducing Sasha to her dad—her mom had backed out at the last second, clearly uncomfortable with the whole thing—that Sasha had never stopped sleeping with her ex, an incredibly beautiful person named Lex whom Maggie had already felt super intimidated by. She'd always suspected something was still going on between Sasha and Lex but it was also the first time she'd ever spent the whole night in someone else's bed, and she thought that maybe her jealousy was just in overdrive. Of course, when she'd turned out to be right, she was humiliated and felt small and insignificant. It was the only time she'd ever slept with a man, and only because she'd thought that maybe it would hurt Sasha worse if she did. He'd been a friend who she could tell had a crush on her, and it was cruel to use him like that. She'd lost him as a friend and Sasha as a girlfriend and had gotten such bad grades that semester—she was perpetually stoned in an effort to mute her feelings—that she'd been put on academic probation.

Lucia is too important, too special, too invigorating for Maggie to lose over a stupid night of drinking. So she tries to swallow her anxiety, tries to think of the hundred reasons she might not have heard from Lucia—she's busy, she's in a bad mood, something is wrong with her phone—and texts one more time. Miss u. Bit worried that I haven't heard from u. How was the opening last night? She wonders whether she can blame grief for her neediness and then feels a terrible guilt sink in. Forgetting about Lucia's show could be chalked up to being distracted by everything that's happening but she was being stupid last night; that doesn't equal grieving, does it?

Focus, Maggie tells herself, and drives back to the post office. She has to park a block away since the spots right in front are taken this time, but she's relieved, because that means they're open.

An old-fashioned bell hanging above the door rings when she walks in. There are two men in coveralls chatting in a corner, apparently puzzled over the requirements of the package slip they're trying to fill out. Three people are waiting in front of the single open window at the counter, two clutching those orangey-pink slips the USPS leaves at people's doors when they're not home, and one holding a big envelope for sending. They're all in their fifties or older, Maggie would guess, and the woman behind the counter is tiny and wizened and reminds her of Justice Ruth Bader Ginsburg.

The wait seems to last forever, and isn't aided by her pounding head or the fact that she keeps checking her phone.

When she finally gets to the front of the line, she shows the woman the letter addressed to Harold. "Hi, so, um, this is kind of strange, but my mom left this letter for someone with this PO box number, and I was wondering if you could tell me where he lives? I'd like to give it to him. In person, I mean."

The woman on the other side of the window just taps the metal plate between them, the kind that people put money and packages into so the clerk can turn it to retrieve them from behind the safety glass. Maggie wonders how many post offices were robbed or how many clerks were attacked to cause this to be the normal system—she remembers hearing about the rash of post office murders in the nineties, the origin of the phrase "going postal," but is pretty sure those were internal, employees shooting colleagues, occasionally customers. Who is the glass meant to protect?

"No," Maggie says, and puts the letter up to the glass. "I don't want to mail it. Just—can you tell me if you know this man? Harold Lake Brooks?"

"Hell, Harold don't live here no more," a voice behind Maggie says. She looks over her shoulder. One of the men in coveralls in the corner is still there, now working on another slip. The clerk is just shaking her head and tapping the metal plate again, as if she hasn't heard a word, so Maggie retreats.

"You know him?" she asks the man, excited.

"Sure I know him. Used to be my neighbor. Retired a couple years back, though, moved away from here to some old folks' home." The man's eyes are a muddy brown and his cheeks are pockmarked and sunbaked red.

"Thank you," she says. "You don't happen to know which nursing home, do you?"

"Nah," he says. "Whatcha need him for?"

She holds up the letter. "My mom passed away a few days ago and wanted me to give him this."

"Sorry to hear that, miss. Want me to ask around?"

"That would be amazing, thank you so much, um—mister—"

"I'm Rhett," he says. "Yeah, like Rhett Butler. My pops loved that stupid movie, and my momma loved the book." He shrugs. "Here, write down your email, I'll let you know if I hear anything."

Maggie is surprised the man is asking for her email address and not her phone. She tends to think all adults above a certain age are technology neophytes, which she realizes is hypocritical, since Peter is far more computer savvy than she'll ever be. She writes down her email on the bit of paper Rhett hands her. "Thank you so, *so* much. You have no idea how much this means to me."

"Sure I do," he says. "My folks died a few years ago, my momma from cancer and Pops a few weeks later from heartbreak as far as I'm concerned. I know what it's like. Last wishes and all."

Unsure if she's going to start bawling right there in the post office or if she's going to throw up on the gray tile floor, she just nods and smiles one more time and rushes back out, run-walking to the car.

When she gets there, she finds a voice message from Allison. "Em, what's up? Your girlfriend is freaking out, says she hasn't heard from you. Something happened to her phone screen, she's been trying to message you on Facebook and you're not answering and she thinks you're like, dead. It's lucky for you I broke my weekend social media detox or I wouldn't have seen she'd messaged me too. Anyway, hope you're doing okay."

Maggie frantically opens her messenger app, sees dozens of unread conversations, and smacks her forehead. "Stupid, stupid," she mutters—she turned off all notifications except for calls and texts the other day, and hasn't turned them back on since. She opens Lucia's message thread, lets her eyes race over the explanation of her cracked phone screen and how she left it to get fixed and so only has her laptop right now, then the tentative check-ins, and hits play on the last one, a voice message from this morning.

"Heyo, love," Lucia's voice comes on softly, and Maggie ups the volume and starts crying with relief. Lucia's tone is warm, not at all angry or upset. "I mean, well, you know, anyway. I hope you're getting by okay, babe, would love to hear from you, hope you've been getting my messages and stuff. I had my group show opening last night. Wished you could be there. Someone bought one of my pieces, though! For a hundred and fifty bucks, which isn't a ton but is damn good for a bowl that took me three hours to make. I miss you. Wish you were here. How is the journey going? Mwah."

"Love." Lucia called her that. The word hovers around Maggie's brain and she listens to the message three more times. Then she sends Lucia a voice message of her own, wondering if the tearful smile in her voice will be audible to her girlfriend. She updates her on the texts she sent but doesn't mention how freaked out she's been. She also doesn't mention last night's events, just that she's a bit out of it and tired. "I wish I was there too," she says at the end. She wants to ask if she and Lucia are okay, if Lucia is upset with her at all, but manages to restrain herself. She learned a long time ago that feeling and showing insecurity were two different things, and that the latter was deeply unattractive to most people she'd dated.

Still, it's with a much lighter heart that Maggie checks how long a drive it is to Vegas and how long to LA. Realizing she's almost exactly equidistant, she decides to go to Las Vegas first and track down this Liam Ainsworth.

As she inputs the address into her phone and turns on its Bluetooth, it occurs to her—five letters. Iris wrote five. None of them to her family. Peter, Ariel, and herself are all chopped liver, apparently. Well, almost. Ariel got the rings, and she got the necklace, after all. Peter got absolutely nothing. Maggie takes a deep breath, trying to calm the pulsing anger beginning to flow through her—her head still hurts, and she's still dehydrated and has a long drive ahead of her, and getting worked up isn't going to help anything at the moment. She considers just going back to Oxnard again, but no matter how mad she is at Iris, this duty she's taken on feels like a reason to keep moving, while the idea of sitting passively in the house for four more days fills her with horror.

She rummages around Peter's glove compartment and finds the trusty emergency kit he always had in the car when Maggie was a kid. She pops a couple of store-brand ibuprofen for her tender head, smears some old and melting sunscreen on her arms because it's approaching a hundred degrees and she's going to be in the desert, and sets off.

FOR THE FIRST half of the drive, Maggie listens to a stand-up comedy podcast and tries to keep herself from paying too much attention to her hangover. Her sunglasses rest heavy on her nose and the contents of her stomach are uncertain of themselves. When she begins seeing signs for Needles, she decides to find a place to pee and get some more coffee.

The ubiquitous golden arches of a McDonald's greet her at the exit. She pulls into a gas station to search for a café, and finds that the closest place is a Starbucks. Another twenty minutes away, though, is a firehouse-themed café, and she sets her GPS to detour there, hoping for better coffee, or at least a more interesting vibe.

The landscape on either side of the road is incredible. She's never lived somewhere like this, where the desert is close enough to be a neighbor. Lucia lived in New Mexico for a while, and she always says she misses it, the majestic beauty of it. But for Maggie, even the suburban-city had been too much, or too little, the man-made isolation uncomfortable to her in a way that she only really recognized once she left and started living in a college town. She likes her elbows brushing up against people, against their realities.

Once, she asked her parents why they lived in Oxnard. She still isn't sure why people end up one place or another. She supposes she could find some good, informative podcasts about this, and decides to dig her planner out once she arrives at the café so that she can make a reminder to look this up. Her parents' answers hadn't been particularly satisfactory. Peter grew up in Massachusetts, Iris in New York City, and Maggie had asked them why they couldn't have raised her and Ariel somewhere cool like New York or Boston. "Why did you have to bring us to this shithole?" she'd asked. Peter and Iris had looked at each other and laughed.

"Oy, baby," Iris had said in that way that Maggie recognized led to a Jewish-sounding phrase. "You don't know from shitholes."

"Oxnard was affordable," Peter had added, shrugging. As a teenager, Maggie was both confounded and infuriated by these responses. But now, there she is, still living in the place she went to college. She supposes inertia is a part of it, lack of funds to move somewhere cooler and more expensive another. But she's also, by now, built a life for herself there, and she likes it; it feels like home. She wonders whether Lucia will want to move away at some point, though—she finished her MFA three months ago, and has a couple adjunct gigs lined up for the fall semester, but Maggie isn't sure what comes after that.

For her parents, she guesses there was also a desire to live somewhere with decent schools and a low crime rate. Then again, what does she really know about the forces that drive people to do anything? Her powers of observation are clearly shit, seeing as how her mother was sneaking off to fuck men and she never knew. She's also beginning to realize that the only way Iris could have had these affairs, especially if the men are so spread out, was if she was lying about at least some of her work trips, which means that the work ethic that Maggie's internalized so well was at least partially a ruse.

She tries to breathe through the renewed tide of anger and reminds herself she's only confirmed one affair, but the fact is she's fully expecting the other men, if she finds them, to tell her similar stories. And she still wants to know why, and how they didn't tell Iris to stop being a shitty person and go back to her husband and kids.

She parks outside the café and spends a good five minutes sifting through the contents of her backpack and duffel before accepting that she must have left her planner back in Oxnard, though she could have sworn she'd brought it with her. Annoyed, she grabs her phone and hopes that caffeine will help her feel better.

The inside of the café looks like a gift shop threw up on a bar. The furniture is all deep, dark wood, and glass-fronted cases full of model fire trucks, hydrants, and firefighters sit next to racks bearing bags of potato chips and peanut-butter cookies and bags of M&M's and snack packs of Oreos. The coffee is thankfully delicious, once it cools down enough for her to drink it.

For the first time since she posted the announcement, she starts looking at the comments on her social media feeds. It's amazing, how little she's cared about the goings-on in other people's lives in the past few days. Usually, she's an hourly or so checker—for notifications, for messages from her friends, for announcements in various queer groups she belongs to, as well as some of the local activist ones Lucia has shared with her.

She's shocked to see the little red notification icon reads 99+. If they have room for the plus sign, she thinks, why not for a three-digit number? She clicks through and begins to read the comments upon comments.

So sorry for your loss, is what most of them read in one way or another.

My mom/aunt/grandpa/cat also died in a car crash and . . . is another common refrain, though these tend to be from people she's not sure how she knows exactly, whose names are familiar to her but whose faces she can't conjure up from their tiny circle avatars.

The messages that mean more to her are the ones that her real friends have left—though many, like Harper and Blair, have messaged her directly and privately instead, and she's not quite ready to check those yet—and the few long memories of family members she barely sees. One of her step-uncles' wives, a woman named Kristen who's a Lutheran pastor, leaves Maggie in tears.

Your mother was a wise and gentle and hilarious soul and she lived a good, full life. It was cut short, and I am so terribly sorry. I am glad, Maggie, that you take after her so much. Did your uncle ever tell you about the first time I met her? It was at our wedding, before you were born, just a little bit after she and your father married. Our wedding was a disaster. The catering truck's refrigerator broke and everything spoiled while they were stuck on highway traffic so we didn't have any food. Your mother, bless her soul, walked around with a Lebanese fast-food menu she had somehow, I don't know where from, and she asked people what they wanted. Thank God it was a smallish wedding! Then she got on the phone while I was putting my makeup back on (I cried buckets, I thought my wedding was ruined!) and by the time I walked down the aisle she already ordered food for everyone. She never let us pay her back! She said she got a good discount and to consider it a wedding present. The next week your daddy called and told us she was pregnant.

"Hey, you okay?"

Maggie is jerked out of the world of her phone's screen and the imagined images of a younger Iris ordering Lebanese takeout to a wedding. A long-haired, red-rimmed-eyed white teenager has two fingers on her table and a look of concern furrowing his orange eyebrows. "Yeah. Yeah, thanks," Maggie says.

"Okay, if you're sure. If you need anything, though—" He pulls a card out of his pocket and puts it on the corner of the table where his fingers were, a respectful distance away from Maggie's own hands. "My aunt, next door," he says, and walks away.

Maggie isn't sure what his deal is, or what the hell he means, but she picks up the card. It's beautiful, heavy card stock with rounded edges. One side is a picture of the Milky Way, a path of dense white dots shining against the black night sky. On the other side, purple calligraphy font spells out MADAME FAUSTI, PSYCHIC, NUMEROLOGIST, STAR CHARTS & TAROT READINGS.

She puts the card down and returns to her phone. A new message from Allison appears. hey M how is things

Terrible and sad, Maggie replies, smiling. It's a question and answer from

Winnie-the-Pooh, which both she and Allison had as books on tape as children. When they first met in college and were exchanging odd facts, this was the best one they had in common.

U taking care of urself? Did u reach ur gf?

Yeah, thanks, Maggie types. And then, impulsively, Thinking of doing a psychic reading. Think I should?

Hell yeah

Which is as ringing an endorsement as Allison is capable of giving in written format as far as Maggie knows. She picks the card back up. Taps it to the table. With one last swig, she finishes her coffee, then places the mug in the brown bin by the door and exits. To the right she sees a barber, but to the left is a private house, a bungalow really, with a triangular banner hanging from it. Maggie walks down the sidewalk so she can see it from the front. The banner says the same as the card, in a more readable font.

She's never been to a psychic before and doesn't think she's going to believe anything she hears, but her head still hurts, and the goth kid was kind of spooky in a way that makes her feel like she should see this through, for the story if nothing else. Plus, she sometimes feels like the last millennial holdout on astrology and energy healing and other things she's been raised to think are nonsense—half her friends seem to be wholeheartedly into it—so she might as well test it out for herself.

She climbs up the steps leading to the wraparound porch and bright blue door. An OPEN sign dangles on the inside of the windowed glass, making it look more like OF–N, but it's ajar, so Maggie pulls it and enters.

"Yoohoo!" a voice calls out.

"Hello?"

"Take a right, please! You don't want to go straight, the kitchen is a mess." The voice has a soft accent that reminds Maggie of her Italian grandfather. She turns right and steps through a thick beaded curtain and into a room that both does and doesn't look like what she thinks a psychic's den should. There's a crystal ball on a shelf and a short, stout woman wearing flared jeans and a floaty purple top sits at the table beneath it. A deck of cards rests on the table, and beside it a miniature set of drawers. But there are also plants everywhere, mostly different shades and shapes of green, though a few carry flowers. A fat cactus holds center stage on a coffee table, and there's a TV in the corner, half-covered with a red scarf. On the walls are painted renderings of tarot cards. "I designed those," the woman says.

"What?"

"Those cards, on the wall. And these." The woman gestures to the deck on the table. "I was an artist long before I was a psychic," she says. "I am Madame Fausti, but you can call me Carolina." She pronounces it in the European way, not like the north or south state.

"Uh, hi." Maggie sits in the chair across from Madame Fausti—she can't possibly call her by her first name, she decides; it would ruin the whole atmosphere.

"You are on a journey," Madame says.

Maggie almost rolls her eyes but manages not to. How often do people make Needles their destination rather than a stop along the way? Plus, surely this woman knows the locals. But Maggie nods.

"You are a skeptic, I can see that. And so tarot will do you no good; you need to believe, and you will think I am just spinning tales. Let's do something more scientific for you, shall we? A star chart. Come." She pulls out a slip of paper and hands it to Maggie with a blunt pencil that looks like it's been chewed on more than once. "Write down your birth date, time of birth, and place of birth."

"How much for the reading?" Maggie asks. She's hoping the woman will say that it's on the house because Maggie is a skeptic, and that she can tip at the end if she likes what she hears. That's the sort of thing that would happen in the movies. But this isn't, and Madame hands Maggie a laminated price chart. "Aren't psychics different than astrologers?" Maggie asks, running her eyes down the list of services. She notes with some pleasure that a star chart is cheaper than a tarot reading—at least the woman isn't trying to squeeze her for every penny she's got.

"I am both," Madame says, and smiles. She has two teeth missing on the right side, but the rest of her teeth look so neat and white and permanent—Maggie can see her gums when she smiles, and they're wet and soft, not the hard look of dentures—that Maggie is sure she must be getting them replaced. Madame Fausti slides the tiny chest of drawers toward Maggie and opens the bottom one. "Please pay now, and then fill out the paper."

Maggie's glad that she has cash for once, procured to pay Gina for the weed. She puts two twenties in the drawer, which Madame then shuts and puts aside. Maggie wonders why she couldn't have just taken the money from her hand and put it in her jeans pockets, but then focuses.

SEX AND/OR GENDER (Maggie appreciates the distinction here,
and that the options are for F/M/OTHER): F
BIRTH DATE: 1/21/1990
BIRTH TIME: 7:51 AM
PLACE OF BIRTH: Oxnard, California

Madame takes the slip and pulls out her phone. She opens an app and plugs all the info into it.

"Seriously?" Maggie asks, getting pissed at herself for spending the money. She could have done *this* on her own. "An app?"

"Do you know how to read this?" Madame Fausti holds up her screen. It's a star map, and as she swipes down, Maggie sees tables full of symbols, planet names, asteroid names, and on it goes, blurring together. Madame yanks the screen back. "This is a shortcut," she explains, her voice as even as it's been the entire time, calm and soothing, as if trying to tame a wild thing. "This way, neither of us is spending time or energy on the math and science and geometry part of the process."

"Okay," Maggie says, and waits as Madame Fausti scrolls up and down her phone.

"Your sun was in Aquarius at your time of birth," Madame Fausti says, looking up from the screen to make eye contact with Maggie. "Which means you don't like to follow the usual way of doing things, but at the same time, you do have some outmoded ways of thinking that you cling to."

Maggie can relate to the first part of this—she's been called blunt before, and she doesn't always adhere to rules. Iris certainly thought Maggie was trying to rebel, sort of no matter what she did. As for the second . . . well, she considers, it's true that she does have a nine-to-five job, a rarity in her group of friends, and she does like the stability of that, which allows her to do whatever she wants elsewhere. She nods, and tries to keep her hands from twisting in her lap.

"You need your space and freedom, and anyone in the past who has tried to keep you in a box has failed miserably," Madame Fausti continues. "Your exes all wanted something from you that you couldn't give."

This is true enough, Maggie thinks. Iris tried to box her into being a straight girl who wears dresses to prom, and that didn't work. Sasha wanted her to accept the cheating, which Maggie wouldn't, and Allison wanted her to be poly, which Maggie couldn't, though she did try. But, she reminds herself, this isn't exactly a shocking revelation, is it? Doesn't everyone think their exes were unfair?

"Your sextile sun is in Moon—unlike many people you know, you had a good upbringing. It was calm, for the most part. Your parents instilled good values in you, harmoniously, and they loved each other and you a great deal."

Maggie can't help interjecting, "Yeah, well, apparently not." She looks away quickly, her eyes filling.

Madame Fausti reaches down and comes up with a box of tissues, proffers it to Maggie. She takes one and blows her nose loudly as Madame Fausti smiles gently. "I was getting to that," she says. "Your square sun is

Lilith. You're concerned about being betrayed, or that you have been betrayed, and your significant other—a woman, yes?—isn't entirely convinced of this betrayal."

Could that be true? Maggie wonders. Is Lucia skeptical about Iris's betrayal? Why would she be? Thinking back, she can't recall a single moment where Lucia condemned Iris for her behavior. She's just been sympathetic to Maggie's feelings, confirming that her reactions are normal, acceptable. So maybe Lucia isn't judging Iris—no, Maggie catches herself. She has no idea what Lucia is or isn't thinking or feeling, because this is a psychic's guess, nothing else. She vows to ask Lucia what she thinks next time they talk.

"Uranus was in Capricorn when you were born," Madame Fausti says, and Maggie can't help snorting, thinking of how, if Allison said something like this, she'd respond with *No, your anus is in Capricorn.* Madame Fausti narrows her eyes at Maggie, as if she doesn't approve of such second-grade humor. "This means making friends comes naturally to you, it's even something you enjoy, and you gravitate toward people like you, progressive thinkers, community makers, but you keep these people at a distance. A shame."

"I don't, really," Maggie says, without much conviction. She doesn't— does she? She doesn't feel like she does. She hangs out with her friends a lot. But a voice—it sounds a little like Lucia, Lucia with her annoyingly sexy maturity and insight that she turns on Maggie ever so delicately, without judgment—asks her why she lost touch with Anthony, who seems like he's pretty rad now, and why she doesn't talk to Gina more often when she knows Gina's been having a hard time for years, and why she hasn't answered the texts from Blair, and Harper, and even Simon from work, and Jolie, her once booty call, who checked in so sweetly. But no, Maggie thinks, this is overwhelming, this is for another time, this is—and she shuts it away somewhere, and tries to listen.

"Your moon is in Sagittarius," Madame Fausti continues. "You like throwing yourself into the unknown and discovering things no matter the possible cost, because you feel like the experience is always worth it."

Maggie's attention wanders as Madame Fausti continues, her thoughts stuck on this last pronouncement. It's true that she's thrown herself into this letters business, and it's true that the reason she's still going is that she has to know the truth. She thinks of last night—is it possible she went out with Nelly and her friends in order to figure out whether she wanted to cheat on Lucia? That she was testing herself to get at this truth? Or did she think that it would be worth it if she had? She thinks of all the times she's gotten high on a whim—on a lunch break at work, occasionally; before a test in college; the morning of the funeral—and then sort of regretted it, but sort of not, because it was interesting to look back later and think of how she dealt with the situation in an altered state. She's yanked back to the present when Madame Fausti says, ". . . goal, slowly and surely."

"Sorry, can you repeat that?" Maggie asks.

"Yes, my dear, of course. I was saying that you are goal-oriented but very patient. You can save money over long periods of time, and you don't lose sight of what you want."

"Financial independence," Maggie says, nodding. "A good pension." She remembers the fantasy she had before she fell asleep last night, of supporting Lucia, taking care of her, so she can dedicate her time to the art and the causes she cares about.

"Yes, security," Madame Fausti says. "For yourself, but more so for others, I think. Well, Venus was in the twelfth house when you were born, which means you care about the sick, the needy, the poor. You maybe work in social services or in the medical profession?"

Maggie snorts. "Wow, no. Never even wanted to be a doctor." But she does, she thinks and doesn't say, want to care more about the world around her, volunteer more. It's why she went to that meeting at the new Pride center—she feels like she's been complacent for too long, coasting, and the political reality of recent months has reminded her that she really can't afford to.

"No, of course," Madame Fausti agrees, as if Maggie's annoyed response didn't even register. "No, that's not quite right, is it." She taps a long nail on her bottom teeth for a moment. "No, you work in something more practical, but there is a service element . . . Ah, insurance maybe?"

"What the fuck," Maggie says, creeped out. She stands up. "What, did that kid you shill out to promote your little operation, did he like steal my wallet or something? Use facial recognition software to get some intel? Fuck this, I'm leaving."

"Ah, yes, with Mars in Sagittarius, you want to run when you're angry, don't you?" Madame Fausti is leaning back, but isn't smiling anymore. Maggie thinks of Peter and his behavior, of the shiva she's escaped. "Oh dear, you have suffered a terrible loss recently, haven't you? You're running from that too."

"You're wrong," Maggie says. "I'm not running from anything." She sits back down, to prove her point. Madame Fausti waits a beat, as if to make sure she's really not leaving.

"Where were we? Mm, yes, with Venus in the twelfth house. So, I'm seeing there's a chance of secret love affairs—perhaps you've been tempted to stray?"

Maggie jumps up again. "No. Nope, that's it. I'm done. Thanks and whatever."

She slams herself out of the house, where the early-afternoon sun beats down on her. She almost expects to see the goth nephew standing there, watching her, maybe urging her to go back inside. Then again, she's already paid, so why should Madame Fausti even care?

In the car, Maggie can't stop sweating. The temperature has gone up, she's sure of it. Something about the desert and heat being released from the ground. She read about the phenomenon once but can't remember what it was called. The air-conditioning vents are all pointed at her, even the ones meant for the passenger seat, but for the first few minutes they just blow hot air and she leaves the window open too. The sandy smell gets stronger as she gets back on the highway.

She isn't running away, she tells herself over and over again as she crosses into Nevada. She isn't. She tries to put the psychic slash astrologer out of her mind. Why should she believe Madame Fausti anyway? It's all bullshit, speculation, guesswork, and common denominators.

HAVING THOROUGHLY DISTRACTED herself by singing along at full volume to the *Wicked* soundtrack almost twice—there was a slowdown on the I-95—Maggie rolls into Las Vegas with the sun still blazing, before the city becomes what she thinks of as its true self. She's been only a couple times with friends, when they all turned twenty-one and then a couple years after college graduation, trips full of drugs and clubbing and light gambling. She remembers the place most for its exceptional ability to cater to hangovers with more alcohol. She's not sure she's been anywhere in the city that didn't have an expansive and expensive bar.

Driving into the city in the daytime is jarring. The highway lets her off somewhere that isn't the Strip, but rather a wide street lined with apartment buildings painted different shades of dust, as if meant to blend in with the rest of the desert's tan and sandy yellows, golden browns, and occasional reds. For a long stretch, the apartments are replaced with walls lining both sides of the road, hiding whatever houses and pools lie beyond. It reminds her of parts of Los Angeles, just strip malls and palm trees and an endless blue sky with barely visible mountains on the horizon.

The sun is ahead, blinding her, and she finds herself suddenly in the middle of an intersection after the light has turned red. She didn't see it switch and sailed through. Cars on either side of her who've started driving honk loudly, and her heart pounds hard as she guns the engine to get to the other side before anyone rams into her.

Before she has time to freak out too badly the GPS chimes in, telling her that her destination is on the right. There's plenty of street parking, so she pulls up right in front. This apartment building is gray and brown, two stories, with a roof that's so red that it looks out of place, like it's meant to live on top of a storybook cottage.

She checks her phone. During the drive, she screened two calls from Ariel, so she calls him back. "Hey, buddy," she says. "What's up?"

"When are you coming home?"

"You keep asking me that. I'm still doing this delivery thing." She knows she sounds like a bitch but can't bring herself to care. Ariel got the wedding rings. He can take care of shit.

"It doesn't matter, I guess," he says, but she can hear the sulk—or maybe the sad—in his voice. "I just . . . It'd just be nice if you were home. Like with Dad. And me."

She refuses to feel guilty right now, not when she needs to focus on the next letter. So she does what she always does with Ariel—she bites. "Isn't Leona there fucking your brains out? I'd only cramp your style, little bro."

"Fuck you, Mags."

"Well, isn't she?"

"We're not—I mean, we—that's not the point. She's just helping me feel better." Maggie can detect the small smile of pride in Ariel's voice. She's pretty sure Leona is his first lay. He must be stoked. Her own cherry popping was pretty revelatory, though she can't imagine women who lose their virginities with men have the same experience. She's heard the painful, awkward stories. She hopes for Leona's sake that she's ridden lots of horses and bicycles before Ariel or that she's had plenty of sex already.

"Good for you, buddy," Maggie says. "Nice manipulation of circumstances. Bet Mom would be proud." She realizes she's gone too far because

Ariel lets out a huff of air and hangs up on her. She calls back but this time he screens the call and sends it to voice mail. She leaves a message. "Hey, I'm sorry," she says. "I'm just stressed. Obviously. I didn't mean to be an asshole." She knows what he'll say—that she absolutely did—but hopes that by the time he listens to the message he'll have forgiven her. She hopes Peter is okay, but since Ariel didn't say anything about him, she assumes he's doing all right, or at least no worse.

Though he hasn't called to check on her himself, she realizes. Peter has never been one to let more than a couple days go by without saying hello, whether through text or email or phone. But she saw him yesterday, she reminds herself. He was fine.

Well.

Relatively.

And besides, she doesn't want to ask Ariel for more details, because then she'll have to hear that Peter probably hasn't asked about her, that he's not worried about her, that he's possibly forgotten her existence entirely.

She pushes home out of her mind, and gets the letter for Liam Ainsworth out of the little stack on the passenger seat. She hesitates, then finds her mother's amber necklace in her backpack and puts it in her pocket. After a moment, she pulls it out again and clasps it around her neck. Something about the browns of the desert reminded her of it earlier, and she wants it close. For good luck, for proof—it was easy to convince Abe she was Iris's daughter, but what if it isn't that simple this time?—or maybe just to have some part of her mother touching her. *Here we go, Mom,* she thinks. *Let's hope this guy is as nice as the last one.*

Out of the car, up the stairs that lead to unit number three, and she's faced once again with a door she isn't sure of. There's no buzzer. She knocks.

"Yeah, yeah, one second!" The door swings open to a slim white man in his fifties with gray hair. "You're not Hugo," he says, and closes the door in her face.

"No, wait—" Maggie says, but the door is closed. She's about to knock again when another man steps up behind her. He has a round face and his black hair is tightly parted and slicked down. The sleeves of his button-down are rolled up, revealing arms covered in swirling black tattoos. He glances at her, but then pounds at the just-shut door.

"Liam, come on, man, we gotta move!" he yells. He turns to Maggie. "Young, aren't you?" The door opens again and he repeats this to Liam. "Young, isn't she?"

"What? Jesus, Hugo," Liam says and comes out. "I don't know her." He locks the door with a key behind him, and he and Hugo begin stomping down the stairs, leaving Maggie still on the landing, looking after them. They're wearing matching outfits, black pants and thick white button-down shirts, with black vests over them.

"Liam Ainsworth?" she calls and starts to follow them.

"Not if I'm getting served," he yells over his shoulder, raising two fingers in a peace sign.

"I'm not fucking serving you!" She jogs down the stairs after them and runs toward the black sedan both men are making a beeline for. "I'm Iris Krause's daughter!"

Liam stops with his hand on the passenger door. He turns, and it looks like he's about to say something, but Hugo slaps his hand on the top of the car and barks, "Ben's going to fuck us right in the ass with a blowtorch if we're late again."

Maggie hovers on the sidewalk a few feet away from them. She can't read Liam's face, but he's torn enough to stay standing as his friend climbs into the driver's seat. He leans down and into the car with his butt still sticking out, and emerges a moment later, banging his head on the door-frame. "Fuck! Okay, get in." When she hesitates, he opens the back seat door for her. "What, you're a lady or something? Come on already!"

Conventional wisdom says that Maggie, a young woman, should cer-tainly not get into a car with two older men she's never met. But she's never been very good at that kind of wisdom, so she gets into the back seat and pulls the door closed—she likes throwing herself into the unknown, isn't that what Madame Fausti said?—and barely gets her seat belt on before Hugo peels away from the curb.

"Man, this is bad. You don't go bringing drama to work," Hugo says, presumably to Liam. He eyes Maggie in the rearview mirror and shakes his head.

"It's not drama," Liam says. "Or is it?" He turns around so his head and torso come out over the center console to stare Maggie down.

"I don't know, really," she says, truthfully. "My mom, Iris, died a few days ago. She left you a letter. I want to understand why she'd do that."

The silence is loud and tense after this, and Liam keeps staring at her until a speed bump makes his body rocket up and he hits his head again. "Fuck," he says, clutching his cranium. "Twice in one day, what is up?" He isn't buckled in, Maggie realizes. "Look, just give me the letter and I'll get you a Lyft back to wherever you gotta go."

"No," Maggie says. She fingers the reassuring contour of her knife in her pocket, there just in case. "I drove for hours to get here, and I want to know how you knew my mom."

"Fuck me," Liam says, and turns to face the windshield again. Another long silence reigns, and Maggie lets it. She doesn't know what Liam is thinking but hopefully he's considering how far she's come, and how maybe a woman in grief isn't the best person to get into a pissing contest with.

At a stoplight, Hugo asks Liam quietly, as if Maggie can't hear him in the back seat, "What, you fuck this girl's mother?" Which confirms what Maggie was suspecting already, but Liam doesn't.

"Just drive, will you?" he says.

The car turns a corner and they're on the Strip. The sun is setting and the lights are all on already, making the street look like a fully decorated birthday party before anyone's arrived yet—prepared, but a little sad. Hugo turns into a garage and drives down the tunnel and turns left at the end, toward a gate marked EMPLOYEES ONLY BEYOND THIS POINT. He lowers his window, swipes a badge in front of a sensor, and the gate rattles open for them. He parks and they all get out, Liam urging her to hurry up and follow them.

Hugo uses his badge on another door and they enter what she assumes must be the service corridors. They pass a kitchen, and Hugo yells a greeting to a couple of guys inside, but doesn't stop to chat. Liam has his hands in his pockets and his face pointed to the floor. He reminds her of a teenage boy, his hunched shoulders sulking like Ariel's not too long ago, if Ariel were this skinny.

"Here, I'll be at a table in a minute." Liam holds open a door that lets out onto the floor of the casino. "Get some chips, you're gonna have to play if you want to chat."

Once again, he shuts a door in her face.

There's nothing distinctive about this casino as far as Maggie can tell, but she's never been good at being able to spot the differences between them. The Strip, to her, is tacky through and through, but she also thinks of it as one of the few places she's been to where no one is trying to be anything but themselves in that particular moment. Gamblers gamble, drunks drink, models snort coke in the bathrooms, old men with big glasses and expensive suits hold on to the waists of escorts and wait for their ears to be nibbled. It's all exactly what it advertises, with no pretense of being anything else.

She hovers around the blackjack tables, nervous about going to get chips before she can make certain that Liam is really going to be where he says he is. The smoke is everywhere, stinking of tobacco and the sickly sweet scent of cigars. She should have rolled a joint to have here. Is weed legal in Las Vegas? She can't remember, but she's certainly brought some over state lines.

Liam comes out from behind a barely noticeable partition wall and taps a dealer on the shoulder. They change places, and Liam pulls out a fresh deck of cards, unwraps it and begins to shuffle vigorously, doing the show-off dealer thing, making shapes on the green table and letting the cards fall in columns between his capable hands. Maggie keeps an eye on him and goes to exchange some cash. She gets chips for forty dollars, figuring that if she can spend that much on a star chart reading that she didn't even finish, surely she can spend that much on trying to learn something about her mother.

There are two other women at the table, both long-haired blondes, their faces made up perfectly. Maggie has a hard time seeing the difference between them. It was something she and Lucia laughed about on their first date—how all the white, long-haired blond chicks on Tinder looked exactly the same, their faces blurring together.

Maggie throws in a five-dollar ante, the minimum—it's a low-stakes area of the casino, this much is clear, full of amateurs—and taps the table twice. Liam deals her in along with the other women. They're both giggling and flicking their eyelashes at him, their tall glasses of booze almost empty. They stay for a couple more rounds, Liam scooping up their money and Maggie's both times, and then totter off in their high heels and short, clinging dresses. Maggie admires the ass of the one on the right and catches Liam doing the same. She's usually creeped out by straight men, but there's something about Liam that she can't put her finger on that makes her think he isn't. Maybe it's his slim wrists or the way the delicate vertical lines on his face seem wise.

Now that the women are gone, she decides it's time. "So my mom."

"Your mom," Liam says, and sighs. "She's dead?"

"Yeah."

"I'm sorry."

"You and everyone else. So how did you know her?"

"What's your name, again?"

"Maggie."

"Maggie," he repeats, and seems to take a long breath. "The gay one, right? Maggie, how about you have a cigarette."

"I don't smoke. Not tobacco anyway," she says.

"Oh-kay," Liam speaks slowly, like she's an idiot, and elbow nudges a pack of cigarettes that's materialized on the table beside him. "How about you pretend to smoke and offer me puffs."

"Uh, sure." She doesn't know why she complies. She could just demand answers. She doesn't have to be this patient. But what keeps holding her back—and what held her back with Abe as well, probably—is knowing that her mother respected these people enough to want to communicate with them postmortem. Unlike her, and Ariel, and Peter, she thinks bitterly as she lights the cigarette and takes in a tiny pull, without inhaling, to keep it going. She sort of smoked for a while in college, but never learned to like the flavor and density of straight tobacco. She offers the cigarette to Liam and he looks around briefly and takes a long puff. He keeps the smoke in for a moment, his eyes closed, and lets it out.

"Your mother and I had an affair, Maggie," he says, handing her the cigarette back.

"When?" she asks. She wonders how many men her mother had going at the same time.

"Fuck, like . . . two years ago? I mean, it ended two years ago. Started about three? Three and a half?"

"You knew she was married." Maggie states this and tries to gauge Liam's reactions. "And had kids. Two."

"Grown," he rebuts. "And yes, I knew she was hitched, but she said it wasn't something I needed to concern myself with and I believed her."

So there it is again, Maggie thinks, her mother managed to charm another man so much that he decided not to take responsibility for his actions or question hers. "So you didn't care that you were a home-wrecker," Maggie says.

He glares at her. "You know nothing about my life, missy. So before you bring your little judgments in here, and before you assume you know diddly-squat about what I care or don't care about, I suggest you take a good, hard look in the mirror and think about what kind of moral standards you expect from your elders that you don't keep yourself."

Maggie feels like she's been slapped. Liam is glaring at her with such intensity that she feels like she's supposed to apologize. But she won't, because she doesn't owe him an apology. She yanks the letter out of her back pocket and slaps it on the table between them. "Here. This is yours. I don't know what the fuck she saw in you." It's a pointless insult that he clearly won't care about, but she's seething. She puts the barely smoked cigarette out in the ashtray between them and gets up to leave.

Everything about this place looks disgusting to her now, the people pulling the levers of the slot machines, the drunk idiots high-fiving each other around a craps table, the absolute and painful straightness of it all. Yes, she thinks, this is the thing about Vegas that she doesn't like: as fun as it can be it reeks of performative straightness at every turn. Each macho man and girly girl walking hand in hand, each painful high heel and golden cuff link, each and every bit of this place is like the 1950s gone wild, with straightness being the only public presentation allowed.

As if to prove her wrong, a pair of drag queens pass by her in glittering dresses, one of them wearing a feather boa and the other a sleek fur stole. One of them winks at Maggie as she passes, and her rage deflates slightly.

In the lobby, she pauses to orient herself—there are several sets of doors she can leave through—when a tap on her shoulder makes her jump violently, and she reaches for her knife and has it in her hand before she's realized she's turned.

"Whoa." It's Liam, his hands up as if trying to calm a horse. Crumpled pages are in his left hand. The letter, Maggie assumes. She crosses her arms and waits for him to say something. "I was real rude back there, and I'm sorry. It's hard to hear she's dead. I'm not really processing it, you know?" He rakes his free hand through his hair. "Look, let me make it up to you. I'm on shift until midnight, but how about I give you the key to my place and you make yourself at home—there's a sofa bed, sheets in the hall closet, it's all easy to find, though my fridge is pretty bare, you might want to order takeout—and then we can talk more later when I get back or tomorrow morning when you're up? How about it?"

"Okay," Maggie says before she can think about it. Here is another man offering her a place to stay because her mother meant so much to him. What is she supposed to make of this? But she'll get a chance to snoop around Liam's place a bit, maybe figure him out. Plus, she hasn't thought about how much staying in Las Vegas, even in a motel, is likely going to cost.

"Here," Liam says, and pulls his keys out of his pocket. They're connected to one of those belt chains like the kind Maggie has, and he unclips them, disentangles his apartment key from the set and hands it over. "I guess you have my address already."

"Yup. Thanks," Maggie says. She's still pissed off, and so before she can say anything shitty, she picks a door at random and walks outside to order a Lyft.

IRIS

Iris lay in bed, awake and aware and scrolling through the news on her phone. It was a recently acquired habit, though she'd had a smartphone for as long as her kids had. But the news was something she'd once preferred listening to in the car or reading in the paper. Liam, though, was attached to his phone like it was a sixth finger some days, and over their mostly silent breakfasts—they both liked long coffees and quiet upon first waking up— he would turn his screen to show her articles and say things like, "Can you believe this shit?" and "Look what the fuckers did today." Eventually, she just downloaded a couple of news apps and became accustomed to scrolling through herself, pleased that she could now nod intelligently and mutter with disgust, "Mhm" and "I know, right?"

Liam wasn't like anyone else Iris had ever been with, for a multitude of reasons, but the one that stuck out most to her, and that weighed on her constantly, was that he was smarter than she was. Not that any of the others had been dumb; Abe was a PhD and a leader in his field, and Peter certainly was incredibly emotionally and otherwise intelligent. But Liam was a dif- ferent kind of smart. He was so well-informed about the forces of capitalism and government and various laws being passed, about the history of oppression both in this country and abroad, about the way speech and action melded together and could cause real, demonstrable good or harm, that she felt ignorant beside him. He had no formal education beyond high school, but he cared about so many things with a passion that could easily tip into rage that she was humbled. And so, humbled and ignorant and impressed, she fell for him. She thought of him, sometimes, as a corrective to Shlomo—Liam wasn't trying to impress anyone with his brain; it seemed more like his knowledge was felt rather than intellectualized.

Quite frankly, of everyone she'd been with, he intimidated her the most. Which was partly why she'd made the decision that she made, and which she would have to carry out once he was awake. Or maybe not right when he woke up, but soon.

Last night, they'd gone out to a bar, at his urging. "I want to show you off, sexy," he'd said, sniffing the back of her neck and running the tips of his fingers up her arms in a way that made her melt. She'd agreed, though she wasn't partial to big crowds, and she was introduced to some of his friends, a couple of whom she suspected were his lovers as well. But she and Liam had an agreement—if she wasn't going to talk about her home life, about her spouse and their relationship, then Liam wasn't going to tell her about what he got up to and with whom when she wasn't around.

She'd been around a lot recently, though. This was the other problem. It was beginning to feel like too much. But it was so easy, with Ariel working on campus most of the summer and starting his second year of college, Maggie long out of the house, and Peter working harder than ever before it seemed on designs for a solar panel company's new marketing campaign. He'd also recently acquired a very demanding client in the form of a medical marijuana pharmacy that tended to give him ridiculously close deadlines but paid very well.

So with the kids both gone and Peter preoccupied, Iris had been spending increasing time in Las Vegas with Liam between her own jobs.

Mostly, they stayed in and talked. It was like going to university all over again, being around Liam. He had radical politics, and while she challenged him occasionally on them, she never won an argument. And she loved it. God help her, she loved it. And she loved him. That, well, that was the biggest problem of all.

She was just reading a piece on the removal of prisoners from solitary confinement in Washington and wondering what Liam would think about that—probably something like, "Prisons are the way the US maintains modern slavery and it's an antiquated system that clearly doesn't help them or society, for fuck's sake"—when he rolled over with a grunt. His eyes were bleary and red, and she could almost hear the way they gummed open sleepily. He'd gotten very drunk last night, and Iris had let herself get tipsier than usual too, but alcohol at night always made her wake up early in the morning.

"Here," she said, reaching over to the bedside table. She handed Liam a tall glass of water and told him to drink it. "All of it," she said with a finger waggle. "I swear, you'd think you were seventeen."

"Honey, I'm youthful at heart," he said, his voice hoarse—there was karaoke last night too, Liam singing terribly but enthusiastically. Iris had nearly peed her pants laughing. He glugged the water from the glass. She watched his throat moving, and ran a finger down it. It was so smooth. Straight up and down, no bulbous Adam's apple in the middle. She had somehow never registered this before. He handed her the glass back and stretched. "Not in body, apparently. Fuck, am I stiff."

"You were a sight last night," she told him.

"A good one, I hope," he said. "Why are you up so early? And why didn't you wake me up? How long have you been staring at me sleeping anyway?"

Iris shrugged. "I wasn't! I was reading the news."

"Ah. A well-informed wife lives a well-informed life," he quipped, chucking her chin. Then he realized what he'd said, apparently, and withdrew. "Sorry, I'm hungover. Coffee?"

Iris didn't say a word, but he was already out of the room, his boxer shorts barely hanging on to his slim hips, his long, willowy torso left bare. His back was narrow, and Iris thought it the most beautiful one she'd ever seen. She wavered. She didn't want to do what she was going to do. But Peter had asked her the other night whether she'd maybe be home more often, because he missed her and one of his projects was winding down soon, and she knew that she was falling in deep here and needed out before it was too late.

She got dressed, putting on her blue jeans and the white top she was wearing last night. She hadn't brought an extra outfit, just another small detail orchestrated to make herself leave today and do what she had to do. In the kitchen, Liam was facing the coffeemaker and rubbing his eyes with the balls of his hands. He yawned widely, his crooked bottom teeth on full display. He'd had braces on the top ones as an adult, he'd told her once, early in their relationship. He was embarrassed by it, though, and said that if he could have chosen over again, he would have kept his fucked-up upper teeth as well, as a reminder to both himself and the world that he came from a small town in Wyoming where his parents worked hard and were too poor to afford luxuries like orthodontia. She loved his teeth, though. She loved that his upper teeth were pristine and straight and looked like a movie star's and the bottom were in the same shape they'd been in for decades. She loved that he carried a flaw like that proudly, and that he was ashamed instead of what he considered succumbing to modern beauty standards. He was so unlike the people in her life.

Except Maggie, she thought often; but for so long she hadn't let Maggie be this way with her, had objected and shut her outrage down, seeing her as childish, a little spoiled maybe, certainly self-righteous and naive. She was all those things, to an extent, but mostly, she was young, and Iris, too, had been young once, going to antiwar protests in high school despite her parents' objections. She should have encouraged Maggie, probably, or at least not gotten so impatient with her. Parents make mistakes, Iris knew, but this was one that rippled inward from Maggie's behavior to her essence. Iris wasn't sure how to rectify it. And maybe, she thought now, mustering courage, that was another reason to do what she had to do. So she could try again, and try harder, with her daughter.

Iris pulled the milk out of the fridge. "Here."

"Thanks," he said, and grabbed her around the waist. He held her companionably beside him, watching the coffee drip into the pot as if hypnotized. Standing quietly like this with him was another of the things she loved. Peter liked to chatter when she was around. And she didn't stop him, because this was one of the things they were good at: giving each other what was necessary. She needed physical space so that she could do her job well and emotional space so that she could be the companion and wife she was to him. And he gave her that. In return, when she was home, she was Peter's sounding board, his best friend, his rock. But Liam could be silent with her in a way that felt rich and intoxicating.

Liam poured them both coffee with milk and brought the mugs to the table. Their ritual had become set: they would sit, Iris with her feet in Liam's lap, and zone into their phones together. Sometimes Iris would read a novel instead, if she wasn't in the mood for the real world. This morning, she didn't put her feet up. Like a fox with a scent, Liam stilled.

"What's wrong?" he asked.

"How do you know there's something wrong?" She didn't bother denying it, because that would make what came next worse, and one thing she refused to do was sugarcoat things. She never had, not since leaving Shlomo, and she never would again. It was part of what made her a good businesswoman too. She was realistic. In the years with Shlomo, business was the only place she could be that way; since leaving him she could spread the outlook to other parts of her life. She fiddled with her necklace, running her fingers over the amber. She'd forgotten to take it off last night. She waited.

"You look . . . different. Shuttered," Liam said. He fluttered his hands in front of his face, like he was playing peekaboo.

Iris let go of the necklace and tried to relax her shoulders. "Well, I do have to talk to you."

"No." Liam got up. He started pacing. "No, you don't. There is nothing to talk about. No."

"Please, Liam, just sit and—"

"I will not sit, no, I won't, I won't. If I don't sit, you won't leave me. If you don't leave me, then there's still a chance."

"A chance at what?" she asked quietly. She'd never seen him like this before. It was like a switch had flipped, and the grumpy man a few years her junior became a child begging his mother not to leave him all alone at the babysitter's house.

"A chance at—at—n-n-normalcy," he spat out. Iris had never heard him stutter, either, and now she was really scared, since he'd mentioned once that a speech pathologist in elementary school had trained him out of it. Part of her was trying to remember whether it could be a sign of stroke, and when Liam stopped dead and stared at the window behind her, his face slack, she really began to panic. Her finger was already dialing the nine on her cell phone when he spoke again and his voice sounded like it usually did. Wry, collected, sane. "Sorry 'bout that."

Iris stayed silent, unsure what exactly he was apologizing for.

He turned his back on her and hugged himself, his hands almost touching on his spine. "I . . . have abandonment issues," he said. "I've been working through them for a long time. And that's all I'm going to say. I think you should leave. Unless . . ." And he turned his head halfway, so that she could see his profile, which looked alien to her in that moment. "Unless you weren't about to tell me that we should end things."

Iris was gripping her phone hard with both hands. She wondered whether she could crack it, break it in her bare palms. "No," she finally said. "I mean, yes, that was what I was about to say, but—" She wanted to say that she thought they could talk about it, that she could explain her reasons, but Liam let out a little yelp.

"No!" He shouted it, but then he took a deep, shuddering breath, and said, more quietly, "No. No buts. I don't want you to explain everything that's wrong with me, but how it's still you, not me. I don't want to hear about what I'm lacking, and how you really just need the real thing, and how you're uncomfortable, and how you'd be ashamed of telling your kids, and how ungodly it all is. I don't care how you couch it, I don't care how you excuse it to yourself."

"That's not—that isn't at all—"

"Stop. Please go."

She lingered. She wanted to hug him, to touch him, to explain. But he wasn't a child, despite his vulnerability. And he didn't need her concern or pity. She could understand that. She picked up her purse. At the door, she wanted to say something more, like, *I love you, I never lied to you, I will always care about you, I care about you too much.* But nothing she could say would be comforting or fair, and it would all be for her own benefit anyway. After all, she wouldn't be able to change his perception of himself, or about why she had to go, and it wasn't her job to try if he didn't want her to. So she left.

In the car, she realized what a brutal mistake she'd made. Not in ending things. She had to do that, and she should have probably done it sooner—the flash she'd just seen of Liam confirmed it, reminded her that there was something feral in him that she never, ever had to worry about with Peter, her solid and adoring Peter. No, the mistake was deeper than that, and was made a long time ago. It was not telling him who she was, where she came from . . . It was not telling him more about her kids. More about Maggie.

It was not telling him how he'd changed her in ways Iris still couldn't articulate, merely by being who he was and allowing her to be with him. She should have discussed things with him more, asked more questions, shown that she cared about his experience—but she'd thought this whole time that he didn't want her to ask, that part of him was tough and closed off like his scar tissue. But maybe he'd been putting on an act for her, the same way Maggie now did, toughness that had nothing to do with how he felt and everything to do with fear of her reaction. Maybe he'd thought that she was pretending he was someone other than he was, or that she was going against her nature and inclination. All this time, had he thought she was disgusted by him? That she thought their union was somehow evil or wrong?

But no, she tried to comfort herself, that couldn't be. She was projecting, mixing everything up. He was her lover, not her child. The sun looked wrong, too bright, and the desert was too beautiful, and she wanted to reenter the concrete of the city again, to be among squat buildings that looked as ugly as she felt.

She could have reassured him more. She should have. She shouldn't have assumed he was always strong.

It's almost one in the morning when Maggie hears Liam's key in the door. She's incredibly drunk and not a little stoned. She really shouldn't be, second night in a row, yet here she is nonetheless. She's in the pleasantly woozy state where she thinks she could be sober if she really wanted to, though a tiny part of her mind is aware that she's very wrong, and long past that possibility. And, to make everything worse, she and Lucia had a fight. Or, at least, Maggie is pretty sure that's what it was.

It started when Maggie was already three shots in. She called Lucia through Messenger to tell her about what she'd found, and without thinking about it, had ranted for a full five minutes, pacing up and down Liam's small apartment.

"Babe," Lucia had said when Maggie finally paused for breath, "I can see why this is throwing you a bit, but . . . well, I guess . . . isn't there part of you that's glad to learn this about your mom?"

"*Glad?*" Maggie really couldn't fathom how Lucia could think that. What was there to be glad about?

"Yeah, I mean, I know she stepped out on your dad, and that's not an easy pill to swallow, but—"

"No, there is no but," Maggie said. "She cheated, and that's shitty, and she was shitty to me, about being gay, and now . . ." Her voice broke.

"Okay," Lucia said. "Okay, you're right. I just—okay."

"Just what?"

"No, nothing, babe," Lucia said quickly. "I'm sorry I said anything, now isn't the time."

But Maggie could tell Lucia had more to say, and she couldn't handle it, didn't want to see how or if she was being unreasonable or judgmental—*like you always said, Mom*—or whatever it was she was being because she had a right to be it, all of it, and she wasn't willing to back down. "I'll talk to you tomorrow," she said after a tense pause, and before waiting to hear what Lucia said, she hung up and put her phone on airplane mode. Then she rolled a joint, and kept drinking.

Now, she's still on the relatively good side of drunk, threatening to tip over into bad, depending on what happens next.

Liam glances at her and the bottle of whiskey open next to her on the made-up sofa bed. "Left any for me?" he asks. Even though just a few short hours ago Maggie hated him, she decides now that she doesn't, really. She's feeling solicitous. No one who wants to share her whiskey could be so terrible.

"There's some for everybody!" she hoots, and passes him the bottle. He raises an eyebrow at her and takes a swig.

"Fuck, that's nasty. Someone needs to teach you about good whiskey. And don't look at me, I'm so broke I apparently bought this shit."

"Then how would you know good whiskey from—of?—from, it's from, right?" Maggie's lost in her sentence and isn't sure how to find her way back, and it seems like just as good a time as any to announce her new under-standing of the situation. "Found your cock," she says.

Liam is very still for a moment, a stag caught in the headlights. But like

a deer will if you wait a moment, his shoulders relax. He hands her the
bottle back and sits in the armchair that matches the sofa. "I guess that's my
fault for letting an angry kid into my apartment."

"So you don't deny it?"

His face registers irritation. "Nothing to deny. What, you think your
generation fucking invented being trans? Fucking millennials, you drive me
crazy."

"But . . ." Maggie's face feels very hot and very red. She blinks hard.
"She was so straight." She feels the tears coming to her eyes.

"I'm a man," Liam says. "So yes, she was. Is. Was. Fuck."

"No, I know—" Maggie realizes what she's implied and she's angry at
herself, but she's drunk, and she's trying to convey something quite else,
something that isn't about Iris at all, or not really, no, yes, it's about Iris, but
not about Liam, really. It's about this, this . . . This sudden entrance of her
mother into this space Maggie didn't know she could occupy. All these
years, Maggie submerging herself in queer culture, hanging out in bars
with other lesbians, with nonbinary pan folx and radical faeries, with trans
men and women, queer bois and womyn, people in drag of all genders.
These have been her people, their spaces welcoming to her, and she took
them in like a drought-stricken land thirsting for a refreshing storm.
Among them, she learned to be herself. To be entirely who she is, not only
as a lesbian but also as a person with a dyke aesthetic and wandering eyes
and a rowdy libido and a queer sense of humor and a love of camp.

All these years, this has also been a space that her mother couldn't take
from her, no matter how much she sneered at Maggie's clothes, rolled her
eyes at Maggie's rants. Many of her friends' parents don't accept them, to
different degrees—some, like Iris, just never really talk to their kids about
any of it and pretend they're straight; others kick their kids out and cut
them off; some call only at Christmas and ask leading and disturbing questions about HIV and AIDS, not that they usually know the difference.
Lucia, as far as Maggie knows, is one of the shockingly lucky ones, with

parents who adore her and who want to meet Maggie. If she has the guts for it. The plan is for her and Lucia to take time off together at some point and visit Puerto Rico, where her parents moved a few years ago when they retired.

Maggie's thoughts run together as she tries to explain again. "No, it's not that she's—it's not that you're not—I mean, what I'm saying is—me, she never accepted *me.*"

And this is the last thing that Maggie remembers that night.

She is lucky, in the morning, that she doesn't remember how she sobbed loudly for a solid thirty minutes, using an entire roll of toilet paper of Liam's—who tells her he isn't the kind of guy who has tissues lying around, because he thinks it's stupid to have two paper products that do the same thing, basically. She doesn't remember telling him about coming out to Iris when she was seventeen, how Iris's face had become cold, how Peter came in after to ask Maggie how it went and Maggie said she wished she were dead, and then said no, she wished Iris were dead. She'd known Peter would be supportive, and she'd known, instinctively, that Iris wouldn't. She doesn't remember telling Liam that it wasn't fair, that her mother cared more about a man she wanted to fuck than about her own kid; that she should have told Maggie about him, about this; that she was a hypocrite, and that Maggie is glad she's dead, she's glad, she's glad, she's so, so, so sad. She doesn't remember how she cried so long and so hard that she began coughing, which turned into serious gagging, which became full-on vomiting very soon, though luckily Liam managed to get her into the bathroom and over the toilet. She doesn't remember how he made her drink three glasses of water, how she threw up again after the second, how he got her to take an aspirin with the third glass, just like Lucia does, just like Iris tried to do for him the night before they broke up, Liam told her, but she doesn't remember that. Or how he got her into bed, and how she asked him, "Why, why, why couldn't she give me one of the rings, why just this stupid necklace?" and how she tried to rip it off her neck, and how he pried open her hand and unclasped the necklace and told her it must have been very, very special to her mother because she gave it to Maggie. She doesn't remember how she then began a barely intelligible tangent, though it was crystal clear in her mind at the time, about how she shouldn't care about the rings because it implies that marriage is the only thing queers want when that's the least of their troubles at this point and that the right to marry is an antiquated bourgeois and/or religious institution that doesn't even matter and, and, and . . . But Maggie doesn't remember any of this the next day, and never will.

SHE HAS A headache when she wakes up, but it isn't as bad as it could be, for which she's grateful, but her mouth does feel like a sock. The last thing Maggie remembers is beginning to cry. When she got to Liam's apartment yesterday, she started snooping. And there in the medicine cabinet she found the patches, and she stared at them for a long moment, and thought, *Surely not,* and then, though she knew she really shouldn't because it was an incredible invasion of privacy, the kind that she would have railed against if she'd heard of anyone else doing it, she went into his room. The door was open, the bed was unmade and messy. There was an empty beer bottle on the nightstand and a big TV across from it. And below the TV, right on the dresser, was a pinkish-beige thing. At first, Maggie didn't register it as what it was—she thought, oh, rolled-up pantyhose? But no, it was one of Liam's penises. She found a few others, in varying shapes and sizes, in the bottom drawer of the dresser, but the one that was out seemed to match his skin tone and was, she supposed, his garden-variety dick.

A person Maggie had dated briefly in college wasn't actually a woman though he hadn't known how to articulate this at the time, and when Gavin had come out as trans the year after they graduated, Maggie had reached out to him. They'd rekindled a friendship until he moved to up-state New York for graduate school, but for a while they were close, and Maggie had learned far more from him than she ever could from the various articles online that he'd sent her. Not because he'd explained things to her, but just being around him and listening to his daily concerns had illuminated his world for her. The ways he wanted to pass and yet felt conflicted about this desire. The way he cried after wrangling with bureau-cracy where he was constantly being misgendered, the exhaustion of cor-recting or deciding not to. The anger he felt at still getting his period, impatient at how slowly hormone replacement therapy was working, and how his skin kept getting ashy though his doctors said that wasn't a usual side effect. She helped him rub shea butter on his elbows and knees some days. It was one of those intimate, extremely intense friendships that fizzled out when they were no longer in the same space. She misses Gavin, she realizes, staring at Liam's ceiling and trying to muster the courage to get up. He sent her a message after her announcement about Iris but she hasn't opened it yet. She should.

A metallic clatter alerts her that Liam must be awake. She pulls her head up from the pillow to see.

"Coffee?" he asks, picking up the top half of a French press from the floor.

"Yes, please," Maggie says, and her voice is so scratchy she doesn't rec-ognize it. "Whoa."

"Yeah. You gave your throat a workout last night," he says. After a pause in which Maggie is momentarily horrified he adds, "Fuck, that sounded awful. I meant you puked. A lot."

"Oh." Maggie gets into a seated position on the bed and that's when the real headache kicks in, like a horse has just hoofed her. "Oooh," she moans.

"Here." Liam gives her a glass of water. "Maybe you should nap a little more."

"Okay," Maggie says, and she falls back into the pillow.

. . .

A COUPLE OF hours later, she wakes up again, this time starving. The first thing she registers is a lingering smell of toast. It's one of her favorite scents— like bread baking, but with a hint of bonfire.

She gets up, and this time she has the sense to feel ashamed of her behavior. She's not sure precisely what she said or did last night but she knows that she confronted Liam, and she knows that he took it well enough that he didn't kick her out of his apartment. Which he was fully within his rights to do.

He's sitting at the kitchen table, immersed in something on his phone. He has reading glasses perched on his nose that make him look older, and kindly.

"Thank you," Maggie says.

"Yeah," he says. "Want that coffee now? Eggs?"

"Sure, thanks."

They're silent for a while as he pours the cold coffee into a mug and puts it in the microwave to reheat, and then quickly cooks her some scrambled eggs and puts in another two slices of bread to toast. Maggie tries to picture her mother here, if Liam lived here back when they were involved. She realizes that Iris may well have been penetrated with the cock she saw last night. The idea is icky, because she doesn't want to think of Iris in the throes of passion—does anyone want to think of their parents that way?— but at the same time, there's something sweet about it. A bridge, a place where her mother experienced something that Maggie has too—even if that thing is a silicone dildo.

"Eat, but not too fast. Chew your food," he says, and Maggie laughs. "What?" he asks.

"Nothing, you just . . ." She reaches for the fork he hands her and touches the tines with her fingers for a moment. "You sounded like a Jewish mother there."

"Like your mom," he says, sitting. Maggie nods. "Okay. So. What do you want to know?" Liam's butt slides down his seat and he interlaces his fingers behind his head and puts his bare feet up on the side of the kitchen table farthest from Maggie, like Humphrey Bogart in *The Maltese Falcon*. "I'm an open book now. Ask me anything, as you kids say on Reddit." He raises his eyebrows. He's so dashing, Maggie thinks, and can easily see her mother liking him. Iris always loved being in control, after all, and when someone questioned her sense of it or poked a hole in it, she'd bristle, unless there was enough roguish charm involved—at least, this is the dynamic Maggie remembers watching as a child, when her mother still occasionally took her to work. She loved watching her mother in that professional space, where she stopped being Mom and became a person to whom men in suits said, *You must be Iris Krause, you come highly recommended*. It was clear to Maggie who was setting the terms in those meetings—unless, that is, something about the client surprised Iris or charmed her, which seemed to happen rarely.

Liam clearly has the gruff charm thing in spades. Maggie herself has always tried to have that same swagger—maybe for more Freudian reasons than she's realized—but she was never able to turn it on Iris. She always got too angry, too hurt, when she and Iris disagreed.

She lets this thought sit as she piles her eggs on the buttered toast, and then asks, "What changed between when you blew me off and when you invited me to stay?"

"Duh," he says. "I read the letter."

"And?"

"And . . . And Iris put to bed, no innuendo intended, a few concerns that I had when we stopped seeing one another." He doesn't explain further, and Maggie isn't sure how far she should push, despite his earlier claim.

"Okay," she says. "So what happened between you? I mean, really."

"What, you want a play-by-play?"

"No, just like, how did you meet? How did you start . . . dating, or whatever it was? How did she explain the fact that she was cheating on my dad and us? See," she says, before he can start, "this is what I don't get. I don't get how she could have done all this and still claimed to love my dad, to love me and my brother. It just . . ."

Liam takes a deep breath. "Hey," he says. "She loved you all. I know she did, because she left me. She left so that she could be in your lives, not leave yours for mine." And then he tells her the rest. How they met at a casino when she was in Vegas for work. Of course, Maggie thinks. And he tells her how he winked at her, because she had a certain something to her. "A classiness," he says, and shakes his head. "No, I don't know what that fucking means, that's a set of ambiguous and probably classist fucking abstracts." Anyway, something drew him to her, maybe just plain old chemistry, and he slipped her his card when he dealt her a hand. She didn't call, but she came back again the next night, and they talked. They went to a bar after Liam finished his shift, and they talked all night, arguing mostly.

He pauses. "What was the next question?"

"What did she say about us?" Maggie asks, and she realizes that yes, this is what she really wants to know most.

"Not much." Liam shrugs. "I'm sorry, kid, but she said she didn't want to talk about her family. She told me she was married, but that I shouldn't take that into consideration, and she said that she had two children, that they were grown-ups, basically. Once we started getting serious, I told her that I felt that things were uneven. That if she was going to have such a private part of her life, then I was going to have to be allowed to as well."

"So you slept around," Maggie interprets.

He shrugs again. "Look, it was a long-distance relationship. It was complicated. And she had another life, so I got back to mine too."

"Jesus . . . Are all old people horndogs?"

Liam laughs, a bit grimly. "Old," he says. "I'm considered old."

They're silent again, until Maggie asks what she's been wanting to ask since last night but hasn't been able to put into words yet. "So did . . . did my mom end up liking pussy?" This is the closest she can come to what she actually wants to ask, which is, *Why didn't she understand me?*

"Oy vey," Liam says. He laughs. "Iris used to say that a lot. 'Oy vey.'"

Maggie murmurs her assent and waits. Her eyes feel odd in her head, dry and too large, staring intently at Liam's face. She can imagine them popping out and hovering right in front of his, trying to read something in his expression that probably isn't there.

Liam sighs and takes his feet off the table. He scratches the sides of his head and mutters, "Should get a haircut . . ." And when he looks up at her, his eyes are moist. "No," he says. "At least, not as far as I know. And I was okay with that. I liked pussy enough for the both of us. Look, Maggie . . ." He leans forward, and something sizzles in the air between them, something Maggie recognizes from the spaces that have always welcomed her, from the people who have always felt like *her* people. Something like understanding, like empathy. "I don't feel comfortable telling you intimacies of our sex life, frankly. It's too weird. But your mother saw me as a man. She knew I was trans, but she didn't ask me a lot about it. She thought I didn't want to talk about it, that I wanted to be cis. She thought that by barely acknowledging that I wasn't, she was letting me be who I truly was without . . . What was it?" He reaches back toward the counter. Maggie hasn't noticed that the letter has been there all this time. He grabs it by the corner, then unfolds the crumpled pages and skims them. "Here it is. 'I thought that my silence on the topic allowed you to be who you were without interrogation.'" He keeps reading to himself for a moment and then appears to remember that Maggie is still there. "It's a nice sentiment," he says. "Shame she never voiced it. Maybe we wouldn't have ended at all."

"Really?" Maggie is taken aback. Was there an alternate universe in which Iris was living a carefree lifestyle as the partner of a Vegas blackjack dealer?

"No, she would have left me anyway," Liam says. He shakes his body like a dog drying itself from a plunge in brackish waters. "I shouldn't dwell. She says in the letter that she couldn't risk her home life any more than she already had."

So she knew, Maggie thinks, and something in her loosens a bit, just enough to be able to keep bearing this. Iris knew that she was risking something here. She cared enough to say that.

Liam tosses the letter back to the table. "So. Like I said—she loved all of you. Anyway," he smiles, not entirely convincingly. "Any other questions?"

Maggie thinks. She wants to ask him what Iris was like, as if they've never met before. But would she recognize the woman Liam might describe or would it only make her feel farther away, more unknowable? But no, there's one more thing. "Wait, when did you say you started getting serious?"

"Hmm. We met in the spring of 2014 . . . So probably the fall of that year?"

That sounds about right. In recent years, Maggie has to admit that Iris had let go of some of her overt judgment. She seemed to have been trying harder with Maggie—she asked about her dating life and refrained from asking about whether Maggie might still find the right man one day. Gender and sexuality aren't the same thing, and aren't always tied together, Maggie knows. But Iris might not have understood this, and it makes sense to Maggie that being with Liam could have broadened Iris's outlook a bit.

It wasn't enough, though, and what loosened in Maggie just moments ago becomes heavy, a sinking stone of sadness. Iris being less homophobic didn't mean Iris being supportive. Like Liam said, if Iris had voiced her understanding, or trying to, if she had told Maggie this directly, maybe things would have been different. And now it's too late, Maggie thinks. Iris had never told her about the men, so she couldn't have told her about Liam, so she couldn't have told Maggie why she was having a change of heart, so she just didn't. She tried, Maggie supposes, to be subtle about it. But after years of unsubtle dislike of Maggie's gayness, it didn't register, not enough for Maggie to open up.

"Thanks," she finally says. "I guess I should get going, then." Her eggs are only half-eaten, since she lost her appetite sometime during their conversation and forgot all about them.

"Are you sure?" Liam asks, and she nods. "For what it's worth," he says, and hesitates. "Look, she didn't talk about you often, but she'd occasionally tell me something she learned from you. So whether or not it seemed that way, I think she was listening, at least sometimes."

"Ugh, this is so stupid," Maggie says as her eyes immediately fill. "Sorry, I just. I don't usually cry so much."

"It's okay," Liam says. "Oh, wait a second." He gets up and rummages through kitchen drawers, grumbling, until he finds what he's looking for. "My card," he explains, handing it to her. "I don't do social media. But keep in touch, if you want. Iris was something special. Plus, you queer kids need to learn that we've always been here. Don't forget that, or else you let the idiots keep thinking we're just rebels sticking it to their Adam and Eve shit every generation all over again. We've *always* been here."

Impulsively, Maggie hugs him tightly. She's never really known older queers. Iris and Peter didn't have any gay friends that she knew of, and the one lesbian professor she had in college for a gender and sexuality course was also a harried mom with young twins and didn't really get close to the students. Liam hugs her back, and this time his eyes are moist when she pulls away. "I will," she says. "I'll keep in touch."

"Thank you, Maggie," he says. "For the letter. You didn't have to give it to me. Hell, you could have opened it and never told me she died. So. Thank you."

Maggie puts on her shoes and collects her bag and returns to her car. The stack of unopened envelopes is shorter.

"Two down," she tells it. "One missing. Two to go."

"HEY MAGS," LUCIA's voice crackles through the car's speakers as Maggie takes a breath, relieved beyond measure that she picked up, that she isn't ignoring her. "You sound exhausted."

"I am," Maggie says. "And also I'm—I'm sorry about last night. About being . . . I don't know. Mean."

Lucia laughs. "That wasn't mean, babe. Besides, you said you were what, three shots in already? At some stranger's house? All things considered, I'd say you're handling all this like a champ."

"But Lu," Maggie says, nervous to bring it up again but deciding to anyway. "You really haven't ever, like, called my mom a bitch for any of this. Or even said she was wrong. Do you think she had a reason to step out on my dad? Like, do you think she's justified?"

"That's . . . It's not my place, Mags. I didn't know her or your dad or their circumstances. I'm so, so sorry she's hurting you, and I'm sorrier that she's dead and that you can't talk to her about it. But judgment? I just don't think I can. Everyone has reasons for everything they do. Good, bad, racist, phobic, logical or not, doesn't really matter. The reasons exist, for them."

"True, but reasons don't mean I should forgive her," Maggie says, trying to keep her impatience with Lucia's ability to see every point of view out of her voice. She doesn't want to fight again, but she wants her girlfriend to be able to say it with her, that Iris was being awful, deceitful, neglectful, gross—anything but this calm and collected understanding.

"Of course not," Lucia replies, sounding surprised. "Forgiveness is a whole other thing."

They hang up soon. It's two hours later in Missouri and Lucia is getting ready to go out to a Sunday evening quiz night at a bar, and they were talking over Skype since her phone won't be ready to pick up until tomorrow. Maggie misses her now ferociously, in a way that she's never felt before with anyone. It's an ache, a physical itching at her fingertips when she wants to touch Lucia's cheek or hair or arm after something she says but can't because there's miles of distance between them and only technology connecting their voices. She wonders whether Iris felt this way about any of these men, about Abe, about Liam. About these others.

She wants this to be over. It isn't just the hangover, the second day in a row, that's making her tired. It's all of this, this trying to understand a person who doesn't exist. When she thinks of it that way, her mind feels like it's shrinking, the corners of her vision going momentarily dark—the same way they do when she's high and tries to contemplate the vastness of the universe. The idea of Iris just not existing, nowhere, nothing, it rocks her, an existential inability to fully grasp the concept.

She's so, so tired.

She entertains the idea of just dropping the remaining letters in the mailbox and heading home, first to Oxnard and then home-home, to St. Louis. She's thinking about getting a cat. For no reason, really, except that the idea of having a cat waiting for her is newly appealing. It would make home feel more permanent. More hers. And Lucia has a cat, so she could teach Maggie whatever she needs to know.

But the curiosity—bone-weary as she is, it still rears up. Who are these men? Why did Iris want them? What did they give Iris that she didn't have at home? What did she give them that she couldn't give to her family?

By the time she merges onto the Santa Monica freeway around six in the evening, Maggie's beginning to feel not just tired but sweaty and unclean, like she's going to jump out of her skin. She's eaten by now, at least, but she's still wearing the same clothes from yesterday and hasn't showered, and her hair feels oily and unpleasant.

She rolls down the windows as she gets onto surface streets. The air has cooled down significantly, so she shuts off the car's air-conditioning. It's rush hour, which it always seems to be in LA, and she slows to a crawl, watching people in neighboring cars fiddle with their phones, pump up or down the volume of their music, do their makeup.

The evening after a hangover is always a tenuous thing. It feels raw and tender, like the new skin below a picked-off scab. She feels a delirious kind of sobriety, her head floaty and her limbs a little loose. The traffic is so bad that as she sits through three red-green circulations in front of a messy intersection, she has time to make her reservation at the cheapest motel in town and text Ariel to let him know she's staying away another night. She knows she could technically drive home to Oxnard but she doesn't want to now, not until she finishes this ordeal. It was easy to leave the first time, and the second time after meeting Abe, but she thinks it'll be too hard to leave a third time and go anywhere but back to Lucia. To stave off missing her too badly, Maggie turns her daydreaming to the bed and its clean, crisp motel sheets, and the shower.

But before that—Karl Jelen. Though she permits herself to hope no one is home so that she can postpone seeing and talking to him until tomorrow and get her body clean, her head high, and both to sleep.

"You've arrived," the GPS chirps.

Maggie wishes she had gotten some more coffee on the way, feels her eyes drooping, but she isn't going to turn back now. She picks up Karl Jelen's letter and walks up the stone steps across a lawn that looks far too lush to be legal in this drought. There's a small nook beside the door with a gorgeously carved wooden porch swing. Next to it is a planter whose damp soil is stuffed with cigarette butts and ashes. The smell of old, wet tobacco rises from it. Whoever lives here, she thinks, must smoke a pack or three a day. Iris always liked the smell, because she said her parents had both been smokers; but maybe she lied, Maggie thinks. Maybe it was about this dude. She grabs at the necklace that's still on her, then self-consciously lets go and knocks.

There's a flickering light in the bay window to her right, so she knows someone's home, but she hears no footsteps. She knocks again, louder. Nothing.

"Fuck this," she mutters to herself, and using both fists, pounds on the door. She isn't sure where this surge of energy is coming from, except that she's been feeling angry on and off for days now, which isn't something she's used to. Sure, she's familiar with political rage, but that's more like a dog's bark—you use it to try to say something, and you don't know if anyone hears you. This rage, though, this is the bite. For a moment, the shows she used to go to and mosh in when she was in high school flash in her mind. She should get back into punk.

"You know the rules, Bill," someone is shouting from inside the house, his voice growing closer. "You can't come in after curfew!" Maggie can see the shadow of a head behind the small pane of frosted glass at the top of the door. "Go to Natasha's and sleep there, fuckhead!" the man inside yells.

"I'M NOT BILL," Maggie bellows through the door. Her fists are clenched, and the door swings open.

"Oh shit, you're not. Who're you?" the man asks. He's white, very red-faced and puffy-looking, of indeterminate age, with a shaved head and sparse eyebrows. A second, brown man walks up behind him, a gold hoop glinting in one earlobe, who looks to be in his early twenties.

A third man approaches behind them. He's tall, older, and, Maggie assumes, of East Asian descent, with a full head of the kind of exquisite gray hair she dreams of having when she gets to be his age. He gently nudges the other two and they move to let him through. "Hello," he says. "What can I do for you this evening?"

"Uh." Maggie is confused now. She isn't sure how these three men are connected to one another but it seems clear that this one is in charge. "Does Karl Jelen live here?"

"Who?" the red-faced guy says. His tone is insufferably rude, even though he's only uttered the one syllable. The gray-haired man in front glances at the speaker and then back at Maggie.

"May I ask why you're looking for him?" he asks.

"I, uh, I'd rather discuss that with him," she says.

"Fellas," the man says, turning to the two behind him. "Go back to the TV room, please. Or wherever, okay?"

"'Kay," the rude one says. The other dude follows without a word but first he turns to Maggie and winks at her. She has no idea why. The man still in the doorway looks after them for a moment then steps outside to the foyer and pulls the door almost shut behind him.

"I'm sorry to have to tell you this," he says quietly. "Karl used to live here and be employed here, but I'm afraid he died about a year ago."

Of all the obstacles she's considered running into, Maggie hasn't thought of this one yet. She assumes Harold is old if he's in a nursing home, but she hasn't thought anyone else would or could be dead. Isn't sixties young to die? Iris died young, everyone at the funeral said so, people at the shiva uttered things of that nature. That's assuming all the men are around Iris's age, though both Abe and Liam seemed a bit younger. She tries to bring herself back to the present.

"Okay, uh, so—" And something about the man's open face and demeanor, the careful way he watched after the others like he was a papa goose and they were his goslings, has her spilling out a brief version of the story. She tells him about Iris's death and the letters and how there's one for Karl.

"That sounds very difficult," the man says. She still doesn't know his name. "I'm so sorry for your loss."

"You said Karl was employed here?" Maggie asks.

"Yes. This . . . well, I shouldn't be telling you, but it sounds like you're really here only about Karl. This is a sober living facility. We don't advertise the fact to our neighbors, though I'm sure most of them have figured it out by now. We like to keep the place anonymous and homey. Anyway, I knew Karl for a long time. We both landed here at difficult parts of our lives, a few years ago, and we both began working here afterward in different capacities. Karl became a live-in manager a few years ago. When he died, they hired me for the same position." The man wipes his eyes, and Maggie recognizes that he is also grieving.

"How did he die?" she asks, though she probably shouldn't.

"Overdose," he says, and shrugs. "It happens. Anyway. I better get back inside. I'm sorry not to be of more help, miss."

"Maggie," she says. "What's your name?" It feels inconceivable, to see a person cry and not know their name.

"Thomas," he says.

"Thanks, Thomas."

"Good night, Maggie," he says.

As she walks back to her car, a white man reeking of booze passes her without a second glance and begins pounding on the door. She wonders if he's the Bill who's supposed to go sleep at Natasha's.

SHE SHOWERS AT the motel, using the entire tiny bottle of shampoo on her hair just so she can run her fingers through it until she feels relaxed. The showerhead has two settings, one that's meant to give a massage effect, and though it spurts badly from the sides, she lets the concentrated stream relieve her lower back muscles, aching from so much sitting still and driving.

By the time she's out, she's gotten a second wind and rolls a fat joint on the room's empty desk to take outside. She stands, smoking, looking at the neon sign for a strip club flickering across the street. It's called Cherry's, which makes her think of small-town diners or beauty salons. The Y keeps flickering out, making it look like a misspelled CHEERS. Slowly, she thinks about the decision she has to make. The Y going in and out doesn't help. She smokes the joint too fast and watches the Y tell her yes when it's lit, then no when it goes out, then yes, no, yes, no. When it sticks in the on position for longer than three seconds, she hurries inside, so she doesn't see it go off again.

The letter. The letter for a man, another man Maggie and Ariel and Peter know nothing about but who gets to have a missive from Iris while they don't. A letter to a man who is dead. Surely, if she can open any of them, this is the one. She can't imagine trying to track down the guy's next of kin, whoever that is. Would they know about Iris? Would they want the letter meant for their father, uncle, brother, cousin? Maybe they would. But Thomas didn't ask to have it, or tell her anything about Karl's family, and she can't bring herself to care enough. Abe and Liam made it seem like their relationships with Iris—which, Maggie realized during her drive from Vegas, didn't overlap—were quite private, even secretive in Abe's case. Maybe the same can be said for Karl. If, when she reads the letter, there is mention of his family, then maybe she'll try to figure out how to find them, or she'll bring the letter back to Thomas for him to deal with.

But damn it, she thinks, if the intended recipient is dead and so is the sender, there's really no harm or foul, is there?

She gets a cup of ice from the machine down the hall to crunch on, a habit she picked up in college to deal with pre-exam nerves. Her freshman RA had recommended it to their entire floor, something about how it was a release of energy that also kept you hydrated. As far as Maggie knows, she's the only one to have taken it seriously.

In the room, she sits cross-legged, leaning on four of the six pillows provided with the bed and places the letter in front of her. Through the wall behind her, she can hear the murmurs of a TV. She wiggles her toes. Cracks her knuckles. Puts another ice cube in her mouth. Feels overly dramatic, and picks up the letter. Her jeans are twisted on the floor beside the bed and she doesn't feel like moving again, so instead of using her knife as a letter opener, she uses her pinkie to get under the envelope flap and begins to yank up. The envelope tears unevenly, destroying the neatly printed address on the front.

Her hands shake as she removes the handwritten pages from the envelope and unfolds them.

Dear Karl,

I hope you read this far in the future, and that you look back from your flying car à la the Jetsons and think of how young—relatively— and naive we were when we first met. You might wonder how I found you—well, you approved me on LinkedIn a couple years ago (I wondered then if you'd even noticed it was me. I know I just usually say okay to all those requests because why not!) and I saw you were working at Hearth Sober Living in LA, and I was so proud of you.

Maybe that's a strange thing for me to say. Nevertheless, it's true.

You may be wondering also why you have received this letter from me. Well, I'm sorry to be the bearer of bad news, Karl, but if you have gotten this letter, it means I have died. I wanted to leave some letters to people who mattered to me very much over the years—people I also might have hurt. You are one of those people, obviously.

Maybe you're old and senile by now, so let me remind you of some things:

1. You asked me out first. You saw my wedding ring and you asked me out anyway. I don't always wear my wedding ring (my finger was getting fat even back then!) but I did that day we met. Can you believe it was 24 years ago? Almost a quarter of a century! I don't know why I said yes when you asked.

2. I'm glad I did. Never forget that, Karl.

3. I think my favorite memory with you is the night we hiked in Griffith Park and watched the sunset and the twinkling lights that came on (they say it's pollution, but I still think it's pretty magical!). We kissed a lot like we were in a movie, remember? It was one of the only nights you weren't high. Or maybe you were and I didn't notice? It took me a long time to understand and notice.

4. I found an old photo booth strip of us a while ago. I think we took it on the pier? Anyway. We looked so '90s! I can't believe my hair used to look like that. Pushed up and big like that. Fashion changes so fast. We all looked like fools in the '90s and the kids today know it too! In the photo strip you're dressed kind of piratey. I don't remember why, though. Was that when you were doing the living statue thing in Hollywood or maybe it was Halloween or you were having one of your days?

5. I will never forget the night we did heroin together. Never, ever, ever. I still dream about it sometimes.

6. I will also never forget the time you stole my pearl necklace, the one my husband gave me, and sold it for more. That was when I knew I'd lost you completely.

You know all this, though. If you're still remembering things, I think you will remember me. But maybe you won't, or not very well. A couple times after we were over I went to Al-Anon meetings and this girl, she was maybe nineteen or twenty, very young to be dealing with that sort of thing, said that it was hard to wait for people to make amends because sometimes they didn't remember what they needed to make amends for, and if you told them how they hurt you, they'd only feel bad about it and then you'd feel worse about yourself. Other people said a lot of very nice things about self-love and accepting and all that crap about God not giving you more than you can handle. I don't know about all that. I just liked how honest that girl was about how complicated it all is.

I'm not going to tell you how you hurt me, Karl. But I know I hurt you too. You wanted to know things about me, and I couldn't tell you. I'm realizing now that my privacy, the way I tried to protect both you and myself was really more self-serving than anything else. I wanted to keep you in a special little pocket of my life. A private space that was nobody else's but mine. Maybe that was cruel? I don't know! I'm not going to apologize either, though, because what happened happened and apologies twenty-two years after the fact don't help anyone, do they?

Apologies are overrated, anyway, I think. I don't know who they're for. Maybe this is an excuse for why I haven't apologized much in my life? Maybe something to talk to my shrink about! Just kidding—I'm not seeing a shrink anymore (I did once, though, and I think he would be proud of me now).

I will tell you something of my life, though, just a few things that I guess I wish I had told you over the years. I think about you, even though it's been so long. You introduced me to many things I never could have imagined before (I'm sure you remember some of that! I think the kids today would add a winky face here, right?). Anyway, here are some things about my life:

1. I am still married to Peter. He makes me very happy most of the time, which is, I think, the most any of us can expect of another person.

2. I am still a corporate witch—remember when you called me that? I think for a while I wanted to put that on my business cards!

3. My daughter is now a beautiful twenty-five-year-old. She works as an insurance agent, and she is apparently very good at it. I'll be honest, I don't understand much about her job, but I am glad that she likes it and is enjoying herself. I worry about her, but she's also my

biggest success. She is very independent (a lot like me?) and strong-willed (like Peter! But in a very different way—Peter is a patient mule; she's a hardheaded rhino sometimes!). She is also gay. For a long time, I felt very conflicted about this. I was, I'll be honest, disappointed. I remember what you told me about your brother, you see, and how he didn't make it. And I confess, that was something I kept thinking about for a long, long time. I was so scared for her, Karl. But things are changing, or they have changed, I guess, and I think I'm finally changing too. I don't understand her, exactly. But I love her, and I am doing my best, finally, to be better.

4. I had another child in 1996. He is not yours! I found out a few months after you stole my necklace, after we ended. That's when I went to a shrink, you know. I worried I was having a second child at least partly to prevent myself from going back to you. I knew I couldn't arrive on your doorstep pregnant, or with a squalling infant. But with the help of my shrink, I figured out the opposite was true, really. I wanted to make sure that what I had with Peter was as sustainable as I thought. And it was. It is. (Also, it was about my mother, but I suppose everything is, in some way or another, about our parents, isn't it?)

5. I have had other relationships like the kind I had with you. I just want you to know this, because I remember a couple times you started beating yourself up about what a bad person you were for seducing me. It was always my choice to be where I was.

6. I never told you at the time, because I didn't think it was something I was allowed to feel and because I didn't think you meant it when you said it. But I did love you, in the way that I could. And I am so glad you finally got clean and well. You deserve nothing but happiness, and I hope you have had that in your life.

Fondly, full of memories and few regrets,

Iris

W hen she finishes reading the letter for the second time, Maggie puts it aside, drained. She started crying several times during both the first and second readings, and each time she'd put the letter facedown on her chest, waiting until she could compose herself, trying to savor the scant pages of her mother's handwriting. She doesn't think she's seen a full letter from her mother since the last long birthday card, on Maggie's thirteenth. After that, Iris always got her joke cards with puns, or the kind that sang whenever you opened it. *Why didn't you leave words for us too, Mom?* Maggie thinks again, rubbing the amber pendant on the necklace, which she put on again after she showered. She likes its delicate weight on her chest, the way it feels warm when she fondles it. *Did you think you had more time? Did you just procrastinate on ours?* After all, the letter to Karl is dated years ago—maybe her mother just never got around to it. It's a comforting thought, but also feels too easy.

Maggie has a million questions after this letter, and she'll never be able to ask them, let alone get answers. Heroin? It's hard to picture Iris's sensitive skin, pinkened so quickly by the sun, resting under the shadow of a needle.

Maybe they smoked it? Allison's cousin smokes it, which Allison always implies is a safer option, though Maggie doesn't know if that's true. What is certain, though, is that heroin is one of the few drugs Maggie has never had even the slightest desire to try—it evokes too strongly the terrors of D.A.R.E. talks at school.

Her mother, in other words, experienced this thing that Maggie never has. Of course, she knows her mother went through a whole life full of things that are unknowable to Maggie, who can barely believe there was a time when people didn't wear seat belts in their cars. But this is different. This is something that, like Liam being part of Iris's life, seems more on brand for Maggie.

But besides the actual drug itself, the idea that her mother could date someone with a substance use disorder without judging him the entire time seems impossible. When Maggie was arrested when she was seventeen, Iris had refused to bail her out that night. She'd waited until morning, making Maggie sit in lockup with a few sex workers, a homeless woman the police didn't know what to do with, and two other teenage girls who whispered to each other like the popular kids in school did and wouldn't talk to anyone else. Maggie had been separated from the guys she was smoking with when they got caught, Anthony and Kyle and some friend of theirs who insisted they call him Buzz, but she saw their parents collecting them, hurrying them out of the station as if they could catch criminal element cooties.

That night, Maggie had learned a few things about herself, and in hindsight, she thinks Iris made the right decision—and maybe, she thinks, Karl is the reason for it. Maggie learned that she was terrified of the concept of being in prison. She learned that she was incredibly spoiled, lucky, and privileged. More than either of these things, she also learned that she was capable of letting go. Yes, she'd been scared, and had felt small next to the sex workers talking about day care and alimony and bad men and worse women—"They call themselves sisters but they snakes," one of them had said, and the words still reverberate in Maggie's head whenever she sees women advocating for making abortion illegal. But Maggie had also listened, settling herself against a wall with her knees curled to her chest. She kept her eyes open for as long as she could, but she did fall asleep, eventually, her head on her knees, hands gripping elbows tightly. If she'd had to, she could have survived confinement for longer. She hopes she never needs to, and knows statistically speaking, her chances are low, despite her constant illegal weed smoking. She's white, after all. Jewish-ish, queer, yes, but still white.

Maggie stares at the ceiling, reliving the tense silence Iris had treated her with for half the car ride home once she'd picked her up before exploding into a lecture whose words were less important than her tone. She'd never yelled at Maggie quite like that, with an edge of hysteria in her voice.

Yes, maybe this, him, Karl—maybe he's why.

If only that were the worst of it, Maggie thinks, curling up on her side and switching off the bedside light. If only she didn't now need to make a decision about whether to tell Ariel that there's a chance her father isn't his father. Iris said he wasn't Karl's—but did she know for sure? If there was reason for Karl to suspect the timeline—and clearly, there was, otherwise Iris wouldn't have made a point of saying that, would she?—then there was reason for Maggie to suspect it too. Iris had been lying to her family for years about the extensiveness of her work trips—last-minute additions to her schedule, often away on weekends, missing parts of Maggie and Ariel's winter and summer holidays from school . . . Maggie had always accepted her mother's apologies, her insistence on the necessity of her schedule. It was normal, really—she doesn't remember a time her mother wasn't always coming and going, except during those six months when Peter was taking care of his father.

She pulls her phone off the side table and its bright screen makes the room eerily glow around it as she asks Google whether it's possible to test DNA without participant consent. The first result—"Can I Do a Secret Paternity Test Without Mom, Dad, or Child Knowing?"—includes an image of a manicured finger held up to bland white-girl lips pursed in a hushing sound. She puts her phone back down. She doesn't want to know if it's possible, because she's pretty certain it's deeply unethical. She'll have to think about that more tomorrow.

If she breathes in slowly and calmly, she thinks she'll be able to fall asleep, and maybe she'll even be able to acknowledge what Iris wrote about her—about her coming out, about her own biases, about Karl's brother who "didn't make it." What does that even mean, Maggie wonders: A hate crime? Suicide? AIDS-related complications? Maggie knows the treatment in the early nineties wasn't as good as it is today, and death was more common.

And what about the other line—she can't help it, she unfolds the letter and finds it again, using her phone's flashlight—"she's also my biggest success, I think." It seems too good to be true and, even if true, it's unfair to Ariel, who always seemed to have such an easier time with Iris. Is Maggie really so selfish and horribly shallow as to forgive Iris just because she said something nice about her for once? And besides, her mother never told her any of this, and Maggie wasn't supposed to see this letter, so does it even count? No, she thinks, she can't forgive Iris, not for any of it. That would mean betraying Peter. Peter who fed her and Ariel, clothed them, helped her buy her first pads because her mother was out of town when she got her period. Peter who has never said one thing against her identity, who hasn't hinted around asking about male suitors or asked pointed questions about the rates of mental illness, incarceration, and drug use in children who grow up without fathers. That one always hurt worst, because procreation was something she hadn't even decided whether she wanted for herself before Iris began implanting those fears in her. Maggie has always known that kids raised by two moms are fine, and she can back up that certainty with all the studies she wants—and she has, on sleepless nights, after bad phone calls with her mom—but she's never yet been able to shake away the fear of the tiny chance Iris was right.

Pain blossoms in her forehead and she realizes she's been furrowing her eyebrows so hard that the muscles ache. She tries to smooth her brow by pushing her fingers down to feel that there are no ridges, but it still hurts. She wraps her arms around herself and begins counting her breaths, waiting for that moment of liminality that she sometimes remembers the next day when, not quite awake nor quite asleep, she can physically sense the nerves shutting themselves off from her brain's grasping fingers.

AUGUST 28, 2017

She sleeps hard and deep, her dreams a jumbled mess that keep pulling her back whenever she begins to wake up. She oversleeps her alarms, turning them off in gummy half-consciousness before sinking back into slumber. When she finally wakes, it's with the feeling that she's been running from or to something again. Images of the dream she was having—Iris's presence, but not her face, long hallways lined with hotel rooms, a lost backpack—seep away as she rubs her eyes and checks the time. Almost eleven already. "Shit," she says, and jumps out of bed, frantic, the tatters of the dream dissipating completely. She doesn't want to pay for another day at the hotel if she doesn't have to.

She checks out in the nick of time, and then sits in the lobby with a cup of tea—the coffee from the complimentary breakfast has already been taken away, but there's still a hot water dispenser and tea bags—and waits for it to cool. She texts Allison a brief update on what's going on, but she's probably at work and not checking messages. But should she tell Lucia? She's not sure she should—what if she doesn't like how Lucia responds again? Maybe she should take more time, figure out what to think and feel before sharing this.

But, Maggie thinks, all this time she thought her parents' marriage was so perfect, that she could never do what they did, have what they have. It was a lie all along, at least on Iris's side—she wasn't being loyal, she wasn't being the perfect wife, she was being selfish and greedy and grasping. So why should Maggie look up to this sham of a marriage anymore, anyway? No, she decides, she's done with that. Lucia's always saying that good relationships—of any kind—require trust and communication. If Lucia gets sick of her or her neediness or her complaints about her mother, it's her job to communicate that. And it's Maggie's job to trust that she will, and to take in Lucia's honestly expressed opinions, and to deal with conflict rather than spend her time trying to prevent it.

With that decision, she messages an update to Lucia too, along with another heart emoji and an I miss u, bb, so much. After a long minute of staring, waiting to see if Lucia will start typing back, Maggie closes the app and makes herself take a deep breath with her eyes closed. *Trust her,* she tells herself, *and try to chill for fuck's sake.*

When she opens her eyes, she texts Ariel, Hows dad? but he doesn't answer right away either. He'd let her know if anything got worse with Peter, she assumes. She hopes.

She checks social media. Her selfie on Instagram from a few days ago has garnered more than two hundred likes. Because her mother is dead? Or because she looked good? Probably the former. Some of the latter. The combination of both is probably what it really is. Tragedy and sex appeal go together.

Finally, Maggie gets back into the car and plugs in the address of Drake & Cardinal, which she assumes is this Eric Baishan's workplace. It's in Brentwood, about a twenty-minute drive away, if there isn't traffic, which of course there will be.

When she switches on KPCC, she catches the tail end of a story about

Hurricane Harvey and the displaced families in Texas. She wonders idly why they always talk about families. Where are all the single people who live alone? Or those with roommates and pets and plants for company? Are they spared the torrent of nature just because they don't have children? Or do they deserve to be forgotten and left out for the same reason?

Traffic is as horrible as she anticipates, though apparently because of an accident rather than the usual LA problem—which is just that too many people have cars—so she tries calling Ariel. He picks up, groggy.

"Hey. When—never mind."

A rush of warmth toward Ariel rises up in her. He's trying so hard to hold it together. Bless him, she thinks. She should be nicer. "Tonight," she says quickly. "I'm coming home tonight. Today. Whenever I can. I have one more errand to run and then I'm there. How's Dad?"

"He's gotten bored with Jonathan Kellerman and is firmly in P. D. James territory now."

"That means literally nothing to me," she says.

"Oh, um, he's gone from psychological thriller to literary mystery," Ariel says. One thing she'll never have is Ariel's connection to Iris's mind through books. She can almost see him rubbing his eyes as he yawns, his silly face with its narrow nose and ears that look a little bent at the top. Being a big sister hasn't always been particularly important to her, but it certainly reminds her of the passing of time. She's known this person since he was born. Since the literal day of his birth, when Maggie's grandparents were still alive and took care of her during the day and took her to the hospital in the evening to meet her new baby brother. She was so disappointed that he just slept the whole time she was visiting that she told Iris she'd never share her toys because he wouldn't know what to do with them. The next time she'll know someone else from the day of their birth like this will be when one of her friends has a kid, or when Ariel does, she thinks— because even if she does end up wanting one herself, she knows it won't be anytime soon.

"What are you doing today?" Maggie asks, trying to get her mind away from mothers.

"Nothing much. Waiting around to see if people show up. Oh, Mom's assistant came by day before yesterday She said she's, like, keeping the ship afloat but that she needs to talk to Dad about what's going to happen next. He was sleeping again so I told her we'll figure it out next week or something."

Maggie realizes she hasn't thought about this at all. Not for a moment. What's going to happen to all of Iris's clients? Are they pissed off that she's dead, that she's not doing the work for them that needs to get done? Do they even know? Did Anya have to tell them? She can't imagine how weird that would be, to have your boss die like that, to have to pick up the slack. "That's good," she tells Ariel. "Next week is good."

"Yeah," he says. Also, some people you knew in high school came yesterday? One of them was that girl I had a crush on when I was in fifth grade. I pretended I remembered her name when I saw her but honestly I always used to think of her as Maggie's Pretty Friend. But it's something with a D?"

"Daphne?" Maggie's voice breaks in a squeak and she starts laughing. "Fuck, I haven't thought about her in years." Daphne was the first girl Maggie kissed. It started during a game of truth or dare, but after that she and Daphne would sometimes hide away and make out, though they never planned it or talked about it, really. Maggie thought she was in love, and that maybe Daphne loved her too. Until the day Daphne's twin brother, who also went to their school, walked in on them in the band room and called Daphne a dirty dyke and said he'd tell their parents. Daphne refused to talk to her after that. "I never knew you had a crush on her. Good taste, little brother."

There's a rushing sound and a thunk of plastic on glass; he must be putting coffee on. "Don't you remember I always tried to hang out with you? You were such a bitch to me."

"I'm sure I was."

"Anyway, she's super nice now, she's like a mom and shit, brought her baby with her and everything. Her husband is this dude who looks like he lives at the gym or is a drill sergeant or something. So weird. Anyway, she said she'd come back tomorrow for a bit, in case you're here by then."

"Awesome, I will be. I promise," Maggie says. The traffic opens up, finally, and her foot presses down on the pedal, merging with the faster current of cars.

"Mags, um, don't get pissed, okay?"

"Sure," she says, but she's distracted, looking in her mirrors. Drivers in LA are crazy, she thinks as a BMW zigs out from behind a trailer to her right and narrowly misses hitting her as it goes into the lane on her left in order to pass her.

"I didn't want to ask because, uh, I dunno, but did you find out what the deal is with those letters?"

"What? Ariel, you're breaking up, look, I'm driving, I'll text you when I'm heading home, okay?"

"Okay," he says, and hangs up.

He wasn't breaking up, and Maggie can certainly drive and talk because she's done it plenty of times before. She just doesn't know what to say. What to tell him. He has a right to know. She doesn't want to do it over the phone, though, that's for sure.

But he also has a right to choose whether he wants to know, doesn't he? It's not as if Iris meant to tell them any of this, clearly. She probably just thought Peter would stick the letters in the mailbox without question. Damn, that's cold, Maggie thinks. *Mom, really? You set up your husband, the father of your goddamn children, to send letters to the men you fucked behind his back?* She remembers Liam called her mother classy and snorts, her arms and chest and face getting hot. This is the unclassiest move she's ever heard of.

She gets off at the exit her phone indicates, and spends the next half hour trying to find parking that isn't a flat rate of $20—she's been spending a lot the past few days, much more than she usually does in this span of time, and though she knows she's going to be okay, she doesn't see any reason to push it. But eventually, she gives up, parks in the too-expensive lot, and walks the long block to the chic, clearly refurbished white building where DRAKE & CARDINAL is emblazoned in small tasteful gold letters on the tinted window. She pulls at the glass door, also tinted, but it's locked. She looks up and sees a camera pointed at her. High security, that's interesting, she thinks. She finds the discreet buzzer to the left of the door and presses it.

"Drake and Cardinal," a cool voice says. "Who are you here to see?"

"Eric Baishan? Bayshan?" Maggie isn't sure she's pronouncing it correctly.

"One moment, please."

Maggie waits. Eventually, a clicking sound comes from the door and she pulls it open.

Inside, the place looks more like a spa than an agency. Tall plants stand in the corners, white couches line the walls and glass coffee tables are stacked with glossy magazines, large art books, and celebrity memoirs. A woman who looks like she's emerged from one of the magazine covers sits at a white desk in the center, in front of an elevator whose doors are tinted rose gold. She looks at Maggie expectantly, like a principal at school waiting for a student to come closer.

"Hi," Maggie says. "Can I please talk to Eric Baishan? I have something to deliver to him."

"There is no one by that name here," the woman says. Her tone is bland, her hands are folded in front of her on the desk, and the space is so free of clutter that Maggie wonders what she actually does all day. Maggie thinks she's going to say something else, but she doesn't. She just looks up at her, fake eyelashes blinking slowly. It's like being stared at by a Stepford wife.

"Well, I have a letter addressed to him here," Maggie says.

"May I ask how you know this person you think is located here?" the woman asks.

"I don't, exactly. My mother did. She died a few days ago, and she knew him, and she left a letter for him. She wanted me to hand-deliver it," Maggie adds, inventing.

"Like I said, there is no one by that name here," the woman says, the tiniest expression coming into her face. "I can give it to one of our attorneys, though," she adds, and holds her hand out expectantly.

Maggie isn't sure what's going on, but clearly the woman knows who this Eric dude is, and either he's one of the lawyers or it's his attorney who works here, not him. "No, I need to find him and give it to him and only him. Like I said, it was my mother's dying wish." She stresses the last two words, hoping for sympathy. Hoping to get this over with. This conversation, this search, this—all of it. "Maybe you can give me his address?"

The woman seems uncertain as to what to do in the face of this tragic story Maggie is telling her. But she knows her lines. "We don't give out clients' addresses, ma'am," she says firmly.

"Okay, so he's a client, see, we're getting somewhere," Maggie says, and the woman has a full-on expression, her hand flying to her mouth in mortification of the precious information she's given away. Maggie turns on as much of her bitchy, customer service, let-me-tell-you-something tone as she can, the same one Iris used to use with the people trying to sell her more internet or cable services, and says slowly, "How about you just call him, how would that be? Or his lawyer, hmm? Maybe if you tell him whose daughter I am he'll agree to see me, okay?"

"Take a seat." The woman won't raise her eyes now.

There's no seat in front of the desk, which puts Maggie in the awkward position of needing to walk over to one of the sofas and sit there, twenty feet from the receptionist, as the woman puts a delicate blue headset over her curly, wet-look blond hair and presses buttons on her phone. She cups the mic of her headset in a hand and murmurs into it so that Maggie can't catch the words. Then the woman takes the headset off, and without glancing at Maggie, turns to her computer screen.

When a couple more minutes go by with no sound other than the occasional clicking of the receptionist's mouse, Maggie decides to speak up. "So, uh, what's the verdict?"

The woman is back to neutral. "He's coming," she says. Maggie doesn't know if she means Eric or his attorney, but she decides not to ask. The receptionist reminds her of the worst of the girls she went to school with. The kind who have a power she's never understood, this apparently feminine ability to be entirely disdainful of all women who don't have their level of normative beauty. Maggie feels infinitely small beside her, even though the woman is physically tiny all over, short and slim, with a button nose and a pursed mouth.

While she waits, Maggie opens the message Gavin sent her. It's so him, so carefully worded and thoughtful, and her breath catches when she reaches the last part:

> Allow yourself to feel whatever it is you're feeling, if you can. Grief isn't uniform. Everyone goes through it differently. I think people judge themselves for how they perform their grief, or don't, and the thing is, it's hard enough without adding guilt. If you're angry, be angry. If you're sad, be sad. If you're giggling and euphoric for being alive, that's okay too. And if you vacillate between those and a hundred other emotions? That's okay. You're allowed. And I'm here. And I love you.

Maggie leans her head back on the wall and opens her eyes wide, trying to dry them out. She doesn't want any tears escaping in this cold room. When she's gotten herself under control, she starts writing back to Gavin, thanking him, ending with, Want to talk sometime soon? I miss you. I have so much to tell you.

She begins to erase that last sentence, but then retypes it and hits send.

Finally, the elevator doors hush open and a tall, square-built white man in a navy-blue suit with no tie comes out.

"Mr. Miller," the receptionist says, smiling brightly. Maggie wonders if she's just a kiss ass, or whether this man might, against all odds, be a good boss. "This is the person I mentioned." She points at Maggie, as if Maggie isn't the only other person in the room.

"Thanks, Crystal," Mr. Miller says. He walks up to Maggie and holds out his hand. She jumps up to shake. "What's your name, honey?" he asks.

Her spine shivers at the endearment, but she returns his handshake firmly, gripping a little tighter than necessary. "Margaret Krause," she says, hoping this version of her name sounds less childish and more like someone who shouldn't be fucked with.

"Wonderful, Margaret, how about you come on upstairs with me?"

"Sure," she says, though the man gives her the creeps. In the elevator, he pulls his phone out and taps at it fervidly, not glancing up at her once. So she glances at her own—Lucia has answered. Come home to me bb, soon?

Maggie's cheeks warm, the request infusing her with courage, but she doesn't have time to respond before the doors open onto a foyer that looks like a bad set for a film taking place in Japan. Tatami mats layer the floor, and the office doors aren't actually paper and bamboo but painted to look like it. She winces to see Mr. Miller walking across the mats in his shoes, feels the need to take her own off. The whole place makes her feel icky, discomfited by its strange design appropriation.

He slides one of the doors open and gestures for her to come in. The inside looks like a mix of the downstairs lobby and the foyer: more tatami mat flooring but the desk is broad and glass and the chairs heavy leather. It looks awful, she thinks, but maybe this is what wealth looks like to some people.

"Now," he says, sitting behind the desk. "Tell me your little story again?"

Maggie bristles, and rather than taking a seat in one of the low chairs facing Mr. Miller's desk, she stays standing in the middle of the room. She wants to be able to flee if she needs to. She breathes through her nose, slowly, trying to keep hold on her temper. "It's not a story. It's the truth. My mother, Iris Krause, passed away the night of August twentieth. She left letters for several people. One of them is Eric Baishan. She wanted me to deliver it to him in person."

"See, here's the trouble I'm having, honey," Mr. Miller says. He looks utterly at ease, leaning back in his big leather chair, twirling a pen between his fingers. "That name is the trouble. You see, very few people know that name these days. And the ones who do are usually close personal friends, or people who work here and who know they will be sued to Timbuktu if they break their NDAs, or scam artists who dug up some records and are trying to get money. Now, you admit to not knowing the man. You don't work here. So what's your scam? What are you trying to get from him?"

"I don't know what you mean or who this dude is," Maggie says, her tone slipping away from politeness now. "I just know that my mom knew him and I want to meet him and give him his fucking letter."

Mr. Miller turns his chair toward the large window that looks out on a lush, wasteful garden hidden in a walled courtyard. "Let's say I believe you," he says. There's a thwacking sound; Maggie thinks he must be tapping his pen on one of the chair's armrests. "Even if I do, the trouble is that the man you're looking for isn't someone who I can simply summon here. But, you know," he swivels back around, grinning wolfishly, "let's see what I can do for you."

He seems so amused that Maggie feels like something terrible is about to happen, but he just turns to his computer and beckons her closer with a large hand. His knuckles look swollen. She approaches the desk and sits gingerly at the edge of a chair.

He clicks something on the computer, and the telltale musical tones of a video-chat program start ringing loudly from surround-sound speakers hung around the room.

A deep, oddly familiar voice replaces the tone. "Let's get this over with."

"Nice to see you too," Mr. Miller says to the person on the screen. Maggie can't see him, whoever he is.

"What's so damn important." Why does Maggie know that voice? Its deep timbre, the almost Southern linger over some vowels.

"There's a young lady with me here, and—"

"Fuck you, Jeff. I don't need a consolation prize, and I don't need a working girl getting in my business."

Mr. Miller flicks his eyes to Maggie and smiles, showing his perfect veneers. "I don't think she'd be interested even if you were," he says, eyes back on the screen. "She says you knew her mother once. What was her name, honey?" he asks Maggie.

"Iris Krause."

Whoever is on the screen is quiet for a while. Mr. Miller says, "Well?"

"That's . . . wow. Her kid's there? Let me talk to her."

"By all means," Mr. Miller says. He turns the screen, with its embedded camera, towards Maggie.

Never before has she considered herself a person who is easily starstruck, but when she sees who's on the screen, the voice slots itself into its rightful place and she finds herself unable to speak for a moment. This man is Mac Lòpez, an actor whose star rose very suddenly a few years ago when he began playing a host of Native American characters on a variety of high-profile, big-budget cable TV shows and giving long interviews about his Oklahoma upbringing, his Apache ancestors on his mother's side and his Spanish and Indigenous roots on his Mexican father's. He talked about his daughter, a servicemember who died in Afghanistan. He was vocally active in the #NoDAPL movement, making appearances at Standing Rock. Just last month, Maggie and Lucia went to see his newest film, a gritty historical drama about Westward Expansion and the Indian Removal Act. It was getting Oscar whispers before it even came out.

"Hi," she says stupidly. She and Lucia cried through the last quarter of the movie and then debated all the way home about a viral tweet that opined that the film, which was written and directed by a white woman, was using the rarely told story of those who refused to walk the Trail of Tears in order to pander to white audiences' thirst for trauma porn. Lucia is going to lose her shit when she finds out Iris slept with Mac Lòpez. Mac Fucking Lòpez. If Iris were alive now, Maggie would be tempted to give her a high five, despite everything—*You had it going on, didn't you, Mom?*

"Wow," Mac says. Or Eric. She isn't sure which is his real name. "You look like her."

"Thanks," she says, uncertain if this is a compliment or not. "Uh, I'm sorry to have to tell you this, but my mom died a few days ago."

He nods, his shoulder-length hair framing his face. He looks older than on the big screen, less smooth-faced, with bags under his eyes. "I'm sorry for your loss," he says after a moment.

"She, um, she left something for you. A letter. She wanted me to give it to you. I guess I can leave it here for you to pick up?" She gestures vaguely at the space she's in, feeling dumb. "Or they can mail it to you, I guess?"

"Sure," he says, shrugging. He doesn't ask her anything else, just gazes, looking a bit sad. She remembers seeing a tabloid headline a couple of weeks ago while in line at the grocery store that his model wife divorced him and took their three-year-old son with her. Maggie dismissed it then, assuming it was a fake story, as so many tabloid pieces appear to be, but now she wonders if maybe he is mourning something too. Maybe it's just his tired eyes that make him look sad, though. Or the quality of the camera, and she's just projecting.

She tries to recall her anger at him, at all these men. "Did you know she had a family when you were fucking her?" she blurts out. Mr. Miller raises his head from his phone and leans forward like he's about to tell her off, but he doesn't get the chance.

"I wasn't," Mac says, and Maggie notes how weird it is to see his lips moving but have the sound coming from around her—just like in the movie theater, she realizes.

"You didn't know she had a family?" she says, trying to focus.

"No, I wasn't fucking her," he says calmly. "And yes, I knew she had a family. She was thinking of sending you to the school my kid went to."

This is a surprise Maggie isn't sure what to do with. "Wait, what?" she says. "But—then—why would she leave you this." She stares at the letter in her hand, feeling confused, deflated.

"She was a good friend for a while," he says. "That's all."

"But," Maggie says. This can't be right. These letters are to the men Iris cheated on Peter with, aren't they? "What do you mean?"

"I need to go now," he says. "Bye." The call disconnects and Maggie is left staring at a white screen with a row of names to one side, several of which she recognizes at a glance as other very famous Hollywood actors.

"Whoops," Mr. Miller says and shifts the screen back. "I guess that's that, huh?"

"Call him again," Maggie says. "I need to know more. This doesn't make sense."

"Sorry, honey, he's a bit temperamental, if he had to go, he had to go."

"Please, just, just try. Please?"

Mr. Miller rolls his eyes but clicks again, and they wait through the ringing until a popping noise tells them no one's answering. "Told you," he said. "Now, you want to leave that letter or what?"

She dithers. "You can't tell me where he lives? Please?"

He laughs. "And let you and every other stalker trying to get to the newly single Mac the Knife? I wish they hadn't given him that nickname, he's already talking about going back to theater." He shakes his head. "No, honey, that's not going to happen."

This is crazy, Maggie thinks. And unsatisfying. At least Abe and Liam told her their story. At least with Karl she saw her mother's side of it. This is like a box she can't open, that has no seams to speak of, but that clearly contains something because it rattles when shaken. She could take the letter with her, open it herself. But that still feels wrong, especially now that she's seen that its intended recipient is real and alive and fucking famous. It feels wrong even though everything her mother has done is worse.

"Fine," she says. "Wait, actually, here—" She reaches for a square of sticky notes and grabs a pen from a jar full of them and scribbles her name, phone number, and email address. She adheres the note to the letter and holds it out to Mr. Miller. He looks a little stunned, as if no one has ever had the audacity to take his stuff without asking. He reaches for the letter and she yanks it back, like a bully pulling a prank. "You promise promise promise he'll get this?" she asks. She hopes Mac, or Eric, has a change of heart, that he'll contact her eventually.

Mr. Miller grins. "Well, I can promise, but you're not going to believe me anyway, are you? You think I'm the big, bad corporate man, but you either have to take my word for it, or leave here with that letter knowing Mac will never get it." This fucker loves to hear himself talk, Maggie thinks. He still creeps her out. She doesn't know why he's played along with any of this. Maybe he's just bored. He plucks the envelope out of her hand. "I'm your best shot."

"I guess," she says.

"For what it's worth, he's not a bad guy," Mr. Miller adds.

Maggie has no idea what that means, coming from this big, bad corporate man, as he conveniently labeled himself. She nods once, and leaves.

IRIS

MARCH 2, 2002

I can't believe we're starting another war," Iris said, fiddling with her necklace. The newspapers and radio that morning had been full of the American invasion of Afghanistan, and Iris was still rattled. Everyone was, after September 11, at how quickly things were changing, shifting, the government's paranoia and warmongering not yet clear to most.

Eric, sitting across from her at a table in the Pho Lantern Cafe in Costa Mesa, nodded. "Tell me about it."

Iris had met him just a few months ago, when she and Peter were trying to decide which high school to send Maggie to. She had a year to go in junior high, but there were waitlists at a couple of the private schools. They were almost sure they were going to go public in the end, but they'd consulted with some parents of other kids in her class who had older children whom they'd sent to private school. One of those parents introduced her and Peter to Eric, whose daughter had just graduated high school and gone into basic training for the air force. Iris knew he must be worried sick about her, about where they might send her now.

The waitress came over to their table and asked if they were ready. "Can I have the vegetable pho, please?" Eric said. "Oh, and what appetizer would you recommend?"

"Our shrimp spring rolls are the best," the waitress said, flashing a grin.

"Then those too, please. Thanks."

"And I'll have the 118, the chicken curry clay pot," Iris said. The waitress poured them both more water and left. "So have you heard from her recently?" Iris asked.

"From Kim? Or Amy?" Eric asked, rueful. He and his wife had gotten divorced not long ago, but hadn't quite let each other go yet. He'd confessed to Iris that they still slept together some nights. The reason they'd gotten divorced was never entirely clear to her, but it reminded her, as other people's marriages falling apart always did, how lucky she was, how utterly blessed, that she had Peter by her side.

"Either, both," she said.

"Kim, no. We've been good since last time. We haven't talked in two weeks. I think I'm really getting over her this time," Eric said, laughing at himself a little.

"That's good!"

"And from Amy, yes, she called this morning, actually. She sounds tougher by the day. Like this grown-up lady. You'll see," he added. "When your kids leave the house, you'll see how they start to sound different." Eric and Iris were the same age, though he looked younger in that way some men did. He'd also married and had his daughter younger than she'd had Maggie. "How about you? How are your kiddies?"

"They're good. Maggie asked me if she was fat the other day, which worried me, but it doesn't seem to be sticking around, so that's good? And Ariel is having a serious train phase. He wants to know everything about them. I'm afraid he's going to become one of those, whatchamacallits, you know, those nutty people who sit around and wait for trains to go by, like in that movie with Ewan McGregor?" Iris snapped her fingers, trying to remember the name.

Eric, ever the film buff, came to the rescue. "*Trainspotting*? Well, it's not always associated with heavy drug use, you know."

They chatted on as the spring rolls arrived, falling into a comfortable silence once the main dishes were served. The food was delicious, piping hot, and best eaten when fresh. They'd first come here with Peter on Eric's suggestion to talk about schools. It was a long drive from Oxnard, but Eric had moved after his divorce and Iris had business nearby, so it wasn't hard to convince Peter to come on out as well. The kids loved nights with the babysitter, because they were rare, and it meant they got to stay up late watching TV.

The three of them had gotten along swimmingly, and Iris wished then that Eric was still married so that they could do this again. She and Peter knew some couples from the kids' schools, but going out with them always felt somehow forced, their lives diverging too much from these people with regular nine-to-fives, or the mothers who stayed home with the kids and the fathers who wore suits to work. Now, whenever Iris was in the area, she'd reach out to Eric and they'd usually go to Pho Lantern because it was so good and because they never felt rushed by the staff when they sat around talking after their meal, sated.

It didn't take her long to realize that she was actually quite all right with Eric's single state. She liked him a whole lot right from the get-go, and soon she was pretty sure she had a crush on him. What drew her to him was that he, like Peter, was creative, a working artist who didn't flaunt his abilities but treated them as a profession and a calling. He was an actor, mostly theater, though he'd played a couple tiny walk-on roles. "Everyone goes on *X-Files* at some point," he'd joked once when she'd asked him about TV. "I got to be the drunk city Injun and Mulder is convinced I've hexed this businessman who got my daughter pregnant because he's found dead with feathers in his mouth. Isn't that nice?" Iris had been rather horrified, but Eric had just laughed at her sputtering, saying that there were some things you grinned and bore and did for the paycheck and exposure and for him, that had been one of them.

When they finished their dinner, they decided to take a walk around the neighborhood before getting back into their separate cars and driving off, Eric home and Iris to her motel. She'd gotten a place closer to Costa Mesa than she really should have; her event was in Anaheim, helping out with a small portion of a larger Disney corporate event. It was an easy job for good money, but she'd have to be up a half hour earlier than she usually would be because of where she'd chosen to stay. She knew she'd done this just to see Eric. Which was stupid, but there it was.

The evening was chilly, and Iris shivered under her thin sweater.

"Here," Eric said, and without asking her he took off his brown leather jacket and swung it around her shoulders, leaving him in just a GOT MILK? T-shirt.

"How gallant," she joked.

He waved her off, embarrassed. "I'm just warm-blooded," he said, but Iris could see the goose bumps rising on his arm.

APRIL 24, 2002

THE NEXT TIME Iris saw Eric was in LA. He'd called her, asking if she wanted to get a meal at a place a friend of his just opened in Studio City. Iris was supposed to help Maggie with a school project that evening, a family tree. She'd been looking forward to sharing with her daughter some of what she knew about her parents and their families. But she'd said yes to Eric immediately, almost without thinking. When she'd hung up, the guilt started to sink in, but she made excuses: she'd had a long week and she deserved to have a night off, Maggie could work on Peter's side of the family tonight, she'd sit with her another time, it wasn't a big deal.

So she told Peter she had last-minute plans and asked if he could possibly help Maggie out and went to get dressed in their room, but he followed her.

"Hey," he said. "What's going on? You promised her. You don't break promises, Iris. That's not like you." He sounded impatient, even upset, and he had reason to be. She and Peter had talked about this years ago, about how they didn't want to be the kind of parents who promised things they couldn't provide. They didn't say *Everything will be okay,* but rather *Let's hope that* or *Odds are that.* They didn't promise to buy things eventually or go places someday, but used *Maybe* and *We'll see.* And they didn't promise to help out with homework or go to a school talent show unless they knew that—barring an emergency—they would absolutely follow through.

Iris pulled her head out of her closet, where she was trying to find a shirt she didn't hate. "What do you mean, what's going on?" She tried to keep her tone light. "I told you. There's a restaurant Eric's friend opened and he wants to show it to me. He's only going to be in LA tonight, so it's a good opportunity . . ." She trailed off. Peter knew her, and while she was a foodie, and the new restaurant featured Sichuan food, which was some of her favorite, she still didn't usually go out impulsively. She planned her life and her schedule carefully, deliberately. And with her job keeping her away so often, she cherished the nights she could spend with her kids. She stood, shirtless, and wondered: what *was* going on with her?

"Love?" Peter said, his voice concerned. He went to her and hugged her naked shoulders.

"I'm sorry," she said. "Let me call Eric and cancel."

"No, it's okay, go," he said. "I know you, my lovely extrovert. You crave people that you can talk to about grown-up things sometimes. I get it."

Iris pushed her head into Peter's chest harder, trying not to cry. He was so good. He never seemed to find homework help boring, which Iris some-times did. He never seemed to need the kind of grown-up time she needed, where she could feel like a woman rather than a mom or an embodiment of a profession. He was too good.

"Thank you," she whispered.

NOVEMBER 8, 2002

THEY WERE TEXTING every night and emailing through the days. Not since the early infatuation with Shlomo had Iris felt this preoccupied. The com-munication was constant to the point where she was beginning to feel dragged down by it, not getting enough sleep, making little and as yet handleable mistakes at work—purple tulips instead of red ones, an error she'd told the client was the florist's fault and told the florist was the client's bad memory; a hall that wasn't set up with the projector that was vitally necessary. She was sure there were others. She was paying and getting paid on time, and so far no one had entirely lost their shit, but she missed her focus.

Nothing had happened between them yet. Neither of them ever ac-knowledged the growing obsession with each other. Once, Eric leaned over their dumplings and chucked her chin and told her she was his best friend. She'd blushed, thinking that he might mean something else. When he put his arm around her outside and they walked down the block that way, en-twined, she was certain of it.

But still, she didn't make the first move. There was something about Eric that prevented it—in person, anyway. He worked as much as she did—auditioning, rehearsing, and performing each seeming like its own distinct job, and he also bartended on the side—which meant they rarely saw one another. But in writing, he was extremely open and vulnerable. He shared his emotional life with her in a way no other man, not even Peter, did: They always talk about the body-image issues women have in this industry, he wrote her one day last month, but men aren't usually allowed to talk about that. Today, during tech, the costume designer told me I had no ass, and that she didn't know what to do with me. I spent an hour staring at workout videos at Blockbuster on my way home, trying to figure out how to get ass definition. I found a bunch of personal trainers in the yellow pages and I'm going to call them tomorrow and find the one who can give me an ass and make an appointment with him. I'm not supposed to care about these things, but I do. She'd wanted to hug him then.

Now she was parking in Boyle Heights in LA, where Eric had recently moved, since he was in a big new production that was paying him a semi-living wage ("I'm still going to be bartending, though, obviously") and the commute had stopped making sense for him. They were going to get lunch and then take a free tour of the Evergreen Cemetery, the oldest one in LA. "It's been around since 1877," he'd told her on the phone, excited. The reason he wanted to go see it was less about its history and more about integrating into the neighborhood. He told her that he always spent his first few months anywhere new making an effort to participate in community events, to show that he wanted to be supportive of it. She'd wanted to kiss him all over when he'd told her that. He was good, she thought over and over again. A good man.

He didn't show up. She waited for fifteen minutes, thirty, an hour. She called him. Repeatedly. She texted. She drove to the cemetery, in case they'd gotten their wires crossed about the plans. The tour group met up and went off without her.

Finally, tired and hungry and pissed, which was better than being worried, she drove home.

SHE NEVER HEARD from him again. It wasn't until years later, when he'd gotten semi-famous and then famous-famous, that she learned that his daughter, Amy, had died in Afghanistan—and that he'd gotten the news on November 8, 2002. She didn't know why he'd decided to cut off contact with her. Perhaps he'd gotten back together with his ex-wife for a while, each of them unable to bear the pain alone. For a long time, she kept emailing him occasionally—angry emails, hurt ones, eventually just once- or twice-a-year check-ins, telling him she hoped he was doing well.

When she sat down to write the letters to those few men she'd loved over the years, the ones she wanted to reassure, to acknowledge the pain she might have caused and explain her feelings, she wrote his without even thinking about it. Of course she'd loved him. Of course.

AUGUST 28, 2017

Maggie calls Lucia in the car on the way back to Oxnard, but Lucia doesn't pick up. So she leaves her a voice message that Lucia will be able to get on her computer. "I miss your voice. This sucks." Then, reminding herself to trust Lucia, and more than that, to trust herself, that she wants to be here, that she doesn't want to sabotage this like she's ruined things in the past, she records another message. "Sorry. I sounded bitchy. I'm not mad, just sad. Okay. Sorry again."

She wants to tell Lucia about the famous man her mother may or may not have slept with. More than that, she wants to be in Lucia's arms, to feel the grip of her flesh and the warm, often orange Tic Tac–tinged breath on her neck. She wants comfort.

When I get home, she decides, *I'll snap Dad out of his shit.* She begins making a list in her head of things to research in order to do this: *How to fix grief; how to snap someone out of mourning; how to make your dad pay attention to the world; how to confront someone about their cheating spouse*; the list goes on and on in her mind as she sits in traffic on the 101.

When it begins to ease and her speed gets back up to seventy, Maggie remembers in a sudden flash a dream that she had last night about Lucia. It's not fully clear, more like a fuzzy photo, and she tries to piece together its story, its context. She's pretty sure Lucia was angry at her in the dream; livid, in fact. Gina was there also. The details slowly emerge:

She was in the playground where she and her friends in high school used to hang out at a lot on weekend nights. There weren't many places to go, after all. It was just her and Gina in the dream, and they were older, the ages they are now. When Lucia arrived, she and Gina started holding hands, and Maggie went up to both of them and kissed them each on the cheek. And that's when Lucia started yelling at her in the dream, using her hands to gesture wildly, chastising Maggie for trying to steal her girlfriend.

Yes, Maggie is pretty sure that's what it was. She smiles. You don't have to be a psychologist to figure out where the dream is coming from. She decides to call Lucia's cell and leave her a message that she'll get when she finally gets her phone back. Maggie will describe the dream to her, the way she and Iris used to do. Those were, she thinks now, some of the least fraught conversations she had with her mom in recent years. They'd speculate, or bullshit really, about what the details of their dreams meant, and Maggie would send Iris funny or weird articles, occasionally memes—often with accompanying explanations—about dream symbolism, to which Iris would reply with smiley faces, WOW!s, hahahaha!s and occasionally a longer missive. These back-and-forths weren't deep in any way, or they didn't seem so to Maggie then, but she wonders what it means that she and Iris communicated by sharing their unconscious minds.

Now Maggie wants Lucia to know she dreams about her, even if it's a twisted, evil version of her—or, rather, a reflection of Maggie herself, probably. But nothing happened with Nelly, she reminds herself, even if it could have. She isn't planning on telling Lucia about Nelly, which might be stupid, but she can't help it—she's still too frightened of losing her to confess to a flirtation. And anyway, Maggie thinks, trying to escape the parallel to Iris she can't unsee, dreaming about someone means you care about them, doesn't it? That you're anxious about them, about what they think of you. That they fit into your life in a way you can't let go of.

In the split second it takes her to glance down at her phone in order to press the microphone button so she can order it to call Lucia, a gunmetal-gray Lexus swoops into her lane to get out from behind a slow sedan. When Maggie looks up, her mouth open, the word "Call—" already uttered, the Lexus is so close to her that she panics and slams on her breaks—her hands, without any conscious decision of her own, turn the wheel left—but there is no more left to go, there is only the concrete barrier between the west-bound and east-bound lanes.

It isn't like people say. Time doesn't slow down. It rushes toward Maggie without pause, and the crash is tremendously loud, the pain excruciating. The airbag inflates. The seat belt cuts into her neck, and her chest slams against it so hard it feels like a ton of stones rather than a strap of fabric. The sounds of cars rushing by outside, a series of honks—these are the last noises Maggie hears before she loses consciousness. Lucia's name is still on her lips.

IRIS

∽

Merry almost Christmas, Mom. Love you. Mhmm. Yes, I'm okay. Really. Yup, bye, bye, say ciao to Papa." Iris waited until she heard her mother click the phone down on her end before beginning to disentangle herself. She had a habit of carrying the landline with the long curly cord around and around the small living room while she talked, pacing, which meant that she inevitably got the cord wrapped around a piece of furniture or, just as likely, around one of her feet. This time, it was twirled three times around her right wrist.

It was a yellow phone, and one of the only cheerful things in this wretched apartment. She wished she could paint it all this color, this bright sunshine color, a crayon color. The furnished one-bedroom otherwise featured dark browns—the couch, the single bookcase—and grayish whites—the tiles, the walls—that made everything look dirty, coated in a layer of soot. At least for her bed she had a light orange coverlet her mother bought her years ago. Shlomo had hated it, so it never went on their bed, which Iris is now grateful for, because there were so many things she used to love and had left behind when she moved because she couldn't stand the association with him.

There were no Christmas decorations, of course, and no tree, because Iris didn't celebrate the holiday and never had. But she and her parents always tried to talk around that day, because the one thing the culture of Christmas seemed to do right, they thought, was making it an occasion to celebrate family. She'd heard all about her mom's new neighbors, who were very nice even if they did cook smelly food, and her father had told her absentmindedly when forced on the phone by his wife that he loved her and couldn't talk because he was listening to a historic game between the Knicks and the Celtics—he said that about almost every game, though, so Iris didn't take him seriously. She didn't mind hanging up quickly; long-distance calls weren't cheap. Plus, Iris couldn't bear when her mother took that tone she'd started on toward the end of the talk, that concerned and slightly passive aggressive are-you-sure-you're-okay-my-divorcee-daughter-oy-vey-what-did-we-do-wrong tone.

But now she was faced with the emptiness of the depressing apartment. Her neighbors across the hall, two model-slash-actresses, were out of town visiting family. The old man who lived upstairs seemed to have company over because for the first time since she'd moved in almost a year ago, she could hear multiple pairs of shoes walking around above her. There must be a child there, she thought, because there was definitely some jumping happening, and a rhythmic sound like a ball being bounced. She couldn't complain, though—for one, it was Christmas, and for another, the occasion of noise from upstairs was so rare that it would be small of her to take issue with it.

She grabbed her library book from the kitchen table and stuck as much of it as would fit in her purse. She'd made a book-buying celibacy vow, because she was in debt to the lawyer she'd had to hire for the divorce—Shlomo hadn't agreed to give her a get at first, even though he was willing to go through with the civil proceedings, and it wasn't until she strategized with the lawyer into near-blackmail regarding how Shlomo treated her that she'd managed to obtain the damn religious document. She would have left it alone, if her parents hadn't insisted, but they'd convinced her that if she wanted to marry in a Jewish ceremony again, she needed to do this. Meanwhile, Shlomo was supposed to be paying her alimony and wasn't, but she couldn't afford more lawyer time.

Iris locked the apartment behind her and got into her used and rather beaten-up Pontiac. She began driving, not entirely sure where she was going. It was early evening, still light from where the sun was setting behind the mountains. The sky was the exact shade of blue as the word-processing program on the computer she'd used at the synagogue. She hadn't used one since then—too expensive—and was back to her typewriter. But she made do, trying to scrimp and save while she worked to find new clients; Shlomo had managed to badmouth her to every synagogue she'd worked for but one, and thank goodness for her friend Dena who'd defended her so vociferously to the board of Beth-El. Still, the careful network Iris had built had come apart, and she was trying to woo some smaller, newer synagogues and expand to churches. She didn't know yet that her first corporate bite would come soon enough, and that from there her occupation would be pretty much set for years to come.

Ten minutes after she set out, after driving a bit aimlessly and watching families and couples going into other people's decorated houses laden with food or drink, wearing sweaters and Santa hats, she decided where to go.

Gold Dragon was one of the restaurants Iris had been going to since she first moved to Los Angeles with Shlomo all those years ago. It was also, thankfully, free of his taint, since his palate ran toward what he was already familiar with. She hadn't been there in a long time, because she was trying not to eat out, but it was Christmas Eve, which meant indulgence, and the perfect time for a Jew to eat Chinese food. It was a cliché that Iris loved. She'd first heard about the tradition in high school, and she'd dragged her Italian and Polish immigrant parents out to the Lower East Side in

Manhattan, where her friends had told her there was a kosher Chinese place. It was one of the only times Iris had managed to make her parents do anything that broke from their routine.

The restaurant was mostly empty when she got there, only one man waiting to order at the counter. The woman behind it was presumably taking an order over the phone, though she was laughing and smiling and talking as if to an old friend in a tonal language, though Iris couldn't presume to know which.

The man looked behind him when Iris came over and shrugged. "She's been on the phone for a while," he said. He had bright green eyes, a rather thin mouth, and thick, well-shaped eyebrows.

"It's okay, it's Christmas," Iris said.

He seemed to think about this for a moment. His posture straightened, and he smiled. "Yeah. You're right." He turned back to the counter with a nod, and the woman put the phone down a moment later.

"What can I get you, sir?" she asked, her words accented.

Iris thought it sounded beautiful. The man's voice when he ordered the beef egg foo young sounded beautiful too. Everything, she realized, was absolutely lovely, from the wallpaper with its curlicue designs to the red lamps hanging above all the tables to the wafting scent of frying food coming from the kitchen behind the counter. She had no idea where this surge of goodwill and cheer was coming from. Maybe there was something to that Christmas spirit people talked about.

"Ma'am? What can I get you, ma'am?"

Iris glanced down to realize the woman was addressing her now. She'd still been staring up at the paper-covered lantern. "Oh, I'm sorry. Yes, can I have the chicken lo mein, please? To go?" She handed over a couple of dollars, got a nickel back, and chose one of the wooden tables to sit at while she waited. She pulled out her book and opened it, ready to settle back into the main character's world.

"*When the Bough Breaks* by Jonathan Kellerman." She looked up to see the man who'd ordered before her scrutinizing her book. "Is it any good?"

"Yeah," she said, smiled, and went back to reading. She heard a scraping and glanced up to see the man turning his chair a little so he could gaze up at the small muted TV that hung in a corner between wall and ceiling. His face looked worn, though he seemed like he was her age. No, not worn, she thought. Sad. He looked sad.

Her desires warred. On the one hand, she wanted to go to him, chat a bit. He was good-looking, and he'd been pleasant to her, hadn't pressed her for more conversation or gotten touchy. But on the other hand, she wanted peace and quiet and to read her book, get her food, drive home, and watch reruns of whatever show was on TV. Maybe *Three's Company*. She kind of hated it but kind of loved it too. Or there would be a classic holiday movie airing, maybe *A Charlie Brown Christmas*, and she could watch that and cry and get into bed early, read until two in the morning, and try to sleep late tomorrow. Maybe she'd even buy a bottle of wine on the way home to make sure she slept through the night this time; she was still having the nightmares that started once she left Shlomo. Yes, red wine and a movie and a book. It sounded heavenly. Living alone was something she used to be terrified of, the prospect of loneliness somehow worse than tiptoeing around her husband, trying to keep him calm between bouts of fire and fury. It was with some rueful self-flagellation that she'd realized, despite the depressing apartment and the nightmares and the tight budget, that she reveled in the privacy.

But even though she liked her independence now, it didn't look like the man was enjoying being alone as much. He got his food from the counter and sat back down, digging into a bowl of rice as if it were his only lifeline. Iris closed her book and went to his table.

"Mind if I join you?" she asked.

"Hey! You bet!" he said, so eager to agree that he'd pouched his food in one cheek to do so. He resumed his chewing as she sat, smiling.

"So," she said. "Jew?"

He shook his head. "Ex-Catholic," he said. "Very ex."

"Oh," Iris said. "Sorry, it's just. Jews and Chinese food on Christmas. It's a thing."

"It's Christmas Eve," he said, and then smacked himself on the forehead. "I mean. Obviously. You know that. Anyway. So, you're Jewish?"

"I guess," she said. "I mean, yes, I am, but I was married to a rabbi for a while and it . . . wasn't great. So I'm kind of taking a break from religion, I guess." She hadn't gone to synagogue for any of the High Holidays, hadn't even lit Chanukah candles a couple weeks ago, or bothered buying a new chanukia, though she hadn't admitted as much to her parents. She just couldn't get the image of Shlomo out of her mind when engaging in rituals he used to dominate; when she reached for memories of her parents, the synagogue in Brooklyn, the summer camp, his face would interrupt, his too-red lips curled, menacing.

The man in front of her, his face clean-shaven and open and so utterly un-Shlomo, put his chopsticks down and looked at her intently, his eyes wide. "I'm so sorry to hear that." He seemed to mean it, too. It made Iris blush a little, this sincerity. She wasn't used to it.

"So why are you all alone and here on Christmas Eve?" she asked. "I'm Iris, by the way."

He put his hand out and she shook it. He smiled. "Peter. Good shake," he said. "And, ah, well, I guess I just really don't like Christmas. Or Christmas Eve. Or any of it."

"Because of the ex-Catholic thing?"

He nodded.

"Chicken lo mein!" the woman at the counter called out. Iris got up and took the plastic bag.

"I hope your night gets easier, Peter," she said.

"Thank you, Iris," he said. Again, his sincerity, as if no one had ever told him to have a good night, did something to her insides. She paused before she got to the door, turned around, and went back to his table. She rummaged in her purse while he looked up at her, mouth full again, confused.

"Forget something?" he asked.

"Yeah. Here." She ripped a piece of paper out of the back of her Filofax, which always went with her everywhere, just in case. She wrote her number on it and handed it over. "Call me," she said, two words she had never spoken to a man before.

He opened the bit of paper carefully, as if it were precious, and looked at the scribbled digits. "I will," he said.

She smiled and walked back to her car and went home for some TV and noshing.

When she got in, there was a message on the machine—an expense, but one that really was a necessity if she wanted to get more work. She assumed it was her mother, maybe making her father call her back after the game was finished, and clicked the play button. As she began unpacking her food and putting it on the coffee table in front of the couch, she smiled at the voice that was very much not her mother's.

"Hi, Iris. It's Peter. You said to call. And I'm a bit of a scaredy-cat, so I thought I better do it before I lose my nerve. Since you may be free during Christmas . . . Want to go out tomorrow? I'm, uh, calling from a pay phone. Here's my number." He rattled it off, and then closed with, "Thanks, Iris. Wow, that was dumb. Sorry. Okay. Bye!" She laughed out loud. The sound reverberated in the empty space—she wasn't sure she'd ever laughed in there yet. Maybe she would be doing more of that soon.

AUGUST 28, 2017

Flashing lights, shouts.

Then nothing.

A loud voice. "Ma'am? What's her name—have you found her ID yet? Miss, can you hear me?"

Then nothing.

The hum of an engine underneath her, the wail of a siren above.

Nothing again.

WHEN SHE'S AWAKE next, it's like opening her eyes into dense San Francisco fog. She blinks.

"Oh shit, Dad, *Dad*, she's awake—"

"Maggie? Maggie, oh my god, Maggie, *Maggie* . . ."

"Hi," she says, and a pain, like the worst kind of muscle ache, shoots through her, but only for a moment. The fog still cradles her. She's vaguely aware of her father's head resting on her stomach, the vibration of his deep voice as he mumbles unintelligibly. Ariel is standing next to the bed looking supremely uncomfortable, eyes wide and damp. "I think I'm really high," she says after a moment.

Peter's head comes up. He stares at his daughter and starts laughing. Big, hearty ha-has that in later days Maggie will recognize as hysteria. In the moment, though, she just finds the noises he's making very funny and begins to laugh herself, but it hurts and she stops.

"Okay, okay, what a cheery bunch, let's see here." A nurse pulls back the curtain around her and Peter and Ariel, letting in more light. "I see you're awake. That's excellent. You've cracked a couple of your ribs and you have a pretty bad cut on your neck, but you were extremely lucky, missy. I can't tell you how lucky."

She tries to nod, which also hurts. "What am I on?" she asks.

"Morphine, but it's temporary. Don't get used to it, eh?" The nurse wags a finger at her, a beaded rainbow bracelet shimmering around his wrist. Maggie wants to reach out and touch it, feel its unevenness between her fingers, but her arms are too tired.

"That's sort of like heroin, isn't it?"

"Pretty similar," he says.

"Good. Like Mom," Maggie says, and drifts off again.

SHE WAKES TO Peter slowly caressing her forehead, his thumb smoothing it over and over. She feels remarkably more sober, though drowsy, and she's aware now of the pain in her ribs every time she breathes in.

"Hey, Daddy," she says. Speaking is painful. She supposes they've lowered her dose now that they know she's going to live and all.

"You scared the hell out of me," he says. His eyes are glistening. "I thought—I can't lose both of you—" His voice catches and he turns his face away, as if to shield her from his grief, his fear.

"It's okay, Dad, I'm okay. I'm sorry," she adds. "I won't do it again," she promises. He smiles at this.

"You better not. You damn near gave me a heart attack."

"Where's Ariel?" she asks. "What time is it?"

"He's getting some coffee. And I think he's on the phone with Leona too—guess he got a girlfriend while I wasn't looking. He was really worried about you, you know. Oh, and it's about eight."

It hasn't even been that many hours—she was on her way back to Oxnard around noon, she thinks. And now she's in a hospital bed, having scared her remaining family half to death. After disappearing for days. "So, uh, how's the shiva been?" she asks.

Peter gives her a watery smile. "It's a shiva," he says. "It's miserable. Your mom had such a love-hate relationship with them. She thought they were probably necessary, a good idea, but she didn't like being compelled into sitting still. She didn't like being forced to do something just because it was how things were done."

Maggie isn't sure if this is meant to be an indictment or praise of her mother's behavior—or her own for that matter. Should she say she's sorry for having skipped out? Should she thank Peter for emerging from his detached state to come to the hospital? She remembers that her plan was to get home and snap him out of it—and now she has, though not intentionally, nor in quite the way she'd meant to do it. Sometimes, she supposes, life is funny that way. "Where's my phone?" she asks. "I need to tell Lucia I'm okay." Her heart begins to pound, worried about what Lucia knows or doesn't know yet, the anxiety about losing her rearing up again—because now Lucia will not only need to contend with Maggie's feelings but with her recovery from this, however long it'll take. Will she want to stay?

"It's okay," Peter tells her, reading the concern on Maggie's face. He pulls the curl at the edge of her widow's peak, like he used to when she was a little girl. He called it her corkscrew and would pretend to try to open bottles with it. It made her shriek with laughter. "Ariel already found her on Facebook and told her. She wanted to fly out, but we told her she shouldn't, that the doctors said you're gonna be right as rain. They think you'll be able to come home in the morning."

"She was going to visit?" Maggie's throat fills. She begins to sputter, which hurts her ribs more, which makes her cry harder. She thinks vaguely that this must be a delayed reaction to the crash, shock finally moving through her system, the awareness that she could have died just like Iris sinking in. But it's not just that—it's also that Lucia wanted to come visit as soon as she heard about what happened. And she knows Lucia is on a tight budget. For a few years, her younger sister had been in bad shape and Lucia loaned her money a couple of times when she was too embarrassed to ask their parents again, and then there's Lucia's student loans from college and more recently the MFA. She often lives on her credit cards, and spending money to fly to California seems like the most pointlessly romantic thing Maggie thinks anyone has ever wanted to do for her.

"Of course," Peter says. He pats his pockets and finds the pack of tissues he seems to always have on him and unfolds one for her. "She's your girl-friend, isn't she?"

"Y-yes," Maggie says. She's glad that Lucia isn't coming, though—she would feel guilty beyond measure and would try to pay Lucia back, which would probably make her angry, and they would get into a fight, and do they even know how to fight yet without breaking up? Maggie isn't sure she ever has, with anyone.

Except, it occurs to her, with Iris. No matter how much they used to fight or fume, or how in recent years they've chatted about little other than dreams and true crime, she and her mom never actually stopped talking to one another. It's not the same thing, but Maggie likes knowing that she didn't bail on Iris.

And, she supposes, Iris didn't bail on her either.

It's a mistake, trying to blow her nose. "Ooooh, fuck that hurts," Maggie moans, panting slightly. Peter frowns.

"I hope they're not trying to rush you out of here too soon . . . Look, I'm going to try to find the doctor, okay? Oh, and here's your phone." He gets it from the little drawer in the speckled gray wheeled bedside table and hands it over. "The screen cracked, but Ariel thinks it's still working."

Maggie rolls her eyes. As if Ariel knows anything more about technology than she does. Iris always went to him with computer issues; Peter did too. Maggie used to get angry about it, this automatic, thoughtlessly sexist behavior, but she saw how exasperated Ariel would get with them and has by now decided she dodged a bullet.

There's a string of texts from Lucia—she finally has her phone back, it looks like—as well as from Allison, whom Lucia updated on what happened. A lot of heart emojis and kiss emojis and get-well-soons. Lucia's last text just reads, ily. A warm, pleasant pain spreads in Maggie's chest, one that has nothing to do with her ribs, and she's about to text back when Ariel comes through the slit in the curtains around her bed that Peter left open.

"Hey," he says. "How are you feeling?"

She puts her phone down. "Woozy, tired. In pain. How are you, kiddo?"

He winces. "Don't," he says. "That's what Mom called me."

"Sorry." She wonders how long this will go on, how many years from now they'll continue talking about things their mom did. It feels like years have gone by already, rather than days. Which reminds her—she clutches at her neck, but it's bare. She starts to panic. "Fuck—Ariel, my necklace, the one I was wearing, it's Mom's, I—"

"Oh yeah," he says, and pulls it out of his pocket. "They gave it to Dad, and he gave it to me. It got a little cracked." He hands it to Maggie, who can hardly believe that it survived with this little damage—there's a thin crack, almost like a scar, running down one side. Quite the good-luck charm, she thinks. She lived, didn't she? She can't clasp it around her neck because it hurts to lift her arms that much, but she holds it tight in her fist. Ariel takes a sip out of one of those brown and ridged plastic cups that come out of a machine. "Where's Dad, by the way?"

"Went to find the doctor," she says. "Hey, actually." She pauses. It's not a good time but maybe it never will be. "Did you want to know what I found out?" she asks. "The letters?"

"Oh, yeah, they gave us all the other stuff that was in Dad's car too. One of the letters was there."

"'Us?'" she echoes. "Like, they gave that stuff to Dad?" Two of the letters were there, she thinks. One was stuffed in her bag, though, the open one. The one she least wants Ariel or Peter to see.

"Yeah, but he wasn't really paying attention, I dunno. It's all in my car. Since his is also totaled now."

"Fuck," Maggie says. "His insurance premiums are going to skyrocket— two car wrecks so close together?" She's needed to tell people this kind of news at work. It always feels like adding insult to injury—and sometimes worse, if someone died.

"Sure, I guess," Ariel says, seemingly bemused at Maggie's bringing this up. "Anyway. Looks like you delivered most of them, huh?"

"Yup. A few," Maggie says. He still hasn't answered her original question, she realizes. "So?" she prompts, and Ariel breathes sharply through his nose, as if steeling himself, but before he has a chance to say anything, another nurse comes in with Peter and a short doctor who looks too muscled for his white coat.

"Hello," he says. "I'm Dr. Cortez. Your dad here seems worried about your ribs. We're certain nothing has been punctured since there's no sign of internal bleeding. Cracked ribs hurt a lot and they take a while to heal, so you'll have to be careful with yourself for a few months. No weight lifting, no hiking, no strenuous activity. Slow walks, plenty of stretches, ice where it hurts for twenty minutes a few times a day, ibuprofen's okay, and if you still feel stiff in six weeks, we'll get you a referral for PT." He speaks quickly, looking at her chart rather than at her, glancing at Peter when he does look up. "We want to do another X-ray just to make sure everything is where it should be now that the swelling has had a chance to go down. Here, Liliane will take you down to radiology." The nurse who came in with him steps forward and Dr. Cortez sweeps out of the room.

Liliane helps maneuver Maggie out of the bed and into a wheelchair. The pain comes unexpectedly when she moves her arm one degree too far in this direction, when her neck bends like that—she'll need to learn how to be still enough not to provoke it. A stab of impatience is added to the pain—how long will she need to deal with this? Will she be able to have sex? She would have asked the doctor if Peter hadn't been there—she doesn't mind embarrassing Ariel. She reminds herself she could have died. Funny, how a near-death experience hasn't particularly altered her priorities, at least so far. Shouldn't it?

"Uh, Dad?" Maggie says, as Liliane unhooks the IV bag from the stand and drapes it over the chair. "I'm sorry I haven't been around. I want to sit shiva with you both tomorrow. Even if it's miserable. Is that all right?"

Peter nods, and Ariel looks relieved. Liliane, ignoring the intimate moment, tells them they won't be allowed into the testing rooms with Maggie so they may as well stay here or go home for a while.

"Okay," Ariel says, just as Peter shakes his head.

"You go," he tells Ariel. "Get some sleep. I'll stay."

Ariel looks between Maggie and Peter, seeking definitive permission.

"Bro-dude, it's fine, go. This is going to be boring. Just pick me up tomorrow, okay?"

"Okay," he repeats, grinning. She hopes he takes advantage of the quiet house and has Leona over.

They all head to the elevator together, and Ariel gets off at the lobby while Peter insists on accompanying Maggie all the way down to the basement where radiology is located and staying in the waiting room while she gets tested. It's nice to have him cling like this, Maggie thinks, as Liliane helps her up onto a table and puts one of those heavy gray vests over her stomach and lap. Mostly, it's just a relief to have him present in the world again. She wonders what Iris would think about this whole thing if she were around.

Maggie feels another set of tears start leaking from her eyes as she re-alizes that no one has chastised her yet. She kind of wishes they would. After all, if Iris were here, she'd be yelling at Maggie to never, ever dare to use her phone while driving again.

The next morning Maggie is sitting in the front seat of Ariel's Jeep eating the McDonald's breakfast she begged him to pick up on his way over—"I can't believe you're asking me to do that," he'd grumbled. "I'm *vegan*, remember? They're like my archnemesis!"—while Peter sits in the back because Ariel claimed that "the front is less bouncy." It's the first time they've been alone and in the same enclosed space since the morning of the funeral.

Maggie recognizes the music turned down low as her mother's *Best of Miles Davis* CD, the only one that's been in the stereo in the living room for the last decade or so. "Nice," she tells Ariel. "Miles, I mean." In the back, Peter sniffs loudly. Maggie can't turn around easily, so she lowers the sun visor and snaps open the mirror, angling it so she can see Peter's face. "Dad," she says. "Were you and Mom happy?"

Peter, whose nose is running and whose eyes are red-rimmed but look quite dry, nods. He opens his mouth, closes it, swallows hard, and tries again. "Very. I think we only got happier with each other over the years." He doesn't ask her why she's asking. Ariel doesn't either. But before silence reigns, Peter speaks up again. "Hey, guys? I want to apologize. For how I've been since, well, just, you know, how I've been. I know it isn't acceptable. I'm your parent, and I shouldn't have fallen to pieces."

"It's okay, Dad," Ariel says before Maggie has a chance. And if he's saying that, how can Maggie be mad, still? She's been gone.

"Yeah, Dad," she agrees. "It's okay."

For the rest of the drive, they listen to the dulcet trumpet tones, saying nothing.

AT HOME, THEY leave the door unlocked so that people can come in for the last day of the shiva. Peter fusses over Maggie, getting her settled on the couch in the living room with two pillows under her back. He gets the electric blanket from his office, and a big wraparound ice pack Ariel got at CVS yesterday for her to start with—she's supposed to alternate heat and cold for the first couple of days. "Dad, I'm okay, it's okay, I promise."

But he won't stop hovering, asking her what he can get her to eat or drink, yelling for Ariel to come join them in the living room for family time. Which rather hinders her, since she wanted to get high before anyone arrives. She regrets not asking Gina for edibles.

Daphne does show up, just like she said she would, without the husband Ariel mentioned. She hugs Maggie gingerly and shows off her seven-month-old baby, still mostly bald, a series of impossibly tiny stitches in his upper lip where a cleft was recently fixed. Peter holds the little boy, and asks Daphne all the right questions that Maggie doesn't know to ask—how he's eating, how he's sleeping, whether he's had his first cold yet or not. Watching him, Maggie hopes Ariel decides he wants kids young.

When they run out of baby chitchat, Daphne tells Peter and Maggie how she remembers Iris being the best parent at fifth-grade career day. "Everyone else brought their dads, remember, Maggie?"

"I honestly didn't until you said it. I totally forgot about that. Oh my god," and Maggie begins giggling, "remember Gordon Efaw's dad?"

"Wait, was he the guy who went to clean up murder scenes?" Daphne puts her hand over her mouth as she starts to laugh. Her teeth are straight now, gleaming with whitening treatments, but Maggie remembers the gesture from when she and Daphne were tweens kissing in the shadows, how ashamed Daphne had been of the crookedness, how she always tried to hide it.

"Yes," Maggie says, "and Mrs. P kept trying to get him to stop talking and he just wouldn't!" They keep swapping stories, and it's almost like everything is normal, just Maggie visiting home and catching up with an old acquaintance, Peter taking a day off, Iris just happening not to be there. It's only occasionally, when one of them mentions something Iris would be doing now, or something she used to do, that her absence becomes the weighty, permanent thing that it is.

Soon after Daphne leaves, Lucia calls and Peter gives Maggie some space. They talked last night, just enough for Maggie to convince Lucia that she's really going to be okay, but they couldn't dwell, since Maggie's roommates were trying to sleep.

"Babe," Lucia says. "How are you feeling?"

"Better, now that I'm hearing your voice. I know, cheesy, so sue me."

"You know, cheesy is a good thing. Corny is when it gets bad."

"But you love popcorn!"

"Not the same thing, Maggie-mine." Lucia pauses on the line. Maggie's face is hot. She wants to squeal into a pillow. "Is it okay to call you that?"

"Yes. Always," Maggie says. "I miss you," she whispers.

"I miss you too," Lucia whispers back. They sit together in silence, each breathing into the phone. Maggie again gets the urge to tell Lucia she loves her but doesn't. Instead, she asks Lucia about the studio, and work, and Isa and her baby, and her other friends, and their mutual acquaintances. "Not that much is different since we last talked," Lucia says, laughing. "When are you coming home?"

In Ariel's mouth, the question needled at her. In Lucia's, it's like a blessing. "Soon," Maggie says. "Maybe a week? I need to heal enough so that I can fly without it being too painful."

"Of course," Lucia says. "Get well first, focus on that. For sure." There's a burst of mechanical sounding voices in the background and a strange ding-dong noise that reminds Maggie of something.

"Where are you?" she asks.

"Nowhere," Lucia says quickly, and Maggie is about to press when she hears the door open.

"Hello?" a creaky voice calls from the hall. "Anyone home?"

"Babe, I've gotta go," Maggie says. "Someone new's at the door."

"Talk to you soon, Mags, yeah?"

"Def. Bye. Miss you. Bye." Maggie shuts off her phone's screen and tries to wipe the smile off her face. It wouldn't do to receive company not only as an invalid but grinning like a fool. She feels so much, too much. She doesn't understand how it can be possible to feel this full—of love, of grief, of anger. It's an exercise in containment.

An old man wearing a pink polo shirt and pressed khakis toddles in, leaning on a very colorfully decorated walker. He has a plastic bag hooked onto two of his fingers that bangs against the aluminum and then against his legs. Maggie remembers him from the funeral.

"Maggie, right?" he asks. "Watermelon," he adds, pausing in the middle of the room to lift up the heavy bag.

"Yeah, hi, I'm sorry, I don't remember your name—thank you for coming," she says. "Just a second, let me call my dad, I can't really get up easily. *DAD!*" She hates feeling this dependent, but she considers the man in front of her as he looks around, patient and watchful. Maybe they're on equal playing fields right now. It's a good reminder that her constricted movement is temporary, while his isn't.

Peter comes into the room. "Here, have a seat," he says, and helps the older man sit down in an upright chair. "I'll go cut this up. Thank you so much," he says. Maggie can tell he's uncomfortable now, eager to leave the room and have something to do. Ariel has been taking a shower for over half an hour, so Maggie is pretty sure he's just hiding in his room for a while. She can't really blame either him or Peter—they've been dealing with this for days, and Peter's clearly doing much better now than he was. It's her turn to step up, even if stepping is currently not very easy.

"So," she says as the man keeps looking around, apparently in no hurry to talk. "I know we met at the funeral but it's all a bit of a blur. Remind me, what's your name?"

"Harold," he says.

IRIS

⟡

I'm Too Sexy" is playing on the radio yet again, and Iris switches the station quickly, heat rising to her face. She really wishes she could avoid the song, because every time she hears it, whether or not she wants to, she thinks of Harold and blushes. It's been only a week since that first, heated encounter in his car—they hadn't even had sex, but Iris had felt more stimulated, more physically alive to her senses, than she had since before Maggie was born—and she already can't wait to see him again.

"Hey, turn it back," Peter says, coming into the kitchen. "I like that song!" He starts mugging for her, swinging his hips from side to side wildly, and Iris starts laughing. "I'm. Too sexy for my hat. Too sexy for my cat. Too sexy for the cat in the ha-at!"

"Is that how you're reading it to her these days?" Iris swats him playfully in the chest. "No wonder she always demands you when I take that book out!"

"Look, after the twelfth time in a row, I have to do something to make it interesting," he says. "Speaking of, she's finally napping now. That was quite the morning."

"I know," Iris says. "Thank you for taking over, love." She'd been up with Maggie since five, when an extremely loud Harley or a car without a muffler drove by, scaring the little girl so badly awake that she started screaming like she was being murdered. It had taken Iris three readings of *Possum Magic* before Maggie allowed herself to be put down without beginning to cry again, but she still wouldn't sleep so Iris had spent most of the morning coloring, playing blocks, and running around pretending to chase her daughter. She was exhausted. But Maggie was usually such a daddy's girl—from the moment Peter first held her at the hospital and she went quiet after crying in Iris's arms—that Iris loved getting her to herself once in a while.

"So, are you excited?" Peter asked as the hourly news came on. Iris was back to watching the pan, waiting for the grilled cheese sandwiches she was making to turn the perfect shade of crispy.

"About what?" she asked, genuinely confused. He wasn't referencing tonight, was he?

"Your favorite serial killer is getting sentenced today!"

"He's not my favorite," Iris whined. "It's not like that, I just find the whole thing so . . . lurid. So awful. How could anyone do the things he did?"

"You're asking the wrong person, darling. Remember, I'm an avowed pacifist. I was all set to return my draft card to the government and go to jail when they abolished the damn thing."

"And took away your self-righteous heroism? How dare they!"

But Peter wasn't entirely wrong in asking about the killer—she'd been reading any article that came out about him since he was arrested last year. She was fascinated by the man being sentenced that day, who'd been convicted over the weekend. They said he'd actually eaten parts of people. She shuddered. She didn't know why it was so interesting, but she usually stuck to fiction for just this reason; she had a feeling she was *too* interested, sometimes. It was embarrassing—she worried people would think she was one of those women who fell for evil men. She'd done it once before, after all.

But she didn't find these killers attractive—she just found their capacity to do what they did so surreal that it became abstract.

"Here we go," Iris said, flipping the sandwiches onto two plates. "Voilà!"

"This is deeply unhealthy," Peter said, spreading more butter on the still hot bread, making it melt immediately.

"Well, yes, but we need all the calories we can get if she's as energetic after her nap as she was this morning. Cheers," Iris added and raised her sandwich.

"Cheers." Peter lifted his own and they touched corners before each taking a big bite. "Mmm," he hummed while chewing. He looked like the happiest man in the world, in that moment.

Iris wished she had a camera around—she could caption the photo "Beloved, with Grilled Cheese, 1992." She didn't want to ruin that blissful expression, but she couldn't help herself from asking. "Are you still okay with me going out tonight?"

Peter pointed to his mouth, still full, and nodded.

"Are you sure?" she pushed.

He swallowed and took her hands. "Love," he said, turning serious. "Yes, I'm sure. But—"

"What? But what? If it's not okay, please tell me, and I'll stay home, just be honest, *please*—"

"No, no, it's not that," he said. "It's just that every time you ask me if it's okay, it makes it feel like a much bigger deal than it needs to be, and then I feel like maybe I shouldn't be. The point is, yes, I'm absolutely fine with you going out tonight. Maggie and I have a big evening planned! I'm going to make tomato soup and she's never tried it before, but since she'll get to dip bread in it, I bet she'll like it."

Iris laughed. Their daughter's love of bread had at first seemed to be tied to how much she loved tossing it at the seagulls at the beach, but more recently she was asking for it at every mealtime. She crumbled it between her fingers, mostly, though some of it did make it into her mouth. Even though her daughter was in another room, asleep finally, Iris felt that surge of love for her that never seemed to deplete, that shocked her with its intensity every time the little girl called her "Mamama," almost always going a syllable too far. Iris grabbed Peter's free hand and squeezed. "I love you so much," Iris said. "I love her so much. I love this, all of this, so much."

Peter tried to smile but had another bite of food in his mouth and could only give a sort of grimace, which made her laugh again.

ON HER WAY out that evening, Iris grabbed her amber necklace at the last minute, the one her mother gave her. Her mother would never approve, but that didn't matter right now. The necklace was good luck, her mother had said when she gave it to her, the day of the small courthouse wedding with Peter. It had survived the war with her, somehow, and the journey to the United States. When Iris had asked why she didn't get the necklace when she married Shlomo, her mother just said that it hadn't felt right and refused to elaborate. Iris never talked in detail about what Shlomo did to her, but they hadn't objected to her divorce, and though they were deeply skeptical of her marrying a Catholic—it didn't matter how many times she told them he was lapsed—their reservations melted away when they met him. When they finally had Maggie, her father had started calling Peter "son" in a boisterous American Dad kind of way that made Iris giggle, even though she knew it was, really, quite the statement.

"Goodbye, my loves," Iris said, peeking in the door of the bathroom.

"Quack quaky quack," Peter said, nodding Maggie's rubber ducky bath toy at Iris. "That's duck for 'bye-bye, have a good time, we love you!' Don't we love Mommy, Maggie?"

"Love Mommy!" the little naked girl squealed and then plopped herself back in the bath, reveling in the water splashing.

"I'll kiss you good night when I'm back, sweetness. And you too," she added to Peter, but didn't get closer, not wanting to get her clothes splashed. She was wearing her high-waisted light-wash Levi's with a sleeveless pink vest tucked into it and a loose navy sports coat to keep warm in the February chill.

"Drive safe," Peter called as she exited.

"I will!" she yelled back.

HOURS LATER, AS she walked into the silent house, she remembered Peter's parting words and felt her face flame up again. She had driven safely, in more ways than one. She'd even brought her own condoms, procured at the pharmacy yesterday, and insisted on using them even though she had an IUD, because Harold had admitted to not having always been careful.

Ah, Harold. Harold was a couples' counselor, though Iris hadn't met him through his profession, of course. She'd met him, of all places, at a singles' night in an LA bar. She hadn't even been there for herself; she was accompanying her friend Dena, a few years younger than her, who believed she had terrible taste in men. Iris was sleeping over at her place because she'd been working on getting everything ready for the rabbi's son's bar mitzvah at Dena's synagogue and it was silly to drive back to Oxnard just to wake up early and come all the way back to LA. Dena had promised a girls' night, which Iris had thought meant they were going to watch a movie and have some wine, but Dena surprised her by insisting they go out.

"I pick the cheaters, guys who take my money, and men who call me fat. Every time. You have to help me screen them, Iris, or I swear I'll bring home another lemon."

So Iris had agreed, and while Dena chatted up a few guys and reported back to Iris, who kept nixing them, she found herself sitting at the bar next to an older man who hadn't tried talking to anyone and seemed to be watching the whole thing at a remove.

"Are you an anthropologist or something?" she'd asked him, sipping her white wine. Dena was drunk by this point and dancing with a man in a tweed jacket, and Iris had a feeling she should insist they go home soon.

"Or something," he'd said. "Psychologist. Harold."

They'd spent the rest of the evening flirting, and Harold, who had only had one beer, drove them back to Dena's place. "Wait here a second," Iris whispered when she got out of the car. She helped Dena inside and to bed and then came back out. Harold was still there, smoking a cigarette with his car off and its radio on playing the kind of sleepy, late-night jazz Iris loved.

She got back in the car. "I'm married," she told him. "And I have a child."

"Okay," he said, affable.

"But that isn't something that should worry you."

"Okay," he repeated.

"I mean," Iris said. "Because, well, it's complicated. But. Are you okay with that?"

"That depends. Are you okay with the fact that I'm a widower and that I have two teenage boys at home? Are you okay with the fact that I'm probably at least fifteen years older than you?"

"Yes, yes, I'm okay with it," Iris said. She leaned forward and kissed him.

Now, BACK HOME, her body felt both relaxed and exhausted. She cleaned her makeup off in the bathroom, undressed quietly, and went to kiss Maggie, who was sleeping with her mouth open and the trunk of her stuffed elephant clutched in one small fist. She gazed at her daughter for a moment longer, feeling boundless, huge, as if she could encompass the world with goodness and beauty and—she didn't have the words for it, so she just tried to feel it as she touched her daughter's cheek once more before padding back to her and Peter's bedroom.

. . .

HE DIDN'T WAKE up fully when she climbed under the covers, but he shifted his body so he could spoon her. He pulled her in close to him and breathed deeply the scent at the back of her neck. "I'm glad you're back," he murmured. "I love you."

"I love you too," she whispered. Sated, grateful, in love with everything, she fell asleep.

AUGUST 29, 2017

The name clicks into place. No. It can't be. Can it? "Harold Lake Brooks?"
Maggie asks.

"Yes," he says, smiles. "That's me!"

"Oh boy." The words slip out without forethought. Harold raises his
eyebrows at her. "Um, will you excuse me for a moment?"

"Of course," he says. "My understanding of this custom is that I'm here
to share space and time with you, without any demands. Please, do whatever
it is you have to do."

Now she has to get up, though. She doesn't want to yell for Peter, because he'll ask what she's doing, and she's not sure she's ready to tell him
about all this. Maybe she can slip the letter to Harold when he's leaving.
She pulls Ariel's number up on her phone and calls. He sounds confused
when he answers. "Why are you—"

"Hey, I need help getting off the couch," she says, and hangs up. Ariel
storms in a moment later, but stops short when he sees Harold.

"Oh, sorry, I didn't know we had company. Hi," he says, "I'm Ariel." He
holds a hand out to Harold to shake. Maggie wonders when he became so

295

grown-up. She has a flash of understanding—how Iris always marveled at Maggie whenever they saw each other once she left home, the way she would remark on anything adultlike that Maggie did with a kind of disbelief.

Ariel helps her get up from her prone position and leads her into the hall. "You're not bailing again, are you?" he hisses when they're out of Harold's earshot.

"No, I just need my stuff. You said you had all my stuff."

"Yeah, it's still in my car, you could have just asked me to get it," Ariel says. "You're not supposed to be getting up just for that."

"It's nice of you to worry and all, but I need to get it myself."

"Why?"

Maggie doesn't know what to say. Her ribs ache. So she tells Ariel the truth. "That's Harold. The letter they found in Dad's car, it's for this guy."

"Wait, what? What the hell, dude. What's he doing here? What does he want? How does he know Mom?" Ariel's agitation is visible as he leans from side to side on different hips, one hand beating a rhythm against his thigh inside his pocket, the other yanking impatiently at a loose thread on his t-shirt.

"Ariel, I'll tell you everything, if you want to know, I promise, but right now, I just want to give this guy the letter and get him out of here before Dad needs to deal with him too much, okay?" The idea of Peter needing to spend a significant amount of time facing a man who cuckolded him—an old-fashioned term that Maggie has always hated, but which somehow matches how icked out she is by this situation—is unbearable. Her anger swells again. She can't believe how *old* this guy is, too.

"Okay, okay, just, yeah, I'll get it, okay?" He walks away, leaving Maggie to slowly head back into the living room. She manages to sit on another straight-backed chair next to Harold—easier to get in and out of than the squashy couch.

"So, uh, how do you, I mean, how did you know Iris?" Maggie asks him. He turns his benign expression on her. She notices a white curl peeking out of his left nostril. She doesn't want to picture him and her mother going at it. There's something terrifying about the notion, as scary as Karl Jelen being dead—it reminds Maggie that she, too, will be this age one day. She too will have ex-lovers whose faces will have changed beyond recognition, bodies aged.

"I'm an old, old friend," he says. "Iris and I reconnected recently. She was a remarkable woman."

"Yeah," Maggie says, fighting off images of what makes a straight cis man call a woman remarkable. "She was."

"Here we go. This is lovely, Harold, thank you."

"Oh," Maggie says. "You know each other already?"

"Yes," Peter says. "Your mom, well, you could say she volunteered at the, ah—what would you call it? You live there, so . . ."

"The old folks' home," Harold says, laughing. "That's what it is! It's a home, and we're all old folks!"

"I think Iris called it assisted living," Peter says, smiling as well. Maggie looks between them, uncomfortable. She wants Harold out. This is her father's home, his territory, and he shouldn't have to share it with one of these awful secrets his wife kept. A part of Maggie feels embarrassed for Peter, just sitting there, not knowing, thinking this is a totally normal situation.

"Ever the diplomat, our Iris," Harold says.

"Excuse me?" She's vibrating now, the adrenaline moving through her body making her forget all about the pain. She's on her feet, though she isn't aware of making a decision to get up, and she's standing over Harold, her fists clenched. "*Our?*" she repeats.

"Don't be rude, Maggie," Peter says. He holds his mouth tight and small, his eyes narrowed at her. He knows Harold as a friend, she reminds herself. He doesn't know what Harold is implying, what Maggie knows is implied by collectively claiming Iris.

The tension is broken by Ariel knocking on the empty frame of the living room doorway. Maggie's anger slides away from her body and the pain comes back. She sits back down, feeling like a chastised child. She shakes her head at Ariel, who keeps his hand, presumably carrying the envelope, behind him.

"Harold, can I get you something to drink?" Peter asks, as if nothing has happened.

"Sure, water, anything," Harold says, but as Peter leaves, the old man turns his gaze between Maggie and Ariel. His blue eyes are keen and clear, and Maggie can't help but hate them.

"Now, Ariel," she hisses. He bounds over, hands her the letter rather than Harold. "This is for you. From Mom," she says, thrusting it over into his lap. "And if my dad wasn't in the other room, I would ask you a whole lot more questions," she adds softly as she hears Peter clinking ice into a glass.

When Peter comes back, Maggie stays silent, letting him and Ariel and Harold exchange empty pleasantries about the weather, traffic, the food at Harold's assisted living. Peter ignores, or doesn't notice, the letter now lying facedown on Harold's lap. He tries to get Maggie involved in the conversation, asking her about the hospital food, wondering if it's equivalent to Harold's dining hall, and though she makes herself stretch her mouth into an approximation of a smile, makes herself answer in as few words as she can manage, the fact is that her skin is crawling. Harold's presence is unbearable.

Soon enough, he gets up to go. When he stretches his hand out to shake hers, and she complies, she notices how soft his skin is, baby soft, Lucia soft. He meets her eyes, intent. He looks like he wants to say something, but Peter is there beside him, about to help him out and into an Uber, so he lets go of Maggie's hand, shakes Ariel's, and turns to leave.

"ALL RIGHT, WHAT was going on there?" Peter comes out the sliding door into the garden where Maggie is sitting with Ariel, rolling herself a joint. She doesn't bother trying to hide it. Fuck it, she figures. She's an adult. "Is that marijuana?" he adds as he comes closer and sees what she's doing. "You still smoke that stuff?"

"What, you mean I was supposed to have been scared straight by Mom? Or the pigs?" she asks, and puts it to her lips. Peter raises his eyebrows and sits down in one of the remaining two rickety metal chairs.

"Pigs? Really? People still call cops that? Some things never change, I guess," he says. He watches quietly as Maggie lights up in front of him, takes a long drag. She holds the joint out to Ariel, who shakes his head and leans back into his chair, as if to put the most physical distance between himself and the incriminating drug.

"It's going to be legal nationwide any minute now anyway," Maggie says. Peter just looks at her. "What?" she says.

"You offer your brother some but not me? In my day we called that Bogarting," he says, and Ariel lets out a snort. Maggie hands it over to him, not entirely believing he'll really take a drag, but he does, a small one, holding it in like a pro, releasing the smoke slowly, no hint of a cough.

"Dad!" Ariel protests. "You smoke?"

"I haven't in thirty years, but it isn't my first rodeo," Peter says. He hands the joint back to Maggie. His gaze is unlike any he's ever aimed at her before, not that she can remember. He's wary, calculating. "Ariel," he says, "why don't you go inside just in case anyone comes to the door."

"Why me?" Ariel says, but he's already getting up. "She's the one who fucking left, I was here the whole time, and I'm still on door duty?" He keeps mumbling all the way inside, where he turns and tries to slam the sliding door, but the rubber stopper set inside just makes it jump back half-heartedly. He tries to slam it one more time and it does the same thing, so he lets out a string of incoherent expletives and walks away.

A moment later, a slam sounds from inside; he's clearly closed himself back into his bedroom. For a moment, Maggie thinks Peter is going to go after him, but he puts a hand over his mouth and she realizes he's stifling laughter. She cracks up too, right in the middle of her second drag, half-inhaled smoke going up her nose, and she starts coughing at the surprising warmth, which makes Peter laugh harder, releasing his hand. They sit there, like idiots, stoned and giggling, cracking each other up each time they try to stop.

Eventually, though, they're depleted, this laughter as close to crying together as they've ever come.

"So? Want to enlighten me? What were you and Ariel being all shifty about?" Peter asks her again, the corners of his eyes damp, though Maggie is no longer certain if it's with mirth or not. She doesn't say anything for a long while, unable to meet her father's eyes.

"Do you really want to know?" she finally asks him. He nods. "Well," she starts. "Mom left letters."

"Letters?"

"Yeah. To, um, some people. And, uh, that's where I went. To deliver them. I wanted to know who they were."

Unexpectedly, Peter smiles. He leans his head back, and a beam of sunlight making its way through a tear in the drab and dusty patio umbrella zigzags across his face. Maggie is reminded of David Bowie. "Your mother was romantic, that's for sure," Peter says. "But honestly, letters . . . It's like something from one of her novels."

"What do you mean she was romantic?" Maggie asks. Peter isn't reacting with any surprise. She's pretty sure he doesn't understand what she's saying.

"Oh, you know, Jane Austen romantic, letters romantic, big signs and dramatic exits," Peter says. He's still smiling, now shaking his head slowly as if recalling the antics of a naughty child. "She left me one too, you know," he adds. "It was in our safety-deposit box. Janice called me yesterday morning to tell me she'd forgotten to mention it to you. Also, she emailed me a scan of a codicil to the will that fell out of the folder or something, I don't know the specifics, but she said she had an update is the point."

"What about us?" Maggie asks. What does it mean that Peter did get one after all? And she and Ariel . . . didn't?

"Oh, sweetheart, Iris would never, ever have been able to write a goodbye letter to you. To her own children. It's . . . I don't know how to explain it to you. I know you hate to hear this, but I think, really, if you don't have kids, you can't really get it. The idea of saying goodbye to these people, these amazing people you've watched as they've *become*." He pauses at this word. Maggie thinks he's stoned, he sounds so reverant. "Well, you don't, you can't, say goodbye to that. I can promise you that if your mom ever tried, she wouldn't have been able to get through it. The idea of parting with your kids, forever, it's—it's impossible to really wrap your head around."

Maggie sits with this as Peter gazes at her. She has the urge to climb in his lap and curl up there like she did when she was little. She thinks he could probably hold her, now that he's back in the world of the living, back to being her dad. But she can't. On a practical level, because it would hurt too much physically, but even if that weren't a factor, she still has to tell him what's going on, and she can't ask him to comfort her while she does that.

"Okay, I mean, that makes sense I guess, but, uh, Dad," she says, trying to push through as her palms begin to sweat. "I mean. These letters. They were . . ." She doesn't know how to say it. She feels evil, breaking this news to her father. She wonders whether she really should. She could just stop now, backtrack.

"To other men, I'm sure," Peter says.

A shiver runs up through her whole body. Her pulse races, and now her underarms are damp too. It feels very much like the panic attacks she used to have when she was in college, before midterms. "Wait," Maggie says. She wants to take it all back, to stop now, not to confirm Peter's suspicions, to keep him ignorant for a while longer. "Dad, I—"

"Oh, honey," he says, putting his hand over hers, his fingers wrapping around where she's holding the joint, careful not to take it from her, not to burn himself on it. "You thought I didn't know?" His eyes are twinkling, and he starts to laugh again.

"Dad!" she protests, trying to understand what's going on, what Peter is telling her.

"Maggie, my dearest one, my favorite daughter," he says, somehow both patronizing and kind. "You . . . you think you and your friends all invented the wheel. You made all these flags, all these names for things that have always been around, and so you thought you made it all up, that you were the first to experience life. Messy, complicated life. Don't worry, my generation thought we invented it all too. You know when I first learned the word for what I am?"

"What you are? What are you? I'm so confused," Maggie says, her head spinning. She brings the joint to her lips and stops. Maybe she's high enough. Or too. Maybe this is a hallucination. A weed-induced dream. She pinches the end out in the ashtray.

"I was in my forties, probably, when I learned that there was a word for it—'asexual,'" he says, spreading his hands as if the word is painting itself in front of him with a flourish. "I assume you're familiar?" He waits for Maggie to nod, to show that she knows what he's talking about, then continues. "Well, I was never really . . . I don't know if you want to hear this from your old man, but I guess it's time, since it appears you've discovered some things on your own, which I don't think Iris intended you to. But it's too late now, so . . . Well, your mother's first marriage was bad. Terrible, in fact. She and I—we had a beautiful, whirlwind romance. We married very quickly, in May about five months after we first met, which her parents didn't approve of, especially since we did it at city hall. But what can I say? Some of us, and I know this isn't true for everyone, but for some of us lucky, lucky few, when we know, we just know.

"We talked about kids during our first date. We both wanted two, hopefully a boy and a girl. We got lucky there, too. And that's how I won over her parents, in the end—they knew I wanted kids, and they liked the sound of that, and then when we had you . . . Oh, Maggie, I wish you could have seen how they looked at you. How Iris looked at you when they held you."

He leans forward and cups Maggie's cheek for a moment. She can feel the tears leaking out of her again, but she tells him to keep going and wipes them away.

"So. Okay. We knew we wanted a family. But I wasn't . . . well, I was never so interested in sex. I loved your mother, don't get me wrong, and I found her the most stimulating being I'd ever encountered, but I just never had much of a drive or inclination. I know some people who are like me never want to have sex, ever—see, I self-educated, Maggie, isn't that what you always told your mom and me to do?" He laughs, but Maggie doesn't, so he hurries on. "So it wasn't like that for me, not quite, but honestly, I could spend one night a year like that and it was enough for me. And, well, she'd only slept with one other man besides me, an awful man she wanted to excavate from her mind and body as much as she could. She was curious to see what lovemaking with other people would be like.

"So, we talked about it, and we agreed that as long as she saw men away from home, as long as she kept them separate from me and from our family once we had one, well, then that would be okay. It took us years to get there, mind you. It wasn't until after you were born, really, that we finally figured out how to make this work for her. I'll give your generation this," he says, a hint of admiration in his voice now. "You definitely do talk about things more, and more openly. Your access to information is totally different too. We didn't know there was such a thing as polyamory—I mean, we knew, but we called them arrangements, and they were kind of secret, not this acknowledged, unabashed lifestyle choice. So we kind of had to muddle through and figure out what it was she wanted, what it was I wanted, what we needed, together. And when you were born . . . Again, Maggie, I really don't know how to explain the kind of joy you brought to our lives. Joy isn't even the right word. Maybe 'purpose' is better?" Peter looks up and rubs his jaw, which is prickly with stubble. "You were bigger than us, Maggie. More important. So we stopped muddling, and we figured out what we wanted, and Iris found someone, Harold, actually, he was the first, ages ago, and then that ended, and she found someone else, and that ended, and so on. I was her man, her person, her . . . I don't know. Her home. And she was mine. I knew she would always, always come back to me. Until she didn't," he adds, lower lip shaking. But he doesn't break down this time, and Maggie can't help it, she has to know—

"But weren't you jealous?" she squeaks. It's useless to try to stop crying at this point, she thinks. Better to let it all out, like hungover vomiting.

Peter laughs a little, rueful. "We worried about it. Your mother certainly did, a lot, actually, until I had to tell her to cool it because it was stressing me out. I never really understood jealousy the way other people describe it, I don't know. I never got the rage, that terrible feeling that men in novels and movies get, that drives them to kill someone or hit someone or . . . Maybe that makes me a pansy, I don't know. A sissy, like my father used to call me. But I was never attracted to men at all, though believe me, when I was young, everyone thought I was gay. I was always being picked on for not being aggressive with the ladies or dating in general.

"But your mother . . . It wasn't about sex for us. It couldn't be, obviously, since that just wasn't a big enough thing for me. You know, not everyone would accept that. Before your mother, no one really had. When I did date, and I tried, I ended up disappointing the women I was with. I tried to explain, but I think they saw me as a freak, really, or they thought I was lying, that I just wasn't interested in them. We've all been taught that men want sex all the time, right? And if they don't, well, there must be something wrong with them.

"I'm not saying that I loved Iris just because she accepted this part of me, mind you, though she worried about that too sometimes. But no, I just . . . She met me when I was very, very sad, and she made me incredibly happy. She was so vivacious, she had so much energy, she made things happen—she made us happen! She gave me her number—"

"I know the story, Dad," Maggie says, smiling through her tears. "I know. Christmas Eve, the Chinese restaurant, you both eating alone. And you left her a message before she even got home. Such a rom-com move." Maggie wonders why she hasn't thought of this story since Iris's death.

"Well, I knew I would lose my nerve if she picked up! It really was just cowardly of me, but it worked. So. Like I was saying," and he gets more serious again, picking up the earlier thread, "yes, she had relationships with other men, of sorts. Sometimes she just slept with them. She'd go for years without seeing anyone at all. And there were a few she felt very intensely about, I know that. But as long as she came back home to me and you, and later Ariel, it was fine. I mean, look, it wasn't always daisies and roses, you know, having two children who only overlap at the same school for one year, there was a lot of driving and birthday parties and all that normal stuff of parenting, and we fought sometimes about her being gone too much, but honestly? I think that really was more about work than about men. I think she felt in control at work, and she didn't always feel in control with you kids.

"It's not a bad thing," he says quickly, reassuring. "It's just, you know, parenting is one surprise after another. And her work including plenty of chaos—something always goes wrong, it was basically her mantra—but in predictable, repetitive ways. I don't think she noticed how much she leaned on that, sometimes. So, yes, sometimes we had issues. But Maggie, your mother made me feel loved every single day of our life together. I miss her so, so much." His voice breaks and his head drops to his hands. His shoulders shake.

Maggie feels frozen, unable to say or do anything to comfort him, to comfort herself. She—everything her father is saying is so utterly, wildly different than the picture she's built in her mind. This woman he's describing, Maggie can half recognize her, but not fully. She can under-stand the Iris who needed control amid chaos. After seeing Abe and Liam and Eric and now Harold, well, she has some frame of reference for her mother's ability to compartmentalize. But she can't picture her own exis-tence making Iris feel the way Peter is saying they both felt. And she can't understand how Iris could accept Peter for who he is, but not her.

"But then . . . why didn't she . . . Dad, what changed? Why did she start hating me?" She knows she sounds petulant, emo, dramatic, and she doesn't care, she doesn't care, why couldn't her mother just tell her that it was okay, that she was okay?

"She did *not* hate you," Peter says, fierce. "Hey, hey, Maggie, look at me." She looks up into his eyes and he looks so intense she can't look away. "She did not hate you. She didn't understand you, but I think that she made it be more about your sexuality than it ever needed to be. I think she didn't understand you because you were a teenager, and because she couldn't reach you there, not because of anything either of you did—just because it's like that sometimes. Especially when you're similar, and you were, you are, whether you see it or not. But she latched on to you coming out, and once she did, she couldn't back down from it for a while. She was scared for you, mostly. She was terrified of what the world could do to you, and she was terrified that she couldn't protect you. So she tried to change you. It was a mistake, and nothing I say will stop it from being that. I thought it then, and I think it now." He breaks the eye contact himself, his face clouding. "I could have done more, probably. I didn't want to meddle, but maybe I should have. Maybe I should have tried to get you to go to therapy together, or maybe I—"

"Daddy, no," Maggie says through sobs. "It's not your fault. It's Mom's. I just wish . . . I wish she wasn't dead, Dad."

He gets up and leans over her, hugging her as well as he can with her stiff posture. "I know, sweetheart. I know. Me too."

May 7, 2017

Dearest,

    This morning, I woke up to the sweetest note on the mirror from you. Thirty-one years. My God! Half my life exactly now. It seems like forever, doesn't it? And no time at all. I don't have much beyond clichés for you today, I guess. But I wanted to write to you, just in case. I do so much just in case, don't I? You always think I'm too cautious. Well, my love, let me tell you this—I am cautious, yes, but it's served me well. Knock on wood, you and the kids are well, and we haven't faced too much trouble in our lives, have we?

    No, I think we've been doing pretty wonderfully. And I hope we keep on that way. If you're reading this, it means that I haven't been cautious enough in some way or another. Or maybe that's not quite right. After all, death does come for us all, doesn't it? Well, whatever the reason, my love, here is what I want to tell you.

    First, thank you. I could say the words for ten straight continuous years and not have said them enough. Thank you for making me the safest, most well-loved, deeply understood and fully accepted woman in the whole wide world. Thank you for making me believe not only in other people again but in myself as well. You let me be who I wanted to be, and you loved me for all of it, and that's rare. My love, you don't know how rare you are. You were, and are, and will always be, the best father I've ever witnessed being a father. You've been the best partner, friend, love, man, person that anyone could hope to meet in their lifetime. You have been my safe harbor, my panic room, my space shuttle. Thank you.

Second, stay strong. For yourself, for the children, and most of all, because I know you too well by now, most of all for me. If there is an afterlife, I will be sternly watching you to make sure you are carrying on. I am under no illusions—I know you will mourn. And I'd be insulted if you didn't! But the truth is that death is part of life. This is part of your journey. Use it—to extend care to others, to comfort our children with your infinite wisdom, to make your beautiful designs and illustrations. Use it to remember that you, you, my love, you are still alive. Don't stop living. You're too vital a man to sit down and give up on life. Take salsa dancing classes (oh dear, I imagine you must be hurling something at the wall now—I know how much you hate group activities!) or pottery lessons or start going to plays, or . . . well, you know what? I trust you. You couldn't give up on life if you tried. And no, that isn't a dare! So don't dare (ha!) take it that way.

You are my favorite person, my love, and always will be. Unless, of course, I find that delicious actor who plays the detective in that show I love so much. Just kidding! I know you won't mind sharing if I do come across him. No matter what, if you show up here, or if our molecules find one another one day, we will be together again eventually.

Never forget me—you with the big brain and long memory, you won't forget a thing, I'm sure—but keep living, my love.

Yours, in life and after and before and always,

Iris

CODICIL TO LAST WILL AND
TESTAMENT OF IRIS JUDITH KRAUSE

I, Iris Judith Krause (the "Testatrix") of Oxnard, California, declare this to be my codicil (my "Codicil") to my last will and testament being dated the 5th day of May, 2017 (my "Last Will").

1. My Last Will is hereby modified by deleting the following clause:

> "8. I bequeath to Ariel Michael Krause my wedding and engagement rings and to Margaret Agata Krause my amber necklace."

2. My Last Will is to be modified by adding the following clause after clause 8:

> "8B. I bequeath to Ariel Michael Krause my engagement ring, and to Margaret Agata Krause my amber necklace and my wedding ring."

3. I hereby confirm and republish my Last Will dated the 5th of May, 2017, in all respects other than those mentioned here.

M aggie wakes up into a dream. The room is dark, but she isn't alone. Someone is breathing on her face. She can smell orange and cherries, faintly. Like Lucia's Tic Tacs and ChapStick. She tries to cling to the dream but can feel herself stirring properly awake.

"Hello, Maggie-mine."

Maggie leaps up in shock and her head knocks against something which yelps. She wrestles with the bedside lamp and gets it on. Lucia is kneeling by the bed and clutching her nose, laughing in that gasping, hiccupping way of hers. "Oof, what a welcome!"

"Omigod, Lucia, what did I do? What are you doing here? Show me, show me—oh no, you're bleeding! Fuck, fuck me, I can't believe I did that! Shit, come on, come on—" She pulls the inexplicably there and still laughing Lucia up from the ground and leads her to the bathroom.

"Shit," Ariel says from down the hall, making Maggie's shoulders grow rigid again with the surprise. She whips her head around and he's standing there with Peter, both of them still wearing clothes, though she thought they'd gone to bed soon after her. But no, Ariel's car keys are dangling from his hand. "We thought you'd be glad to see her. What, you beating on your girlfriend, sis?"

"Fuck you!" she calls. Lucia is already in the bathroom, sitting on the closed toilet lid with her head leaned back and a wad of tissue held up to her bleeding nose.

"Hey, be nice," she says, starting to laugh again. "Your brother picked me up from the airport and brought me all the way back here and saved me a late-night Lyft."

"Yeah, say thank you!" Ariel yells.

Maggie feels torn in a hundred directions. She wants to kiss Lucia, and hug her, and hold her. She wants to go flick Ariel in the forehead and also hug him fiercely and say thank you. She wants to go ask Peter if he knew, if he helped make this happen.

But her body, running on the surprise of the moment, remembers suddenly that it was in a serious accident less than forty-eight hours ago. "Fuck," she says as her back and neck seize up. She tries to bend down to Lucia, but the pain is so intense that tears well up in her eyes. "Okay, okay," she mutters, and breathes in deeply. "I, uh, can't move so well yet," she adds sheepishly, keeping her head very still as she swivels her eyes down to Lucia.

"Baby!" Lucia gets up and tosses the tissue in the trash. She holds Maggie's shoulders gently. "Can I?" she asks, widening her arms.

"Yes, oh god, yes, just gently," Maggie says, and Lucia hugs her as if Maggie were a delicate or maybe dangerous thing, and perhaps she is a bit of both in her volatile emotional state and weakened physical one.

"Come on, let's say thank you to your dad too, for keeping it a secret," Lucia says.

THEY END UP doing a lot more than say thank you—they sit with Ariel and Peter around the kitchen island as Peter pours them glasses of red wine.

Lucia explains how she had friended Ariel on Facebook, how they'd put together a plan for her to come a few days ago when Ariel was still worried about Maggie never coming back. Peter paid for the ticket after convincing Lucia that it was her birthday and Christmas present rolled into one for that year, because of course he would get her those because she was Maggie's girlfriend. He makes it sound like he's always given Maggie's girlfriends birthday and holiday gifts, and Maggie raises her eyebrows at him. Peter winks at her, as if to say, *Shh, it'll be our little secret.* After Lucia gets the bottle of wine from the counter and pours them all a little more, she and Ariel begin exchanging rap lyrics from a band they listened to on the way from the airport and fist bump, laughing.

Maggie watches them all, this, her family, born into and chosen. Minus her mother. Her mother who will never get to witness this. She begins to cry again, but quietly, and no one notices, or they pretend not to.

Finally, around three in the morning, they all get ready to go to bed, Maggie for the second time. While Lucia is brushing her teeth, Ariel calls Maggie over to his room.

"Here," he says. "Dad showed me the codicil thingy. This is yours. Just, you know. You should keep it close, just in case." His face is red with the wine and maybe with some other embarrassment, but he pats her awkwardly on the arm, and holds Iris's wedding ring out to her.

Maggie takes it and closes her hand tightly around the smooth surface. It's strangely hot, or maybe that's just her own skin. "Ariel, the letters," she starts, but he waves a hand.

"Tomorrow," he says. "We'll talk about it tomorrow." He shuts his door, and Maggie feels her stomach clench. This isn't over yet, she thinks. Maybe it never will be.

Hobbling into her room, she finds her backpack hanging on the hook on the back of the door, and she puts the ring in a mint tin that she always keeps in the smallest pocket. She'll put it somewhere safer when she and Lucia get home. In the same pocket, she finds the necklace, which she asked Ariel to put there yesterday, and she holds the cracked amber for a moment before putting the chain around her neck and clasping it.

Lucia helps Maggie settle on her back with a thin pillow so she can lie flat and then curls up to her in the narrow bed, throwing a thick, warm leg over both of Maggie's own. "What's this?" she asks, touching the necklace.

"It's the one from my mom," Maggie says. "It's, well, she originally gave Ariel the rings and she gave me just this, the necklace. It was her mom's, I know that much."

"So she gave him the future, and she gave you the past?" Lucia asks, tracing her finger over Maggie's collarbone, careful to avoid the bandage covering the stitches in her neck. "That's nice."

"I didn't really think about it like that. But, well, she changed her mind. She gave me the wedding ring, too, and left the engagement one for Ariel," Maggie says. *I guess you gave me a bit of the future after all, Mom.* She doesn't know who she's thinking it to, but she adds, *Thank you.*

"Good, engagement rings are always ugly," Lucia says, and Maggie snorts. "Babe, how are you doing, though? Really?"

In a soft voice, Maggie starts telling Lucia about what her father told her. Lucia listens, occasionally interjecting a clarifying question, all the while tracing her fingers along Maggie's skin. "So, yeah, I guess . . . I guess you were right not to jump to conclusions," Maggie says, finally finished, feeling depleted.

Lucia is silent for a moment before saying, "Damn, Mags. Your family is so cool." Maggie is so surprised by this reaction that she doesn't know what to say. She supposes her parents' relationship is . . . well, it's certainly not what she expected, that's for sure. But cool? "Wait, so what about Harold?"

"What about him?" Maggie isn't sure what Lucia means.

"You said he was the first, but your mom was hanging out with him again recently, right? Gotta say, I'm impressed with the dude," Lucia says, nuzzling up to Maggie's neck and heaving a sigh. "I hope I still got it when I'm that old."

"Oh—ew, no! I mean, I don't think it was like *that* at this point." Maggie can't imagine Harold, with his walker and his wrinkles and his slow movements being capable of any kind of sexual activity. She doesn't want to picture it. Instead, she thinks about Lucia getting older, her skin sagging slowly, face gaining wrinkles, and she smiles in the darkness. She wants to tell Lucia how beautiful she'll be when she's eighty, but then Lucia asks the question that's plaguing Maggie.

"What are you going to tell your brother?"

"I don't know yet," Maggie says. "I really fucking don't." They're quiet, and Maggie can feel how they're both sinking into the mattress, sleep coming for them. She nudges Lucia. "Kiss?" she asks.

Lucia lifts herself on an elbow and looks into Maggie's face intently before kissing her deeply, and when she pulls away, Maggie thinks she's about to say it, but she wants to say it first, to make this promise, even if it's temporary, even if it's just for now.

"I love you," she whispers, and feels Lucia tense and then relax beside her, feels her own banged-up and bruised body shedding something too, as if a layer of thin ice that's encased her skin since the night her mother died is melting. Part of her is aware that this can't last, that surely it isn't this easy, that the ice—and the anger, the sadness, the frustration, all of it—will come back. But in this moment, Maggie feels calm, even secure, in this bed with her beloved, in this house she grew up in, where something of her mother's essence will likely linger forever.

"I love you too," Lucia whispers back, and kisses her again. "And when you get better," she continues, grinding her pelvis into Maggie's side, "you better believe I'm going to show you how much."

It takes Maggie a long time to fall asleep. Her underwear is fairly soaked.

ACKNOWLEDGMENTS

My first acknowledgment is to you, reader. Thank you for being here.

I read the acknowledgments of most books these days, and they almost always make me cry, because they're a testament to something I wasn't aware of as a young writer dreaming of publishing a book—which is that while the physical act of writing is solitary, everything around it isn't, and community is one of the most important assets we have as writers. No one who gets to see their book published—be that as physical pages bound with glue, as digital formatting, as audio recording—does it alone. There are many, many people along the way, and I'll do my best to thank each and every one of them. If I haven't thanked you but you think I should've, you're probably right, and any negligence to do so is purely due to faulty memory and a tight deadline.

In chaotically chronological order, my abiding thanks to:

My small first family—Ima/Andi, Aba/Uri, David, Aunts Michelle and Vero, Grandma Ronna whose voice I recall so clearly, Grandpa Jerry for letting me jump on the couches, Saba Zvi for the pearl necklace we drew together, Savta Helen for the stories of swimming and breaking the rules— for keeping books around, for reading to me until I snuck away to read on my own, for encouraging my love of stories, for believing in me.

And extended family—Dani, for joining us and letting us in; Libby, for thinking I was writing a book about rainbows during Pride month (you weren't that far off) and for being a miraculous human; Uncle Jack and Aunt Nancy, for the trips to Barnes & Noble when I was little and the dinners when I was big and a love of Harry Potter everywhere in between; Aunt Candy, for gifting my brother the first three HP books (they're mine now; sorry, David) which I've worn to tatters over the years; Jonathan and Peter, talented artists and gracious cousins, for all the love and humor and conversations over the years; Hilda, who isn't a cousin though for years I thought you were, for the books you recommended when I was too young; and Joe(y), the first person who ever came out to me, long before I was out to anyone about anything, for being patient with your loved ones while always fighting for what you believe in.

My seventh grade literature teacher, whose name I'm unsure of but whose habit of sitting on the desk, boldly showing off striped orange-and-black tights I will never forget, for assigning us to write "novels" that year, and for teaching me how to close-read the first piece of flash fiction I'd ever encountered, Etgar Keret's "Break the Pig." ‏אם אשכחך פסחזון, תשכח ימיני!‏

My first girlfriend, Gal, for the introduction to my first-ever poetry reading, showing me a world I hadn't known I yearned for, where I was also introduced to performance art when a long-haired metalhead dude breathed deeply, centered himself, yelled (in Hebrew) *bitch son of bitch* as loudly as he could into the microphone, bowed, and left the stage.

Amanda, whether or not you were who you said you were, for spending time with my writing, telling me you were impressed with it when I was all of sixteen and self-loathing and feeling impossibly ugly.

My friends throughout high school (and prior) and to this day for letting me be who I was, who I am, who I became, and for never telling me how nuts my dreams were: Orin, Yael, Maya, Omri, Lia, Keren, Erez. I love you all so very much.

Amos, Miki, Tami, and Aya, for being a second family, for loving me, for supporting me in tough times, for giving me some doses of reality without scaring me away. It's what Aba would have done if he was around, and I'm grateful.

Brian Morton, teacher, mentor, friend, for believing in me from that very first writing workshop in college, for continuing to champion me throughout the years since, for the conversations and disagreements and challenges and warmth, for sharing invaluable advice about publishing anxiety, for being a true mensch.

Teachers and classmates of every writing workshop or class I was lucky enough to take in undergrad, for your wisdom, your words, your enthusiasm, your writing, your reading, your inspirational selves, including (but not limited to): Kieron Winn, for encouraging me to play with language and read scary-big books; Kit Haggard, for sharing early morning coffee and writing and late night dance parties in Oxford; Amy Hempel, for leading the kindest of groups at the New York State Summer Writers Institute, and Rowan Hisayo Buchanan, whom I met there, for the friendship and advice and camaraderie ever since; David Hollander and the Enemies of Fiction for letting me be amongst you.

SLC family and friends—whether we connected then or after—for solidarity, artistic talks, general weirdness, inspirational work, amazing style, and love. There were many of you, and we've lost track of one another over the years. I want to especially thank India, Matt, Jean, Laurel, Ben, Emma, Montana, Gemma, Rob, Alec, Laura, Lukas, Tasha, Anna, and Will—all of you have taught and given me so much, in so many realms. And to instrumental teachers who changed the way I read and thought: Joe and Ann Lauinger, Lyde Sizer, Ilja Wachs, and Marvin Frankel.

Michael Mejias, for telling me the truth (and being right, goddammit. Look, I did it!), and everyone I interned with and learned from at Writers House.

Leigh Feldman, for friendship, employment, knowledge, laughter, gossip sessions, trust, not to mention invaluable email addresses and a deep, abiding faith that I could do it.

Joy Parisi and Paragraph: Workspace for Writers, for the space, the friendships, the wisdom, the coffee, the employment, the events, the drinks, and the company, including, but not limited to: Will, Maya, Ryan, Rebecca, Sarah-Jane, Kavita, Aurvi, Danielle, Anne-Sophie, Caroline, Laura, Matt, Julia, and Jane Hoppen (who is no longer with us, but who I think, I hope, would have approved of this book). I'm sure I'm forgetting some people; if we shared coffee and space and conversations across rickety tables and mutually-agreed-upon silence, thank you. You all made New York City and being a writer feel real and tolerable even in the depths of imposter syndrome and a sense of doom.

Natalie Zutter, writing-date pal extraordinaire and early reader, for the many early mornings, bites of doughnut, profound (and petty and silly and fun) conversations, and sustained friendship.

Chelsea Laine Wells, writer-wife forever, inspirational teacher and tattoo goals, for the texts and the writing prompts and the forever support. Ily.

Residencies where I didn't work on this book, but where I wrote other things, because each bit of writing somehow leads to the next one: 100W Corsicana, especially Kyle Hobratschk for the incredible building and sharing Pinto Bean, and Katie Ford and Adam Raymont for the company, the art, the conversations, and the tattoo. And Vermont Studio Center, where I met so many incredible people and feasted my eyes on art, with special thanks to Brenda Peynado, Lena Valencia, Michael Badger, Mo Davieu, Eloisa Amezcua, and Kelly Johnson.

All the people I've ever slept with, crushed on, kissed, obsessed over, been ghosted by, for the life experience. I mean it. No regrets.

Garth Greenwell, workshop leader and Dalloway-lover, and all the fellows at Lambda Literary's 2017 Writers Retreat for Emerging LGBTQ Voices, for your fully emerged and wondrous voices, for sharing nighttime cigarettes and daytime space, for getting me to my room that time I fainted in the elevator, for all you taught me and still do.

Grad school colleagues, friends, and writers who've shared workshop space and presence, for all the support, community, belief, poetry, smarts, and love. Special thanks to early readers Rachel Cochran and Scott Guild for their encouragement, cat-sitting, and abiding friendship; early reader Zamira (Zamy) Atluhanova for the honesty and presence and love; Stevie Seibert Desjarlais and James Desjarlais for the introduction to Lincoln, Bachelor Nation, home-brews, and so much more; cohort mates Claire Jimenez, David Henson, and Alex Ramirez, for the education, empathy, beer, and incredible writing. And more, for sharing coffee, tea, intelligence, booze, kindness, stress-hugs, cards, stickers, department meetings, office space, friendship, and conversation: Jamaica, Jess, David, Katie, Katie, Ángel, Kate, Kathrine, Raul, Teo, Charlotte, Saddiq, Linda, Linda, Christian, Gina, Cameron, Adam (and Tiff!), Adrienne, Michelle, Jordan, Jessica, Anne, Nicole (and Pumpkin, may she rest in peace and doggy treats, and Sheila), Robert, Ashley, Damion, Keshia, Regan, Jeremy, Maria, Zoe, Alex, Gretchen, Maria, Emily, Emily, Nick, Dillon, Erin, Rosamond, Natalie, and if there's anyone I've left out, it's probably because you're smart and have left Facebook. I am so grateful to you all for being my community.

University of Nebraska-Lincoln faculty and staff for welcoming, educating, and sharing wisdom with me, especially Timothy Schaffert, advisor and early reader of this book, for the care, open door, cocktails, and friendship; Hope Wabuke and Stacey Waite, early readers and committee members with valuable notes and incredible minds; Joy Castro, for encouragement, grace, and empathy; Amelia María de la Luz Montes, for blowing my mind with theory I loved; Julia Schleck, for giving me the call and for incredible teaching; and Jennine Capó Crucet, for plucking the weirdest, most ambitious writing I've ever done off a pile, seeing what I was going for, and insisting I deserved a spot here. Thank you all, also, for your incredible writing in your various fields—what gifts your words are to the world.

Catherine Goldberg, for the shipments and care.

Sharon Holiner, early reader, best friend, writer and artist, kindred spirit, beautiful soul, for being you. We are so lucky to have found each other, and we've worked hard to keep each other. To dentures and beyond, love.

Josh Langman, early reader, design expert, keen eye, for the unwavering belief that I could and that I would, for the advice and friendship and fonts and heffalumps.

Alexandra Franklin, early-early reader (before we even met), for the friendship, advice, faith, bookish nerdery, constant texts, literary conversations, intellectual stimulation, anxiety soothing, and for knowing this was the one before it was done, before I believed it, before it was possible.

Mike Cahill, my partner and beloved, my Peter, for the eggs, the cuddles, the Friday night pizzas, the Sunday morning diners, moving with me, making home feel like home, and everything else that makes you family—I love you. And to Mike Sr., Deb, Brendan and Staci and Martin, for welcoming me so wholeheartedly.

My many literary communities who've filled my mind and fueled my body with words and thoughts and opinions and kindness, through Twitter and Facebook and other extremely-online-venues, for letting me in and teaching me more every single day. There are far, far too many of you to name, but if we've interacted about books, writing, feelings, impostor syndrome, residencies, etc., it's you I'm thanking here.

Virginia Center for the Creative Arts, where I wrote a big chunk of this book, and NaNoWriMo, for the physical and virtual spaces, for the invitation and the inclusion, for the communities both IRL and online.

Eric Simonoff, for being the best agent a queer Jewish weirdo could have, for the phone calls, patience, faith, and friendship. Here's to many more years and book talks! Taylor Rondestvedt, thank you for the kindness, the check-ins, and the cover talk—I can't wait to see what you do next. And everyone at WME who has been involved behind the scenes, without my knowing your names, thank you.

Maya Ziv, editor of wonder—they say it only takes one, and I'm so glad you were it!—for seeing, getting, and loving this book from the start, for making the editing process exciting and invigorating, for pushing me to fill in the gaps and letting me stand up for what I needed, for creating a space of mutual trust and admiration, for meeting me where I'm at even in the depths of anxiety, for believing in me, this book, this work.

Folks at Dutton without whom this wouldn't be possible: John Parsley, Christine Ball, Hannah Feeney, Natalie Church, Sarah Thegeby, Susan Schwartz, LeeAnn Pemberton, Erica Ferguson, Christopher Lin and Lynn Buckley, Elke Sigal, and Maria Whelan, thank you all—some of you I haven't met or spoken with yet, because the structure of how this all works separates us and because I'm just one of many, many people for whom you make dreams come true, but please know that I so value and appreciate your work, skills, judgment, flexibility, and think you all deserve a raise.

And, finally, writers everywhere, whose imaginations, words, and books shaped me, whose careers and paths have demonstrated a way forward, for the empathy, the heart, the words, and the endless hours of pleasure, pain, and deeply felt narratives you've given this eternal reader.

ABOUT THE AUTHOR

Ilana Masad is a queer Israeli-American fiction writer, essayist, and book critic whose work has appeared in *The New York Times*, the *Los Angeles Times*, *The Washington Post*, *The New Yorker*, *The Paris Review*, NPR, *BuzzFeed*, *Catapult*, *StoryQuarterly*, *McSweeney's Internet Tendency*, as well as others. She is the founder and host of *The Other Stories* podcast and a doctoral student at the University of Nebraska-Lincoln, where she also serves as the assistant nonfiction editor for *Prairie Schooner*. *All My Mother's Lovers* is her debut novel.